THE HOLLAND FAMILY SAGA

PART SIX

DAWN OF AN EMPIRE

ISBN:978-0-9892445-1-0

This is strictly a work of fiction. Any references to actual events, real people, living or dead, or actual localities, is to enhance the realism of the story. Events within the novel that coincide with actual events id purely coincidental.

All material copy-written and filed on site at The Library of Congress.

ACKNOWLEDGEMENTS
11:37 a.m.
April 25, 2013

I picture this ride on The Holland Express as that part of the journey where we hit the Great Plains. If you know the area, you know it to be expansive and versatile—which is how I would like to describe this particular read. We cover a lot here and the family will grow exponentially. As you sit, the rails click-clacking under your feet as you stare out into the beautiful land, which is the story written, grasp hold of the fact that this saga is morphing into more than just street-fiction. Understand that I wrote this particular story to really convey love of family. Of course the drama is there, but let us take a different journey this go around. Let's leave behind the skyscrapers and concrete sidewalks in the bustling inner city for a moment and visit a new setting for the most part while we get to know and understand The Holland Family even further.

I would like to thank everybody that has supported this project and it is my every intention to deliver another quality read. Hopefully an Epic one. I see the posts, I get the messages and you all's eagerness for the next installment has me on edge I must say. With that aside, I would like to welcome you into Naomi's world. Take on her journey and come to know her and the people that have shaped her personality. Interesting characters here if you ask me, and a lot of surprises within. I hope each and every one of you enjoy this read as much as I enjoyed writing it.

I would also like to thank all my readers from the Northeast, New Jersey, Maryland, DMV, Connecticut, New York, Philly. Much love to the south, Louisiana, Florida, Alabama, Mississippi and Georgia. The Midwest has my heart. Hello, Ohio, Michigan. Wisconsin, Illinois, Missouri, Kansas. Much love to Oklahoma. Colorado I see you. Vegas and Cali where you at? Thank you all for the love. Happy Reading!

Clever Black

CHAPTER 1
MATRIARCH

Naomi Holland-Dawkins if you had to sum her up in one word could best be described as being versatile—but many more attributes lay beneath the surface of this particular Holland female persona. She was a dignified woman with a laid-back disposition. Socially liberal, but fiscally conservative. A forty-five year-old married woman with eight children living on a huge ranch in Ponca City, Oklahoma, she stood 5' 8" and weighed 145 pounds and had smooth, caramel-complexioned skin, dark eyes and thick, coarse, black hair that she often wore in two thick plats that were braided to the back whenever she was on the ranch. Naomi, like her sister Mary and Mary's identical twin Martha, and every other living Holland female, had a birth mark under her left eye and could produce the most gorgeous smile that would give way to very pronounced dimples and pearl white teeth. She was a voluptuous woman with a somewhat rugged appeal due to the labor she often performed on the ranch over the years, but she was feminine just the same.

It was August of 2001 and Naomi was walking across the field of her ranch back towards her mansion, which the family had named Ponderosa, where a celebration was getting underway for Martha Holland, who'd been released from prison several days earlier with her friend, Irene 'Twiggy' Charles. Twiggy had done time with Martha in Grenada, Mississippi and was released a few months before Martha. When Martha got out of prison, she linked up with Twiggy back down in Jackson, Mississippi, and the two women headed to Ponca City to join the rest of the Holland-Dawkins Family and start life anew on The Holland Ranch.

Naomi was overjoyed to have her sisters back in her life; but she also had a conflict within herself that she was aiming to resolve. Forty-two year-olds Mary and Martha were under the impression that their oldest sister was a corporate lawyer; but the truth was, Naomi, although keeping her license up to date so as to run the finances within the family, had actually sat her practice aside seven years ago in order to support her husband's endeavors and to also live on the ranch where she could raise her kids in a privileged environment. She and her husband had talked about the matter shortly after Martha and Twiggy arrived on the ranch on this day and Naomi had decided to not tell what Doss Dawkins actually did for a living because she sincerely believed that if she told her sisters the full story they would leave her home having learned such terrible truths. So rather than be open and honest with her sisters, Naomi decided to keep the harsh realities surrounding her and her husband's success hidden from Martha and Twiggy in the same manner in which she'd been hiding the secret from Mary, Dimples, and her youngest five kids.

Dressed in denim jeans, a white, tight-fitting tank top, black boots, and wearing a black cowgirl hat, Naomi slowly walked through Mary's onion patch under the hot sun, across the field towards Ponderosa, eyeing her family proudly as she approached the huge theatrical-style patio behind the home. The backside of the home was where the family mainly spent most of their time when the weather was right, just as it was on this hot summer's day in August of 2001. Neatly trimmed spruce trees and tall shrubs on either side of the patio provided extra shade and a large grill sat to the far left of the patio at the edge of the stairs; an outside cooler/freezer that held beer, soda and ice cream was on the patio as well. There were six marble benches sitting around a marble fountain that sprayed cold water into the air and back down into the pool below. All a person had to do was place a cup under the falling water. f and drink as it was naturally filtered spring water fro aqueduct that ran below the land, some of the

Oklahoma, and it was cold year round, even in the summer. The backside of the mansion and the entire ranch itself, including the stockyard and barn, looked like a well-maintained park with its beautiful landscapes and picturesque architecture.

Naomi reached the top of the patio and she couldn't resist stopping to dance with her six daughters and her niece Dimples as they danced along with Siloam Bovina, Naomi's twenty-eight year-old unofficially adopted daughter, to Chic's song *Good Times*.

...*"Let's cut the rug...little jive and jitterbug...we want the best...we won't settle for less...don't be a drag participate... clams on the half shell and roller skate, roller skate...Good times...these are the good times..."*

Naomi jammed with her daughters the duration of the song, gyrating her hips and dancing around in one spot, dipping and swaying in perfect rhythm, showing her daughters a thing or two on how to step before she made her way across the patio over to Mary, Martha and Twiggy, who were sitting in lounge chairs near the grill talking to nine year-old Walee Dawkins, Naomi's youngest son, and seventeen year-old Dawk Holland, Naomi's oldest son and the oldest of Naomi's eight.

"Dawk, can I borrow your aunts for a while?" Naomi asked as she wiped her head with a scarf.

"Can't you see we talkin'? Sheez!" Walee remarked, as if he were annoyed at his mother's request. "Always buttin' in on somethin'."

Naomi smiled at her son as she walked towards him slowly, checking her flowers and dipping her hand into the water fountain as she eased her way over towards Walee. The youngster had a tendency to run off at the mouth, to speak when not spoken to, and it agitated Naomi to the highest just about every time he did so.

"Take off. Better take off, boy," Dawk warned as he laughed slightly, recognizing that his mother had something in store for Walee, like a headlock or the infamous jaw grab and one minute lecture. The kids all hated the jaw grab because their mother's nails would sometimes dig into their skin and it would sting when she moved their heads slightly.

Walee jumped down the patio stairs and ran into the field before Naomi even made it half way. He turned around and stopped and waited until his mother came into view at the foot of the stairs and remained silent.

"You gotta come home tonight, li'l boy!" Naomi yelled through laughter. "You stay out there! Stay right out there and don't even think about comin' this way no time soon!" she added as she did a quick two step and sipped cold water.

"You play too much!" Walee yelled from a distance.

"And you have a Smart Aleck mouth! So there! We're even! You know I don't play with you like that, boy! You just stay there until I'm outta sight!" Naomi yelled back as Walee kicked the ground.

"Naomi, don't be so hard on him." Mary said.

"He'll be fine. He just has to learn to tame that mouth of his. We're not staying here long anyway. Mary, Martha, Twiggy? Walk with me over to Ne`Ne`s Hill will you all please so we can have some grown folk's time alone."

Mary, Martha and Twiggy, along with an unauthorized Dawk, began following Naomi as she made her way back across the patio. When she descended the stairs and headed out into the open field, she reached for Mary and Martha's hand, Twiggy following the sisters and Dawk followed Twiggy.

"Now, first I want to say that—" Naomi stopped mid-sentence when she saw Dawk following closely behind. "Where are you going? I don't recall asking you to join us."

"I'm going with y'all. I just wanna hear you tell those stories, Dad got everything covered on the grill and don't need my help really once Walee get back." Dawk stated seriously.

Naomi sighed and shook her head. Dawk had heard the stories before, but in spite of that fact, Naomi really wanted to be alone with her sisters and their friend. The look in Dawk's eyes however, couldn't be ignored by his mother. She relented and said, "Okay, just let me talk, and you remain quiet."

"Already! Momma, it's a li'l warm out here. Nahh, it's hot. Martha and Twiggy might want some beer. I'm a go get the golf cart and put some ice and beer in the cooler." Dawk remarked before he turned and jogged back to the patio, never waiting for his mother's reply.

"Awww, he's nice. I could really use a beer. Naomi, this ranch is like paradise."

"Thank you, Twiggy. I want you to feel at home here always, because this is your home now for as long as you want to stay. And I can promise Dawk wasn't being nice to you. I guarantee he'll have drunk at least two beers before he gets back to the hilltop."

"You let Dawk drink, sis?" Martha asked.

"He's mature enough. And he only drinks here on the ranch." Naomi remarked happily.

"This is truly a time for celebration, sis. After seven plus years behind bars, I'm ready to celebrate my freedom, my family, and life itself."

"You got that right, Martha." Twiggy said as she and Martha high-fived one another and continued walking towards the crest of Ne'Ne's Hill.

When they reached the hilltop, Martha and Twiggy stared at seventeen year-old Rene 'Ne'Ne'' Holland's grave. Mary and her surviving daughter, twenty-three year-old Regina 'Dimples' Holland, Ne'Ne's surviving identical twin, had placed white marble benches on either side of the grave and had planted numerous flowers around the white marble headstone. A picture of Ne'Ne' standing outside of Twiggy's black Impala with her hands on her hips and smiling on the day before she was killed was encased in Plexiglas and sunken into her headstone and an inscription that read, "*Always loved. Forever missed. And never forgotten*", was inscribed with the dates, *June 22, 1977—March 22, 1995*. The area was sweet-smelling, pleasant and tranquil. It was a place where one could reflect on matters while over-looking the land.

Laying eyes upon Ne'Ne's grave for the first time had moved Martha to tears. Seeing her beloved niece's final resting place had really hit home for her. The sun was shining down brightly on Ne'Ne's picture, breaking through the numerous trees that lined the hillside and hilltop and the picture seemed to glow.

Martha took off her hat and slowly dropped to her knees and closed her eyes and cried. "That's my niece right there," she said lowly as Mary knelt beside her. "Rene. God knows I miss you, baby girl."

Mary and Dimples, and various members of the family visited Ne'Ne's grave every Sunday morning to tend to it. Mary's pain had healed, but she, too, cried from to time, this day would one of those days.

"She loved you Martha. She's still with us, too. Here," Mary replied lovingly as she pressed her index finger gently to Martha's heart. "And here," she then said as she kissed the left side of her twin's temple and hugged her tightly.

Naomi and Twiggy knew both sisters were hurt all over again at that moment. They said nothing, only bowing their heads and swaying side to side, trying to hold back tears of sorrow as they reflected on the young life that lay in the grave before their very eyes. Naomi didn't have the chance to know Ne'Ne', she'd only heard stories, but through Dimples, she'd somewhat come to know her niece.

Twiggy, however, had watched Ne'Ne' grow up from a newborn. She was the one who had given Rene the nickname Ne'Ne'. Twiggy knew Rene Holland before Rene had even known herself. She wasn't Twiggy's real niece, but she might as well have been, because Twiggy loved her all the same. Those thoughts caused Twiggy to breakdown and cry. She was hurt for Mary and Martha's lost. She wiped her teary eyes and said, "When you lose someone you care so much about, some days the pain feels just like the first day you realized you have lost that person. Today is one of those days, sisters." Mary and Martha agreed with Twiggy, and for a brief moment, all three women went back to March 22, 1995, the day Ghost Town, their old neighborhood in Jackson, Mississippi, was forever changed.

"You three ladies," Naomi remarked somberly, "I understand believe me. But don't either of you feel guilty for surviving in that place. And the people who hurt—" Naomi quickly caught herself; she was about to speak out on the people Rene Holland and her friend Sandy Duncan had killed before they met their fate the same night, but what was transpiring on Ne'Ne's Hill at the time was not about who killed who, or what went down on March 22, 1995. It was about missing a loved one and Naomi knew that so she quickly changed her statement. "We all miss Ne`Ne`, and I hope to God that another day like that never arises within the family."

Martha sat back on the heels of her boots and stared through watery eyes at Ne`Ne`s grave and said sadly, "I'm not supposed to be here. I, I should be where Ne`Ne` is today. My niece shouldn't be dead," she ended as she leaned forward and hid her face, realizing that the fond memories she and her niece shared in Jackson, Mississippi, were all she had left to remember her by. Martha had the full understanding that creating new memories with her niece would never come to pass, and it pained her to the core. "Ne`Ne` took my place." Martha said as she clutched her stomach and stared at Ne`Ne`s picture and heaved and sat back up to try and regain her composure.

"Why you say that?" Naomi asked as she and Twiggy knelt behind Martha and Mary.

"All the wrong I done? The people I hurt? People I killed? I shoulda died the day I got shot on Friendly Lane. I lived, but death came back and got Ne`Ne`."

"You don't believe that, Martha," Twiggy said. "I lost all my people in Ghost Town but I don't think death passed over me and came back and took my nephew Simon. Peter Paul, Kenyatta, Sandy, Urselle, Sidney and Paulette, a lot of people died back there, but don't you feel guilty for living."

"I don't Twiggy. I just wish Ne`Ne` could've lived long enough to see our family now you know? We got a family that love us and I'm glad to be here in Oklahoma. I'm just sorry Rene is missing these times, you know?"

"Well, we're all together now. Back intact, Martha. Rene may not be here in the flesh, but she's always here in spirit. That helps me carry on," Mary stated with a smile and tear stained cheeks as Dawk came up the hillside toting a cooler full of beer. The four women could see Dawk was sucking on a peppermint and right away they knew he'd drunk some of the beer and they all laughed to themselves.

"Told you, Irene." Naomi remarked as Dawk handed her, Twiggy and Martha a cold beer.

Dawk then handed a beer to Mary, who said, "You know I don't drink that, Dawk. Where's the wine coolers? Did bring any wine coolers?"

Dawk opened the cooler and handed Mary a *Bartle's and James Passion Fruit* wine cooler and spread out a blanket for the females. The women then sat in front of Ne'Ne's while Dawk sat on the bench and popped open a can of beer.

"Hey, don't get drunk out here. I swear you'll spend the night right out here with Rene if you do." Naomi stated to her son.

"I'll just go to the guest house with Mary." Dawk said lowly.

"What was that you said, son?" Naomi asked politely, but doing little to hide her mounting angst.

"I said I'm not gone get drunk." Dawk replied, knowing his mother was prepared to scold him over the remark he made.

"That's what I thought I heard from that bench." Naomi said before turning her attention back to her sisters and Twiggy. "Now, Martha, Mary and Twiggy, it's time you hear and learn some things. Mary, I told you about the murder of our parents, you heard that too when we visited you in Grenada, Martha. I left a lot though, because some things I couldn't speak on while you were locked up. So now that we are together, I wanna tell you my story. How I grew up and what me and my friends and family went through early on. Do you girls mind?"

"I really wanna hear this, sister." Martha said as she swallowed a squib of her beer.

"Okay, well, you know we were split up in Alabama in 1965."

"Yea, you told me that in a letter. Plus I remember from the journal you wrote. What happened to that journal anyway, Mary?" Martha asked.

"I put it in a laminated scrapbook. Naomi only wrote on the front pages of the journal so it is perfectly preserved word for and page for page. I keep it in the family room inside the small house. The kids read it from time to time."

"Okay. I wanna read it again myself. I'm glad you kept it,

Mary. That's our history. Holland history. How you get to Chicago, Naomi?" Martha then asked. "Wait," she then said before Naomi could reply, "first tell us what happened to you after we left the orphanage in Selma."

"Well, the events that unfolded in the orphanage after you two left actually took me to Chicago in 1966."

"How?" Martha asked inquisitively.

"I remember the day you two were taken from me." Naomi said as she rested her elbows on her knees and looked to the ground. "I ran behind that car, holding on to the side while begging that man to stop. Please stop!" Naomi said through a smile as she looked towards the ground, tears forming in her eyes. "I lost my grip and fell down and watched helplessly as you two rode away. Watching my two baby sisters being driven away to God knows where had left a wound in my heart that didn't heal completely until I ran and grabbed Mary in that driveway behind her home back in Ghost Town. But they day you two were taken, I fell down screaming and out of control...and then..."

Selma, Alabama—August 1965

...Ten year-old Naomi Holland lay flat on her stomach in the middle of the dirt road leading back to the Orphanage in which she resided. It was a hot day in August of '65 and the ten year-old husky-framed 4' 5" 115 pound little girl with thick, dark hair was screaming to the top of her lungs because she had just witnessed her two youngest sisters, Mary and Martha Holland, being driven off from the orphanage.

Naomi had lost her brother Samson Holland to an adopter six months earlier and she had promised herself that she would keep Mary and Martha with her always and not lose them the way she had lost Sam. She was devastated to not be able to fulfill the promise she had made to herself and her sisters. The ten year-old had been to hell and back and her nightmarish existence was only getting worse as time wore on. She had witnessed the murder of her parents three years earlier in Sylacauga, Alabama and was the only sibling that knew the truth behind the murders at the time and others were unwilling or unable to help bring justice to her family.

13

To cover their heinous crime, town officials in Sylacauga spread rumors to the orphanage's officials that Naomi's parents were heroin junkies and had robbed the city bank to earn money to support their habit and pay the mortgage on their farm. They also had members within the orphanage's staff to further fuel their propaganda. A conspiracy was underway against the Holland family's children. Their parents were killed, and all that remained was for the officials to separate the siblings. They'd succeeded up to the point of removing Sam, Mary and Martha and now, only Naomi remained. Sam, Mary and Martha were too young to fully comprehend what had transpired; but Naomi knew all-too-well what happened. She saw the officer who had shot her mother only feet away from her and she remembered his last name—Eastman. She silently vowed revenge someday, but on this day, the ten year-old was torn apart having lost all her siblings. They were all she had left and now they were gone.

Naomi didn't trust anyone at the orphanage except a man by the name of Kevin Langley. He was an assistant manager at the orphanage; a white man around Naomi's parents' age when they were killed. Naomi, who had come to somewhat fear and hate white people, had come to trust Kevin for two reasons: he was the only one at the orphanage who called her by her name and he never uttered the words 'nigger' or 'savage', two words the child had come to abhor because they'd been used by her family's killers.

For those two reasons alone, Naomi was drawn to Kevin, but he wasn't at the orphanage on this day in August of 1965, however; Naomi believed had he been there, her sisters would not have been taken. She put up a serious struggle as staff members picked her up from the ground, kicking up at the staff members as she lay on her back, knocking her shoes off in the process. Her dress was above her waist revealing her underwear and the two plats she wore were now frayed. She was dusty from lying on the ground, and she screamed to the top of her lungs as two white male staff members got the best of her. One man grabbed both her wrists, the other wrapped his arms around Naomi's legs and both men carried her back to her room where they threw her down on the bed and quickly locked the door. Naomi ran to the window and beat on the pane furiously while looking to see if she could see the car that held her sisters but it was out of sight.

For two days Naomi stayed locked in the room. She didn't eat the food that was brought to her, nor did she bathe. The weekend staff could care less about her welfare and they never bothered to check on her the entire weekend. Tired of being mistreated, Naomi lashed out early Monday morning when she awoke from her sleep by trashing the room. She smashed the desk beside her bed, pulled the curtains down, and took a chair and broke the two windows in the room and then tried to escape. That loud shatter startled thirty-nine year-old Kevin Langley, who was down the hall in his office, having just arrived for his shift. The man leapt from his seat and ran to Naomi's room, unlocked the door and entered and saw the little girl jumping up and down on the bed in her panties. Urine was running down her legs, her hair was a mess and both of her hands were bloody because she had cut herself on the broken glass trying to escape.

Kevin ran over to Naomi and grabbed her and asked, "What's going on here? What're you doing, Naomi? What is this?"

"They took Mary and Martha! They took my sisters! We gotta get 'em back!" Naomi yelled hysterically as she lay in the clutches of Kevin's arms.

"Calm down. Come on now Naomi." Kevin said softly as he held her tightly and looked at her hands.

Kevin saw that Naomi had a gash in her left hand and a puncture in her right hand. Knowing the little girl needed medical attention, he wrapped her in a sheet and took her to the nurse's office. The nurse began attending to Naomi's hands and Kevin began to leave the room to phone members of the weekend staff to find out what happened to Mary and Martha. Naomi saw him leaving and she leapt from the chair and ran behind him, nearly tripping over the long sheet that draped her body. The nurse ran after her, but Naomi made it to Kevin and grabbed the man around his waist, staining his clothes with her bloody hands. "Don't leave me!" she cried aloud. "They gone kill me! Don't leave me, please!"

Kevin turned around and knelt down and said, "You're safe here, Naomi."

"No I'm not! They killed my momma and daddy! They took Sam, Mary *and* Martha! They gone kill me! That's why they took them away! So they can kill me!"

"I won't let anything happen to you. I promise."

"You promised me and my family would stay together but we didn't! You're just like them! You're on they side!" Naomi side as she backed away from Kevin.

The nurse grabbed Naomi from behind and she turned and kicked the lady in her shin. When she bent down and grabbed her leg, Naomi punched her in the face and knocked her down to the floor and quickly grabbed her injured right hand and grimaced from the pain. The jab she had given the nurse had reawakened the wound, but it didn't prevent her from kicking at the nurse, who crawled away and pulled herself up and leaned back in a corner.

"She's an angry nig—" the nurse caught herself when she noticed the glaring stare coming from Kevin, as if he were daring her to say that word.

Kevin really felt for Naomi. To him, she had a rage within her that was hard to contain, a burning desire to hurt those around her who were causing her so much pain. He grabbed her and called for more medical staff in order to treat her wounds. Naomi had to be held down and sedated with a tranquilizer, which quickly put her to sleep. When she had awakened a couple of hours later, she saw that she was strapped to the bed. Her left hand was stitched, and her right hand was bandaged. Naomi began screaming again and she didn't stop until Kevin entered the room.

"Why you let them do this to me?" she asked loudly as she continued to kick and scream.

"The nurses had to stitch your hand, Naomi."

"Now what?"

"You need to eat." Kevin answered as he got up to grab Naomi's lunch from the cafeteria. As he headed for the door, Naomi began screaming again.

"Naomi! I'm only going get your food."

"Say you promise! Tell me you promise! And mean it this time!" Naomi screamed as she choked on her tears.

"I promise. I will be right back, Naomi." Kevin replied before he turned and walked out the door.

When Kevin returned, he was with a staff member from the cafeteria. The lady sat the tray that held a bowl of chicken noodle soup on the stand beside the bed as Kevin unstrapped her and Naomi sat up and just stared at the bowl as if it were a mere brick. The cafeteria worker waited to see if she was going to eat the soup, but Naomi wouldn't budge. She looked over to Kevin, and then looked at the cafeteria worker, letting her eyes do the talking. Kevin understood Naomi's silent talk so he turned and nodded his head towards the door and the worker left.

"Okay, go ahead and eat, Naomi." Kevin said once he and Naomi were alone in the room.

"It's poison! They tryin' to kill me!" Naomi yelled angrily as she went to knock the bowl of soup off the tray.

Kevin grabbed her arms and held on tight. "No," he yelled as he held her arms at her side. "Not another temper tantrum! Not this time, Naomi! No one's tryin' to kill you here! Now eat!"

"You eat it first." Naomi snarled as she sat back down to watch Kevin's reaction.

"Fine!" Kevin said as he picked up the spoon and dipped it into the bowl and ate a portion of the soup. "See? No one's tryin' to kill you Naomi."

Naomi sat back and opened her mouth and Kevin looked on in surprise, sensing that she wanted to be fed. She was ten years old—fully capable of feeding herself—but her actions had caused the man to do a quick evaluation of the troubled child. Kevin had a degree in Child Psychology, and his quick assumption was that Naomi was trying to forge a bond with him. He knew that Naomi, by allowing him to feed her, was placing her full trust in him. Whatever the reason behind her actions, Kevin was willing to oblige because Naomi was truly a troubled child who needed special attention lest she not survive her stay at the orphanage. Kevin had seen kids taken away to mental institutions and many of them entered into a psychotic state, some never speaking again, others setting fires, and several had even committed suicide. He was determined not to let Naomi be removed from his care and become another statistic.

"My birthday is November 29, 1954." Naomi said, breaking Kevin's silent thoughts.

"I know, Naomi. I have all your records," the man answered as he dipped the spoon into the bowl and slowly brought it up to Naomi's mouth. He picked up another portion and fed it to the little girl and she smiled as he did so. It was the first time in months that Kevin had seen Naomi smile, and she'd even managed to thank him, words that had touched Kevin's heart. On this day, a bond was beginning to form, too bad it took Naomi losing her siblings, but at least Kevin had finally committed fully to making sure Naomi was okay, at least that's how Kevin Langley viewed the matter.

The next few weeks saw Kevin spending more and more time with Naomi. There were seventy-two orphans inside the home, but he'd made Naomi his top priority because he knew she needed the most attention. On top of that, he really wanted to be near the little girl. Naomi repeatedly told Kevin that her parents were murdered. He believed her, but there was nothing he could do. He knew all- too-well that trying to solve a racist-fueled murder in the heart of the south would only endanger his and Naomi's life, but he did try to find out what happened to Sam, Mary and Martha.

When Kevin discovered the kids' records were missing later that afternoon, he, too, had come to believe that a cover-up was on-going. He also began to believe that Naomi may be right about people trying to kill her. To prevent the little girl from being lost in the system or worst, Kevin carried her portfolio with him wherever he went, and for over a year, he looked after the child very cautiously, working seven days a week and locking her in her room at night and taking the spare keys home with him. Those times were frightening for Naomi. She felt that on any given night, her door would be smashed in and she would be taken somewhere and killed, maybe burned like her parents were. She rarely slept at night, and she wore clothes all the time, ready to jump out the window and run if anybody besides Kevin tried to enter her room.

Kevin and Naomi had grown so close to one another by October of 1966 staff members working for town officials back in Sylacauga had decided to put in orders to have Kevin moved to Chicago, Illinois. When he got the news, Kevin knew if he were to leave Naomi behind, she would suffer a tragic fate. He fought the move for as long as possible, denying requests to fill out his transfer papers while filing State reports for Child Study on Naomi Holland that would keep him involved in the child's welfare. The more Kevin hung around, however, the more he could feel the noose tightening around his neck so-to-speak. Staffers were beginning to treat him harshly; they were trying to get rid of him, offering to work weekends on his behalf and inviting him to vacations, all so they could be alone with Naomi.

Kevin didn't know who was pulling the strings, but he sensed that most of the staff was involved in what he viewed as a plot to kill an innocent child. His beliefs were solidified when a short message that read '*Nigger Lover Beware*' was placed in his mailbox on Halloween night of 1966. That was it for Kevin. He now knew for certain that he and Naomi's future, better yet, their lives were at stake. Whoever was pulling the strings had just upped the stakes and Kevin was not about to stick around to see how the end would unfold in this subtle game of xenophobic chess because checkmate would mean certain death. He had all the files on Naomi, and if he was leaving, he was taking the child with him. He would not sit by and let Naomi be killed.

On a cold and rainy Sunday night in early November, Kevin, after filing out his Request for Transfer papers, snuck into the orphanage and went to Naomi's room and woke her and told her to remain calm and quiet. He placed a coat on her and shuffled her to his car and took her to his home just outside of downtown Selma, Alabama where he would hide Naomi in his basement until he could make the arrangements to move away from town. The following day, when Kevin returned to work, the staff was up in arms over the fact that Naomi was missing.

"Where is she?" Kevin asked in mocked unawareness.

"How about you tell us?" a man in a neat, dark brown silk suit asked matter-of-factly.

"Mister, umm, who are you, sir?" Kevin asked, having never seen the muscular black-haired white man before in his life.

"Eastman's the name. Sylacauga Sheriff's Office. We have orders to remove Naomi Holland from this orphanage. She's being relocated to Huntsville, Alabama."

"Show me the documents."

"There are none, but this case began in Sylacauga, so it's my business to know what happens with that child. I want to make sure she is being taken care of the best way possible. The managers here tell me codes are being violated because Naomi Holland refuses, or rather, you refuse to have her bunk with the other kids. Three to a room here and you know that. We'll move her to a better facility and free up three additional beds here."

"This makes no sense. Anyway, she's gone. If you wanna be helpful, you'll go and track her down yourself. I guess she was smart enough to get the hell outta here before you came for her, umm, Mister Eastman."

"Are you interfering with official business, Mister Langley?" Eastman asked as the manager stood beside him, both men staring angrily at Kevin.

"No, sir," Kevin replied as he began to get nervous. "But until you show me official papers, not from this orphanage, but from the Birmingham Department of Child Services, I will not sign off on moving that child. And I most certainly won't hand her over to a complete stranger. And like you've told me, she's not here. You'll have to find her to move her. I would like to help, but I no longer work here. I'm turning in my resignation as of today."

Kevin knew the rules and procedures like the back of his hand. And something inside was telling him that this man Eastman had no intentions on taking Naomi to Huntsville, Alabama. He would make sure she was taken care of alright, but she wouldn't be going to Huntsville. Kevin was glad he'd moved Naomi the night before; otherwise, he would have never seen or heard from the child again. He eased pass the two men and began removing contents from his desk, a bone of contention rising from within as he knew he'd done a good thing for Naomi.

Eastman looked over to the manager and extended his hand to Kevin as if to say to the manager, *"Are you're gonna take care of this?"*

"Look here nigger lover," the manager of the Orphanage stated angrily. "We know you responsible for this little mishap! Now, what will happen here is that you will leave this facility. Take the little half-breed nigger-bitch bastard! I don't give a shit! What I do care about is you ever, *ever*, mentioning this orphanage or showing your face in Alabama again!"

Kevin's jaw was clasped shut as he stared at the manager and Eastman in fright. He was not a violent man, and it was fair to say that he feared for his life at that moment. He literally held his breath, turning red in the face as Eastman stared at him coldly. The perceived racist pointed at Kevin and produced a smirk. "That letter you got in your mailbox is all the warning you get, boy," he said to Kevin as he placed his right hand on the barrel of his gun. "You better make a move and make it soon—because if we find out you're hiding that little girl? I'll have your nigger-loving ass arrested for interfering in official business. And Naomi," he said as he chuckled, "Naomi will only be a fond memory and your ass'll have your own troubles to deal with when you're placed into gen-pop with niggers who can't stand your ass. See ya' 'round, Mister Langley. But for your sake? It's best I don't."

When Eastman and the manger turned and left, Kevin gasped for air and vomited onto the floor. On this day, he had come to understand fully the hatred that some whites had towards blacks as he cleaned up the mess he had made. He was relieved that Eastman and the manager had walked out of his office without inflicting bodily harm. This Eastman guy and the manager were undoubtedly aiming to rid the world of Naomi, and if they got to her, Kevin knew he would be killed right along with the little girl. The shaken man gathered Naomi's documents, his entire body trembling as he knew he'd just stared Naomi's potential killers, and possibly even, one of the killers of her family in the face as he cleared out his desk drawers and went home and began planning his departure.

The week leading to his leaving was the scariest week of Kevin's life. The man stayed locked in his home with Naomi tucked away in the basement and walked around his home with a loaded twelve gauge, rarely sleeping. Kevin had never even fired a gun in his life, but the fear he had within himself compelled him to purchase and wield a weapon. The people at the orphanage had forced him into a life he cared not to live. Kevin wasn't a killer, and truth be told, he wasn't sure he would even fire the gun if he was confronted with animosity. He simply had to get away, that was his only option, because restless nights and countless shots of Whiskey to build up his courage to kill another human being was not the life he wanted to live.

Naomi, during that period of time, had seen the protectiveness within this white man and she wanted to aide him. In her eyes, she and Kevin were now in this fight together, because if Kevin was willing to risk his life over her safety, she would do all she could to partake in the battle because she herself wanted the both of them to survive and get away. Naomi would sneak up from the basement when she knew Kevin was asleep and she would silently stand guard. Kevin would often awake to find a blanket over him, or an extra box of bullet shells. He knew Naomi was looking out for him as best she could at her young age, but she was just a child. If her attackers came, she would basically be helpless to defend herself. "*I have to get her out of here. Soon!*" Kevin would often state to himself.

Halfway through the week, Kevin had brought Naomi a plate of steamed rice covered with fried sausages and green bell peppers and topped with grilled onions down to the basement. All had been quiet around town. No threatening letters or phone calls, and the movers had begun boxing Kevin's items and breaking down beds. The move was going along smoothly and Kevin had finally felt comfortable enough to begin moving around the house a little more, so much so, he'd fixed Naomi a special dinner and sat and talked with her in a peaceful atmosphere in order to ease her anxiety.

"I never had sausages and peppers before." Naomi said as

she mixed the meal.

"It's an Italian dish. My mother was Italian."

"My mother was a Creek Indian."

"I know, Naomi. I bet she was beautiful."

"How you know that?"

"Because *you* are beautiful. You get your looks from your mother I bet."

"I don't gamble."

Kevin laughed as Naomi tasted the dish. "This is good. How you cook so good?"

"Well, I haven't a woman in my life. You learn over time."

"My grandmother was a good cook." Naomi stated in between swallows of food.

"Can you cook?"

"I don't know. I like to eat though." Naomi quipped, bringing about a smile to Kevin.

"Why white people don't like black people or Indians? Did we do something wrong?"

"No, Naomi. Those types of people are just ignorant. And all white people don't behave in that manner. I'm white and I like you."

"I know. I like you too. You my only friend."

Kevin smiled again and touched the back of his hand to Naomi's cheek. The ten year-old sighed, dropped her fork and held Kevin's hand close to her cheek and said through tears, "I loved my family! They was, they was the best family in the world! And they gone now. They all gone!"

Kevin's heart went out to Naomi constantly. Her words, just about every time she spoke, impacted him greatly and he really wanted to see her make it in life. He hoped for it. "You'll do great things someday, Naomi. I'm gonna make sure you do great things. Make sure you're okay, my child."

"I believe you, Kevin." Naomi said as she picked up the fork and continued to eat, she and Kevin lightly talking.

It was during this time of further bonding in Kevin's basement that he and Naomi heard a thud upstairs and then tires screeching a few seconds later. Kevin grabbed his shotgun, ran upstairs and looked around nervously, cautiously walking towards his front door. He cracked the door slightly and found two nooses on his porch. He picked them up and quickly locked the door.

"What is it?" Naomi asked.

Kevin jumped. He thought Naomi was still in the basement. He hid the nooses, but Naomi had already seen them.

"It's them again, isn't it?" Naomi asked as she ran back into the basement crying. "Why they don't like us?" she could be heard asking repeatedly as she descended the stairs. "We did nothing to them!" she cried aloud.

Kevin sat down on the couch, poured a full glass of whiskey, downed it and placed his head in his hand. He had become troubled and depressed once again, tired of the harassment and growing weary. The man couldn't go on living like this. Naomi didn't do any wrong to anyone, but because she was Creek Indian and Negro, she was being persecuted. The next two days were nerve-wracking for Kevin. The man found bullets placed in his mailbox, and 'nigger lover' was spray painted on his car. He hid those things from Naomi, but even she had seen hooded men riding pass Kevin's home on three occasions, not to mention the nooses she had seen Kevin hiding behind his back. On the sixth day the moving company had all of Kevin's furniture loaded into a moving van and he and Naomi left for Chicago in the middle of the day a week before Thanksgiving in 1966.

Kevin believed had he stayed longer than that week, he and Naomi both would've been killed. He'd come to understand that Naomi was right all along—if she'd stayed in Alabama, she wasn't going to go to a foster home like her brother and sisters, she was going to be killed because she was the only surviving Holland family member that knew for certain that her parents were murdered.

Kevin and Naomi set out for Chicago to start a new life; neither knew what lie ahead, but Naomi was glad that Kevin believed her and cared enough to save her and she would be forever grateful; but she would never forget what happened to her and her family in Sylacauga. Ten year-old Naomi Holland would leave Selma, Alabama with forty year-old Kevin Langley, telling herself that she had a score to settle with the state. By letting her and Kevin live long enough to escape their wrath, those responsible for Naomi and her family's plight had given her the opportunity to exact revenge—but even more important than that—they gave her a chance to find her siblings and reunite the Holland family once again...

****

..."What was perceived as running a 'nigger lover' and an orphan out of town would over the years become a blessing." Naomi said as she sat atop the blanket on Ne'Ne's Hill.

"A blessing it has been, sister." Mary stated proudly.

"Yes it has been, Mary," Naomi replied. "Kevin tried to pretend he didn't know where I was the day after he moved me but that tactic didn't fly. Those white racist were onto him big-time."

"At least y'all got away from there." Martha remarked as Twiggy and Mary nodded in agreement.

"Umm hmm. But the road was still rough for us two."

"Y'all struggled?" Martha asked.

"Not in the way you and Mary did back in Ghost Town, Martha. Kevin was financially well-off. I grew up around money and it rubbed off on me as you can see," Naomi answered as she extended her arms outwards towards the open land. "Kevin and I had, we had emotional problems. Well, *I* had emotional problems. But this woman Kevin met? This really wonderful woman named Serena—"

"You talkin' about grandma right, momma?" Dawk asked.

"Yes, Dawk. The lady that became your grandmother. See, girls? I had a family too. They weren't blood, but they treated me like their own. That woman of Kevin's did something for me that helped out a great deal." Naomi said.

"Ohh lord, the dolls!" Mary stated as she laughed.

"What's the dolls?" Martha asked as she opened another beer.

"Well, Mary knows—but let me go back a bit to when we first got to Chicago. Actually we lived in Cicero, a few miles

25

outside Chicago limits, but it's all the same, Chi-Town, Cicero, whatever!" Naomi said as she opened another can of beer and told the story of Serena and the Dolls.

CHAPTER 2
SERENA AND THE DOLLS

"King of diamond beats your queen of heart! I win!" Naomi yelled aloud.

It was December of 1966, a month after forty year-old Kevin and Naomi, now age eleven, had moved to Chicago. Kevin stayed at a hotel for a week until he was able to find a home for sale in Cicero, just outside of Chicago, a week after Thanksgiving. The home was a luxurious two story red-brick home with white shutters, a huge porch with a swing, and a neat front lawn, although the backyard was somewhat small. It was a three bedroom two and a half bath home with wooden floors and raised ceilings. The dining room and kitchen were connected and the adjoining living room with the fireplace made that part of the home real warm and cozy.

It was there, in the dining room, on this cold December night in '66 that Naomi and Kevin were sitting at the table playing Battle. Naomi had just beaten Kevin at the card game and she went to gather all the cards and set them aside to prepare the table for dinner. Kevin, unbeknownst to Naomi at the time, had her going through therapy. He knew Naomi had serious emotional problems and he was trying to help the child overcome the misfortunes that held her back from becoming a productive and sociably viable individual.

Kevin also had to find a job. He had four months' worth of savings left, so by March of 1967 he had to be working in order to support him and Naomi. The job he'd supposedly had with an orphanage in Chicago was denied to him when he arrived in town. The administrators back in Selma had called and told the orphanage not to hire Kevin; they also gave a bad reference for the simple fact that they did not want the man to be a part of the system anymore because they knew he knew too much about what went on in Alabama. Kevin didn't get angry; instead, he came to view the job denial as a blessing. He wanted a complete career change anyway and he was now searching for a new job venture.

Naomi, once Kevin moved into the house in Cicero, seemed to begin heading towards becoming emotionally stable, but it was a slow process. She still had issues that arose from time to time, but they were becoming more infrequent. She was prone to snap at any given moment, however; the littlest gesture, comment or question could easily cause another psychotic episode to rise from within. Kevin came to see that it took very little to set Naomi off; she had sort of a manic-depressive disposition and she was hard to figure out at times.

Kevin often wondered what was going on inside that little head of hers, but when he asked, Naomi would shut herself off emotionally most times. The eleven year-old could go from happy to angry, or from aggressive to subservient in a matter of seconds and she often lashed out at Kevin, who had the hardest time figuring out why Naomi often tried to attack him. He soon observed that Naomi grew angry whenever he asked her about her family and concluded that the child wasn't ready to talk about the matter because she was still angry and hurt by what had happened.

Naomi's pain was often reflected in her behavior, but Kevin never stopped prodding. He'd asked her about her family the second night they spent in the home trying to spark conversation, and she only sulked, cutting her eyes at him as she headed upstairs. It was the calmest Kevin had ever seen Naomi respond to his questions about her family and he was surprised when she came back down the stairs with a stack of papers and handed him the top sheet.

Kevin took the sheet of paper and saw that Naomi had written down what happened to her family, explaining: "*I don't know why a policeman by the name of Eastman had shot my mother in the back two times. The police killed my father and grandmother. I had a gun pointed in my face when I ran to help my mother and it scared me. I couldn't move. In the end, I, Naomi Holland, a Negro and a Creek Indian little girl eleven years old, now find myself apart from my brother and two sisters with a White man in Chicago. His name is Kevin Langley and he's my only friend in the world."*

Kevin looked over to Naomi as she stood beside him with her head bowed. He ran his hands through his silky brown hair, tapped the floor with his wing-tipped shoes and stared down at Naomi, holding back tears of pity, but also tears of joy. For the first time since he'd taken her away from the orphanage just over a month ago, Naomi had expressed herself towards him. It was curt and to the point, but the words she had written spoke volumes.

"I left my journal in Selma. I know they probably destroyed it, but I wrote it over again. This is everything right here," Naomi then said as she held up the new journal she had written. "But that's all you need to know for now," she ended as she turned and marched back up the stairs, never losing eye contact with Kevin.

Naomi's thick, dark eyebrows curved downward and her brown eyes were squinted as she traversed the stairs. She had an angry look on her face as if it pained her to tell Kevin what she had told him. Naomi had her reasons to be angry, however; she was mad at Kevin for not doing anything to seek justice for what had happened to her family in Sylacauga or Selma. Even at her young age, she knew Kevin was afraid of the people in Alabama, and truth be told, Naomi was somewhat afraid of the people down there herself; but she thought that because Kevin was a grown up, he should have been able to do something to help her out. Naomi was just too young to understand Kevin's fear, however, and that lack of understanding had just forced her to give up on the hope of Kevin ever helping her seek justice for her parents' murders. Kevin need not worry any longer, because when she was old enough, Naomi would take care of that portion of her life herself—at least that's what she was thinking as she walked up the stairs the second night in the new home.

Naomi placed the cards in the drawer and washed her hands

and placed mitts on them and grabbed the baked chicken from the oven as Kevin gathered glasses and plates. He turned on the water in the sink to rinse the glasses and asked, "Naomi, how do you feel about attending school here in Cicero?"

"I never been to a school. My mother and grandmother taught me all I needed to know."

"I know, but maybe with you going to school you can make friends."

"You're my friend. That's good enough for now."

"I mean friends your age, Naomi."

"I want my brother and sisters to be my friends!" Naomi said loudly as she threw the chicken on the floor, shattering the dish and ruining the meal in the process before running out the kitchen crying.

"Dammit!" Kevin yelled as he slammed the glasses and plates on the counter. The plates shattered and Kevin cut his hand. He leaned back and screamed loudly, "God, Jesus!"

Naomi ran back into the kitchen, and when she saw the blood dripping from Kevin's hand, she began to scream. "Kevin! I'm sorry! I'm sorry!" she said hysterically as she ran and grabbed a towel and wrapped his hand.

Kevin drove himself to the hospital and Naomi cried the whole way, apologizing repeatedly. When he was taken into a private room to have his hand stitched, Naomi went into a fit. She thought the man wasn't coming back and she began calling out for him hysterically until the nurses finally relented and let her in the room.

Later that night, as Naomi lay on the sofa asleep, Kevin began analyzing his life. He questioned whether he could deal with Naomi until adulthood as he stared at his stitched hand. Things were easier the year they spent at the orphanage because other staffers who weren't involved in the plot to kill the child were around to help when he needed. Naomi was a serious task for Kevin on his own he had to admit—but he had willingly taken her to Cicero so he had to finish the job he'd started with the eleven year-old. The man hoped he could change Naomi and help her transition into adulthood, but he also worried that when she was grown, would Naomi be mentally sound enough to function on her own? Or would she forever need assistance because of her mental instability? Kevin began to think that maybe taking Naomi away was a bad idea. He believed at the outset that he could help her, but the task was becoming a serious battle that had the man questioning himself as to whether he was up to the challenge. Putting Naomi back into foster care would destroy her for certain in his eyes so he was now stuck with the child. Kevin then laughed to himself. Naomi was a minor and he'd dealt with troubled kids before. What was it about this child that was causing him to be so lenient when a strong hand and more importantly, a stern voice is what she needed in order to govern her properly? *"Who really is in control here?"* Kevin asked himself. He then answered his own question in silence, *"I'm in control! Naomi should do as I say! I'm the adult! And I call myself a psychologist!"* he ended as he laughed to himself.

Whatever the reason or status of the current situation, Kevin was in too deep with Naomi and he couldn't back away. He was a smart man, but Naomi was a perplexing personality; a personality he had not encountered during his twelve year career in Child Psychology. He wanted to learn from Naomi, and he hoped that by doing so, he could give her what she needed in return to make it in life. Naomi said she didn't want to go to school, Kevin would respect her request and would home school the eleven year-old. Yes, Naomi was indeed running things in Kevin's life, but the man knew of no other way at the time how to get through to the child who he'd diagnosed as being abstruse.

Naomi knew Kevin as well. She knew he cared and he only wanted to help, but the fact that he was scared of the people in Alabama was causing her conflict. She would try and push Kevin to do her biding, conform him into the person she wanted him to be, and the more she pushed, the more things would go her way as Kevin had no answers to combat Naomi's difficult personality. Just like in her life, this entire experience was new to Kevin as well. Taking on a troubled child who'd witnessed horrible atrocities inflicted upon her parents at a young age, being stripped from her once happy existence and placed into a figurative pit of hell, which was the orphanage, and having loss the only surviving family she had left in the world would drive any normal adult, let alone a child, completely insane. A great deal of people would have given up on Naomi, viewing her fits of rage as an act of ungratefulness, believing she would never get better and only destroy the lives of those who were trying to help. Luckily for Naomi, she had Kevin caring for her. A resilient man who was not one to admit defeat, and would not give up on a child who he knew was at a serious disadvantage in all phases of her life. She didn't deserve a beating for her behavior, Kevin knew that, he also knew Naomi cared for him; she just had to find it within herself to get past what happened in her life and open up to him to allow him to help her from a mental aspect. Kevin, however, knew for an eleven year-old, that task would be nearly impossible. If anybody could do it, however, he believed that Naomi could do it. The man stared at the little girl for several minutes as she slept peacefully on the sofa before he got up to prepare for bed. When Kevin turned the light off, Naomi jumped from her sleep and ran and turned the light back on. She stared at Kevin with her trademark cold stare as she walked back to the couch and laid back down to go back to sleep. Kevin left the light on.

For Christmas Day of 1966, Kevin had bought Naomi a couple of gifts and was sitting on the first floor of the home awaiting her first appearance of the day. He'd been waiting for nearly a couple of hours when she finally walked down the stairs fully dressed. Naomi paused in the mid-drift when she saw Kevin sitting at the dining room table with a female around his age, the two of them drinking coffee. She hurried down the remaining stairs and ran into the dining room, placed her hands on her hips and asked in a stern voice, "Who's this person?"

"Well, good morning to you too, Naomi." Kevin said as he added cream and stirred his coffee.

"I said who is this person?" Naomi asked again as she stared at the green-eyed white woman harshly.

"This is Miss Serena Wales. She lives across the street."

"She needs to go back there!" Naomi snapped as she turned and walked back up the stairs, never acknowledging Serena, or even bothering to look at her gifts under the tree.

Kevin was embarrassed, but he and Serena, who was a forty-three year-old Sociologist for Cook County Department of Health and Human Resources, which encompassed the city of Cicero, had been discussing Naomi earlier in the day so the woman was somewhat aware of the situation and Naomi's disposition.

Serena was embarrassed for Kevin as well, but when he got up to go and correct Naomi, the short and petite woman brushed her blonde hair aside, stood up and said, "Let her be, Kevin."

"Serena? I know we've talked about Naomi's idiosyncrasies, but she had no right to speak to you in that manner. She has to learn to be dutiful of others. It's one of many things she has to learn and this can be used as a teaching point. I'm not going to scold her, just make her aware of how contemptuous she was towards you."

"She wasn't disrespectful, Kevin. I take no offense."

"Well, you should," Kevin replied. "She pushes me around with her pugnaciousness and now, her first time ever seeing you she's passing that attitude right along. I won't tolerate it."

Serena picked up her coffee mug, walked a few feet away and turned and looked up at Kevin and said, "If you don't mind me interjecting, I think she wants me to leave. No matter what you say when you go up there, she will never assimilate it into rational thinking because she wants me to leave."

"Well, I want you to stay."

"Okay, I will. And she'll be okay. Let's sit and finish our coffee. Tell me more about the business your parents ran in Philadelphia. Let's continue on and see what happens the next go around."

"Fine, but if she does it again…"

"We'll deal with it." Serena added.

Serena liked Kevin, and she wanted to help the man with Naomi. She knew gaining Naomi's approval would be key to her and Kevin maybe becoming intimate, but Naomi was of the utmost importance. Even if the two of them didn't connect,

Serena believed she could help Kevin as she herself often dealt with troubled youths in her occupation. She expressed her desire to help out with Naomi to Kevin and Kevin, who was having a hard time dealing with Naomi on his own, accepted the woman's offer.

"I'll just come over from time to time. I think she has to feel me out, so-to-speak. But I won't press anything. I promise."

"Serena, you won't have to press, Naomi does a fine job at that as you've already seen."

The two laughed and Serena gently tapped Kevin's arm as they continued spending time together before they were interrupted again by Naomi later that afternoon. She came down the stairs and eyed Kevin and Serena, who were now sitting in the living room as she went into the kitchen and grabbed a piece of sliced ham.

"Your gifts are under the tree Naomi." Kevin stated.

Naomi didn't reply. She just stared at Serena as she ate her piece of ham while the two adults returned to their conversation as if she wasn't even present.

When she was done eating, Naomi headed for the Christmas tree and grabbed her gifts. "She likes you," she turned and stated to Kevin.

"Excuse me?" Kevin asked.

"She wouldn't be here all this time if she didn't like you." Naomi remarked as she took the two boxes with her name on it and walked up the stairs eyeing Serena. "Don't you ever be mean to him because that's my job," she told Serena before she disappeared from sight.

Serena grew flush as Kevin looked her over. "I, I don't know what to say. She speaks candidly," the woman said as she coughed slightly and patted her chest, having been choked by Naomi's words.

"Well, is she telling the truth?" Kevin asked.

"She is telling the truth. It is her job to be mean to you."

Kevin laughed lowly as he slid to the edge of the sofa cushion. "That is her job from time to time I have to admit. But you know that is not what I was referring to."

Serena herself scooted to the edge of the cushions and looked Kevin in the eyes and said with a bright smile, "Ever since I watched you two move into this neighborhood I've had my eye on you two. You two are an interesting pair."

"What do you mean?"

"Well, I'm from Roanoke, Virginia as you know—and you know all-too-well that the south is full of prejudice, more so than the north, in my opinion. The day I saw this handsome white man drive into this predominately white neighborhood with a little black girl, a child I just knew wasn't his, I said to myself, 'He's a special man. He has to be. Or else he's going to harm that little girl'."

"So, it was more out of concern for *Naomi* that you spied on us." Kevin said as he poured Serena a glass of wine.

"Of course! As I watched or spied as you say? I noticed how you two interacted. You really do care. And the way Naomi cried that night you took yourself to the hospital showed how much she cared. She might not say it, but she loves you. After that, I said, 'I have to meet him. I have to meet them both'." Serena said as she turned to Kevin and sat her glass down and turned to face him. "I think you're wonderful. I want to be a part of you and Naomi's life. Can I, Mister Langley?" she asked sincerely as her face grew nearer to Kevin's.

"You most certainly can, Serena. You're a very pleasant and beautiful woman," Kevin replied as he began to draw closer to Serena's lips in preparation of a kiss. As their lips grew nearer, right before the moment they were about to touch lips, however, loud thuds began to be heard coming from upstairs.

"Naomi!" Serena and Kevin said in unison as they leapt from the couch and ran up the stairs to see what the commotion was all about.

When the two entered Naomi's room, they saw the eleven year-old had opened her gifts. Kevin had gotten Naomi a boy and girl baby doll set, only both were white. Naomi had laid the two white baby dolls on the floor and was jumping from her bed directly down on top of the dolls. When she saw Kevin and Serena, she jumped on the dolls one last time, picked them up, and hurled them at the two adults. "My family doesn't look like that!" Naomi yelled loudly before she ran up and slammed the door in both their faces.

Kevin clasped his hands to his forehead as he stood in the hall outside Naomi's room. Right away he knew he made a mistake. Naomi wasn't the typical child. She had suffered losses at the hands of white people and here he was, giving her white baby dolls to play with. The average child, black or white, would've loved the dolls, but Naomi, who was an angry child, had taken out some of her frustration on the toys. Serena grabbed the dolls and hid them from sight as Kevin slowly turned the knob on Naomi's door and entered her room in order to apologize.

"I hate Christmas! What's good about this day? What's good about it?" Naomi yelled as she ran and fell onto her bed and hid her face with a pillow and screamed to the top of her lungs, her body heaving from the pain and anger she was feeling at that moment.

It took almost two hours for Kevin and Serena to get Naomi to stop crying. It was during that time that Serena saw a chance to gain favor with child via an idea that she would bring to fruition the following day. In the meantime, however, once Naomi had calmed down, Serena and Kevin sat just outside of her room the remainder of the day. They sat on a chaise in the hall and talked real upbeat and loud. At the behest of Serena, they began to tell jokes and funny stories. Serena believed laughter was needed in order to help Naomi get over what had taken place a couple of hours ago. She felt Naomi's Christmas had been ruined, but she was trying to make it better for the child. Serena decided to tell a story about when she was a little girl in Virginia and how she had tied a sheet together and made a homemade parachute and jumped off the roof of her home believing she would float down like a feather.

"What happened?" Kevin asked.

"I plummeted to the ground like a rock! Broke my leg as well! Stupid gravity!" Serena said as she and Kevin laughed.

"That was dumb." Naomi said softly as she sniggled while sitting on her bed Indian style with a pillow tucked beneath her chin.

Kevin and Serena both looked at one another with their mouths slightly open in surprise as they smiled. They were making progress. The adults continued on talking in an upbeat fashion, cracking jokes whenever possible as Naomi sat quietly on her bed and listened. Serena would look into Naomi's room on occasion and when she did, Naomi would quickly shift her head away as if she wasn't listening and laughing. Kevin and Serena heard the little gasps and sniggles of laughter from time to time, however, so they knew she was listening keenly.

As night took over, Kevin and Serena had finished their bottle of wine outside Naomi's room and were about to start a second bottle. It was a little after eight and the snow was coming down heavy outside. Just as they uncorked the bottle of wine, Naomi, who had laughed often and even managed to smile at Serena when she peered into the room one time, finally grew tired. She got up and walked to the door, stood in the threshold and said softly, "Thank you."

"What are you thanking us for, Naomi?" Kevin asked.

"Thank *you*," Naomi said as she pointed to Kevin, "for the ham." She then pointed to Serena and said, "And thank *you* for making me laugh today. And I'm sorry I disrespected you, Miss Wales." Naomi then closed her door, but it quickly reopened. "I have something else to say also."

"What else do you have to say, Naomi?" Kevin inquired whilst smiling, proud of the fact that Naomi had apologized for her indiscretions and had also managed to show gratitude without being coaxed.

Naomi wiped away tears that were forming and said lowly, "I really didn't like today at first, but you two made it better. Good night," she ended as she stared at the two for a few seconds and gently closed the door. Naomi didn't receive any toys that she liked for Christmas, but the gift that she received from Serena, the gift of laughter, was good enough. It was highly appreciated.

Kevin and Serena smiled and hugged one another. They also had finally gotten to finish the French kiss they had started before Naomi had to be tended to earlier in the day as they sat on the chaise outside Naomi's room.

"Well, I should be going." Serena said as she pulled her face back from Kevin's.

"Yeah. We'll finish this bottle later. For New Year's maybe?"

"I would love to. But tomorrow, I'll have something special for Naomi—if you don't mind of course."

"No, not at all. Not at all. I think having a female in her life would do Naomi some good." Kevin remarked as he guided Serena towards the front door.

"You know," Serena said as she turned and looked into Kevin's eyes, "I've never kissed on the first date?"

"This was a date?"

"Well by all means! You don't think I just came here for the coffee, dinner and wine did you? I'm *courting* you mister!" Kevin and Serena laughed and hugged one another tightly before she stepped out into the cold where he watched from his porch as the woman made her way across the snow-covered ground to her home and entered her domicile.

The following afternoon around one 'o' clock, a light tap was heard at Kevin's front door. He answered and Serena quickly stepped into the foyer, knocking the snow off her boots and coat as she did so. She kissed Kevin's cheek and undid her scarf; it was then that Kevin noticed she had a huge shopping bag in her hand.

"What's this? Gifts? For moi?"

"No, Mister Langley. These are for Naomi." Serena said as she reached into the bag and pulled out a Raggedly Anne doll.

Serena had in all, two Raggedly Ann dolls and one Andy doll, and all three were black. "She said yesterday that her family 'didn't look like that'. Maybe, maybe she'll like these. What do you think?" Serena asked as she breathed heavily and looked out into the rest of the home. "Where is she," the perky woman asked as she peered into the house with wide eyes and a huge smile, her button nose and cheeks all rosy red and flush.

Kevin looked at Serena and it was at that moment that he knew she was going to be a part of his and Naomi's life for a long time. Black dolls were hard to find, and they cost a good bit of money. Serena went out of her way for Naomi and she didn't have to do so. The woman was sincere in her concerns for Naomi. "You're a good woman, Serena. Naomi's lucky." Kevin remarked in humbled voice.

"I'm the lucky one. I always wanted a daughter." Serena replied as she looked into Kevin's eyes and smiled. She then bowed her head when she realized the statement she made. "I'm sorry. I'm rushing things. I should—"

"No, no, it's okay. Really, it's okay." Kevin stated as he went to hug Serena.

Serena was bundled up and could barely move and Kevin was a little too far from her. He moved closer in order to hug her, but he stumbled over the bag and fell onto Serena. Serena fell against the door and she and Kevin slowly slid down to the floor. The two were laughing aloud just as Naomi entered the foyer and stared at them. Serena tapped Kevin's shoulder and when he turned and saw Naomi, he quickly stood up and grew silent. Naomi peeked around Kevin and stared at the dolls that were on the floor and then made eye contact with Serena. The woman balanced herself on her knees, slowly picked one of the dolls up and handed it to Naomi.

"I thought you might like these." Serena said cautiously as she held the doll out before Naomi, her hands shaking as she was nervous, hoping she didn't upset Naomi by buying the dolls.

Kevin sat and watched silently as Naomi slowly grabbed the doll and stared at it.

"Mary," Naomi said lowly.

Naomi quickly scooped up the other two dolls and held all three tightly and began to cry as she stared at Serena. She then dropped to her knees and fell into the woman's arms and wept. "Thank you, Miss Wales." she said through tears as she lay in Serena's arms.

Serena rubbed Naomi's thick platted hair, kissed her temple and said, "You're welcome, baby. You're so welcome."

Kevin moved over beside Naomi and the three embraced one another as Naomi turned on her back and said, "This Mary, Martha, and Sam. That's their names. Mary, Martha and Sam.

Me and Kevin were about to eat a ham sandwich, you can come in if you want." Naomi said happily to Serena as she stood up and walked into the house holding the three dolls.

While Kevin was helping Serena remove her coat and scarf, Naomi skipped happily into the dining room and pulled the chairs from under the table and sat 'Mary', 'Martha', and 'Sam' into a chair next to one another and she sat in between them. Kevin and Serena soon joined her and Naomi began to talk to the dolls as if they were human, stating that she loved them. She told the dolls about their mother's heritage. "She was a Creek Indian. You and Martha look just like her, Mary. Sam, you look like momma too, but you got daddy eyes." Naomi stated as she laughed.

All day long, Naomi walked around the house holding all three dolls. She would sit in the living room with Kevin and Serena, ever so often looking over to Serena and smiling. She hugged Kevin often, sometimes making him hug the dolls. Serena had even talked to the dolls, telling them how pretty their oldest sister was.

"This is one of the best days since I left Sylacauga. Thank you both." Naomi said later that evening.

Serena had helped out a great deal on this day and she had won favor with Naomi, who in turn, had loosened up a bit and had become more receptive from that point forth. And as 1967 came in, Naomi began to grow more and more comfortable with her new life in spite of the turbulent history that was still fresh in her mind.

CHAPTER 3
LUCKY AND FIN

"I loved those dolls so much." Naomi stated.

"She still got 'em inside too." Dawk stated.

Naomi rolled her eyes and smiled. "Yes, and even though the real Mary and Martha are right before my eyes, those dolls are still a big part of my life. I don't even think Serena knew at the time how much she helped me. You know, people can be so sweet, and so damned cruel. But with Serena and Kevin in my life? Things got much easier over time."

"Naomi, you had any friends when you were young," Martha asked. "Because me and Mary didn't have many friends until we moved to Ghost Town. Mary was my only friend for a long time. Then we met Twiggy."

"You're right, Naomi," Mary chimed in as Dawk cracked open another can of beer.

Naomi eyed her son, "You better not start wobbling, son."

"I'm okay, momma. I'm waiting to hear 'bout Lucky and Fin." Dawk replied.

"Who's Lucky and Fin?" Twiggy asked.

"Those are my two friends. I had friends at the campus where Kevin worked too. I had quite a few friends, but Lucky and Fin were real good friends. What was I right about, Mary?" Naomi then asked.

"About how sweet people can be sometimes. I don't know cruel people personally, but those people who killed our

41

parents were cruel."

"Who's sweet, Mary?" Martha then asked.

"Well," Mary said humbly, "when we got to Ghost Town we knew nobody, but Twiggy was a Godsend. She could have chosen to make life real difficult for us back there. Instead she befriended us. We owe a lot to Twiggy."

Twiggy looked at Mary and said, "That's one of the nicest things someone has ever said to me. Thanks, Mary."

"No, thank you, Twiggy." Mary said as she smiled.

"Well, *I'm* sure glad for Twiggy," Naomi chimed in. "We can't pick our relatives, but we most certainly can choose our friends. Twiggy was a damn good choice. And you chose good friends, Twiggy. Me myself? I chose some oddballs for friends. Why? I don't know—because Fin and Lucky are completely different. Maybe that's the reason—but anyway I decided one day that"...

April 1967

..."I'm going outside today," eleven year-old Naomi stated matter-of-factly to Kevin.

Naomi had given Kevin a hard time when they first arrived in Cicero in November of '66. When Serena entered their lives, however, things got easier. Serena and Kevin was a couple now. Kevin was also working. Serena had used her contacts in downtown Chicago to help the man get a job as an Assistant Professor of Psychology at Northwestern University. Kevin was earning good money and he was now home schooling Naomi. He took her to the college campus and laid out her work each day and she would sit in his small office and complete her assignments. When she was done with her work, usually right after lunch, Naomi would sit in the lecture room and listen to presentations by Kevin, or the tenured professor in charge of the Psychology Department.

At the young age of eleven, Naomi was benefiting greatly from the lectures she was hearing and she was learning a lot about herself, her peers and society in general. A privileged child she was to be sitting in a college setting at the prestigious Northwestern University at her young age. The experiences eleven year-old Naomi Holland was undergoing at the college campus would unknowingly benefit her greatly later on in life because of the undeniable fact that she was growing up around financially-fit, mature-minded, educated benefactors and it was causing her to mature at a rapid pace. Naomi sometimes used words kids her age could not understand and she always spoke in a confident tone. Real blunt was her attitude when she spoke and when coupled with the experiences she was witnessing at Northwestern, along with Kevin's and Serena's guidance, an intelligent female was definitely in the making.

Naomi and Kevin left the campus on this warm Friday in April of '67 and got into Kevin's Volvo and were headed home for the weekend when Naomi announced her desire to go outside.

"You are going outside today? I haven't seen many kids in the neighborhood, Naomi. You wanna go to a park or something like that?" Kevin asked.

"No. I'm just going outside. I saw some kids outside and I want to know who they are."

"Okay. How's about I bake some hamburgers later on?"

"Okay. My friends will come over so make one for each of them. There's two of them."

Kevin looked over at Naomi in wonderment and asked, "What are your friends' names."

"I don't know yet—but they *are* going to be my friends!"

Kevin chuckled to himself as he turned on the radio. He knew Naomi didn't have friends in the neighborhood at the present time, and before she'd even met the people who *may* become her friends, she'd already labeled them as friends and had invited them over to the house. The two made it home and Naomi quickly leapt from the car and ran down the block. Kevin watched Naomi run across the tree-lined street through two lush green lawns and cut through some shrubs and run up the stairs to a brown-bricked house and knocked on the door. Kevin somewhat knew the people, so he let Naomi go on with whatever plan she had formulated for the day.

Naomi knocked on the door repeatedly until a young male answered. "I'm Naomi Holland. I want to be your friend and I think that you should be my friend," she stated bluntly.

"I'm Faustino Cernigliaro. My friends all call me Lucky. My first name means lucky," the kid answered with a heavy Italian accent.

"What does Cernigliaro mean?"

"I don't know. My grandparents were from Sicily, though. The last name is Sicilian. That's all I know about that."

"Okay, Lucky. Can you come outside?"

"Sure!" Lucky replied as he stepped out of his door.

Faustino 'Lucky' Cernigliaro was a slender, olive-complexioned kid thirteen years of age. He had slick, jet black hair and dark eyes. He was taller than Naomi, but Naomi had more weight. Lucky thought Naomi was cute, so when she asked him to come outside he had no problem with her request, if only to be in the presence of the pretty girl who wanted to be his friend.

Lucky was a street-savvy young lad who resided with his mother and father in Naomi's neighborhood. He spent a lot of time with his father, who was a mafia hit man, who often hung out in another part of Cicero. Mendoza Cernigliaro, Lucky's father, had ties to Murder Incorporated, a notorious squad of hit men based in New York in which Bugsy Segal was also a member. Mendoza later became an enforcer for the Gambino Mafia Family and was acting on orders of his boss, Albert Anastasia, until Anastasia was gunned down in a barber shop in 1957.

It was after his boss was killed that Mendoza, who was in on the hit with the approval from Captains inside his own family, who felt the same as he, that the family's boss was outdated, moved his family to Chicago as another Italian took control of the Gambino Family and took the heat for Mendoza, who was a respected man in his organization. When Mendoza touched down in Chicago, he was able to continue his criminal career. Mendoza's wife, Francine, was a full-bloodied Italian woman who willingly went along with her husband's lifestyle. She was a loyal mafia wife that held true to her husband's mafia family ties and the married couple's son, Faustino, was being reared in the same fashion as his father and Francine approved.

Naomi knew not the facts behind Lucky's family history at

the present time; but she had often watched the man and his wife from her bedroom window and to her they seemed like some nice adults; and that led Naomi to believe that this particular family's son would make a good friend.

Lucky stepped out onto the porch and jumped from the stairs down onto the sidewalk and turned and faced Naomi. "You know, I have a friend around the corner named Finland Xavier. Black boy! He's all right, I guess. It's not a lot of kids around here so I just hang with him sometimes."

"I saw him. He acts like a girl."

"I thought I was the only one who thought that! Hey, he's a smart kid though. We only shoot basketball sometimes. You play basketball?"

"No. I play with baby dolls. Maybe Finland would like to do that." Naomi said as she and Lucky laughed.

"Come on," Lucky then said, "let's go and see Fin. I call him Fin for a nickname. You have a nickname, Naomi?"

"No. I'm Naomi. Just call me Naomi."

"Okay, Naomi. Call me Lucky." Faustino stated as he and Naomi walked down the street side by side.

Kevin had watched the scene unfold. He smiled as he went back into the car grabbed he and Naomi's belongings and brought them inside, happy that she was beginning to open up more and more. When he returned to the porch about ten minutes later, Kevin saw Naomi walking in between the young lad's door she had knocked on minutes ago, and a young black male around her age. Naomi and her two new friends walked over to Kevin's house and up the stairs onto the porch. "This is Faustino Cernigliaro, everybody calls him Lucky. This is Finland Xavier, we can call him Fin." Naomi stated and then turned to Fin and Lucky. "This is Mister Kevin Langley. He takes care of me. His fiancée is named Serena Wales and she stays right there across the street."

"You made a perfect introduction, Naomi," Kevin responded as he extended his right hand and shook the two young lads' hands.

Twelve year-old Fin was a black male with a slender face, a low haircut and brown eyes. He told Kevin he resided with his aunt Chloe and her husband Lester. Fin also wanted to tell Kevin what he often tried to tell his aunt about his troubled relationship with her husband, but her husband had always threatened him not to do so. Fin was having problems with his aunt's husband, but he was too afraid to tell anybody the problem that was a constant burden being thrust upon him. It would take time for Fin's troubled relationship with his aunt's husband become known to those around him. Kevin told Fin of a cookout he was planning soon and that Fin and his family should come and Fin agreed.

Kevin then mentioned that he had a conversation or two with Lucky's parents and asked Lucky their names again. Lucky replied by telling Kevin that the next time he sees his parents, to ask *them* their names again. Lucky wasn't about to give up his parents' names to a man he'd never met before. He quickly surmised that Naomi and her family were working people, but they were cool. Still, he wasn't going to give up his parents' names. He did want to be friends with Naomi though, because she was pretty to him. Lucky had a cocky disposition about himself; square jawed with a somewhat rugged appearance.

Kevin had to admit that Naomi had chosen two peculiar individuals to be friends with, but if she was comfortable with them, he would accept them for what it was worth. Naomi walked into the foyer and turned around and said to Kevin, "I'm going to get my dolls. Me and Fin will play with those," before she ran upstairs, leaving Kevin in the foyer with her two new friends.

Kevin welcomed the two boys in and sat them down in the living room and went into the kitchen to prepare the ground beef in order to bake the burgers. When Naomi came back down the stairs with the dolls, Lucky got up and walked into the kitchen. Lucky didn't play with dolls, and if Naomi and Fin wanted to play with dolls, that was their business.

"Mister Langley, what are you making? Pasta?" Lucky asked coolly as he walked into the kitchen and looked around whilst slowly nodding his head. Lucky had walked around the entire first floor of Kevin's home and was impressed with its layout. It wasn't as fancy as his parents' house, but the home was still nice in his eyes.

"No, Lucky. This here will be baked hamburgers." Kevin answered as he used a spatula to chop up the ground beef on a wooden chop board on the kitchen's counter beside the sink. "You like the home?"

"It's nice, Mister Langley. You should check out my parents' home the next time you talk to them. I'll tell them you may stop by to give 'em a head's up. I woulda used that ground beef for spaghetti, or lasagna, by the way." Lucky remarked then asked for a soda.

Kevin went into the fridge and handed Lucky a bottle of Coca-Cola. "You have an Italian accent, Lucky. Where are you from originally?"

"New York. My grandparents were from Sicily."

"Oh, okay. What do you know about baked hamburgers?"

Lucky yawned and said, "Booorrrinnng!"

"Alright, Lucky," Kevin said through light laughter. "We'll see about boring. Italians have good cuisine. I should know, because I'm part Italian. I love spaghetti, but hamburgers? You haven't had a burger until you've had a Langley burger. My parents owned a popular deli back in Lansing P-A, just north of Philadelphia. Cheese steaks were our specialty—but we had this four pound burger we used to make. I'll make two of those and the four of us can split them both. Quick math! How many pounds would each of our burgers weigh after I cut them in half?" Kevin asked as separated the meat into either side of the sink.

"We each get to eat a two pound hamburger?" Lucky asked in disbelief.

"That's right. What do you say now? Still boring?"

"Aww man! This is unbelievable! Now this I gotta see!" Lucky stated with a smile as he watched Kevin prepare the baked hamburgers.

Meanwhile, back in the living room, Naomi and Fin were playing with her dolls. "Do you like boys or girls?" Naomi asked as she eyed Fin.

"Why you ask me that?" Finland responded as he platted one of the dolls' hair.

"Because, you act like a girl."

"You don't know how girls act!"

"*I'm* a girl! Of course I know how girls act."

"Well there's your answer."

"So you like boys?"

"Do *you* like me, Naomi?"

"Yes. As a friend."

"Well, I like you as a friend—but what if I *did* like boys?"

"I don't care. I just wanted to know if my assessment of you was in accordance with my assumptions."

"Can you even spell those words you're using? In accordance with your assumptions? You can't shake me with those words."

"I wasn't trying to shake you. I really wanted to know if I was right. Am I?"

"You may be right, you may be wrong—but the way I act has nothing to do with who I like, okay, Naomi?"

"Okay, Fin. I'll never ask you again. You're a smart person by the way. I can see we'll get along fine. But just in case you do like boys? Don't like Faustino. He likes girls all the time. I can tell." Naomi whispered.

"Believe me, Naomi. I won't like Lucky, and I know he likes girls." Fin replied as he and Naomi continued to play with the dolls. "Just in case," Fin then added, "don't like Lucky, he likes *every* girl he sees. Today he'll like you, but tomorrow he'll like someone else."

Naomi chuckled as she watched Fin plat the doll's hair, knowing she would never like Lucky in that manner, and Fin neither. She only wanted to be their friends...

****

..."In April of 1967 I became friends with Lucky and Fin. Fin had a little problem with his aunt's husband Lester, but it took a while to figure that scenario out. And slowly we learned about Lucky's daddy Mendoza. Mendoza was a good man that did bad things. That's what Kevin told me about the man shortly after he got to know him."

"I kinda understand." Martha replied. "I'm a good person that has done some bad things."

"We all have done some bad things in the past Martha." Naomi stated. *"And some of us still are doing bad things,"* she then thought to herself.

"You made friends with an Italian in the sixties? How'd you do that?" Mary asked. "I mean, we had racist in the south and I know there were racist up north as well."

"There were racists up north—but the Cernigliaro family was down to earth. They didn't look at a person's race. If you were real, you were 'amico', which means 'friend' in Italian."

"I remember this lady that moved into our neighborhood in the early eighties," Martha then chimed in. "Mrs. Washington was her name. She was prejudice, but you know? I don't think she perceived herself to be that way."

Naomi smiled and then laughed. "What's funny?" Martha asked.

"Mary told me about that. The dog named 'Blackie' and what you did. That was funny Martha, but I had a similar experience in Cicero in the sixties that wasn't so funny. These three white women called me names, and girls? That little small group of friends on my block took action! It was a special moment for me too because I got to see just how much Serena cared during that time. And I, too, had finally confessed how I felt about both Kevin and Serena." Naomi said as she began to relate the Little Sambo Story.

CHAPTER 4
LITTLE SAMBO

"So, I got this fuckin' guy in the headlock, right? And he's pleading with me, 'Mendoza, Mendoza, you gonna break my neck!' So I reply, 'I know you fuckin' son-of-a-bitch, that's my day's ambition,'" thirty-six year-old Mendoza Cernigliaro told Kevin and Serena as he stood beside the grill pit in Kevin's backyard on a hot summer evening in July of 1967.

Naomi had become quite close to Lucky and Fin over the past few months and Kevin had come to know Lucky's mother and father quite well. He also came to know Fin's aunt Chloe and her husband Lester somewhat, but he was closer to the Cernigliaro family. Kevin was having a cookout this day and he thought it would be nice to invite Mendoza, his wife Francine, and Fin's aunt, Chloe and her husband Lester over to hang out and get better acquainted.

Mendoza Cernigliaro was a grey-eyed Italian with a head full of jet-black curly hair that stood an even six feet and had numerous tattoos on his forearms. He was a muscular, clean-shaven guy who was a heavy drinker during social events and could get real loud sometimes, and this day was no different. The adults listened to the man's story in a somewhat unnerved state, feeling a little bit at odds about hearing him discuss how he'd placed a man in the headlock and was preparing to snap his neck. Basically telling of a crime he'd committed on the streets. Only Francine could relate to what her husband was talking about, however; she was laughing loudly at times and adding to the story herself, reminding her husband of certain details he'd left out, willingly coasting him along with the telling of his gangster tale.

Lester had grown tired of Mendoza's braggadocios talking. "Come on Fin," he said as he stood up and stretched, "let's go and get another bag of ice from home for the drinks."

"Eh, that's a great idea, ole Les. The scotch is getting watery. You have any ginger ale?" Mendoza asked aloud.

"I'll check. I think we do. Be right back." Lester answered as he placed his fedora onto his bald head and trailed Fin out the side gate.

Kevin, Chloe, and Serena had thought things had settled down with Mendoza, but after speaking with Lester, he merely went back into his story. "I mean this guy is stomping the ground, slapping at my arms and—"

"Tell him when he passed gas, Mendoza!" Francine yelled through laughter. "Tell him how almost crapped his pants!"

"Oh yeah! This guy was all over the place! He smelled like rotten eggs let me tell ya'!" Mendoza said loudly as he erupted into laughter.

While Francine and Mendoza were engrossed in the story, Kevin looked around and noticed that Naomi and Lucky were listening intently to the conversation. "Mendoza," he leaned over and said in a near whisper, "I think maybe we should change the subject here. There are young ears listening," he ended as he pointed the spatula over towards the kids.

Mendoza looked around at the kids, and then towards his wife, who threw her arms up and said in her raspy, slow-pitched voice, "They don't understand, dear. They're right though, young ears are listening. Change the subject, Mendoza."

"You right, Kevin. You're right," Mendoza remarked. "But hey? Just to let you know? That guy had it comin'. And if I had ta' do it again? I would beat the brakes off that muther—"

"We get the point, Mendoza." Kevin said in a calm voice, cutting the man off.

Mendoza chuckled, patted Kevin on the arm and went and sat beside his wife and popped open a can of beer. The man meant no harm, telling a story was just a part of his personality. He'd been a member of the Italian-American mafia since he was eighteen, and had been affiliated with the mafia since he was his son's age. He was merely conducting himself as he always did whenever he got together with his Mafioso comrades in east Cicero.

"Hey," Lucky said to Naomi as he stood with her under the shady hickory tree in Kevin's backyard, "my dad likes your family. If he's telling stories like that? He definitely likes your family."

"What happened to the man in the headlock?"

"Go ask my dad and see what he says."

Naomi walked over to Mendoza and asked him what happened to the man in the headlock and Kevin had witnessed her walk over to the man. Mendoza felt eyes on him so he peeked from around Naomi and saw Kevin watching him closely. "I let him go, we talked it out and I let him go," he said to Naomi, who turned and skipped back over to Lucky.

"What did he say?" Lucky asked.

"He said he let him go—but I think he broke the man's neck. That's what he said his ambition was that day so why would he not do it?"

Lucky knew Naomi was right in what she was saying. He liked her and considered her a friend so for the first time, he shared a dark secret with her. He turned his back to the adults and said lowly, in a whisper that was nearly inaudible to Naomi, "My dad did kill that man. I was in the car that day with my momma and I saw it. We both did. Don't you ever tell no one what I told you, Naomi."

Naomi knew Lucky had just revealed a serious crime that his father had committed. One in which he bore witness to. She wondered why Lucky would tell her what his father had done as she would have kept that a secret forever. "You shouldn't tell what you and your father did. That's a serious secret, Lucky."

"I know, Naomi. But I trust you. You wouldn't say anything, right?" Lucky asked as he and Naomi walked back towards the concrete patio.

"I won't tell anyone, Lucky. Not even Fin. Still, you should keep your business to yourself." Naomi replied as Lucky nodded in agreement and the two sat down and drank a soda.

Mendoza soon got up, grabbed another can of beer and walked over to Kevin and apologized for being rude. "I was out of line earlier il mio amico (my friend). And I didn't tell Naomi anything else about what happened when she came over there. I respect you. Mister Langley. You *and* Serena. I just like to have a good time that's all." Mendoza stated just as Fin and Lester returned with bags of ice.

"I understand, Mister Cernigliaro. What does il mio amico mean?"

"It means my friend. I thought you were part Italian."

"I am—but I was born here in America. My mother was born in Philadelphia. My father in Italy. The two met at a train station, married and opened a deli. My father died from some illness years later and my mother sold the deli shortly thereafter and moved to the south and joined the Civil Rights Movement. She 'needed a new purpose' is what she always said to me during her time down there before she died a peaceful death in her sleep."

"Civil Rights, huh? That's a good thing. Seems like a little bit of your mother rubbed off you."

"What do you mean?"

"Are you kidding?" Mendoza asked with slight laughter as he looked over to Naomi, who was bouncing a basketball back and forth with Lucky. "Not ta' get in ya' business, Kevin, but something tells me that kid over there ain't yours naturally."

"I've told you about some of the things that happened in Selma and what Naomi has told me about her past in Sylacauga," Kevin said as he flipped the chicken breasts over and coated them with his homemade bar-b-cue sauce. "She may not be mines biologically, but I love her like my own. Serena and I both do."

"That really is a good thing you two are doing, man. Not many people would be able to fill your shoes."

"What about you?"

"What? Would I do what you are doing now?"

"Yes," Kevin replied as he closed the lid on the smoking grill, "I'm not tooting my own horn or anything, but I'm a good judge of character, I believe. You seem like the type of guy that would do the same thing Serena and I are doing if you were ever presented with such a predicament."

"Hey," Mendoza said as he handed Kevin a beer, "I have nothing, absolutely nothing against people of other races. Religion, sexual preferences, none of that bothers me. We're all human. Ya' got me?"

"I told Naomi something similar a couple of years back. I guess people like us really are a rare breed in these chaotic times. I sometimes get stares at the university when me and Naomi are walking hand in hand. I can always tell when they're wondering what we're doing together. Who says a white man can't raise a black child that's not his? Societal rules are only a façade that keeps people in their comfort zones and uninvolved in what's actually going on around them."

"Forget what other people think. You two are doing the right thing and it's more of a standup thing I've seen done in years. More than a lot of the men I ran with back in New York. A lot of my guys hated Negroes. I used ta' tell 'em black people can be more loyal in this business than a lot of our own kind. And that's why I did business with them back then—and that's why I do business with them now."

"What did your guys back in New York have to say about you doing business with blacks?"

"Some of 'em called me a, a, I don't used the word, but they called me a 'blank' lover. They used to say it in a joking type of way but I knew they were dead serious. I used ta' joke back and say fuck 'em all—but they knew I was dead serious too when I would joke back and tell 'em what I'd do to 'em if they ever got in my business and disrespected anybody I did business with. And 'til this day, one of my closest associates is a black guy and I love 'em like a brother. Him and his kid. So, I guess my answer to your question is yes. I would do what you are doing if ever it came to it."

"I knew it along," Kevin said as he smiled at Mendoza and

the men toasted with their beer cans. "And maybe you were right about a little bit of my mother rubbing off on me. If I had to say, when I decided to have a role in Naomi's life, I myself had found a new purpose."

"I needed a new purpose, too. That's what brought me here to Chicago." Mendoza responded before gulping his beer.

Kevin laughed to himself over Mendoza's last remark. He knew all-too-well that his new friend was a made man, and whatever 'purpose' it was that had brought Mendoza Cernigliaro to Chicago was not the same purpose as his. In spite of that fact, Kevin knew he and Mendoza both had left a chapter of their lives behind that dealt with violence in one form or another—walking nearly the same path—although taking different routes that had landed them both in Cicero just south of 16th Street in this quiet tree-lined neighborhood.

"I understand, Mendoza." Kevin replied, removing himself from his thoughts as he raised the grill to check the meat and coat the chicken with another helping of bar-b-cue sauce. "I tell, ya', though, I miss the deli back east. That's where I developed my love for cooking outdoors. Grilling especially— reminds me of those four pound burgers we served outta our deli right across from the train station in Lansing where my parents first met."

"Get the fuck outta here! The Langley Burger Deli?" Mendoza snapped as he laughed. "Your parents created the four pound burger and ran that deli? I loved that joint! I went there all the time when I was on business in Philly!"

"Yeah? Well we have crossed paths early on in life, il mio amico!" Kevin replied as he and Mendoza laughed and began talking about various eateries in Philadelphia.

Kevin wasn't too keen on Mendoza in the beginning, but after talking to the man on different occasions, he came to understand his demeanor. He didn't condone Mendoza's behavior or actions not one iota, but Mendoza really cared about his family. Kevin felt the same way about the people in his life, and although he and Mendoza had different occupations, they both cared about family and that it was made Kevin befriend Mendoza Cernigliaro—a man Kevin could only describe as a good man, who did bad things.

Chloe and Lester were more laid-back than Mendoza and Francine. They talked infrequently, sometimes laughing with Kevin and Serena, but the two mainly kept themselves while remaining cordial. The day ended on an upbeat note and before long, the adults would begin spending more time at each other's places during the summer.

Mendoza's mafia associates never came to his home. Only one man out of his crew, a black man nick-named DeeDee, knew where he resided at the time. DeeDee was Mendoza's 'go to guy' whenever he had a problem with Black Gangsters in Chicago and surrounding areas. DeeDee was also a contract killer. He and Mendoza often took on assignments together, killing Italians, blacks, whites, and any other race of human being that meted extermination. Mendoza liked DeeDee a lot— he wished he could have made the man, but DeeDee was black —and for the Italian Mafia, that was definitely a no-no. Still, Mendoza trusted DeeDee more than his made mafia affiliates. The two were not only business partners, they were best friends, and had been for years.

****

As winter of '67 approached, Naomi, now twelve, was nearing completion of her eight grade year of home schooling and was preparing to start her ninth grade assignments. She often helped Lucky, who wasn't too book smart, with his school work and would charge him a small fee in order to make a few dollars. Things were going well in Naomi's life, and on Christmas Day of '67, while everyone was over to the Cernigliaro's home enjoying the Christmas Holiday, things got even better when Kevin and Serena announced that they were getting married. They were congratulated by all, but no one was more excited than Naomi. It was one of the best Christmas' the twelve year-old could ever remember.

In May of '68, Serena Wales married Kevin Langley in a small ceremony in Kevin's backyard and moved into the Langley home that very night. The woman kept her home and had converted the living room into a luxurious casino-style lounge where she could get together with other sociologists that worked for Cook County in order to play Bridge and had her first game scheduled a month later.

Naomi was in the front yard of Kevin's home with Fin and Lucky hanging out and chatting about much of nothing that day, when Serena emerged from the house with a tray of sandwiches. "You need help, Misses Langley." Naomi asked with a smile.

"Misses Langley sure does. I have another tray, a punch bowl, and a set of glasses on the dining room table. Could each of you grab an item please?" Serena asked with a happy grin and a bright smile.

As they transferred the items from the Langley home to Serena's home, Fin merely asked aloud, "Serena, why couldn't you make the sandwiches at your place?"

"We had to move all the refrigerated items from my house to Kevin's house last week. The refrigerator is broken and they haven't delivered the new one."

"This makes sense if that's the case. I was just wondering." Fin replied as the group crossed the street.

"No harm, no foul, Finland. It really was a good question." Serena replied as the group walked up the sidewalk towards the home.

Once inside, the three kids sat their items down inside Serena's kitchen. "Naomi," Serena then called out as she walked towards the lounge, "follow me. I have a favor to ask."

"What, m—" Naomi caught herself at that moment because she'd almost let a word slip from her mouth and she didn't know what kind of response it would provoke. For a while now, ever since Serena and Kevin had announced that they were getting married, Naomi had wanted to ask, rather, she wanted to say something to Serena. She feared being rejected or rebuked, however, and for those reasons, she held back. When the time was right, however, Naomi told herself she would say to Serena what had been building up in her over the past few months.

"What do you need me to do for you, Misses Langley?" Naomi asked kindly with a wide smile.

"Well," Serena replied as she folded napkins and placed wooden rings around them, "I need for you to put out the leather place mats and matching coasters. There's a wicker basket filled with fresh cut flowers on the front porch, too. Could you bring that in?"

"Yes, ma'am." Naomi replied in a somewhat dejected tone.

Serena sensed the downtrodden spirit emanating from Naomi. "Are you okay, baby," she asked as she pulled Naomi close and sat down in a chair to check her temperature. "You're not getting sick or anything are you?" she inquired as she placed the back of her hand to Naomi's forehead.

"I'm fine. I just wanted to say to you that I would like to—" Naomi was cut off when Fin and Lucky ran into the lounge area and bumped into the bar Serena was setting up.

The woman scrambled and grabbed three long-stemmed glasses just before they were about to plummet to the tile floor. "You boys!" she yelled. "Running is not allowed in the house across the street nor is it allowed in here! If you wanna wrestle and run around do it outside. Get along now! Scoot!" Serena said as she ushered Fin and Lucky towards the front door.

"We stayin' for the game, Misses Langley!" Lucky snapped.

"No you're not. This is a ladies only affair so you boys will have to leave."

"We helped carry food over here and we can't stay? Awww, man! You shiested us!" Lucky remarked as he threw his hands up.

"No one has been shiested, Faustino. Now, you and Finland can have some sandwiches if you like, and you can stay until the guests arrive, but you'll have to leave when they do. Bridge Club rules states that no males are allowed."

"We don't want no sandwiches. Come on y'all, let's go outside and play baseball." Lucky said as he and Fin headed for the front door.

"Can I stay?" Naomi asked Serena.

"You most certainly can. Would you like to learn how to play?"

"Yes ma'am. I'll walk Lucky and Fin out and grab the flower basket."

"Bridge is boring," Fin said once the kids stepped onto the

porch. "If you get bored, Naomi, we'll be across the street." he ended as he and Lucky jumped down the stairs and ran down the sidewalk.

"Okay. But I think I'm gonna like this game. See you guys later," Naomi replied as she grabbed the flower basket and walked back into the home.

"Okay, Naomi, set that basket in the center of the table."

"What kind of flowers are these?"

"Those are white tulips," Serena replied as she placed white napkins around the basket. "I don't know why I'm creating this center piece when all we'll do is remove it once the game starts."

"I think it's pretty," Naomi remarked as she placed brown leather place mats and their matching coasters before each seat at the table. "While we're eating it'll be something to talk about and I can say I helped make it."

"Yes you can, sweetie," Serena said loving as she kissed Naomi's forehead. "Come on, let's prepare the sandwiches. We have to add pickles and tomatoes. Viola likes tomatoes."

Naomi was learning how to conduct herself as a woman from Serena and she simply loved being around this person who was slowly becoming a second mother to her. Serena treated Naomi like she was her own daughter, and to this twelve year-old child, it meant the world.

A half hour later, Serena's colleagues arrived over to her home in a pristine champagne colored four door Mercedes. Kevin was out with Lucky and Fin, watching the kids play ball as he eyed the car, which had vaguely sparked his memory. He'd met the women when Serena invited them to their wedding, but he'd drank so much champagne that night, he barely remembered the trio. One thing he did remember, though, was how discourteous the women seemed to be during the reception.

A few minutes later, three white women, all dressed in paisley skirts of various colors and sporting neat, silk scarves that matched their leather purses and shoes, exited the car and walked up the sidewalk, talking and laughing loudly on occasion as they looked over to Kevin's porch from time to time before sniggling to themselves.

To Kevin, the ladies were just a bunch of over-the-top women that only wanted to get together with Serena and gossip. Playing cards was just their excuse for getting together in order to discuss office issues, sort of like the 'meetings' he held with other professors from Northwestern at a bar near campus on most Fridays. The women were harmless in Kevin's eyes, but everybody didn't view things the way he did.

"They racists." Fin stated matter-of-factly as he eyed the women.

"You don't know that, Finland." Kevin remarked.

"I know a racist when I see one!" Fin snapped.

Lucky thought the women were not like Serena because they seemed a little wild, but, he, too, was wondering what the women were laughing at whenever they looked over towards Kevin's porch. Fin said that they were racist, and Lucky had a feeling something was not right about the ladies, but he didn't think they were racist. "How you know they racist, Fin?" Lucky asked as he threw a baseball up into the air, catching it a few seconds later with the baseball glove he wore.

"When they pulled up they was pointing over here while they was sitting in the car. I remember them from the wedding that day and they was making fun of me and Naomi."

"That don't mean they racist. They just some mean people." Lucky said as he watched his mother walk over to Serena's home.

"But they was talking about me and Naomi that day."

"What did they say, Finland?" Kevin asked.

"They was actin' like, like, they was acting like we was y'all maids or butlers or something because Naomi was pouring drinks."

"We were, well, the adults were all a little tipsy that night, Finland. I'm not fond of them either, but to call them racist may be an overstatement."

"Okay, watch and see. I know people." Fin said as Mendoza made his way over to Kevin's front porch with a six pack of beer.

Mendoza had watched the women walk up the sidewalk as he crossed the street. He'd come out just in time to get a good look at Serena's friends and he remembered them from the wedding as well. They seemed okay, just a little too rambunctious for Serena's liking in his opinion. "Hey Kevin, I brought over some beers for us," he said as he pulled a beer from the plastic ringer.

"Thanks, Mendoza. What do you make of Serena's friends?"

"I don't care for 'em. They work over to Serena's office, right?"

"Yeah. Finland thinks they're racist. I just think they are obnoxious."

"Obnoxious could be another word for racist, you know? All I know is...they better not start no trouble on my block." Mendoza replied as he popped open a can beer.

The three women, meanwhile, had knocked on the door and were waiting patiently when Naomi answered. "I remember you! Is the lady of the house available," one of the women asked with a silly smirk on her face.

Naomi smiled and politely and said, "Yes she is," as she stepped back to let the women in. "My name is Naomi Holland. Welcome to our home."

"We didn't ask your name or if you lived here, little sambo. We asked if the home's owner was in the house and was she available," another woman remarked as she and her friends giggled.

Naomi didn't know exactly what a "little sambo" was; but she surmised it was a derogatory term because of the way the women laughed after the woman had said those two specific words. She dropped her smile, slammed the door shut in the women's faces and went to call Serena from the kitchen, leaving the women feeling insulted and in stunned silence with their mouths agape. The loathsome trio was talking amongst themselves when Francine walked up the sidewalk wearing a tight-fitting lime green silk pant suit and matching eel skin shoes. Her silky red hair was styled in curls with a bun in the back and she had on a diamond necklace and matching bracelets, along with diamond studded earrings and her wedding ring.

"Are we in Vegas?" Viola, a slender, short-haired brunette, and the leader of the pack asked rhetorically as she eyed Francine walking in their direction.

"No, Vie...we're in little Italy. Remember her and her husband? The sexy Italian over there holding the beers?"

"I do! I wanted to drop to my knees and service him right away!"

"You're a slut, Vie!"

"You taught her everything she knows!" the third lady remarked before bursting into laughter. "Can you believe how rude it was to us? Slamming the door in our face?" she then asked.

"I can't believe how rude it was! Serena will hear about this!" Viola replied and then shushed the ladies as Francine approached the stairs.

When Francine introduced herself, Viola and her girls gave her a quick nod and remained silent. Francine, however, had heard the women talking about how rude "it" was and she quickly surmised that the women were using the word in mocked tone. She didn't fully understand what was going on and had missed a great part of the conversation, including Viola and her friends' mocking of her appearance. Something about these three women was not sitting right with Francine, but before she could dig any further into their demeanor, Serena opened the door and greeted the four.

"Everybody's here!" Serena said happily. "You ladies come on in! Welcome to the Langley Bridge Club," she said in a way that invited for more conversation as she went and stood behind Naomi. "I have everything we'll need and the snacks will be ready shortly. You ladies take a seat in the lounge and we'll get things underway in a minute. You all remember Naomi, right?"

Serena had just introduced Naomi to her three co-workers, but they never acknowledged her. She paid it no mind, however, because she was overjoyed at having friends over to play Bridge and felt that she was being an excellent host. She was also quickly distracted from the introductions when Viola asked her about the lounge as she stared around with a wide pretentious smile.

"Serena? My God this place is beautiful!" Viola remarked. "We didn't get to see this layout on your wedding day, no?"

"No, Viola. We were across the street last month. I turned the dining room into a lounge for us all. This is where we'll play. Come see!" Serena replied as she began guiding the women around, giving them a tour of the downstairs.

Francine remained behind and bent down and hugged Naomi. "You gonna stay around, Naomi?" she asked.

"No. You and Serena have fun." Naomi replied nonchalantly as she left the home.

Naomi, at the out-set, was planning on learning how to play Bridge, but her attention had been shifted all of a sudden. She now had a new agenda—instead of learning how to play Bridge, she wanted to know what a "little sambo" was; and if what she believed about Serena's friends was true, she would have her say in the matter. What happened in Sylacauga still had a deep impact on Naomi. She still had an inclination to get angry and vindictive at times. She crossed the street and walked up to Lucky, Fin, Kevin and Mendoza where she sat beside Kevin on the porch swing.

Kevin had seen Naomi slam the door on the women and couldn't help but ask, "Is everything all right over there, Naomi? I thought you wanted to learn how to play Bridge with Serena."

"I do. Everything's fine, but I wanted a treat. Can I have some ice cream, please?"

Kevin got up to enter his home to fix the ice cream whilst Naomi remained on the porch. She watched through the screen door until Kevin disappeared from sight and then turned to Mendoza. Even at her young age, Naomi Holland was perceptive and manipulative. She'd managed to remove Kevin from her presence so she could ask Mendoza one question, "Mister Cernigliaro, what is a little sambo?"

"I told you they was racist!" Fin stated to Lucky.

"Who called you that?" Mendoza asked as he popped open another can of beer.

"One of Serena's friends."

"Serena can't know about her so-called friends," Mendoza said as he looked over to Serena's home. "The word sambo is another way of saying what Kevin always tells you is a derogatory term, Naomi," he said with a serious look on his face.

"They called me a nigger?" Naomi asked disheartened as she turned and looked over towards Serena's home.

Ever since 1962, when Kevin had told her that 'nigger' and 'savage' were never to be accepted nor used in her presence because they were meant to degrade her and her heritage, Naomi had acquired a disdain for the words. She quickly learned on this day, however, that there were other ways to berate her and it infuriated her to know that she had been insulted on the sly—she now sought revenge and began looking around for a rock in order to break the windshield on the nice Mercedes the women had ridden up in until Mendoza stopped her and told her he had another idea, one that wouldn't get her into trouble. He, too, was angry that grown women had called Naomi a derogatory term and he was going to help her attain a little payback.

When Kevin came out with Naomi's ice cream, Mendoza asked him would he like a Whiskey Sour and Kevin answered to say yes. Mendoza then asked Naomi, Lucky and Fin to help him carry the items needed to make the drinks from his home back to Kevin's house and the kids followed him over to his home. The moment Mendoza closed the front door, he turned to the kids and said, "Eh, Naomi, go over there and serve them three bitches those sandwiches you threes brought over there! And when you do, you spit all over them mutherfuckas, understand? All over them bastards and give it to 'em, understand?"

"Yes. I'm going and do it now!" Naomi replied as she headed for the door.

Mendoza then handed a switch blade to both Lucky and Fin. "Son," he said calmly, "you and Finland take these knives and slit all four tires on theys Mercedes and meet me in Kevin's kitchen right after ya' done. Got me?"

"No problem, dad." Lucky answered as Fin nodded in agreement.

Mendoza grabbed the blender and the liquor and headed back to Kevin's house where the two men went in and mixed the drinks, and when the coast was clear, Lucky and Fin went about with their portion of the plan.

Meanwhile, back inside Serena's house, Naomi had just walked into the lounge area when one of the women remarked, "Look, it's back," the three women began laughing amongst themselves as Francine, who'd just poured herself a shot of scotch, asked what was funny.

"Ohh nothing. Just something that was said on the way into the home," one of the women replied.

Francine had an inkling Naomi was being made fun of; she was incensed that one of the women had called the child "it", only she wasn't sure that they were actually mocking Naomi. In order to confirm her beliefs, she went along with the women, joining in on their perceived mockery.

"I can't stand that little spear chucker!" Francine said as she laughed.

"Oh my! I knew you were in agreement," Viola said as she squeezed Francine's arm. "When I saw that little sambo answer the door? I said to myself, 'Gosh! She's a little young to be a servant.' But when you're blue-gummed, the best you can do in life is to become a maid-servant. She's gonna be good one because she's learning early."

Francine squint her eyes and smiled slyly as she began unwrapping a fresh deck of cards. She was planning on showing Serena what her friends were really like by getting them to mock Naomi in front of her because she believed Serena didn't and couldn't know about her so-called friends. The woman was certain Miss Serena Wales would not sit by and let three bimbos insult the person who she had on several occasions told Francine, was "the most precious little thing in her life".

Naomi, meanwhile, had gone back into the kitchen where Serena was placing sandwiches onto plates in preparation to be served and had offered to help and Serena accepted. They placed sandwiches onto plates and whenever Serena had her back turned, Naomi let saliva drip from her mouth onto the meat and folded the sandwiches back. A few minutes later, Serena and Naomi entered the lounge area with plates in hand and kindly served the women, Naomi making sure that Serena's "friends" had saliva-laced finger sandwiches in front of them. Serena then removed the center piece she and Naomi created and sat down and the women began to eat and play cards.

When Francine reached for a sandwich, Naomi quickly shoved a napkin filled with untainted sandwiches in front of her. Francine had picked up right away that Naomi was up to something. She'd done the 'spit-play' herself a time or two as a teenager back in Brooklyn when she worked at an eatery where she first met Mendoza. The alert woman watched with delight as Serena's so-called friends all bit into saliva-laced sandwiches and she laughed to herself, right along with Naomi, who was bursting with joy on the inside. It felt good to have a little payback.

The women ate as they played cards until Naomi asked if they wanted more sandwiches. "No, we're fine, little sambo. Return to your duties," Viola replied.

"What did you call my child?" Serena asked in shock.

"Ohh, come on Serena! You know if you weren't in love with Kevin you would have nothing to do with anything or anybody that was from the Negro species!" Viola said matter-of-factly.

"The word species is often used in reference to animals, Miss Viola. And your implications are leading me to believe that you have me mistaken with members of the white supremacy movement. I love Naomi like my own child. You work with black kids every day! How could you say those things about a child?"

"My job is just that—a job! Look, I never had intentions on helping *those* kind." Viola responded as she pointed towards Naomi.

"Those kind," Serena said as she stood up from the table. "Well, 'those kind' are just the type of people I intend on helping, Viola. It is what I signed up for and it is what I love to do. Naomi has given me an opportunity to put forth my best work and I wouldn't have it any other way."

"That's what you've been brainwashed into believing, Serena. But deep down inside? You know you have no sincere interest in helping a bunch of unwanted niggers. Even if you are married to a man who loves them so. Which is the source of your vainglorious act of righteousness," she ended in a harsh tone of voice. "Now sit! Come on and let's play cards, please, ma'am!"

After being totally disrespected, Serena, who wasn't a violent person, nor all that strong for that matter, grabbed hold of the table and flipped it over, forcing Viola and her friends up out of their seats.

"What the hell is wrong with you?" Viola asked. "You're acting like what I said wasn't true."

Serena grew even more infuriated over Viola's unwillingness to comprehend how sincere she was when it came to Naomi. She walked around the table and grabbed Viola by the head and began yanking hard on the woman's long brown hair. "You take back what you said!" she yelled as she and Viola flailed about in the lounge.

Francine, at that moment, began slapping the other two women and Naomi gave her a hand. She and Francine were throwing a series of hard punches at both women and kicking at them as they began running to the front door. When the door opened, the brawl quickly spread out like a heated rash onto the front porch. Kevin immediately leapt from his swing and ran down his stairs towards his wife and Naomi while Mendoza, Fin and Lucky stood up and erupted into laughter.

"What is going on? You all were supposed to be playing cards and now you're fighting? I thought these were your friends, Serena!" Kevin yelled as he got in the middle of the brawl that had by now fanned out onto Serena's front lawn.

"They called her out her name! They will respect my daughter always!" Serena cried aloud as she pounded Viola's skull with her fists.

Kevin pulled Serena off the woman, but Francine and Naomi

were still active in their dealings with their opponents. Although Francine was capable of taking care of both women herself, Naomi's presence was welcomed. She was kicking one of the women on the ground while Francine had the other woman on her knees repeatedly punching her about the head and face.

"Bash her fuckin' skull in, Francine!" Mendoza yelled as he and his son walked casually across the street with Fin trailing close behind. Mendoza could feel no pity for the three racist women, and coupled with the alcohol he'd consumed, he was enjoying the scenery that lay before his eyes—that of his wife and Naomi kicking ass on the front lawn.

Kevin soon brought the fight under control and the women were all separated. Viola and her two friends gathered themselves, backed away and headed towards the car. "We're going to tell everybody what happened here today, Serena! You people are a bunch of animals! Animals!" Viola yelled.

Just then, Mendoza walked up and slapped Viola across the face, buckling her knees. "Get the fuck from 'round here ya' fuckin' bimbo!" he yelled as Viola stumbled and clutched her right cheek. Mendoza then charged the second lady, but she broke and ran, joining the third woman as all three ran to the car. "If you threes come back here? I'll fuckin' go fishin' with ya' fuckin' livers and kidneys the next mornin'!"

"We're calling the cops!" Viola remarked as she rose up from the ground and ran towards her car.

"Go 'head! And be sure and tell 'em how you called a black kid out her fuckin' name, too, ya' three fuckin' mutts! Ain't no fuckin' racists on this block! Not on my block ya' bunch of incestuous dick-sucking, malaria carrying hicks! Go home and fuck your fathers! Get the fuck outta here!" Mendoza yelled again as he charged the women.

Viola and her two friends hopped into the car with Viola behind the steering wheel and made a hasty attempt to flee the neighborhood, but as Viola rode off, she realized her tires were flat, all four of them. Everybody in the group, with the exception of Kevin, laughed as the women tried to pull away.

Just then, Naomi ran back across the street to Kevin's house and grabbed the rock she knew was lying in his yard and was about to hurl it at the car, but Kevin ran and stopped her as Viola and her two friends rode down the street on four flat tires. The women stopped a few blocks away and called a tow truck from a pay phone and never even bothered calling the police.

Naomi then wrestled free of Kevin's grip. "Naomi, calm down! Calm down!" Kevin yelled.

"I gotta go! Before she don't say it ever again I gotta go by Serena!"

"Why? What did she say that has you so worked up?"

"She, she called me her daughter! She might not say it no more if I don't go now!" Naomi said as she struggled to free herself from Kevin's grip.

Kevin let go of Naomi and she took off running across the street back towards Serena's home. He watched as she made a beeline for Serena and grabbed her tightly the moment she'd reached her. "You called me your daughter! You mean that? Say you mean it, please, please!" Naomi said through tears as she hid her face in Serena's bosom.

Serena looked down at Naomi and stroked her hair. "Yes. I meant that, Naomi," she replied lovingly. "For as long as I live you'll be my daughter. I didn't even think you heard me say that, but yes, I meant it, baby."

"Thank you, momma." Naomi cried as Serena held her close.

Kevin walked over and he began to slowly clap. Mendoza followed, and before long the whole group applauded Naomi and Serena.

"Well, this is certainly one for the record books. I don't think they'll be back. How will you deal with them at your job?" Kevin asked as the tension eased.

Serena merely fanned off Kevin's question as she and Naomi stood in a warm embrace. "Viola and her two friends are not going to be around long, dear," she said through a slight smile of contentment. "I'm over the entire department Viola works in and I'll file a report and a recommendation for dismissal on Monday. Racism by anyone on my staff will not be tolerated."

"Naomi are you all right?" Kevin asked.

Naomi replied by nodding her head up and down as she held on tightly to Serena, who in turn, rubbed her thick braided hair as she apologized to Francine for ruining the game.

"You did right not to let them stay, Serena. And they deserved everything they got today because they had no right to disrespect you and Naomi." Francine remarked.

Later that night, after seeing Naomi off to sleep, Kevin and Serena sat up in bed and talked the matter over. "You know," Kevin stated, "today, what you did, in spite of the fighting, meant a lot to Naomi. Me too. That was real special what transpired between you and her. A real mother-daughter moment set against the backdrop of an all-out brawl. That was crazy." Kevin remarked lightly before he sipped his decaffeinated coffee.

Serena caught on to her husband's last remark and was a little shocked and insulted that Kevin had called her crazy. She sat her novel down before she removed her reading glasses and asked, "Is that what you think, dear? Do you think that I'm crazy for loving and wanting to raise a child whose parents were murdered? Do you think that *we* are crazy for doing what we're doing, Kevin? I don't think what we're doing is crazy. I would like to think that we are two caring adults raising a child the way all children—no matter their race should be raised— with love and care. Isn't it what you think? Or am I wrong in my assumptions?"

"You're correct in all that you are saying, Serena. And I don't think you're crazy by a long shot, baby. It's just Naomi."

"What about Naomi," Serena asked anxiously as she leaned forward. "Did she do something wrong? We didn't scold her for hitting those women! I should've–I mean I did tell her to not let her anger get the best of her. You're worried she's, I mean, we can, we can talk—"

"Baby," Kevin said as he leaned over and kissed Serena on the cheek, "I'm not reconsidering."

"Are you sure? Because I know what happened today was unbecoming. We're not angry, aggressive people. But you should have heard that conversation, Kevin."

71

"I hate to even think about it after hearing you tell it. I can't say that I wouldn't have flown off the handle either."

"Then, what is it that has you agitated?

"Naomi called you 'momma' today. I've *been* waiting for her to call me 'daddy'—or, or maybe 'father'. I even have dreams about her saying that to me, but she never did or does. But you, you come along and she has this big spot in her heart for you right away. I wonder what I'm doing wrong for her not to call me 'dad'."

"You *are* 'dad' to Naomi, Kevin. But to daughters? It's like, it's like, ohhh look! There's dad! Okay, hmmm. But on the other hand, with mothers? It's like, momma! Momma! As she runs into your arms and hugs you tightly. That's beautiful. But don't worry, my love, Naomi loves you as if you were her real father." Serena said she leaned over and kissed Kevin and ran her hands through his silky brown hair. "You're a great father to Naomi."

"Thank you, baby. Hey, you think *I* should call her daughter? Maybe then she would call me dad."

Serena chuckled and said, "You sound like a little kid that has just devised an ingenious plan, dear. I think you should just let it happen, Kevin. Let it come natural. I said what I said and did what I did today out of heart-felt love and conviction. Naomi, God I love that little girl. She's, she's special. She's going to be a great woman someday and I just—"

"I said the same thing five years ago." Kevin said cutting Serena off. "I love that child, Serena. I want to see her make it in life. Why? Why did *her* family suffer in the manner in which they did, and *are* suffering now?"

"Prejudice. Just like Viola and her two friends. God knows I never wanted to believe Viola and her friends were truly like that, but there are men and women much worse. Naomi's family just happened to encounter some very cruel people. Whatever lies ahead in Naomi's future has to be better than her past. I sincerely hope for that to be true." Serena ended before she kissed Kevin and turned off her lamp.

The next morning when Kevin awoke, he saw Naomi lying in between him and Serena on her back in her pajamas. She lay sound asleep until Kevin's movement awakened her.

"I'm sorry for the way I behaved yesterday." Naomi said to Kevin sleepily as she turned away from him and hugged Serena tightly.

"Naomi, you don't have to apologize for protecting your dignity." Kevin said lowly.

Twelve year-old Naomi turned and faced Kevin, opened her eyes and said through tears, "My father's name is Rutherford Holland. My mother's name is Nituna Holland. But if, if I had to choose besides them? I want you to be my daddy. And I want Serena to be my momma. I like this new family," as she wiped her tears. "If there's a God, why he let the mean people in Alabama take my real father and mother?"

"Sometimes bad things happen beyond our control, Naomi. But in time, God will make it right someday."

"I hope that's true because I really miss my brother and sisters. I want to find them someday."

"I know you do, Naomi. No matter how long it takes, never give up hope that you will find them. And just know that God has your best interest at heart."

"Your father, and I have your best interest at heart, too, Naomi." Serena said as she now lay on her back listening to the conversation, gently rubbing Naomi's stomach.

"Momma, I think about my brother and sisters every day. I miss them. I know, I know y'all not my real parents, but I like it here."

Kevin went to speak, but Serena, in complete harmony with Naomi's emotions, silenced him. That last remark warranted no response. It was confirmation that Naomi was now beginning to accept her lot in life at the present time, while at the same time not forgetting where she'd come from. The disdainful acts of others who dared to impede upon the relationship Serena had with Naomi, others who unwittingly tried to put the woman's love to the test—had failed tremendously. Their berating of Naomi had only served to intensify the bond between the three individuals and the rest of the friends—and it would be a bond of love that will remain intact for all times.

CHAPTER 5
FIRST KILL

"You had a lot of people that cared about you back in Cicero, Naomi." Martha remarked.

"I truly did," Naomi replied through a proud smile. "Those were some good times let me tell ya'. I felt so safe. And being called daughter meant the world to me, Martha. After our mother was killed my heart ached for so long to hear somebody call me daughter, the same way mother used to. Serena said that word the same way mother used to say it—with heartfelt love and conviction. I love that woman."

Mary sipped her wine cooler and said, "Twiggy and Martha had a lot of people that cared for them in Ghost Town."

Twiggy widened her eyes and looked at Mary with a puzzled look on her face. "You talkin' about Folk Nation," she asked before she and Martha erupted into laughter.

Mary tapped Twiggy's leg playfully and responded, "Some of 'em cared, like Sandy Duncan. Clark's son and those two sisters, Urselle and Sidney? They cared."

"Okay, I give you that. But most of them didn't care about us. It was more to it than that." Twiggy replied.

"Most of 'em was scared of y'all right, Irene?" Dawk asked.

"They was more scared than caring. You right, Dawk." Twiggy answered.

"Dawk, go and check and see how your father and the rest of the children are doing. DeeDee and the friends from Chicago should be here pretty soon, too. Call and see where they're at, will you please, son?" Naomi asked.

"Timing the drive? I say they just south of Kansas City right about now. I'll go check on things, momma." Dawk said as he got up and walked down the hill and hopped into the golf cart and drove towards the mansion.

When Naomi saw the golf cart emerge out into the open field, she sighed and said, "I just had to get him away."

"Why?" Mary asked.

"This must be something more serious than that little sambo story, Mary." Martha answered matter-of-factly.

"You're right, Martha. And Mary you have never heard this tale either," Naomi said. "Twiggy? You spoke of fear earlier. Well, in 1962 when my parents died, I was scared to death when a gun was pointed at my face right after Nituna was shot dead. I was scared when I lost Samson and my sisters at that orphanage—but I was never held hostage by that fear because I had too much anger to just sit back and accept what they had done to us. And because I loved my brother and sisters all so much I was determined to find them no matter what. Fate stepped in for me and made that happen, though, so my fight wasn't hard, just long-suffering. But my friend Fin had great fear. And his situation had shown me how fear can hold one hostage. I also saw two people who had no fear what-so-ever during that time, too. It was a little cool out in 1969 and it was Mary and Martha's birthday. Me and Lucky was out in front Kevin's home..."

March 22, 1969

..."Lucky? Where's Fin today?" Naomi asked.

Thirteen year-old Naomi was in front of her flying a kite on this cool, windy and cloudy day as fourteen year-old Lucky stood beside her bouncing a tennis ball. Over the nearly two year period Naomi had known Lucky and Fin, she'd become real close to the boys, especially Lucky, who was always around to share in some of Naomi's stories about her life down south. They hung together just about every day.

"He says he has a math test this week so he's probably studying. I have homework myself." Lucky replied. "I gotta write a three page essay on what the affect of the riots last year during the Decratic Conviction had on Chicago and the Demcratic party."

"You mean the Democratic Convention of 1968 and the affects that it had on the Democrat Party. I did a five page essay a month after it happened and got an A-plus in Civics. Give me a dollar and I'll do an essay for you." Naomi replied.

"A dollar, Naomi? Come on, you overcharging!"

"Since we became friends I been doing your homework and barely charged you if at all. Today I need some money to buy cupcakes and cards because it is Mary and Martha's birthday. They are ten today!"

Lucky knew of Naomi's sisters and brother because she talked about them repeatedly. "Ohhh. Okay. I have a dollar. Man, I know you miss your sisters."

"I do, Lucky. But just like this kite? They flew away from my life." Naomi said as she watched the stick in her hands twirl around quickly until all the string was removed and the thick knot she had tied came into view, wedging the stick in between her fingers. She then began reeling the kite back towards her and said, "Someday though Lucky? Someday I'll get them back."

"Let's go see Fin." Lucky then said. "Hey, when you find your family will you leave Chicago?"

"I don't know. Who knows? Maybe, maybe not. I do plan to make a lot of money someday though—that way Mary and Martha can stay with me forever. Wherever I'm staying." Naomi replied as she and Lucky walked over to Fin's home.

When the friends arrived over to Fin's home they knocked on the front door and Fin opened. Right away Naomi and Lucky could see that he had been crying. Naomi asked what was wrong, and Fin was about to respond until Lester, Fin's aunt Chloe's husband, walked out of Fin's room. The man seemed surprised to see Naomi and Lucky and he quickly headed in the opposite direction. Naomi and Lucky looked at Fin, then back at Lester.

"What happened?" Naomi asked lowly.

"Nothing. We was playing and he got a little rough that's all, but I'm okay." Fin stated in a soft voice.

"Finland! You need to finish your homework! Close the door, boy." Lester yelled from deep within the interior of the home.

"I'll be out later." Fin stated as he quickly closed the door and locked it.

Naomi and Lucky talked about the awkward situation with Fin and Lester as they walked back to Kevin's house. To them, it looked like something more than a little horse-play had taken place between the two.

"What you think's going on over there, Lucky?" Naomi asked.

"Something weird is all I can say. Finland don't really like Lester and I can't say I feel any different about the guy."

"Me neither. And you're right, he is a weirdo. I hope he's not hurting Fin."

"For his sake I hope he isn't either," Lucky replied.

When Naomi and Lucky made it back over to Kevin's house, Serena was pulling into the driveway. She waved excitedly towards Naomi from behind the steering wheel as she opened the car door, got out and opened the back door of her car and grabbed two white boxes.

"What's that, momma?" Naomi asked.

"Cannoli, ice cream, and cake!" Serena answered with a smile.

"What's cannoli?" Naomi asked.

"All this time and you never had cannoli? Aww, man! That's the best dessert ever!" Lucky said loudly as he rubbed his hands together excitedly.

Serena also pulled out candles and birthday hats and it was at that moment that Naomi had realized what was about to transpire. She had been telling Serena and Kevin that her sisters' birthday was coming up on March 22, and she wanted to have a party for them. Serena had brought her wish to fruition.

Naomi ran into the house yelling Kevin's name as she ran through the dining room and the living room, up the stairs to her bedroom, and grabbed her three Raggedly Anne and Andy dolls. She then hurried back down the stairs to the dining room and sat the dolls at the table as Serena, Lucky and Kevin gave her a helping hand. Lucky called his parents and they came over. Naomi called Fin, but got no answer so the party merely continued on.

Soon, the table was set for Naomi's sisters. She had the two Raggedly Ann dolls in a chair in front the cake and she held the Andy doll in her arms. She was all smiles when Kevin snapped a picture of her. The lights were dimmed and Naomi said a prayer, thanking God for her family and friends and asking God to protect her brother and sisters until she was, "Old enough and able to find them, someday, Amen," was how she ended the prayer.

Everybody sat and ate and chatted after Naomi blew out the candles on the cake. The overjoyed teenager had her first taste of cannoli and she fell in love with the Italian pastry dish right away. It was a school night so Lucky had to leave early, Naomi had to turn in as well; but she remembered to save a piece of cake and cannoli for Fin.

The next day, when Naomi and Kevin returned home from Northwestern University, Naomi went over to Fin's house to deliver the cannoli and the piece of cake she had saved him. When she got there, however, she saw Lucky in the alleyway beside the house. She crept down the sidewalk and when Lucky saw her, he placed his finger over his lips to silence Naomi, who tip-toed over and stood beside him.

"What are you doing?" Naomi asked lowly.

Before Lucky could respond, voices could be heard inside the home. Naomi could tell it was Lester yelling at Fin, and amidst the yelling, Fin seemed to be crying and pleading. Lester's rant against Fin was clearly heard by Naomi and Lucky. He was yelling that if Fin wanted to dress like a woman, he would be treated like a woman. Naomi covered her mouth and widened her eyes as Lucky opened his jean jacket and showed her a .38 revolver that was tucked in an inside pocket.

Lucky had been having suspicions about Lester for a while. And when he witnessed Lester walk out of Fin's room the day before, he had a gut feeling something wasn't right. He only went to check on Fin this day, and he happened to hear the commotion from outside and he followed the argument to the back of the home from outside.

Once the quarreling had ceased, faint sounds of grunting and groaning slowly began creeping into Naomi and Lucky's ears minutes later. At that moment, Lucky pulled out a pocket knife and he and Naomi walked to the back of the home and crept up the stairs where Lucky stuck the knife in the back door and jimmied it open. Fin could be clearly heard yelling and pleading with Lester the moment Naomi and Lucky entered the back of the home.

"You're hurtin' me!" Fin could be heard yelling. "Get off of me!"

Fin's constant grunts and pleading for Lester to stop hurting him was sickening to Naomi. She could only imagine the fear and pain Fin was experiencing as she followed Lucky, who now had the gun in his right hand, through the kitchen towards Fin's bedroom. When the two entered Fin's room, they knew not what to say. Fin was naked on his back, his legs being held open by Lester, who lay in between pistoning back and forth rapidly.

Just then, Mendoza blew pass Naomi and his son and went and snatched Lester off Fin. The pedophile was surprised into a state of shock at the sight of the three individuals in the bedroom, and Mendoza wasted no time in taking action. He punched Lester in his stomach, dropping him to his knees and then began kicking him in his groin repeatedly, trying to detach his dick from his body completely.

"Come on, man! We wasn't doing nothing!" Lester screamed as he writhed about on the floor.

"You fuckin' piece of shit! Make you feel big? It make you feel big doin' that shit to a kid you fuckin' homosexual?" Mendoza asked angrily, his face nearly turning burgundy from the rage he carried.

"He asked me to do it!" Lester yelled as he clutched his groin and rolled around on the floor. "What the fuck you doing, man," he asked pitifully.

"Fin," Mendoza asked never taking his eyes off Lester, "you asked this scumbag to do this to you?"

"I never asked him to do this to me. He been doing this to me since I was eleven." Fin said through tears as he hid his face from sight.

"Eh, you know what, Ole Les?" Mendoza said in cool and calm manner as eyed him coldly, "even if the kid did tell you to do it to 'em, it still don't make it right you child molestin' faggot! Lucky, kill this mutherfuckin' mutt!"

Naomi's eyes widened and Fin hid his lower face behind the pillow as his watery eyes gazed upon the scene unfolding in his bedroom. Lester pleaded, but before his voice could reach a crescendo he was silenced by Lucky with a gunshot to the forehead. Everything in the room then went silent. Naomi and Fin looked at one another without saying a word as Lucky stood beside his father, the two staring at Lester's trembling body.

"He ain't dead. Hit 'em again son." Mendoza said lowly.

Lucky shot Lester in the forehead again and the movement stopped. Mendoza then looked around at Naomi with a cold stare and said nothing as he eyed her.

"What are you going to do now?" Naomi asked.

"Don't worry about that. Lester is no more. And you and Fin better not feel sorry for this piece of shit. He deserved what's happened to him." Mendoza replied as he began pulling the sheets from Finland's bed. "If anybody speaks about what happened here today? They'll have me to deal with, understand?"

Naomi only nodded. For a while she had the sense that something was not right about Lester. Now she knew what it was—he was a child molester—and a gay one at that. He had been abusing her friend for over two years, but Fin was too scared to say anything. Fin didn't deserve to have this happen to him, Naomi thought; but thankfully, he was freed by Mendoza.

Fin knew the moment he told Mendoza the truth, Lester would be killed; but he didn't care. He hated Lester for abusing him. Naomi, however, didn't see it coming. She thought they were only going to scare Lester and call the police. Mendoza was an exterminator, though; he had no dealings with the police in no shape, form, or fashion. *He* was the law on the streets of Cicero.

Lucky told his father about his suspicions with Lester and Fin after noticing Lester's behavior the day before and Mendoza responded by telling his son that if what he was saying was true, then he would get to kill his first mark. Mendoza had been watching Lucky from the woods in Fin's backyard. When Naomi came onto the scene, he almost aborted the initiation; but when Lucky had her join him, Mendoza stuck to the plan for one reason, and one reason only: the man had come to that conclusion the year before when Naomi told him that if she ever had the chance, she would kill the people who'd destroyed her family. Naomi didn't know it at the time, but Mendoza was not only training his son to become a killer-for-hire, he was preparing her for what he deemed, 'a day of reckoning'. He knew of Naomi's desire to avenge the death of her parents, and should that day ever arrive, Mendoza wanted Naomi to know what she would be up against. This would be the only time Mendoza would kill someone in front of Naomi, but it would eventually become a life lesson. And as for Lucky, he had been initiated into the art of killing by his father in March of 1969. His criminal career was now underway…

…"You saw somebody get killed?" Mary asked.

"Why you so shocked, Mary? You saw people die in Ghost Town." Martha remarked.

"I know, but Mendoza and Lucky didn't have to do that." Mary stated.

"There she go! Righteous Mary!" Martha remarked as she threw up her hands.

"No, Martha. I'm just saying that that was a little bit *too* harsh."

"You may be right, Mary," Naomi remarked, "but Mendoza was a killer back then and he was rearing Lucky to be that way. But that is the past. We've moved beyond those times. I'm just letting you girls in on some things that I know will never leave this hill, right?"

"We cool, sis." Martha replied as Twiggy and Mary nodded in agreement. "I mean, it's not like we ourselves don't know of

—" Martha's voice trailed off at that moment as she bowed her head and reflected on the two people she'd killed and countless other murders she knew about. "We just talking. And these are just stories, sister."

"Right," Naomi replied. "These are just stories. Now, Lester was a perfect mark for my friend Lucky. I soon learned from him that it wasn't much the *act* of killing, but Mendoza wanted him to get the *feel* of killing. That's what Lucky told me later on. Anyway, Chloe said she would have killed Lester herself once Mendoza and Fin broke the news to her concerning what he was doing to Fin. Mendoza and Lucky later took Lester's body to a scrap yard in the trunk of a car and had the car crushed and Lester eventually became a cold-case. His killer went unknown and things returned to normal in the neighborhood."

"About Fin," Twiggy then chimed in, "was he really gay?"

"No," Naomi answered. "The truth of the matter was that Fin's aunt Chloe worked twelve hours shifts as a dispatcher for Southern Pacific Railroad and her nephew was left home alone with Lester for extended periods of time. That guy had been under the impression that Fin was gay shortly after he was dropped off at Chloe's home."

"Whatever gave him that impression, Naomi?" Twiggy asked.

"He caught Fin dressed in his aunt's clothes, including make-up and shoes when Fin was only eleven and he took advantage of him that day. He'd been secretly molesting my friend for over two years."

"Why would he wear woman's clothes if he wasn't gay?" Martha inquired.

"Finland just had a fetish. A weird fetish, but hey, people can be weird. When I first met Lucky and Fin, Kevin said they were oddballs. We were a motley crew to the fullest extent of the word, too. A black girl, black boy and an Italian boy in the sixties calling themselves friends? It was a rare mixture, but I can honestly say that we sincerely cared about one another. And Fin turned out okay. He hid his fetish from Lucky for almost two years after that incident with Lester, but for whatever reason, he suddenly wanted to tell Lucky. Mind you, by now Lucky was a bona fide gangster, but Fin insisted on telling him."

"How did that unfold?" Twiggy asked Naomi.

"Well, I'll tell you. Wait, let me tell you all 'bout my friend's fetish and the problem it cause first and then I'll tell about the day I met Doss. Let me see—oh! There was the bar and when I first met 23rd Street Mafia, too! Those were the days! Let me see, it was in August of 1970 when…"

CHAPTER 6

DOSS DAWKINS AND THE 23rd STREET MAFIA

Fifteen year-old Naomi hopped into sixteen year-old Lucky's 1968 Dodge Charger on a warm summer night in August of 1970 and showed him three pictures of Fin dressed in girl's clothes as the car idled in front of her home. Lucky, at first, thought it was one of the girls from the neighborhood that Naomi rode the El with some days, and when she told him it was Fin, he laughed it off and denied it.

"No, Lucky, it's really Fin." Naomi said seriously.

Lucky looked closer and when he realized that it was Fin indeed, he grimaced and asked, "What the fuck is you showin' me this bull shit for, Naomi?"

"Finland said he wants you to know everything about him so there won't be any surprises. He says he's not gay and I believe him. I think he just likes dressing as a woman sometimes."

Naomi really didn't believe Fin was gay; to her, he was only role-playing. When Fin and Naomi were alone, he liked to dress up for Naomi, who didn't mind role-playing with Fin either; she was truly his friend, and to her, that was just Fin's way of having fun. He and Naomi talked a lot about sex in Naomi's room, but Fin never talked about liking boys. He answered Naomi's questions about male behavior to give her insight, and he talked a great deal during their time spent together about becoming a big-time lawyer in Chicago as he sat in his clothes. In Naomi's eyes, Fin wasn't gay at all, he just had a weird fetish.

Lucky on the other hand, believed Fin was outright gay. "What kind of man would dress up in women's clothing," was the next thing he asked Naomi.

"I don't know what kind of man they call that, Lucky. But I think Fin only has what I believe is a fetish. Lester took advantage of what our friend viewed as harmless fun."

"Harmless fun my ass! Look where it got 'em, Naomi!"

"He only does it in front of me—but he wanted you to know. Let's just leave it at that."

"How can I look at that fuckin' guy the same way, Naomi? I killed a man for him and he still doing that shit? He's settin' his self up for trouble I'm fuckin' tellin' ya' right now!"

"Fin could have any girl he wants to have."

"What about you, Naomi? Can Fin have you?"

"I don't want a boyfriend that wears girl clothes. But that's beside the point."

Lucky leaned over and got in Naomi's face and said sternly, "Fin is gay, Naomi! He's gay!"

"It's just a fet—"

"Naomi!" Lucky screamed, startling the fifteen year-old and causing her to jump in her seat and lean against the passenger side door a little frightened. "Finland Xavier is a man that wears women's clothes," he then said in a low but angry tone. "And in my eyes that makes him gay."

Naomi said nothing more. She took the pictures and exited the car quietly and went home and called Fin and told him he dare not show up in drag before Lucky lest he wanted to get himself killed. Fin was hurt over the things Naomi had told him that Lucky had said about him, but he understood. Naomi, however, would not relent because she felt Lucky was wrong for treating Fin so harshly when he'd been his friend long before the secret ever got out into the open amongst the three.

Naomi and Lucky discussed the matter repeatedly for days on in while Fin stayed out of Lucky's eye sight, and each time the two friends debated over Fin's fetish, Lucky would always tell Naomi that since she said she didn't want a man in women's clothes, she had to agree with him that Fin was indeed gay; but Naomi always reminded Lucky that Fin only wore the women's clothes in front of her and he had only seen a few pictures of Fin dressed as a woman. Lucky and Naomi's debates sometimes erupted into big arguments about hanging with Fin during the entire month of August in 1970 and Lucky always ended the conversation by saying, "Fuck it! He likes it in the ass, he likes it in the ass! Keep that mutherfucka from around me!"

Naomi knew Lucky was now involved with his father's crew, and she was also aware of the fact that he had a reputation to uphold. Lucky was a stone-cold gangster and Fin's fetish could easily destroy the three's friendship, something Naomi did not want to come to pass. She knew no other way, because Lucky was strict and obstinate on the matter, but to just plea for forgiveness on behalf of Fin. Naomi could be persuasive when she needed to be, and now, more than ever before, she had to be as cunning as possible in order to slowly wear Lucky down.

Over the next few months, Naomi often begged Lucky to forgive Fin. Lucky would listen, but that was about all. Naomi, however, knew she was having an effect on Lucky with her subtle persuasions. She reminded Lucky that it was *he* that was friends with Fin first.

"You did all that for Fin and now after he came clean with you, you turn your back on him? A friend is friend, Lucky! If Fin's your friend, he's your friend no matter what! And he never did nothing to you!" Naomi, who had turned sixteen a month earlier, said aloud on a cold December day as she got out of Lucky's car and walked towards her home.

Lucky watched as Naomi walked away in tears. Ever since the summer, the two had been arguing about Finland. So much to the point that the three friends hadn't hung out since the day he'd learned of Fin's secret. It was something he wish he'd never found out about. Fin should have just kept his little thing to himself. Lucky missed being around Naomi more than anything though, and he knew in order for the two of them to maintain their friendship, a friendship he'd come to love and appreciate, he would have to accept Fin. Fin wasn't a bad guy, he just had a fucked up way of getting his rocks off, at least that's what Lucky thought of the situation. Just before Naomi entered her home, Lucky blew the horn, stuck his arm out the window and waved her back over to the car.

"Yeah," Naomi asked as she leaned into the passenger side window.

"Look, I'm really disappointed in Fin—but so long as he never dresses up or act like a female in front of me? He's okay."

"Thank you, Lucky. Thank you."

"I'm not just doing this for Fin, you know?"

"What you mean?"

Lucky leaned over and opened the door. "Sit down for a minute," he said. Naomi climbed into the car and looked over to Lucky in wonderment. "I was thinking while you were headed home. You really care about people, Naomi."

"I care about my friends, Lucky. Remember that day I ran over to your house?"

"I do."

"What was one of the first things you said to me?"

"I have a friend named Finland Xavier." Lucky said as he looked out the window and laughed. "You remember what you said to me, though, Naomi?"

"That he acts like a girl. You agreed with me, too, Lucky."

"I did," Lucky said as he turned towards Naomi. "But I never knew until that day the reason behind it. You're a good friend," he said lowly as he leaned in closer to Naomi, who began to get nervous.

"Look, I have this friend, my dad's friend DeeDee's son named Doss. He's a cool guy and I think you twos should meet someday."

Naomi sighed and ran her hand through her thick, platted hair and then laughed as she covered her lower face.

"What's funny?"

"I thought you were going to try and kiss me." Naomi said through laughter.

Lucky was beyond kissing. He'd lost his virginity a couple of years back. Getting laid wasn't a problem as the mobsters down at the bar where he hung with his father often turned him on to females inside the establishment. He did, however, take a little offense at Naomi's laughter because he considered himself a lady's man that could have any woman he pleased. "What if I were trying to kiss you? Would you have done it?"

"Maybe," Naomi replied as she exited the car. "But my rule is friends can't kiss."

"I never heard that rule from you before in all the years I been knowing you."

"I just made it up, Lucky. Let's agree to never do anything like that, okay?"

"Fine by me. I'm going see my dad."

"Call me later." Naomi ended as she ran through the snow back towards the warmth of her home...

..."Lucky's a rare breed. Most gangsters wouldn't have accepted Fin." Twiggy stated.

"Right. But persistence paid off. I swear I was about to give up on the matter. I think Lucky came to the realization that our friendship would have been altered had he remained on the defensive. I began to admire him so much after that. And we became even closer as a result."

"So what happened next?" Martha asked.

"It wasn't too long after that when I met Doss. I'd actually forgotten that Lucky had wanted him to meet me because a little time had passed and he never brought it back up. I didn't know Doss was even coming over that day and when I first saw him from my window I thought Lucky was trying to set me up with some young hustler or something—and he was. But I was glad Lucky brought *that man* by the house *that day*. Those three years or so from '71 to '74 was fantastic let me tell ya'!" Naomi said as she laughed. "It all started back in April of '71. We were going to a Cubs game at Wrigley Field that day and..."

April 1971

..."Fin! What the hell are you doing still dressed like that?" sixteen year old Naomi snapped as she stood in her bedroom and stared at her friend.

"You like it! I'm wearing it to the game today!" Fin remarked as he fanned out the bottom on a blue sundress. "How you like the red sandals?"

"You can't go out with Lucky like that! He already told you about that, Fin! You tryna get yourself killed, boy? Go change!"

"Naomi I'm just playing."

"You go too far sometimes!" Naomi said as she heard Lucky's four door black Dodge Charger pull up in front of the home. "You need to change back into your regular clothes!" she snapped as she eyed Lucky from her bedroom window.

Lucky was dressed in neatly pressed black slacks, white gator shoes and a white silk shirt. Naomi briefly eyed his friend, whose face couldn't be seen because of the white fedora he wore. He was dressed neatly in light grey slacks with a pair of white and grey gator shoes with a button up shirt that was white on the left side and light grey on the right. Naomi had to admit that the outfit was sharp, but still, she didn't know the young man. She ran from her room, shoving Fin into the bathroom in the process, and hurried down the stairs where she flung her front door open and asked loudly, "Who did you bring to my house, Lucky?"

"Calm down, Naomi." Lucky said in low and calm tone of voice. "This is Doss. My dad's friend DeeDee's son. I told you a while back that I thought you twos should meet," he said as he stepped aside and let his friend Doss come into view.

Naomi was prepared to give Lucky a piece of her mind, but when she eyed Doss, her entire demeanor had quickly changed. She immediately felt butterflies as she stared at Doss. The handsome young man took off his fedora and nodded, extended his hand and said, "How you doing? I'm Doss Dawkins and it's nice to meet you, Naomi."

Doss Dawkins Junior was an eighteen year-old contract killer just like his father DeeDee, or Doss Dawkins Senior. Mendoza and DeeDee had reared their sons to be just like them, and Lucky and Doss had adapted well to the path that their fathers had put them on early on in life. The two also had style and class, and both qualities were being put on full display by Doss Dawkins on this day.

Naomi stretched her hand out and when she touched Doss' hand, she nearly melted. At age sixteen, Naomi Holland stood 5'6" and weighed around 140 pounds. She was a thick, buxom teenager with slender brown eyes and a contagious smile. She wore her hair in two thick plats that she often braided to the back and had ample breasts, curvaceous hips and legs, a flat belly, and what could only be described as a glorious, round, soft-looking ass.

She was a compact, well-built, voluptuous young woman whose lips looked inviting to Doss, and instead of shaking her hand, he wanted to press his lips to hers and hold her soft-looking and sweet-smelling body and all its delectable parts tightly in the palms of his hands.

To Naomi, Doss was a man—*thee man*—and she knew right away that she would have him someday as it was an instant attraction.

Doss, who wasn't much taller than Naomi at 5' 9" and weighing around 165 pounds, was a few shades darker than she with dark, slender eyes, neatly-trimmed sideburns and a sexy smile. His muscular physique was what captivated Naomi the most and in her eyes, Doss was fine and sexy. She wanted to be taken by him at that moment. To press her body into his and rub his well-toned biceps as she slowly kissed his lips and licked his earlobes. She wanted to feel his hands on her body, and wanted to be held close by Doss. She grabbed his hand, naughty thoughts racing through her mind as she stared at him while smiling.

"Hey. baby," Doss said, "you know, you don't need a beauty mark under your eye to state your splendor because you're already gorgeous."

"Smooth talker," Naomi sighed as she leaned in her doorway in a dream-like state.

Naomi was still clutching Doss' hand, and when he raised it to his lips and planted a soft kiss on the back of her palm, she became like butter in a hot skillet. She excused herself and walked back into the home trembling slightly with joy and readiness. When she was out of sight, she grabbed her stomach trying to contain the excitement she was feeling. She then peeked back and saw Lucky and Doss walking into the foyer. "Y'all stay there! I be right back, Lucky," she screamed as she trotted up the stairs, eager to tell Fin.

Naomi ran into her room and saw Fin, now dressed in his normal attire, and she closed her door, raised her skirt and pulled off her panties, which were wet from what had transpired between her and Doss. Fin had seen Naomi naked many a time, besides that fact, he acted more female than male around her most times and for that reason Naomi felt comfortable undressing in front of him. She shared her innermost thoughts with Fin, and she often got good advice from a male perspective. Naomi often shared things with Fin that she didn't even tell Serena.

Fin stared at Naomi as she stood naked from the waist down and asked, "Girlfriend, just what on earth are you doing?"

"Ohh Fin, he's, he's so sexy."

"Who? Lucky?"

"Lucky? Boy, please! I'm talking about his friend, Doss." Naomi said as she went for another pair of panties and headed for the bathroom to clean herself. "I swear I had a small orgasm just by touching him, Fin. I'm feeling that brother right there!" she ended as she walked out the room.

"Don't make it too obvious, sister." Fin said with a smirk on his face.

Naomi then ran back into the room. "You think he noticed how I was acting?"

"I didn't see that—but tell you what? We'll spy on him and see how he acts and at the end of the day? We'll match comparisons and see what we come up with." Fin replied.

"That's a good idea, Fin." Naomi said before heading towards the bathroom.

Fin and Naomi straightened themselves and headed back down the stairs, Naomi smiling sexily as she eyed Doss who returned the gesture by tipping his hat. When Fin came into view, Doss turned and asked Lucky, "Is that him?"

"Yeah that's him. He's a cool guy, though. And he's a friend of mine." Lucky replied.

Doss nodded towards Fin as he and Naomi approached the front door and said, "What's up, guy?"

"Hello. I heard your question. I take it Lucky told you all about me?"

"Yeah, umm, Lucky told me that you were—"

"Gay?" Fin asked, cutting Doss off.

"Actually I was going to say tall."

"Tall?" Fin asked in a sly tone as he looked down at Doss, who was slightly shorter than his 6'1" slender frame.

"Yeah, I was going to say he told me you were—tall."

"Ohh okay," Fin stated with a wry smile. "Well, thank you but I'm not, umm—tall."

"Me neither!" Doss stated as he and Fin laughed.

The three walked out the door and Naomi locked her home and smiled at Doss as he grabbed her hand and walked with her to Lucky's car where he opened the back door for Naomi and helped her in. Fin stood by the front passenger side door, meanwhile, standing by idly and waiting as if his door was going to be opened. Doss eyed him, chuckled and shook his head as he hopped into the backseat beside Naomi, who chuckled herself when she saw Lucky look back at Doss because she knew what was coming.

"Eh, what the fuck are you doing back there?" Lucky asked Doss.

"I'm on a date, brother. Sit up there with the umm, with the tall guy." Doss said through laughter.

"Eh? We rode here together you should be up front, Doss."

"Come on Lucky we gone miss the start of the game! Fin? Get in and stop playing!" Naomi requested.

Fin opened the door and Lucky eyed him seriously. "Stay on your side too ya' mutherfucka you! Here, put this wine in your purse while you're at it," he told Fin as he pulled off from the curb.

"I don't carry a purse, Lucky."

"Yeah? I coulda swore otherwise ya' weird, no ya'—hey Doss what you call Fin a minute ago?"

"Tall."

"Yeah. Ya' tall son-of-a-bitch!" Lucky stated as he laughed and nudged Fin and turned up the song *Bad Moon Rising* by Credence Clearwater Revival that was playing on the radio.

For a while now, Lucky had been teasing Fin, who'd resented Lucky's taunts at first, but saw that he really meant no harm. The four made it to the game in time, grabbed cups of ice and Lucky led the way to the seats, which were in left field. When the group made it to their seats, Lucky opened the wine and everybody got a cup full as the players ran onto the field. The game got underway and mid-way through the first inning, amidst the thousands of cheering fans, hot dog vendors and peanut servers, a pretty, light blue-eyed red-head Italian female and an older man with a bald head and a thick grey beard sat in the two empty seats beside Lucky.

"Hey! Look what we got here," Lucky said as his eyes widened. "Hey toots! Takin' the old man out to the ball park, eh? That's good! Let 'em stretch his legs and get from in front the TV at the old folk's home! You doing volunteer work or something?"

"That's my granddaughter ya' bum!" the old man snapped.

"Hey! Pops? I'm talkin' ta' ya' granddaughter right here! Do ya' mind?"

"You most certainly can not talk to my granddaughter. Ignore him, Mildred," the old man ordered. He then leaned forward in his seat, eyed Lucky and said, "And don't try any funny stuff ya' fuckin' hoodlum! I'm a Word War Two vet and believe me when I say I'll kick your ass."

"You fought in the War? Where?" Lucky asked as he eyed the man and then stood up and cheered for his favorite player, Billy Williams, who played left field for the Cubs, who were playing the St. Louis Cardinals on this sunny day in April of 1971.

"I fought in Italy. Ground infantry. I was the best First Sergeant in my platoon in the Eighty-Sixth."

"The Eight-Six? They were legends! My family is from

Sicily and I heard of you guys from my grandmother. I appreciate what you done for us over there." Lucky said seriously as he extended his hand to shake the veteran's hand. "My name is Faustino, but everybody calls me Lucky."

The man responded in kind and introduced himself as Sergeant William Delmont and then introduced his granddaughter, Mildred, to Lucky afterwards. Lucky sat down and talked to Mister Delmont, asking numerous questions about the war. What could have been a verbal confrontation or physical altercation had turned into a peaceful and friendly conversation that soon had Mister Delmont telling numerous stories of the battles he'd fought and survived. The man had come to like Lucky once the two got to talking. As the game wore on, the group continued to drink the bottle of Cold Duck that Lucky had snuck into the park. Mister Delmont even had a sip.

By the seventh inning stretch, Lucky had gotten Mildred's phone number. He learned she resided with her grandfather and mother in Chicago, not too far from the bar on 23rd Street where his father and other Mafioso hung out. Mildred was a voluptuous red-head female standing about 5'8" weighing a hefty 150 pounds. She had big breasts, and Lucky couldn't wait to get his hands on the busty pair. All through the proceedings Lucky and Mildred flirted as her grandfather became enthralled with the game.

Naomi and Doss were hitting it off as well. She'd had her first taste of liquor this day and to her, the wine was sweet, just like Doss, was her thinking, and she really was infatuated with her new friend. Early on during the game, she told herself when she was ready, Doss would be her first. She and Doss talked about everything from Martin Luther's King Junior's assassination, to her long-lost siblings. They learned a lot about each other as the game wore on.

Fin was ready to leave. To him the game was boring. He had brought along an English book to read, but he scolded himself for being foolish enough to believe that he would actually be able to concentrate and read during a Chicago Cubs baseball game.

The game ended its regulation play and entered into a tenth

inning tied 2-2. Lucky, who had gotten a serious buzz from the wine, stood up and yelled aloud when his favorite player came up to bat. "Hey, Billy! Billy, sock it this way and end the game with a walk-off homer!" Lucky yelled.

"That would be awesome if he were to hit a homerun this way! Too bad he can't hear you, Lucky!" Mister Delmont yelled in return as he stood up.

"He might not can't hear me—but I just got a feelin'! If he hits a homerun, I got a feeling it's comin' this way, Mister Delmont!"

"I would love to catch that ball—but I'm afraid I'll miss it," the sergeant stated as he looked at the old glove he held in his hands.

"You been to hell and back, Mister Delmont—and you scared to catch a baseball?" Lucky asked.

"Me and some of the men in my company used to play baseball when we weren't on the front lines. A lot of those guys, a lot of those guys never made it back home, Faustino. Holding this glove brings back a lot of memories. I may get nervous catching that ball and just drop the darn thing."

Lucky now understood Mister Delmont's fear about catching the ball. He also wanted to do something nice for the sergeant, like getting a baseball hat signed by one of the players. The crowd sighed when Billy missed the first pitch and Lucky tuned back into the game.

"Dang it! That wasn't a strike!" Mister Delmont yelled aloud as several other fans agreed loudly.

"I know! The Cards may just walk him." Lucky responded. "Hey Mildred, you been real quiet. You not a Cubs fan?" he then asked.

Mildred smiled and said, "Well, they're really good."

"So you a Cubs fan? Or maybe you a Cards fan. I can't tell with you wearing red and all."

"What is wrong with red?" Mildred asked.

"That's the Cardinals' colors!" Lucky remarked. "I bet you a secret Cardinals fan!"

Just then a loud cracking sound was heard throughout the

park. "And it's a fly ball to left field by Billy Williams!" the announcer shouted as Mildred, Fin, Naomi, Doss and all the fans surrounding the group stood up with Lucky and Mister Delmont and began cheering.

"That's his ball! That's the sergeant's homerun ball right there and I'm gonna catch it for 'em!" Lucky stated as he slid pass Mildred and her grandfather and stood in the aisle.

"Lucky you need a glove!" Mildred yelled.

"Here, Lucky! Use mines!" Mister Delmont yelled as he threw Lucky his mitt. "Catch that son-of-a-bitch!"

"Got it sarge! Everybody out the way! Out the fuckin' way!" Lucky yelled to the crowd as he shoved people aside.

The ball was headed directly to the group's section and Naomi, Fin, Doss, Mildred and Mister Delmont were all screaming at Lucky, telling him to catch the ball.

"To the left! Left, Lucky! It's going left, man!" Naomi yelled.

"Okay, Naomi! I got the mutherfucka! I got it!" Lucky yelled as the ball sailed towards the group's area.

An old lady had her mitt and the ball was headed straight towards the woman. Some people backed off as the lady called for the ball, but Lucky broke through the crowd and trotted down a few stairs and shoved the lady aside in an attempt to nab the winning homerun ball. Lucky had his right arm fully extended, pressed against the old lady's head, forcing her over to her right side as she struggled to free herself. Lucky caught the ball with his mitt-covered left hand and snatched the lady's wig off with his right hand at the same time. "Ohh shit! What's this, old gal? A fuckin' squirrel? Eh everybody? She gotta' squirrel on her fuckin' head! Doss! She wearing a fuckin' squirrel!" Lucky stated through laughter as he ran back up the stairs amidst people's boos. "Eh, fuck off! I got the ball fair and square! Forget that old broad!" Lucky yelled at people who witnessed what had just transpired in the aisle.

"What if it was your mother ya' scumbag?" a fan yelled to Lucky.

"My mother don't wear squirrels on her fuckin' head!" Lucky ended as he made his way back to his seat.

Naomi, Doss and Fin were still there laughing to the top of their lungs as Lucky handed the ball to Mister Delmont.

"You shoved an old lady out of the way for me, Lucky?" Mister Delmont asked through light laughter as he shook his head. "It really meant a lot to you to catch this ball for me, didn't it, son?"

"It sure did! Billy Williams is the best guy on the team and I got that ball for *you*! All's fair in love and war! You're gonna get it signed?" Lucky asked as he gasped for air.

"No. You are." Mister Delmont replied as Lucky stared at him in a perplexed manner.

Mister Delmont smiled at Lucky as he handed him the ball. "Get it signed," he said. "Get it signed and bring it to me. Mildred will tell you how to get to our home. You have been invited to meet my family."

Lucky shook the sergeant's hand and hugged Mildred and watched as she and her grandfather made their way towards the exit. He'd been given approval to see Mildred and he was head over heels. "Eh, let's go get this ball signed and go over to 23rd and see my pops!" Lucky said happily as the group began to make their way out of the ball park.

An hour and a half later, after getting the ball signed by Billy Williams, the four were parked out front of *The Eastside Bar and Social Club* on 23rd Street, just west of South Cicero Avenue. *The Eastside Bar and Social Club* was a small, green-bricked grocery store that had been converted into a bar. It sat in the middle of the block in between 49th Avenue and South Cicero Avenue and it was where the 23rd Street Mafia was head quartered.

The outfit started out as a group of men hanging out in a parking lot on the corners of 23rd and 49th Street. When members of the Egan's Rats gang, a mob organization based in St. Louis approached a group of Italians in the year 1922 and asked them to do a hit back in St. Louis, the four men took the job, completed it, and were compensated. The gang of four then returned to Cicero, brought the grocery store and opened the *Eastside Bar and Social Club* and formed the 23rd Street

Mafia. The Egan's Rats used the four men for various jobs throughout the mid-west for two years until the Egan's Rats were dismantled through death and imprisonment; but the 23rd Street Mafia had become well established as the Chicago version of New York-based Murder Incorporated by the time the Egan's Rats were dismantled.

The gang grew rapidly, and by the early 1930's 23rd Street Mafia was highly respected by a great majority of mobsters, including Lucky Luciano based in New York, and Bugs Moran and Al Capone whose operations were headquartered in Chicago. No one fucked with 23rd Street Mafia. They operated under their umbrella, but they were close allies with Al Capone and the Purple Gang out of Detroit. Unlike Capone and the Purple Gang, however, who were primarily bootleggers, members of 23rd Street Mafia only took hits—and it didn't matter who ordered the hit or who was the mark. There had been stories told that the gang would set out to kill a person, and if the person they intended to kill had the cash on hand to pay 23rd to kill the people who placed a hit on him, 23rd would still kill that person, but they would return and kill the person who paid for the hit at the out-set. No one knew if the rumors were true or not, but when 23rd came on the scene in the mid 1920's, men who knew they could possibly end up on someone's hit list were known to carry what came to be known as 'return the favor money' from time to time, just in case 23rd came calling.

The founders of 23rd Street Mafia, all who'd died violently during the Bugs Moran/Scarface Al Capone prohibition war, were highly efficient killers, and they willingly trained the ones coming up behind them to be just as proficient as they were.

Lucky's father, Mendoza Cernigliaro, was already a hit man when he arrived in Cicero in the late fifties. He'd heard of 23rd and he merely walked into the bar and asked for a job. The current boss, Zell Verniche`, checked Mendoza's credentials and got the okay from Carlo Gambino back in New York and Mendoza got made a second time and had been a member of 23rd since 1957. Mendoza's right hand man, Doss Dawkins

Senior, or DeeDee, came on the scene in 1960 when he approached Mendoza and asked for a favor.

DeeDee was having problems with his landlord. His wife, Doss' mother, had been raped and killed in her own home and DeeDee believed his landlord, an Italian Mafioso that worked for a notorious gangster by the name of "Mad Sam" DeStefano, was behind the slaughter. Knowing he, too, would be killed for touching a made-man, DeeDee went to 23rd and offered to pay Mendoza for the hit.

Mendoza took the job and killed the man, but DeeDee was arrested for the crime. DeeDee never told what actually happened, though; and would have willingly taken a life sentence rather than roll over on the mob. DeStefano was a killer in his own right. He sought out DeeDee to have him killed behind bars, but when 23rd caught wind of the hit and vouched for the man, announcing that DeeDee was a friend of theirs, "Mad Sam" took a more gentlemanly approach and let sleeping dogs lie in order to avoid going to war with 23rd Street Mafia.

The charges against DeeDee were soon dropped because of lack of evidence and he was released eight months later. From there, Mendoza and DeeDee formed a partnership and completed hit after hit on various gang members and Mafioso. Mendoza moved up in the ranks quickly and he kept DeeDee by his side. DeeDee couldn't get made because he was black, but he was a bona fide affiliate who came to be loved and respected by the 23rd Street Mafia.

Lucky, Doss, Fin and Naomi exited Lucky's car and let their eyes scan the crowded neighborhood that was tucked in between the Chicago El and Interstate-55 to the south, and West Cemak Road to the north. There were delis and pizzerias everywhere, right alongside rundown three, four, six, and ten-level apartments. There were well-known drug dens in some of the buildings and obvious prostitutes walked the streets in broad daylight. The people in this bustling part of Cicero operated under an umbrella peace, and so long as 23rd was in power, police were not a problem in this section of town because they were being paid off handsomely. The people here were free to do as they pleased so long as no one was killed—that was 23rd's job to rid the neighborhood of 'pot-stirrers'. People of all races could go to the bar and have a problem rectified within hours or days. 23rd didn't discriminate. They took all comers so long as the person requesting the hit had the cash on hand.

The group followed Lucky towards the bar's entrance as he spoke to various mobsters dressed lavishly in tailored silk suits, sporting matching shoes and fedoras with pinky rings on both fingers. Mobsters were all over the outside of the establishment; some were leaning against shiny Cadillacs and Lincoln Continentals, others were standing in groups of three or four smoking cigarettes and cigars as they conversed. This was one of the most organized locales in the Chicago area, and the men here were involved in a serious business—the extermination of life for unspecified amounts of money. It was a dangerous profession to say the least, but a profitable one none-the less for the men who'd chosen this treacherous way of life.

After Lucky chatted with several made men outside, he and his friends entered the bar. A neatly dressed Italian opened the door and tipped his hat to Lucky, who handed him a twenty dollar bill. Naomi and Fin, who had never been to the place, saw that the bar was directly ahead, to the right was five tables where more of 23rd's soldiers sat. In the middle of the crowded bar, between the tables and the bar counter was two pool tables that had games being held by Italian and Black men alike while women of various ethnicities paraded around in skimpy outfits vying for drinks and attention. Naomi grabbed Doss' hand as the group slid past a dozen or so sharp-dressed, rough-looking Italian gangsters; she was somewhat unnerved by the power emanating from within *Eastside Bar*.

The bartender noticed Lucky and yelled aloud, "Hey, mutherfucka? I saw ya' knock that old lady down on national TV ya' lucky son-of-a-bitch!"

"Eh, that's my name! That's why they call me Lucky! Where's pops?"

"In the back with Zell and DeeDee!" the raspy-voiced

bartender replied as he wiped the counter.

The group walked to the back of the club and Naomi eyed Doss' father for the first time when he pointed him out standing beside the bar talking to a young, attractive black woman. DeeDee was a six-foot four, tall, slender man with a thick, but neatly-style Afro and had a thin mustache and pearl white teeth as he was smiling when Naomi laid eyes on him in his black, pin-striped silk suit and white and black alligator shoes as he stood before the woman, obviously trying to woo her with kind words as he rubbed her thigh. He wore a shiny diamond ring on each pinky finger and had a shiny watch on his left wrist. He emanated success and had a distinguished appeal in Naomi's eyes. She was impressed with the man and had a brief glimpse into the future as to what Doss would look like should they remain a couple and she liked it.

Naomi then eyed Mendoza, who was in the middle of a story. "So, I walk up to this guy, right? I like ta' look a man in the eyes right before I kill 'em, so I call out to 'em. I said 'Hey muther'—the mutherfucka turned around and punched me in the neck before I could finish my fuckin' sentence!" Mendoza said over the song *Mustang Sally* sung by Wilson Pickett, as various gangsters laughed aloud. "I'm going down now fellas," he said as he took to one knee, "I'm clutching my neck looking up at DeeDee and he askin' me 'Doza! You all right? You all right?' I'm like 'fuck me—kill the son-of-a-bitch'!"

"Man," DeeDee remarked through laughter, "I had that cat in my eyesight, but you, you looked like you was about to fuckin' die!"

"Any of you hoodlums ever been punched in the neck? It'll make ya' feel like ya' dying. At least it did for me." Mendoza replied as he stood up and sipped his drink and pointed towards the dance floor.

DeeDee turned and saw his son walking his way with Lucky. "Hey, son! Who's the fine young sister you got with you?" he asked Doss over the music.

Doss walked towards the back of the bar where the top members of the crew hung out and introduced Naomi and Fin. Several ranking mobsters within 23rd were hanging out with

DeeDee and Mendoza this day as well. Combined, these guys had more bodies under their belts than the total number of spots on a pack of leopards. Fin knew most of the members of 23rd were contract killers. He nervously shook the men's hands and Naomi did the same, only she was all smiles now. She was beginning to actually like being around such intriguing and dangerous men. The men smiled at Naomi and tipped their hats in respect in return as she greeted each of them. When she got to DeeDee, she smiled and did a curtsey. DeeDee eyed his son and his eyes widened as he sipped his whiskey and pointed to Naomi.

"Nice move, young lady."

"Thank you."

"Naomi! I didn't expect to see you in here! You like the hangout?" Mendoza asked as he lit a cigar.

"It's a better place now that I'm here! How do I become a made woman?" Naomi asked as the men chuckled to themselves.

"She got spunk!" Zell, the crew's leader yelled. "Doss, don't fuck this up ya' son-of-a-bitch!" he ended as he puffed on a cigar.

"Hey son," Mendoza then yelled to Lucky, "why you knock the old broad down at the game?"

"I would've knocked my own mother down for that ball pops!" Lucky yelled aloud.

Just then Lucky was grabbed from behind by the ears. "Ya' would knock ya' own mother down for some stupid baseball?" Francine remarked as she placed her son in a headlock.

The men laughed again as Naomi and Fin took a seat at the bar and enjoyed the gangsters' conversation. The mobsters were real nice to Naomi and Fin, asking if they wanted a drink or a plate of food and repeatedly telling them to make themselves at home, which they did by sharing an order of deep-fried Italian chicken wings. The two were eating and discussing college when a member of 23rd walked up to Naomi and told her that the Don of 23rd Street, a man named Zell Verniche`, wanted to meet her personally.

Naomi looked at Fin, who only shrugged, and got up from her bar stool and was escorted to the last booth in the bar. She had seen Zell briefly, but she hadn't spoken a word to him since entering the bar. She went and stood before his table and the heavy-set gangster stared at her with a faceless expression. Zell reminded Naomi of Santa Claus with his thick, black and grey beard and huge round stomach; but she knew the gifts this man often brought to people were gifts they cared not to receive.

Zell stretched his hand, signaling Naomi to sit and she slid in the booth opposite the man. He leaned back in his olive green silk suit and rested his hands on his stomach and just stared at Naomi. His dark eyes were intimidating for a brief moment, but Naomi felt very safe inside the bar and at Zell's table. She began wiping the back of her neck and reached for a napkin to wipe her forehead as Zell watched her.

"I said you had spunk earlier and you didn't reply," he finally said.

"Am I supposed to thank you?" Naomi asked.

Zell knew Naomi wasn't being sarcastic or facetious, but only trying to figure out what to say in response to his statement made earlier. "That's why you didn't reply," he asked as he stared at Naomi. "Because you didn't know what to say? You don't seem like the type of person to be at a loss for words, young lady."

"I'm not really. I didn't feel worthy."

Zell frowned and leaned forward, resting his arms on the table. "Worthy of what? To speak to me? I'm no one special, Naomi. And don't you ever feel that you aren't worthy to speak to anyone. I don't care who they are. There are no aristocrats on this planet."

"You're right. I'll never do that again—Santa Claus." Naomi stated as she covered her mouth and laughed.

Zell smiled at Naomi and said, "My three daughters and all of my grandchildren along with their friends all call me Santa Claus. Only family and friends can call me Santa."

"Can I call you Santa?"

"It sounds nice comin' from you, il mio amico. Do you know

what that means? Il mio amico?"

"You called me your friend." Naomi said lowly.

"Right you are. And today it is what you have become. Learn from me today, Naomi, when I say that DeeDee's son is a good kid. Doss needs someone special in his life. And you wouldn't be here if you didn't care for him."

"We just went on a date." Naomi said as she played with the salt and pepper shakers on the table.

"That's how it starts. First a date, then a dinner, then breakfast. What happens in between or afterwards is left to the imagination."

"Why you tellin' me all this, Santa?"

"Because I think you and little Doss would make one helluva pair. I wish the two of you well in life—together in life. Take my advice and love that man." Zell said through a smile.

"Okay. But you know what? You are a little late." Naomi ended as Zell patted her hand and then extended it outwards to allow her to exit the table.

"You ever need a favor, you just come and talk to me. You're a friend of mine now." Zell ended as Naomi thanked him and left his presence.

That day Naomi had grown to love the *Eastside Bar and Social Club*. She spent the summer of 1971 attending baseball games and heading over to the bar afterwards to sit and talk to various mobsters, and she'd learned a lot about the mafia-lifestyle and its many traditions from Zell Verniche` during the summer months.

Kevin and Serena didn't come to learn of Naomi's doings until the summer of 1972, but by then they were too late. Naomi, who was almost eighteen at the time, told Kevin, the most vocal about her hanging out with Lucky and Doss in July of '72, that she wasn't going to stop seeing Doss, nor was she going to stop hanging out at the bar.

Forty-eight year-old Serena asked her in front of forty-six year-old Kevin if she and Doss were having sex and Naomi truthfully replied that they were not. Serena then pleaded on behalf of Naomi, telling Kevin that she could be doing worst.

"She goes to baseball games and listens to music at a bar with Lucky and Fin, what's the harm?" Serena asked Kevin.

Kevin didn't answer, he merely walked off shaking his head in frustration.

Naomi had Serena's support, but she warned her not to destroy her future. "You're going to be attending Northwestern tuition-free in the near future, Naomi. Don't move too fast or too soon, child. Sex will be there, and if Doss loves you, he'll wait. You're doing fine. Just, just be careful okay? The game, the bar, and then straight home, alright?"

"I promise, momma. I just like being around Doss that's all. I, I love—"

"Shh, shh, I know," Serena said lowly. "I know you love him —but you take care of yourself first, okay? Kevin only wants the best for you. Being friends with Lucky, and loving Doss? That's the decision that you're making for your life. Kevin would rather you be friends with some of the kids on the campus and prefers that you love a doctor or a lawyer or some other professional, but you have the power to make your own decisions on who you want to be with and that is what you're doing, and that is the freedom you have."

"Me and Fin, we, we both plan on being lawyers someday. Everybody is not meant to go to college. Why should I stop loving Doss because he doesn't attend a college? I remember I got out daddy car that day and ran over to Lucky's house and introduced myself. Lucky took me by Fin's house that day and we been friends ever since. Why should I stop being friends with Lucky now because we are taking different paths in life?"

Serena then smiled at Naomi and kissed her cheeks. The woman had *been* a part of Cicero, and she had known of Mendoza before Kevin and Naomi had even entered the neighborhood. She also knew of the bar and the people who hung there; they weren't the nicest of people, to outsiders, but Naomi had befriended the men at the *Eastside Bar*, who didn't hurt their own and Serena knew that; she had even been to the bar a time or two and had a drink herself and discovered how sociable the people were inside the place. To Serena, the bar *was* Cicero in its purest form. A small slice of Italy brought to America on the outskirts of Chicago. As long as Serena approved of what Naomi was doing, she would have no problems hanging out at *Eastside Bar*.

Naomi finished her home-schooling in February of 1973 and entered Northwestern University's School of Law in September of '73 with eighteen year-old Fin by her side. She took up Corporate Law while Fin had decided on studying Criminal Law. Naomi had goals, and she knew exactly what she wanted to do in life, and not only did she have Serena's backing, but by 1973 she was in good with the mobsters inside the *Eastside Bar and Social Club.*

CHAPTER 7
SURRENDER

It was now April in the year 1974 and nineteen year-old Naomi was now spending most of her time over to Serena's house. Kevin wanted Naomi only to focus on her education so he would give her an allowance, thus enabling her to remain job-free throughout her early college years. The nineteen year-old was also receiving gifts of cash from DeeDee, Doss, and other mobsters at the *Eastside Bar*—gifts she kept secret from Serena and Kevin.

When the mobsters in the bar learned that Naomi and Fin were attending Northwestern University's School of Law, they donated to both their tuitions with the intent of having free counsel when they earned their licenses. Naomi told the men that she was attending college tuition free and aiming to practice Corporate Law, but Fin was studying to become a criminal trial layer and he could really use the money. Members of 23rd paid for Fin's tuition in full and that allowed him to quit his job at a local deli and focus on his education. Fin knew full-well that the mobsters wanted him to become their on-call lawyer and he openly agreed to do so when he started accepting their money.

Serena had given Naomi free reign over her house so long as she kept the home clean and cared for its needs. She and Doss, now twenty-one, were going strong in 1974. Doss had other girls he slept with because Naomi wasn't ready for sex when the two of them first got together in 1971. Serena was a constant deterrent and safe guard for Naomi also, but by 1972 the sexual tension between Naomi and Doss was reaching a boiling point.

Doss would sneak over to Serena's house after dark and he and Naomi would kiss and pet one another heavily. Naomi almost gave in during the latter part of the summer of '72 when she was seventeen years-old, but she held strong, telling Doss she wasn't ready and she didn't want to betray Serena's wishes. Doss didn't mind, he had other females that Naomi didn't know about, but Naomi was the woman he really wanted. He would wait until she was ready, careful not to get any of his other women pregnant.

To prevent the sexual tension stirring within her from getting the best of her in 1972, Naomi had decided to grow a garden in Serena's backyard in order to take her mind off of sex. She quickly became a natural; although it had been years since she had even tended soil. Serena and Kevin loved the garden Naomi had planted during the summer of 1972. They would walk over to the backyard every Sunday morning in the fall with their huge straw basket and pick the fresh tomatoes, green bell peppers, cucumbers and onions that Naomi had grown and they would use them in their salads and dinners. Francine and Mendoza also partook of the vegetables Naomi was cultivating as they were the freshest around, even fresher than the ones at the Farmer's Market, and they had such robust flavor that was perfect for seasoning pork, chicken and various cuts of steak and sauces.

Naomi bought a rooster as well—much to nineteen year-old Lucky's disdain. She kept the bird in a huge coop, and when Lucky asked her why she'd bought a rooster, Naomi had no solid answer. She could only attribute her agricultural skill and desire to raise a bird to the life she was beginning to live back in Sylacauga before things were tragically uprooted. Eileen and Nituna Holland where excellent agriculturalists and were quite adept to tending the land the family once owned; and Naomi and Ruth had spent a lot of time with their mother and grandmother in the field in Sylacauga and were fast learning the way of the land. Years later, the things Eileen and Nituna had taught Naomi were still fresh in her mind and were of great value now at this particular juncture of her life, for what started out as a release to sexual tension, had slowly morphed into one of the most beloved projects Naomi had ever undertaken. She often cried when she was alone in the garden because working the soil often brought back the few scant memories she had of the life she once lived in Alabama. She would look around and swear she could feel her biological mother's spirit helping her along in the garden. Nituna often hummed whilst working, and Naomi, the first day she dug into the soil, began to hum the same hymn her mother often hummed, although she had no clue as to what was the name of the hymn.

Pretending to talk to her mother was another activity Naomi often delved into when she worked outdoors. She often imagined her grandmother, father and her brother and sisters milling about as she worked the garden. Naomi's emotions were so overwhelming during this period of time she'd gone so far as to set up a small, white plastic table and four chairs in the back of the garden where she would often set out her Raggedly Anne and Andy dolls and talk to them as she worked the garden.

The garden had unwittingly become therapy for Naomi, and even though they weren't there when she'd started the project, the love she had for her lost siblings had grown even deeper; and her desire to find them had grown stronger. Sam, Mary and Martha may have not been there in the physical sense, but Naomi, whenever she was in the garden, could feel her siblings' spirits flowing through her soul. She would work in the garden, wearing a sundress and apron, and smile to herself as she turned soil with her small garden shovel. She would tell herself that someday was getting closer and closer with each day that went by. Those two years or so from 1972 until 1974 had given Naomi some of the fondest memories. Her sexual drive was subdued for a while as well, but by the spring of 1974, nineteen year-old Naomi Holland again began to have strong urges, urges that working in the garden could no longer suppress.

During the middle part of April '74, Naomi was again

preparing to work her garden. It was a warm and sunny Saturday morning around 5a.m. and in spite of hanging at the Eastside Bar the night before, she was bright-eyed and bushy-tailed as she enjoyed a cup of coffee while sitting at the poker table in Serena's lounge. This year, Naomi was planning on growing turnip greens, green bell peppers, cabbage, tomatoes, and onions. She sat in silence inside the poker room with only the tick-tock of Serena's grandfather clock stirring the quiet as she wondered what her brother and sisters looked like at the present time. Sam would be seventeen now, and Mary and Martha would be fifteen in June. Were they okay? Did they know she existed? Were they still alive? The last question Naomi asked herself had put tears in her eyes. She got up and looked at herself in the mirror in Serena's lounge and saw the image of a young Creek Indian and Negro woman staring back at her. Her hair was platted into two thick plats that hung on either side her head, gently touching her shoulders. Her dark eyes radiated a look of delight and passion, but they also held a certain kind of sadness and a sense of loss. She touched the birthmark under her left eye and thought of Ruth, knowing that as she stared at herself, she was looking directly into the eyes of her murdered twin whom she missed tremendously. Naomi then remembered Mary and Martha's appearance the day they were taken away from her; and she reflected on the unawareness of her brother Sam as he stood and watched the assistant at the orphanage button his coat just before he was taken away. Tears ran down her cheeks as she stared at herself, remembering how distraught she was when she ran and grabbed her, Mary and Martha's coat, in an attempt to save Sam the day he was being taken away. She remembered how the door was locked on her and her sisters and the heartache she endured as she watched from the window of the orphanage while Sam was being led away with an unknown woman. Naomi then thought about the way Mary stared at her as she ran alongside the car that held her and Martha, telling them that it wasn't over. She soon wiped her teary eyes and smiled, knowing that the words she had spoken to Mary in 1965 were true—it was not over—and if they were alive—she would find them someday indeed.

Naomi picked up her three Raggedly Anne dolls and headed

for the door just as her rooster began to crow loudly. She entered the backyard and sat 'Mary', 'Martha', and 'Sam' down at their table, opened a pack of tomato seeds and knelt down in the dirt and began to plant her seeds for the summer growing season.

Just after six, Naomi looked through the opened back door of Serena's home and saw Doss moving about in the kitchen. He'd spent the night. The two slept spooned against one another in their under garments, Doss behind Naomi hugging her tightly, breathing lightly on the nape of her neck. Naomi told Doss before he even entered Serena's home that she wasn't having sex with him that night, but as she watched him open a few cabinets she couldn't help but to lament over not giving in to her desire. Those feelings of regret now let Naomi know she was ready to surrender her love to the man she'd fallen in love with during the summer of 1971. She left her garden in order to set out to do what she felt she should have allowed happen the night before. She entered the kitchen through the back door and smiled at Doss, who sat and stared at her as she went to the sink and washed her hands and placed a pot of water on the stove.

"You want some oatmeal this morning?" Naomi asked Doss in a sweet tone as she smiled at him.

"Yeah, that'll be nice, baby."

As the water boiled, Naomi walked over to Doss and sat in his lap facing him and the two began kissing one another hard and passionately. To Doss, Naomi was very soft to the touch; she felt good pressing her body to his, her hardening nipples could be felt through the silk bra she wore underneath her brown sun dress. She opened Doss' shirt and leaned down and kissed his chest. Her lips covered his nipples and sucked gently. Doss moaned slightly and reached out and ran his hands through Naomi's plats, twisted them loose before she sat up and twisted her head releasing her thick black mane of hair. Doss was lost in pure in admiration of his woman's natural beauty. She was gorgeous to him—the quintessential perfect woman in his eyes—highly intelligent, strong-willed, compassionate and responsive. He leaned forward and kissed Naomi and her body trembled from arousal and anticipation.

The two pulled apart and Naomi stood up, her hair now spread across the entirety of her head, draping down and touching the tops of her shoulder blades. Her deep, dark eyes, that were radiating sheer love, spoke only two words at that moment— take me.

Doss stood up and turned off the stove and turned back to Naomi, who was slowly backing away from him, biting her lower lip like the shy little girl she had become when she reentered the house just moments ago. She backed into the threshold and stumbled into the poker lounge as Doss caught up with her and grabbed her around the waist and shoved his tongue back into her hungry mouth. Naomi held on to Doss' neck as she backed up to the stairs, climbing them backwards as Doss trailed her, the two never relinquishing their passionate kiss.

Halfway up the stairs, Doss removed Naomi's sundress and she removed her bra and allowed her exquisite physique to come into view. The nineteen year-old's body trembled with anticipation; her nipples were erect, dark and throbbing, aching for attention. She pulled Doss' head to her breasts and he took a nipple into his mouth and sucked hard, forcing a moan of delight to rise from within Naomi.

Naomi had worked in the garden for almost an hour, she was a little sweaty, but the perfume she wore still emanated a delightful, sweet smell that turned Doss one even more. Dressed in only her black silk panties now, Naomi reached out and clutched Doss' member through his slacks. "Make love to me, Doss," she pleaded. "Take me and make me into a woman this morning," she begged as she unbuckled her man's slacks as the two climbed the rest of the stairs and now stood in the hall on the second floor of the house.

Doss stripped off his clothes and his hardening member stood at full attention before Naomi's eyes. She pulled down her panties, her fluffy black bush now in full view, and placed her hands on her hips and spread her legs slightly, putting on full display all of what she possessed and was willingly giving over to Doss. She turned around slowly, revealing her glorious derriere to Doss in all its nudity for the first time. Her perfectly round and smooth ass quivered from excitement, her thin, pink pussy lips were light and fluffy, like an opened rose petal glistening in the morning sun. Naomi was aching in a good way. She wanted to be touched, needed taken, and had to be fulfilled. She looked over her shoulder at Doss as she walked into the bathroom and disappeared from sight.

Just as Naomi turned on the shower and set the water's temperature just right, Doss walked in and grabbed her from behind and turned her around. The two kissed again, this time, rougher, hungrier than they were before. Naomi clawed at Doss as she raised her right leg and rested it on the side of the tub. She reached down and grabbed Doss' hand and placed it to her opening and began gyrating on his hand. "Put your fingers inside me," Naomi panted as she stared at Doss sexily.

Doss rubbed Naomi's clitoris and when his fingers slid into her tight opening, she shuddered and came in less than a minute. Doss then grabbed Naomi's hands and pinned them against the shower stall as the water beat down on the two. Both lovers knew that this was not just a fling, that this was neither lust nor the mere satisfying of a curiosity, Naomi and Doss both understood that this was the start of a life-long relationship. The two were coming together as one this morning, forming a bond that they hoped would be an impossible one to break.

Doss pressed his body to Naomi and kissed her again for a couple of minutes underneath the warm running water and when he gently turned her around, Naomi knew what was coming and she wanted it—badly. She spread her legs and bent slightly forward as the water continued to cascade over their bodies. Doss wrapped an arm around her waist and held his rod and moved it up and down the crack of her ass, rolling his throbbing knob in tight circles around her opening before she could no longer hold out in anticipation and began to ease back slightly. When Doss' thick, fully erect dick slowly slid inside Naomi's slickened pussy the two moaned in ecstasy.

Doss placed his hands over Naomi's hands, pinning them to the wall once again as his member sat snugly inside her tight opening that had just been penetrated by a hard dick for the first time ever. Her legs trembled from the pleasure and pain she felt. Doss' member throbbed, just a few inches inside and

Naomi was soon breathing hard and crying out in delight. Never had an experience felt so good.

Doss held his body still to let Naomi get comfortable with his girth as he tended to her in a sincere and sensual manner by rubbing her back gently and planting soft kisses on the nape of her neck. He rubbed her stomach from behind and ran his hands along Naomi's thighs and gently kneaded her ass cheeks.

Naomi looked back at Doss and stared at him, her mouth slightly agape, thighs quivering, and her eyes displaying a pleading look as she slid back ever so slowly, impaling herself on her man's shaft and allowing herself to be slowly filled with a hard dick that was in her thoughts, 'magnificent'. She stared back at Doss one last time and closed her eyes and turned and faced the wall and cried aloud as she pressed her pelvis tightly against Doss' pubic hairs. She was fully mounted now and ready to be fucked good and hard.

Doss began stroking with a rhythm and depth that caused Naomi to literally see sparks in her closed eyes as she screamed aloud and received her first penis-stimulated orgasm. The nineteen year-old was sure her screams could be heard throughout the block as she stood trembling in awe at the pleasure that she had was receiving.

Naomi wanted to be nowhere else at this moment, and she wanted no other man to do what Doss was doing to her. She literally cried and begged to be fucked harder, faster. Doss released Naomi's hands and wrapped his arms around her stomach and lay against her back and drove into her, lifting her onto her tiptoes as he ground into her from behind while calling Naomi's name as he ejaculated inside her snug opening.

Naomi, her wet hair now wildly splayed over her face, came again, calling out to Doss and a higher source as their bodies convulsed repeatedly from the orgasms they had just given to one another. The two then kissed softly and professed their love for one another before they washed each other's body and exited the shower, where they walked naked hand in hand to Naomi's room amidst the crows of Naomi's rooster.

"Lucky hates that rooster." Naomi said to Doss as she entered her room.

"I see why, he been at it for over an hour now." Doss remarked.

"That's where we're headed." Naomi said as she spread herself out on her bed.

Doss knelt over Naomi as she grabbed his rod and stroked it to hardness. He leaned down between her legs and held them up to her chest and began tonguing her pussy fiercely. Naomi ground her pussy against Doss' lapping tongue, rubbing his low-cut hair, cupping his chin and guiding him to where she wanted him to lick and suck. When her orgasm approached, Naomi threw her hands back and spread her legs high and as wide as possible and thrust her hips up and down on Doss' lapping tongue and surrendered completely, telling Doss that she was his. Naomi was a very orgasmic woman. She came quickly and easily at the hands, dick and tongue of twenty-one year-old Doss Dawkins Junior.

As she came down from her third orgasm, Naomi sat up and laid Doss on his back and straddled his face and got into the sixty-nine position. Doss thrust up at the feel of Naomi's hot, snug mouth encasing his over sensitive member. She was licking and stroking her man hungrily and taking hard swallows keen on tasting all of Doss. She looked over her shoulder and asked her lover did it feel good, did he like what she was doing and Doss could only muffle a sigh of approval as his tongue was busy going from Naomi's clitoris to her smooth asshole as he teased and tantalized her for almost thirty minutes.

Naomi, unable to return the favor to Doss at first because of the pleasure he was giving to her, finally managed to give her man long, deep-throated head that caused him to shoot three thick wads of sperm down her throat. The love-hungry nineteen year-old was going for broke on this day; having made up her mind that she would be everything to Doss for the simple fact that she didn't want him to have to look for satisfaction in some other place. With that in mind, Naomi got down on all fours and spread her ass cheeks and let her man eye her most private parts, opening herself up completely. Doss stared at Naomi's opened ass crack, eyeing her pink puffy labia, her smooth, brown sphincter and staring at the pretty pink pussy that had just been given to him.

"Do me there." Naomi said in a low sexy tone as she lay before Doss holding herself open, exposing her entire crevice that was slick with her juices.

Doss gave Naomi a few long, slow licks across her smooth sphincter before he lined his member up against her rear end. He leaned forward and pushed slowly until he eased inside of Naomi and remained still as she had placed her hand on his hips to prevent him from going further. She could feel the vein running beneath Doss' shaft pulsating as it rested just inside her ass, throbbing in anticipation of going further into the tight, warm passageway it was slightly nuzzled in at that moment. Naomi was giving all she had this morning. She was willingly surrendering her entire body to Doss, offering up every orifice for her man's own personal pleasure. The feel of Doss' throbbing vein pulsating inside her sent waves of pleasure through Naomi, waves that that only fueled the young woman's desire to submit fully to the man she loved. She eased back slowly, feeling every ridge, and every throb as her sphincter slowly engulfed Doss' dick. Her ass came to rest against Doss' pelvis, the back of her thighs pressed tightly against the front of Doss' thighs and the two could only gasp over the sensation. Naomi grabbed the covers tightly, clutching her jaws tightly and slowly eased forward, and then back, slowly forward, and then back, fucking herself on her man's thick tool. With her body in a constant orgasmic state, Naomi reached back and pulled Doss into her and he got the point, she was ready now. With raspy grunts being forced from her lungs, Naomi pressed her face down into the mattress with her arms spread and Doss began to move in and out of her gripping ass quickly, picking up the pace and driving harder and deeper each time he sexed Naomi, who was thrusting back and screaming aloud how good it felt. The two were sweating profusely, two bodies meshed together in perfect unison and rhythm, creating a harmonious chorus of flesh slapping flesh. Naomi pounded the bed with her fists and gyrated her ass furiously, trying to milk Doss' semen from his rigid pole as she rubbed her clitoris for extra stimulation. Her pussy was leaking at this point, juices running down her labia and over her clitoris and dripping onto the bed like a peach that had been bitten into on a hot summer's day. Naomi cried tears of pleasure as her pussy, throbbing in pleasure, squirted fluid and her body began to shake all over as she came multiple times. The bewildered teenager shot vaginal fluid onto Doss' stomach and thighs and it dripped onto the mattress like a leaky faucet as Naomi lay feel down with her ass in the air, eyes tightly closed, her mouth agape, her hair matted to her head from the body sweat and her body convulsing uncontrollably.

Doss had never come so many times in one session from one woman and Naomi had done things to and for him, and allowed him to do things to her that had the young man wanting more and more. No words were spoken as Doss lay behind Naomi, spooning her again, but unlike the night before, the two were jay-bird naked this early morning and left awe-struck over the love-making and severely exhausted, so much so the two of them had drifted off into a deep, comatose-like state of sleep with smiles of contentment plastered across their faces.

A couple of hours later, Naomi, her body feeling achingly delicious, awoke, nudged Doss and asked him was she good enough as they now lay face-to-face.

"I have to ask am I good enough for you, baby." Doss replied before he kissed the tip of Naomi's nose.

"I suppose your playthings will no longer be playing with you, right?"

"I gave them up a long time ago, baby." Doss stated.

Naomi didn't know if Doss was telling the truth or not. Her instincts were telling her he was insincere with that statement, but she believed that now that she had given in, Doss would not stray. She knew she'd done everything for Doss and he now had no reason to look to another woman for satisfaction. With those beliefs in mind, she sat up and leaned into her man and said, "Doss? If I ever catch you with another woman after what we did here today? You'll lose me forever. I'm not playing with you either."

Doss knew Naomi meant what she said and he would not risk losing this woman. Naomi was better, far better than any of the females he'd dealt with; not because of her sexual prowess, but because of her intellect, loyalty and strong-will—although her bedroom manners weren't to be ignored. Doss believed that a woman of Naomi's caliber would be just the type of woman he needed by his side to aide him in his profession. The two were good together in his eyes and the possibilities for the future were boundless. Naomi was a strong woman that knew what she wanted and wasn't afraid to give of herself; she was a sexual being, a giver as well as a taker, a complete woman. Doss was not aiming to loose Naomi from his life and he promised her and himself that he was in it for the long haul. Naomi was on birth control, she didn't want kids as of yet; but she promised Doss that she wanted to have his kids someday. That was fine by Doss because he wasn't' ready for kids either.

As the two lay in bed naked, they listened to Naomi's rooster's constant crows that were stirring the neighborhood. Lucky, who hated that bird with a passion, finally raised his bedroom window and yelled out aloud from the second floor of his parents' home three houses down, "Hey, Naomi! I know you over there! Listen—and listen good! If that mutherfuckin' rooster lays there and cock-a-doodle-doos one—more—muther —fuckin'—time—I'm gonna walk over there and blow that bird's brains all over Serena's backyard! You hear me? You, you—ohh! Shut that mutherfucka up before I come over there and kill that son-of-a-bitch!"

Naomi and Doss laughed aloud as they lay cuddled in the bed for a while until Naomi got up to begin her day all over again. She showered, fixed breakfast, and she and Doss ate before she went and worked her garden. Naomi had entered Serena's home that morning a girl—she came out four hours later a full-grown woman. She returned to her garden with a smile of contentment on her face and went about planting her turnip seeds. As she knelt in her garden, she looked over to the three dolls and began to speak to them, imagining Sam getting angry over her taking Doss as a lover. "Sam, you can't fight Doss! You may be well-built for seventeen, but Doss is a grown man, besides I *wanted* that to happen," she said aloud as she smiled and turned the soil.

Naomi then imagined Mary and Martha speaking, asking her

questions about what her first time was like. "You two are only fifteen," she said as she eyed the two female dolls. "You'll have plenty of time for sex Mary and Martha; but I'll tell you a little bit about what happened later okay? Nituna will be fine. When I tell her Doss loves me and I love him she'll be fine. Daddy will be furious if he finds out! We can't tell him. He'll want Doss to marry me right away! It'll be a shotgun wedding!" Naomi said as she chuckled to herself.

Naomi then sat back on her heels and looked around. All was quiet. Her three dolls were smiling at her as if they were blushing over hearing her speak about Doss. She eyed the dolls momentarily before bowing her head and she began to cry silently. Acting out what she believed would have transpired had she been with her family in Sylacauga, Alabama had stirred her emotions and she was now wishing for the real thing. She wished all that she was speaking was true-to-life. She wished she could have been saying the words she'd spoken, the conversation she'd had with herself, with her living relatives, no matter the outcome. Just having them there would have meant the world to her, angry father and all. An argument with her father, a blessing from her mother, her siblings' mocking of her plight. She wished it were all real. She told herself that someday she will have those conversations with her siblings being that her parents were deceased, and she continued on in her pretend world, expressing thoughts to her parents openly. "Momma, he makes me feel good," she said as she sprinkled seeds into the soil. "I love him. I love that man inside that house. Daddy? When I marry, can you give me away to my husband?" Naomi smiled, imagining her father getting angry that she hadn't waited until marriage to have intercourse, while at the same time welcoming Doss into the family.

Moving back into reality, Naomi rested back on her heels again and looked to the ground and said, "Mary, Martha, Sam, God I miss y'all to death. I can't wait for the day when we're all back together. Umm, when we're together again, I promise to be a good sister," she said as she eyed her three dolls, let out a flood of tears and continued speaking. "Wherever you are in this world, may God keep you safe until I'm able to find you.

Please God, let someday come. No matter how long it takes, just let it come, please God. Amen." Naomi ended through her tears.

Just as Naomi was ending her prayer, Fin and Lucky entered the backyard. "That damn rooster's gonna end up on my dinner table one of these days, Naomi." Lucky snapped.

Naomi cut her eyes at Lucky in slight disapproval of his intrusive remark. She was enjoying time with her family and she really didn't want to be bothered. Still, she smiled at her friend and told him Doss was in the kitchen eating and reading the newspaper. Lucky went inside while Fin walked to the garden and knelt beside Naomi.

"You're glowing young woman," nineteen year-old Fin stated as he knelt down on one knee.

"Yes. I am a young woman today."

"You and Doss? Finally?"

"Yes!" Naomi stated as she grabbed Fin's arms. "Ohh Fin it was—"

"Uh, uh. This ain't something you tell Fin. You should share it with Mary and Martha."

"Would you do it, Fin? Today? I mean once Lucky and Doss leave?"

"I'd love to."

"Thank you. I don't wanna seem rude, Fin, but I was here with Nituna, we were, we were umm—"

"Say no more, Naomi. I'll be inside. Hey, Mary and Martha," Fin said as he waved at the dolls. "Sam you're getting big! Don't try and fight Doss because he slept with Naomi. They love each other, brother." Fin said as he stood up.

Naomi stood up and hugged Fin and kissed his cheek and said, "You're such an understanding young man. You understand the empty space I have in my heart."

"We all do. See you later, Naomi." Fin ended as he headed towards the house.

Naomi did get to share her experience with Mary and Martha in 1974, courtesy of Fin. She enjoyed a great portion of the day alone in the yard with her dolls and went out later that night with her friends. She would share some of her experience with Serena, but kept it a secret from Kevin, just as she would have done her real father. The spring and summer of '74 was a time of love and peace for Naomi and 1974 was one of the best years of her young life up until that point...

.... "Yesss, indeed." Martha remarked as she fanned herself. "Now I gotta hit the club and find a tree trunk! Like Loretta used to say."

"You and Doss sound like you're made for each other, Naomi." Twiggy remarked.

"We are—although we were different—we were in love. And as for as the loving, with Doss? Every time is like the first time. I didn't tell you all the things we did, but imaging it my mind brought it back just like it happened yesterday. Believe me when I say through eight kids and over twenty-five years of loving it's still good. And today, I did what I wanted to do all so badly in 1974, to share my first time with my sisters, today that dream was just fulfilled."

"I wish I had settled down." Mary then stated lowly.

"You still can, Mary. You're only forty-two and you look years younger. If Martha and Twiggy go out to the club in the city you should go." Naomi remarked.

"I like my life, Naomi. It's just hearing that story brings back memories from my past. Remember that night in Vicksburg?" Mary asked Martha and Twiggy as the three sniggled and blushed.

Naomi eyed Dawk ascending the hillside and she looked at her watch. "Time is going by slow today, but Doss should be ready to grill soon. You ladies hungry?" she asked.

"Yeah," replied Twiggy. "Naomi? That guy Lucky? He ever killed anybody else? Him and Doss?" Twiggy then asked as Dawk handed her another beer and sat down with the group.

Naomi thought quickly and answered, "No, Irene. Doss owns a warehouse in Chicago where our freight is sometimes delivered or shipped. From time to time he takes my oldest three up there to show them the business so they can take control one day. Lucky is a gangster—always was and always will be—but he's my friend no matter what. He and Doss are on different paths now."

"Hey sis, what happened to that rooster you had?" Martha asked.

"Lucky ate 'em." Dawk answered as Naomi turned and eyed him seriously. "What I said? Uncle Lucky ate 'em right?" Dawk asked as Twiggy and Martha laughed.

"What did Lucky do?" Twiggy asked through laughter.

"Irene? That bird, we umm, we couldn't find any turkey for Thanksgiving in 1975. We waited too late and a lot of shipments couldn't make it to town in time because we had four huge snowstorms that month. Lucky came to Kevin's house with a huge bird that he *said* was a turkey, but when I bit into it, I knew. I knew right away. Lucky killed my bird in 1975 so we could have Thanksgiving. I was mad at first, but I got over it."

"What Lucky doing now?" Martha asked. "I mean, you say he not a killer no more, right? So what he do?"

"He runs a booking operation in Cicero. Look, I know you girls are wondering about that, but believe me, Lucky is my friend, but I have no ties—neither I nor Doss have ties to his criminal endeavors. He's our friend. Nothing more."

Dawk knew his mother was construing the truth this day in order to hide what was actually going on between his father and Lucky. He said nothing as his mother looked her sisters and Twiggy over and watched as they shrugged their shoulders and shook their heads, believing what she had told them this day.

From that point forth, Mary, Martha and Twiggy had come under the belief that Doss was a warehouseman in Chicago and Lucky was Naomi's childhood friend who just so happen to be a gangster. Mary even spoke in favor of Lucky, saying she never knew he was a gangster until Naomi revealed his lifestyle. Naomi had just succeeded at deceiving her sisters and Twiggy, and the family's dark side would remain hidden and intact.

"Hey, it's almost time to eat and DeeDee and the rest of the friends should be arriving soon. You ladies go ahead and I'll be right down." Naomi said as she hugged her two sisters and

Twiggy and watched them with a wide smile as they descended the hill.

When her sisters and Twiggy were out of Naomi's sight, she slowly stopped smiling. She felt bad for having to lie to her sisters and their friend, but at the time, she felt she had no choice. She was so afraid to lose her younger sisters she would rather lie than be truthful. Naomi knew exactly what she was doing. And right or wrong, she was making sure that her family would never have to struggle again.

Dawk knew all that was going on. He understood his mother's motives, but he couldn't help but to ask, "Ma? Don't you think it's best you tell them the truth?"

"No, son. Not now. You and your sisters are coming along fine and we do no business here. Just, when the time arises, no matter where you are going, you are always, *always,* going to Chicago. Okay?"

"Yeah, we cool on that. I'm just thinking that they might not really care if they were to know the truth."

"I don't wanna take that risk right now, Dawk. We're gonna keep the family members not involved out of the loop. They are safer not knowing. And I don't want them to get involved. The less people who know, the lower the risk of gettin' caught or worse. Understand?"

Dawk nodded his head in agreement and said, "I'm going join the rest of the family. You okay, momma?"

"Yeah. All that talking brought back so many memories, Dawk. Go on down to the house. I'll be down shortly."

Naomi had grown up around mobsters and the gangster lifestyle had rubbed off on the woman. To her, what Doss was doing was normal; just another form of business. She couldn't change this part of her upbringing because 23rd Street Mafia was indelibly ingrained into her psyche. On top of that, Naomi felt that she was only getting back the things her family was owed for the way they had suffered early on in life. She sat down on one of the benches beside Ne'Ne's grave and rested her elbows on her legs as she looked sadly to the ground.

Naomi Holland at her core was a very loving woman, but she could be highly vindictive at times. She was intelligent, methodical in her dealings, and shrewd to the point of obsession. Her business sense kept the family's businesses and personal wealth on an even keel and in good standing before the eyes of the law. It wasn't much if anything that the woman missed when it came to handling finances. She knew how to wash dollars proficiently; and the family up north never revealed their deadly side to the family members down in Oklahoma.

In August of 2001, the Holland Family owned five trucks that ran livestock to slaughterhouses and transported freight to and from Chicago and to various points across the country. The Holland family had come a long way, along way indeed. And the road to riches had been paved with many a blood stain left behind by those who lied in its path to success.

For Naomi, being a corporate lawyer has its perks, one was that of enabling her to put forth a lie to cover up what really lay behind the family's successes. She'd given glimpses into her extraordinary past, spoke of crimes committed by her friends, but there was much more to her story. As she sat on the bench atop Ne`Ne`s Hill, Naomi began to reflect on some of the events that had gotten her and her family into the position they now found themselves in the month of August in the year 2001.

CHAPTER 8
INSIDE A MOB HIT

It was June of 1976, a mild summer's day and twenty-one year-old Naomi, twenty-three year-old Doss, and twenty-one year-olds Fin and Lucky, and Lucky's girlfriend Mildred, also twenty-one, had just come from a Cubs baseball game and entered the *Eastside Bar*. Everybody spoke to the group as Naomi gave forty-five year-old DeeDee and forty-three year-old Mendoza generous hugs and went to the bar to have a drink with Fin. Doss and Lucky, meanwhile, went and sat with Mendoza, DeeDee, and sixty-eight year-old Zell Verniche` to talk business.

Zell Verniche` was second generation mafia Don of 23rd Street Mafia. Standing only 5'7" and weighing in at two-hundred and eighty pounds, the pepper-haired, pony-tailed wearing Mafioso rarely moved from his seat once he entered the bar. He wore lavish suits and pinky diamond rings, used a cane to assist in walking and had a chauffeur and three armed body guards with him at all times. Zell and his old underbosses, all of whom were dead now, trained nearly every member of 23rd that was in the crowded bar on this night; a score of killers who readily dished out death for the almighty dollar.

Zell had made Mendoza the new underboss a couple of years

back as he was sometimes in ill- health, which could be contributed to his weight and heavy cigar smoking. On top of that, he loved slaw dogs, pepperoni pizza, Alfredo, calamari, and every other fat-saturated and high calorie dish that was slid before his face. He wasn't a sloppy man per say, just extremely over weight. A menace to society he may have been to those in opposition to 23rd Street—but those who knew the man personally knew one thing was certain about Zell Verniche`— he was exceptionally nice to his friends and would help them earn money whenever possible; even if it involved breaking laws and bloodshed, which was his most preferred method of earning a paycheck.

On this day in June of 1976, Zell had a job lined up for Mendoza and his crew, which now consisted of Mendoza and his son Lucky, DeeDee, and DeeDee's son Doss. The men were all seated at the last booth in the bar with Zell preparing to take on the new assignment.

"You remember that guy with the church on the west side of Cicero?" Zell asked Mendoza as he stirred a plate of scungilli, an Italian dish consisting of large marine snails drenched in marina sauce and spread over pasta.

"Yeah," Mendoza replied lowly as he leaned into Zell. "The preacher guy with the renovation project. I told him we'd do the church for forty-thousand dollars, but he went with some other guy from East Chicago."

"Yeah I know," Zell replied. He then paused when his chauffeur came over to the table and uncorked a bottle of 1967 Elvio Cogno red wine and poured all the men a glass. Lucky handed the guy a twenty dollar bill and when he left, Zell continued. "But that 'some other guy' took 'that guy's' money and ran off to Cleveland you see? Now the good preacher wants his money back, and he's come to us for help."

"What'll we have to do, boss?" Mendoza asked casually as he sipped his wine.

Zell wiped his mouth with a cloth napkin, sipped his wine and said, "I need you and your crew to go over to Cleveland and meet with that 'some other guy' and take care of 'em. Here's the deal—he's an usher at a church over there in Ohio and he's looking for an investment banker to wash the money he stole clean."

"He's an usher involved in crime?" asked Lucky.

Zell laughed slightly and said, "The bishop on 26th Street gets blowjobs from the local, from the uh, from the local hooker who hangs out on the corner right there across the street from his church. Nobody gives a fuck what those religious people do. What *is* important is that we get to keep the forty thousand. And the good preacher is willing to pay another forty thousand to give some of our boys some work to show his appreciation for what we're gonna do for 'em. Now, that's gonna sit well with the Union boss back in Chicago who can put in a good word with the mayor. Bring me twenty thousand out of the forty thousand, and you fours can split the rest and take another twenty percent of the total cost of the project, which is gonna go up to about eighty or a hundred grand once we book the union guys over in Chicago to remodel the church. That's at least another sixteen thousand you all can split amongst yourselves."

"Doesn't sound like the preacher is getting his money's worth if ya' ask me." Mendoza said.

"Since when do we care about how another man outside of here fairs in life? That son-of-a-bitch had a chance to break more than even but he chose another way. Now that he's gotten screwed over he wants our help. So you damn right I'm gonna tax his ass for the simple fact that he's stupid."

"To say the least," DeeDee remarked.

"To say the least and to say the most. He knows what we're charging, but he wants that guy that ripped him off out of the equation no matter the cost. We'll tax him, he'll tax the working stiffs that are crazy enough to pay the tithes on this new church he wants and everybody makes money. We're just gettin' our cut upfront. The preacher will have his job fulfilled and money from the congregation will come pouring in. He'll have his money, and his 'flock', if that's what you wanna call it, they will have their god."

"We on it boss. You got a plan working?" Mendoza asked.

"Yea. We're gonna need a couple of gals to go over to New

York and set up a phone line." Zell replied. "This here guy in Cleveland is gonna wanna call to verify some things. Now, he's under the impression that DeeDee here works for Morgan Stanley over in New York. DeeDee flew into town and met the guy once and as of now he has him under the impression that he's putting the papers together to get this guy in on the ground floor of the investment firm. He's awaiting DeeDee's return to Cleveland with the documents. We can't use the numbers here when the usher makes that call of verification because of the, the uh, the area code thing. He knows he's dealing with stolen cash and I don't want him to get suspicious. A Chicago area code may make him suspicious. So we needs two or three gals to go over to New York and meet up with Johnny and his crew."

Everybody then looked at Doss.

"Naomi? You want Naomi to go to New York?" Doss asked.

"Why not? Mildred ain't too bright. It wouldn't fly. Naomi will be able to pull this off, Doss. And I'll owe her a favor in return." Zell replied. "No offense to Mildred, Lucky," he added.

"Hey, I know she a dingy broad. I can't count on that fat bitch not ta' burn the garlic bread, let alone handle a business call." Lucky replied as everybody at the table chuckled.

Doss then looked over to Naomi and saw her sitting at the bar with Fin sipping a drink. She eyed him through the crowd and raised her glass and smiled and blew him a kiss. Zell noticed her gesture and smiled at Doss. "She'll do anything you ask," Zell remarked. "She'll even kill for you because she loves you that much, il mio amico," he told Doss. "Don't worry about her safety. Johnny's a friend of ours. It's totally safe up there. Naomi, she'll, she'll be there for like fifteen minutes. Then, she and Francine can go shopping on my dime."

"I'll never ask my woman to kill for me. I do a good enough job myself," Doss answered. "And as far as Naomi going to New York? I'll ask, but if she says no I won't force her."

"Okay, but just ask her. I'm positive she'll do it, il mio amico." Zell remarked as Doss got up and walked over to Naomi.

Doss pulled Naomi on the side and said, "Baby, I need a favor."

Naomi smiled at that moment. Doss rarely called her 'baby'; for him to do so signified to her that he had a serious question on his mind. "Who do you want me to help you kill?" she asked bluntly as she stared Doss in the eyes seriously.

Doss was caught off guard. He didn't think Naomi would have ever ask him that question if his life had depended on it, but he was glad she did so because that let him know that she was willing to help him out where needed. "The mark is not important," he said as he leaned into Naomi, who rested gently against the brick wall beside the bar. "I only need for you to fly to New York with Francine and pretend to be a banker from Morgan Stanley."

Naomi laughed aloud at that moment, much to Doss' surprise and wonderment. She was under the belief he'd ask her to do something for more dangerous. "What's so funny?" Doss asked as he leaned back and looked into Naomi's eyes.

"That's, that's all you need me to do? I thought you were going to ask me to drive a get-a-way car, or maybe pretend to like someone so you can get close to him. A phone call? Sure! I'll be a banker for you, baby." Naomi replied through laughter as she kissed Doss on the lips.

Naomi thought Doss was going to try and pull her into his occupation by asking her to go on a hit with him this day. She was prepared to do more than just make a phone call. She would have done anything Doss asked of her, including killing someone, just as Zell had stated. "You, umm, you know if you need me to do more I'm willing to help you, right?" Naomi said.

"Leave this portion of our life to me. You just continue in law school and look forward to being the mother of my kids someday. You got me?"

"I will and I do, Doss. But if ever you need me, I'm here."

"I know—but I would never ask you to kill someone for me. I love you too much to put you at risk like that. Johnny's a cool guy. It's safe up there. And Francine will be there with you all the way. Make the call, and get out of there, understand? Zell's gonna give you some money to go shopping when you two are done."

Naomi was eager to help Doss; and truth be told she could care less about going shopping. She'd been curious about the inner workings of 23rd for a long time now, and she was finally able to get an inside peek into a mob hit without actually getting her hands dirty. The thought of being involved in a mob hit was a severe turn on for Naomi. She reached down and grabbed Doss' dick through his silk slacks and pulled him into the women's rest room, locked the door and raised her skirt and leaned forward over one of the sinks.

Doss got behind Naomi and pressed up against her wide, curvy ass. "Bad men turn you on don't they?" he asked as he kissed his woman's neck softly and kneaded her ass cheeks.

"Only you, bad man."

"So, this is all mines," Doss asked as he pulled Naomi's panties down and began smacking her ass. "You're a bad girl."

"A bad girl in love with a bad man. Take me, Doss. Take me now," Naomi moaned as she felt the head of Doss' dick slide up and down her ass crack.

****

Naomi and Francine were filled in on what they had to do that night by Zell. Mendoza and his crew also had all the information they needed, and three days later, they were on a flight that had landed in Cleveland on a Saturday morning. The four spent the day at a ball game and scoped out the church later on that night in order to layout their plan more fully, and a phone call from Francine in New York on Sunday evening had put all the pieces in place and sealed the deal.

Early Monday morning, Mendoza and the crew headed over to the church in a car that was delivered to them by 23rd members the day before. The usher, which was the crew's mark, was a man in his mid-thirties. He'd told DeeDee when he first met him a week or so back that he felt safe meeting with the bankers inside the church, which "was a good cover front", is what he said.

Mendoza, DeeDee, Doss, and Lucky were neatly dressed in silk suits and gator shoes upon arrival to the huge Methodist

Church, which was located over in Cleveland Heights, about eight miles east of downtown Cleveland. The four were sitting in the parked car across the street from the church in a Burger King parking lot watching the building intently as they waited their mark's arrival. With numerous stairs ascending towards a white marbled, five-columned tan-bricked building that could easily accommodate seven hundred or more people, the pristine church with its neatly-kept front lawn, well-sculptured trees and shrubbery and extravagant billboards emanated a royal appearance. The parking lot was void of cars this early Monday morning and Mendoza and DeeDee took the time to give their sons, who were still in training, a few last pointers.

Lucky and Doss' first contract was on a guy who ran a booking operation that was cutting into DeeDee's Poker Room profits back in Chicago. The two cornered the guy in his parked Jaguar outside of a restaurant on the south side of Chicago and gunned him down in cold blood. They'd also killed a man who'd owed Mendoza money on a loan. In that case, they broke into the man's home and forced him to open his safe and hand over his cash and jewelry before they executed him in his own bedroom.

Besides murder for hire, Lucky and Doss also handled 'juice loans', which were loans to those who couldn't borrow money from the bank. A high weekly interest was put on the loan payments, and the people who borrowed money, often working stiffs with gambling and drug habits, were rarely able to pay on time. Lucky and Doss would then put 'the squeeze' on the person owing money, whereby they would demand payment, or threaten bodily harm. In some cases, their threats had to be made a reality. The two often beat the person who owed them money, and within a week's time, they would receive payment. Lucky and Doss were truly involved in a serious and dangerous occupation and knew how to perform their duties, but this job, however, was in new territory.

"You two know what to do once we enter the place and I give you the code, right?" DeeDee asked as he looked over the backseat towards Doss and Lucky.

"Yeah, dad. On your word we open fire."

"Will you be able to do it is what he's asking." Mendoza said as he sat behind the steering wheel.

"Why wouldn't we?" Lucky asked.

"Son, Lucky," DeeDee said, "in the past we've had you kill other gangsters. Criminals. This here," he said as he turned and extended his hand towards the church across the street, "these aren't gangsters. What we wanna know is, when you see these people, once we get to talking to lure them in, will you not be softened by their citizenship? They're church-going folk after all. They lead normal lives and have families that care for 'em and have good standing within the eyes of public."

"Well, they must've done somethin' fucked up or else we wouldn't be here," Lucky said. "Don't worry about me and Doss. Yous taught us well and we do our job without remorse."

"Lucky's right," Doss chimed in. "And we have family that care about us too, so that's a moot point, dad. We get what you tryna say, though. No remorse."

DeeDee looked over to Mendoza and smiled just as a white Stingray Corvette entered the church's parking lot and slid into a 'reserved for church staff' slot.

"There's our mark," DeeDee said once he eyed the usher, who was dressed casually in a white silk jogging suit and sporting a neat Afro. Just then, the passenger side door of the Corvette opened and a woman stepped out.

"Who's the broad, DeeDee?" Mendoza asked.

"Shit," DeeDee said as he scratched the side of his face. "That's his wife. She was there when I first met the guy. Asking questions about this and that as if she knew what the hell she was talking about. It's a non-issue. Let's go with it."

"Okay," Mendoza replied. "You boys ready?" he asked Lucky and Doss.

"Let's do it." Lucky replied as he and Doss picked up their briefcases and placed them in their laps.

"Okay, gentlemen. Job's on." Mendoza said as he backed out the parking spot at Burger King and headed towards the church.

While Mendoza and the crew were riding over to the church and preparing to enter the building early on this Monday

134

morning in June of 1976, Naomi and Francine were entering The Raven Night Club located in the borough of Queens, New York. Francine walked in wearing a tight pair of blue jeans, white ankle boots, and a white tank top with a white b-bop leather cap. Her hair was pressed down her back and she wore thin-framed sunglasses. Naomi was trailing close behind in a tight-fitting red and black paisley all-in-one dress and black three-inch heels with large gold earrings dangling from her ears along with a gold bracelet on her right wrist. Her hair covered her head entirely, hanging down over her shoulders and she wore little make-up, only a light coating of eye shadow and lip gloss.

The two women walked into the bar and stared at four men who sat a table as Pink Floyd's song *Money* played in the background. The place was void of people, minus the four men who sat at the table just to Naomi and Francine's left. Chairs in the club were all upside down on the tables, except for the four the men were sitting in. The place was a little dark inside, but it wasn't uninviting. Naomi liked the place, she knew it was a gangster's hangout and it aroused her as she was used to being in this particular type of setting. The only thing different about this club was that it just didn't have a large crowd that often accompanied the hangout back in Cicero; but she wasn't expecting to see a bar filled with gangsters since it was an early Monday morning. She figured that most of the men affiliated with this particular crew, who she knew to be factioned to the Gambino Crime Family, were most likely home with their families on a day and time such as this.

Two of the men took off their hats and greeted the women as they remained seated at their table, the fourth man, however, got up and went and locked the door and walked over and kissed Francine on both cheeks.

"Francine, how you doing? How's life in the Midwest," the man asked.

"It's good, Johnny. Real good. A little slower than what we used to, but we're doing okay." Francine replied.

"Sweet Mother of Mary. Who's this lovely black woman standing in my bar?" the man then asked upon eyeing Naomi.

"This is Naomi, Johnny. She's a friend of Zell's."

"A friend of Zell?" the man questioned as his eyes widened. "Well, on this day, heaven has to be missing an angel. Right boys?" the man asked his crew as he grabbed Naomi's hands and squeezed them tightly.

"Johnny speaks the truth." one man stated.

"She's the most beautiful black gal east of the Mississippi," another replied.

The third man didn't answer. He only stared at Naomi with a look of uncertainty. "Who are these broads?" he asked as he leaned back in his chair and took a drag off his cigarette.

"You have to excuse Sammy over there. We call him the bull because he can be very stubborn at times. Not to mention rude!" the man who had locked the door stated loudly, directing his statement towards his counterpart, who merely got up and walked to the back of the bar.

The man greeting Francine and Naomi then turned back to the two and said, "How ya' doing, Naomi? I'm, Gotti. John Gotti."

"John Gotti? Your reputation precedes you, sir."

"Hey, don't you sir me! A friend of Zell's has a reputation all its own. Nice to meet you, Naomi. Make yourself at home. You and Francine make yourselves at home."

The women walked across the floor and sat down at the bar where Francine pulled a telephone out of small leather satchel. Gotti inquired as to what was so special about the phone the two women were using and Francine responded by telling him that the phone had a wiretap detector as she walked behind the bar. "If the line's bugged, it'll fry the line." she told Gotti.

"No shit? Where'd you get that from?"

"We got an inside man with the police force back in Chicago. You want us to turn you on to him?" Francine asked as she searched around for a phone jack.

"I'll find a guy here. I never knew they could do something like that. Technology gives us the tools we need to stay ahead in this here business we're in. In the meantime, let me keep that phone when ya' done will ya'?"

"Sure thing, Johnny."

"Alright we got ourselves a deal. The phone line's behind the counter near the sink. What time are your people supposed to call?"

"Ten minutes. In exactly ten minutes, so we need to get everything hooked up and do a test run. Naomi give me a hand."

When Naomi got up to walk behind the counter, two of Johnny's cohorts began to sniggle. Johnny shushed them, but he, too, was eyeing Naomi's ass. "You interested in moving to New York Naomi?" Johnny asked.

"Only if my husband asks me to."

"Eh, we haven't even begun our affair and you two timin' me already." Johnny said as he laughed and Naomi chuckled. "Here's to you beautiful gal," he then said as he raised his glass to Naomi.

Naomi looked around the back counter of the bar and found a stack of shot glasses. She grabbed one from the back counter and poured a shot of Jack Daniels Whiskey and turned back to Gotti. "To friends!" she shouted from across the bar.

"And to love!" Johnny remarked as he and Naomi both tilted their heads at the same time and drunk the liquor.

Naomi then assisted Francine, who was smiling as she plugged the line into the phone jack. "To friends? To love? Wait until Doss hears you and Johnny shared a drink together. You know how to leave a mark Naomi—that you do, girlfriend —that you do." Francine stated as she and Naomi went about their business as Johnny and his men sat and talked amongst themselves.

****

Meanwhile, back in Cleveland, Mendoza, DeeDee, Doss and Lucky had just walked into the church and were greeted by the usher's wife, who escorted them to the church's office. "My husband will be with you in a minute," she said. "Can I get you men anything? Coffee? A soda or orange juice?"

"No thank you," DeeDee answered with a wide smile. "I was thinking we can all go and have breakfast when we're done here. My treat. A way of saying thank you for investing with Morgan Stanley."

"Well, that is really nice of you! I know a place near here that has the best steak and eggs in Ohio."

"Make me a believer," DeeDee chided as he and the woman shared a quick laugh.

"I most certainly will, mister! Now, you all have a seat. You two can place your briefcases on the desk if you'd like," she told Lucky and Doss. "I'll be right back."

The woman left to retrieve her husband and the four men sat down on two sofas in the office, which was more like a condominium with its small kitchen, island counter, and living room, where they were all seated and waiting patiently for the usher. The place was dead silent, and none of the men spoke during this period of time as they were all mapping out what was to come. Time seemed to move like molasses. The men were checking their watches and lightly discussing a town to stop in and have breakfast when three voices were heard approaching the office from outside in the hall. Mendoza and DeeDee placed their hands on their guns inside their suit jackets while Lucky and Doss went over to the desk and opened their briefcases and placed their hands on their weapons. The door slowly opened and this time, the woman entered with two men. Doss and Lucky closed their briefcases and their fathers removed their hands from inside their suit jackets upon realizing the people posed no threat.

"Hello," the unknown man said to the men as he stood just inside the doorway eyeing the four men. "I'm pastor over the church. My beloved and faithful associates informed me of a good deed they were doing for the congregation and I came by to bless the Cause."

The crew hadn't counted on the woman being present, but they were willing to work around her presence. The pastor of the church being on the scene, however, had upped the ante tremendously. The man spoke on how proud he was of the usher and his wife as he requested the group to stand in a circle in the center of the room so he could recite a prayer. The job was now going off kilter; Mendoza and DeeDee had it in their minds to just kill all three right away, but Doss and Lucky hadn't picked up on their gestures because they were already in the circle with their heads bowed. The two men joined in the group and when the pastor was done with his prayer, everybody exchanged pleasantries once more and immediately got down to business.

"Well, gentlemen," the usher said calmly and politely as he went over to the island counter, grabbed a suitcase and returned to the office, "what we want to do here is find a real good investment for this," he stated as he laid the suitcase down and opened it, giving the crew an up-close look at the forty grand he'd taken weeks earlier.

"Alright here's the deal," Mendoza said, sliding into his role, "you all's investments will be handled by my staff. These two young guys right here," he said as he pointed to Doss and Lucky, "they work me and this guy here is my boss," he said as he pointed to DeeDee. "His name is William Preston, as you already know. We have a couple of things lined up that we can discuss after your wife makes the call, but I assure you, these investments will turn a sizeable profit for the entire congregation. We have stock in General Electric, Zenith, IBM and oil exports—and all of our investments are guaranteed and low risk."

"That is exactly what we want," the usher remarked. "A low risk fund that will guarantee dividends at a high percentage rate."

"You will get what you ask for, my man." Mendoza replied.

"You say you have the money invested already. How's that so when the money is laying on the table?" the pastor asked. "Not being nosy, I'm just trying to understand the inner workings of a major investment firm."

"What we do," DeeDee stepped in and said, "what we do is put the future investment money up ourselves from our own investment fund. Once everything is verified and we receive the money agreed upon, that money then goes back into our investment fund and the account is officially transferred into our client's name. What we're doing today is the final step in that process."

"Ahhh. Interesting job you guys have."

"Yes it is," Mendoza replied. "And we deliver without fail, my friend."

"Okay then," the usher said. "Baby? You wanna do the honors so we can get things squared away?"

DeeDee handed the usher's wife a letterhead with an embossed Morgan Stanley emblem on it and said, "The number to call is circled in red."

"Thanks, Mister Preston," the woman answered and began dialing the number.

The phone rang and Francine answered back in New York. "Morgan Stanley how can I direct your call?" she asked politely.

"Yes ma'am, I know it's early, but I really need some information on an account that was established a little under a week ago?"

"Well, ma'am, offices aren't scheduled to open for another hour. I'm only working the boards, but there's a few people here early though so we may be able to help. Who's your banker?"

"William Preston from Morgan Stanley."

"Hold on ma'am." Francine stated as she placed the woman on hold and gave the phone to Naomi.

Naomi waited a minute, picked the phone up and said, "Thank you for calling Morgan Stanley you've reached the office of William Preston who's not in today. How can I help you?"

"Hello?"

"Morgan Stanley how can I help you?"

"Yes, I'm inquiring about an account that was recently established under the name of Victor Lorraine?"

"May I ask who's calling?"

"This is Cybil Lorraine. I'm calling from Cleveland and—"

"Ohh yes, Cleveland! Mister Preston told me someone from Cleveland may be calling today. Your investment plan. That's why you're calling, right?"

"Yes! That's exactly why I'm calling!" Cybil stated as she grew excited.

"In what way are you related to Victor Lorraine?" Naomi

then asked.

"He's my husband."

"Is he there? Because I can't give you any information being that your name isn't on the account."

Naomi was passing herself off as a true secretary; but she never knew what trouble she had just stirred. Cybil was now eyeing her husband with a look of contempt and was wondering why her name wasn't on the account. After all, the two had stolen the money together and without her help, this entire deal would not be transpiring. Since the bankers were present, Cybil decided to wait and question her husband concerning his actions later on; because if he thought he was going to wash the money clean and run off with his mistress, a woman in the church whom she knew about, well Mister Lorraine had a new day coming. That's what Cybil thought about as she handed the phone to her husband.

Victor gave the account number to Naomi and she told Mister Victor Lorraine that he had a balance of $40,000. The usher thanked her and hung up the phone and smiled as he began thanking his "investors".

Naomi and Francine had completed their task. They shared two more drinks with Gotti and his crew and then went shopping and would catch a flight home the following day. Naomi had no worries at all because she knew she had fooled Cybil and Victor both; it was up to 23rd to do their part now. She laughed to herself as she and Francine hopped into a taxi, unable to believe how gullible the man and woman back in Cleveland had appeared to be.

The three church members just couldn't see that they were being set up. Victor and his wife knew what was going on was a little unscrupulous, but the pastor was clueless. Either directly involved or not, all however, would suffer the same fate. Victor was all smiles over the deal, but Cybil was seething inside. She was planning on blowing this whole act of thievery wide open to the congregation and take down her husband at the same time because she was tired of his lies and deceit.

The pastor of the church, who was under the belief that

Victor and Cybil Lorraine had received the money in all honesty through donations from a sister church in Chicago, smiled and thanked God for the blessing as he put on a fresh pot of coffee.

"Alright peoples," Mendoza stated as he stretched lightly, "here's the rest of you threes documents. Faustino, Doss, give the good people the rest of the work will you, please." he requested.

Doss and Lucky smiled politely as they opened their briefcases. Each of them then produced a Ruger .9mm with a silencer on the barrel. The pastor's eyes widened when he saw the guns Doss and Faustino were holding. "What's going on? What is this?" he asked in a confused manner as he stepped out of the kitchen.

Not a word was uttered as Lucky fired upon Victor and Doss shot the pastor. Each of the men received two double tap shots to the forehead and their bodies dropped to the ground. Doss and Lucky then walked around the table and stood over the men and shot them three times each in the heart.

Cybil was silent the whole time, believing she would be let go because of what her husband had done. "I'm gonna tell the whole congregation what my husband has done. He was going to rip off the church and he got killed for it."

"So did you," Lucky said in a cool manner as he aimed his weapon at Cybil.

Cybil then understood that the murders committed seconds ago was not just about her husband and the pastor. "I, I'm innocent! I didn't know anything about this! I'm just a woman who sings in the church choir!"

"Correction! You used to sing in the church choir!" Lucky remarked coldly. Cybil pleaded and tried to scream, but she was silenced by a bullet that passed through her opened mouth and exited the back of her skull, courtesy of Lucky.

Mendoza and DeeDee complimented their sons on their work before Mendoza grabbed the suitcase of money off the table. DeeDee went and removed the fake letterhead from Cybil's lifeless hand and Doss went and picked up the fake documents that Victor was holding onto while Lucky wiped down each and every spot the crew had touched with a handkerchief. The four men exited the office and walked down the hall through the foyer, calmly exited the church, got back in their car and drove back to the hotel, discarding the guns along the way and shredding the letterhead and documents and scattering their pieces. The crew checked out that same day and drove home to Cicero, each of them now several thousand dollars richer. The three bodies were found later that evening by a cleaning crew, but by then their killers had vanished into thin air. Mendoza, DeeDee, Doss and Lucky's job in Cleveland, like all of their previous jobs, would become a cold case.

This was Mendoza, DeeDee, Lucky and Doss' method of operation, and it worked to perfection each and every time. The crew from Cicero hunted men and women down, set them up, and eliminated their mark, or marks without remorse and were proficient at their profession. Hands down, they were the most prolific crew of killers coming out of 23rd Street Mafia. Zell had five more jobs lined up in the Midwest that summer for the crew as well, so they would be real busy the next few months spying on their marks in preparation to take them down.

****

During the latter part of the summer of 1976, while Doss was in Milwaukee working with Lucky, Naomi and Fin, who were spending a lot of time together, had taken two trips to Sylacauga, Alabama to try and find her siblings, using money Doss had given her shortly after the Cleveland hit to fund the expeditions.

Naomi was full of hope as she headed down south during her first trip, but her heart was broken when she learned that her family's history had been erased from the annals Sylacauga history entirely. No record of anyone with the last name of Holland was found in the City Hall's chamber of records. It was as if the Holland Family had never existed. Naomi also saw that a lumber warehouse had been erected on the land where she once resided, land Eileen, Rutherford and Nituna once owned. She grew furious at the sight and promised to return someday soon and exact revenge.

On another occasion, towards the end of August, Naomi and Fin drove to Selma and found out that the orphanage had closed. She then drove to Birmingham and searched the state's records, but she came up empty there also. Sam, Mary, and Martha were lost in the system, and that began to fuel an increasingly uncontrollable rage and prolonged sorrow within Naomi. She entered her senior year at Northwestern University in September of 1976 a depressed and angry woman. She cried often, alone most times, sometimes in front of Doss, expressing her anguish and desire to find her siblings. Doss wanted to help, but the resources were scarce, nearly non-existent in the seventies. They searched archives, old newspaper articles from down south, obituaries and wedding announcements, anything they could find; but Sam, Mary, and Martha Holland were nowhere to be found.

Naomi had seen firsthand what Sylacauga had done to her family and she just couldn't rest knowing the people who had destroyed a once honorable and peaceful existence were living happy, comfortable lives while she lived nearly every day of her life wondering where her siblings were; or even if they were alive. She had to let the town of Sylacauga know she hadn't forgotten what they had done to her family back in 1962. Her family history had been erased and the orphanage was destroyed. Naomi couldn't do anything about those things —but she knew of one name in Sylacauga, Alabama— Eastman. He had murdered her mother. Now, fourteen years later and much more stronger and knowledgeable, twenty-one year-old Naomi Holland was determined to let the man feel her presence. She knew she couldn't make the whole town pay, but she was determined to let her mother's murderer feel the pain that she had been carrying with her ever since 1962.

The thought of revenge lingered in the back of Naomi's mind throughout the fall of 1976 and gnawed at her soul continuously. No longer could she just sit by after learning what the town's people in Sylacauga had done to her family and chalk it up to bad fortune or a tragedy to be put out of her mind. No. Naomi had to answer. And the people involved had to answer to her for what they'd done to her family.

Naomi knew what Doss did for a living. She also now knew how her man operated. The desire for revenge was so strong within Naomi, that on New Year's Day of 1977, she had finally made up her mind that she would ask Doss for his help. And as fireworks soared into the night sky in west Cicero on January 1, 1977, Naomi, as she celebrated with Doss and the rest of the crew inside *Eastside Bar*, now had a hit of her own in mind—one that she felt needed doing—and one that had been a long time coming.

CHAPTER 9
FOR MY PEOPLE

Naomi threw her graduation cap high into the air on a warm Saturday evening in late May of 1977. She had just graduated Magna Cum Laude from Northwestern's four year introductory law program, the highest honor one could receive. She and Fin both hugged one another tightly while laughing aloud. The two friends since childhood were now on the path to success.

"The first phase is over, Misses Magna Cum Laude. Now the hard part begins." Fin stated as he and Naomi walked through the dispersing crowd to find their family.

Kevin and Serena greeted Naomi and hugged her and congratulated Fin, telling them how proud they were of both of them. Loud whistling and clapping was soon heard off in the distance and Naomi and company turned around and spotted Mendoza, Francine, DeeDee, Doss, Lucky, Mildred and Zell Verniche` through the crowd. Zell looked the old gangster he was as he stood in his white silk suit and fedora with his cane and three body guards behind him.

Kevin grew weary at the sight of Zell. He sighed and looked towards Serena and asked, "What is that gangster from the bar doing here?"

"Kevin, he's her friend. Mendoza's a gangster too. Why not question him why he's here?"

"The rest have *been* around, except for Doss. And to be honest, I don't know what she sees in him."

"She loves him, Kevin. Let's not talk about that now. This is a special day for Naomi." Serena said lowly as she watched Naomi run in her gown towards her friends.

Naomi hugged them all and said to Zell, "I didn't expect to see you here today, Santa Clause."

"For you my friend, I've cleared my schedule. You're going to celebrate with us at the bar," sixty-nine year-old Zell stated matter-of-factly.

"I'm having dinner with my parents first, then we'll be right there. I promise."

"Those ain't your parents! You're parents are named Nituna and Rutherford." Zell stated as he chewed his un-lit his cigar.

"I know Zell—but they're doing what Nituna and Rutherford can't do now. Respect them please."

"I'm just making sure you don't forget."

"Believe me, every day of my life I talk to my parents, my real parents. Thanks for caring," Naomi said as she hugged Zell one last time, kissed Doss on the lips and returned to Serena and Kevin.

"Make sure you come right after dinner! Bring your parents! Everybody's invited to the Eastside Bar on 23rd Street in Cicero for a celebration later this evening!" Zell yelled aloud to the crowd.

"I'm not going there." Kevin remarked as Naomi walked in between he and Serena and clutched their arms.

"Dad, he's just being nice. It's not good to turn down an offer from the—"

"The Boss of Twenty-third Street Mafia doesn't run my life, Naomi. If I don't want to go, I don't have to go."

"I'll go." Serena said.

Kevin and Naomi often argued about her choice of friends because he didn't like them all that much. Serena always said it was Naomi's life, and whenever she sensed an argument coming on, she tried to keep the peace just as she was doing today. Naomi, however, was becoming more vocal with Kevin because she felt he didn't care what was going on in her life. She also felt that her surrogate father was trying to match her with someone she didn't care about by constantly suggesting that she maybe think about dating one of the many men on campus who often asked her out on dates.

Kevin cared deeply about Naomi's feelings, though; and he truly wanted the best for her, but his way of caring was perceived by Naomi as disapproval of her choice of friends and the man she had fallen in love with, Doss Dawkins Junior. Kevin actually understood what Naomi was feeling, though, he just never succeeded at finding the right tact to use to get Naomi to understand his point of view; a task he'd been struggling with ever since the day he first met Naomi.

Every time Kevin tried to talk to Naomi, he would see that helpless little girl he fell in love with back in Selma, Alabama. He'd realized several years ago, however, that Naomi had become a grown woman with her own personality. In spite of that fact, he still felt the need to protect her. Serena often told Kevin that he should be proud of the way Naomi turned out as she was strong and very independent. Kevin came to understand that it was because of Naomi's strong sense of self that the two rarely saw eye to eye; but in spite of it all, they loved one another deeply. They just had a hard time communicating.

Naomi reflected on the somewhat-strained relationship she had with Kevin as the three walked towards the car and she said to him, "Nobody runs my life, dad. Zell's trying to be nice. Anyway this is my day. Can we do what *I* want to do today? I want you to come to the bar—just show your face, please. For me?"

Kevin was thinking of the difficulties he had in communicating with Naomi as well. He was looking directly into her eyes when she asked him to join her at the *Eastside Bar* and he was broken. He couldn't resist his daughter's beautiful eyes and lovely smile no matter how hard he tried. "Only because you asked," he said as he touched Naomi's cheek.

"Thanks, dad."

Kevin didn't want to admit defeat, so he gave ulterior reasons for joining Naomi at the bar. "It was not that sweet smile of yours that has won me over, Naomi, if that's what you're thinking. I have to go in order to keep an eye on my trophy wife."

"You are being disingenuous at this moment, daddy. Admit it —my smile floors you and makes you weak for me." Naomi replied as she hugged Kevin tightly. "I love you, dad. Thanks."

****

Two hours later, Naomi, Kevin and Serena walked into the *Eastside Bar* and cheers erupted. "Hey everybody, Naomi's here!" a mobster yelled aloud as the crowd paused and began to clap.

Norman Greenbaum's 1971 hit song *Spirit in the Sky* blared across the bar as mobsters patted Naomi on the back and kissed her cheeks. A banner that read, "*Congratulations Naomi and Fin*" was hanging from the ceiling and the sight of it made Naomi's eyes water. She was very happy this day, but she couldn't help but to start thinking about her mother, father, grandmother and siblings, wishing they were present to share in the moment; but before she drifted in her thoughts, she, along with Kevin and Serena, was whisked through the crowded bar towards the back and placed at a specially decorated table that held a bouquet of flowers and a small jewelry box that had a card from Doss underneath. A bottle of champagne was brought over for Naomi along with three glasses. "Complements of Mendoza Cernigliaro, Naomi and family," the mobster stated just before he kissed Naomi's hand and nodded towards Kevin and Serena.

The man then handed a box of cigars to Kevin tipped his hat and said, "Complements of DeeDee, Mister Langley. He says you've raised a wonderful daughter. Serena, DeeDee also says he hopes someday, that Naomi grows into the special woman you are right now. Salute," the mobster ended as he shook Kevin's hand and walked away.

"Flattery!" Kevin said as he sniffed a cigar. "Nice. This is nice, though."

"Well, I just love flattery. The way you called me your trophy wife earlier? What flattery!" Serena said as Kevin chuckled and loosened up a bit.

"They're nice to certain people, okay? But, Naomi I still think you should—"

"Not now, Kevin. Later, my love." Serena said in Kevin's ear. "Our daughter has graduated Magna Cum Laude," she then yelled aloud.

"Dad's just being dad mother. He doesn't realize as of yet that he can't make me love someone I don't want to love. Let's drink." Naomi said as Serena uncorked the champagne and poured while Naomi opened her gift.

Naomi was stunned to silence when she saw the glistening tennis bracelet Doss had given her. An inscription that read, *"To a Great Woman"* was engraved underneath. She began searching for Doss, but was held back by Serena as the glasses were topped off. While Serena poured, Naomi was preparing to propose a toast to both she and Kevin before she went and thanked Doss.

At the same time, Zell leaned over and whispered to Mendoza in a low raspy voice. "The Boss has something to say! Let me say what I have to say on *this* day."

Zell had been watching Naomi and waiting for the right time to speak, and when she had her glass full of champagne, he felt the time was right for him to acknowledge the young woman in a special way. And acknowledging Naomi wouldn't be all of what sixty-nine year-old Zell Verniche` would have to say as he slowly stood and stepped outside of his booth.

"Everybody listen up! The Boss is about to speak! Everybody listen up! Listen up! I said the Boss is about to speak!" Mendoza yelled aloud on his feet, causing the crowd to grow quiet and the music to be turned down.

Zell slowly walked to the center of the room and stood in between the pool tables and braced himself with his cane. He looked over to Naomi and nodded his head, cleared his throat and said aloud, "My parents, Mister and Misses Salenio Verniche`, they came over from Sicily in 1903 and I was born here in Cicero in 1907. My parents had wanted nothing but the best for me when I came into this world—but their dreams weren't recognized—because of prejudice. My father couldn't go here, get a job there. When he did get a job at the steel mills in Gary, Indiana—my father busted his *balls* to help out in the industrial revolution. But in the end, he died penniless, and disappointed in the so-called 'American Dream'. I said long before that point and time that that'll never happen to me. I did what I *had* to do to make something of myself. So don't judge me, for the man I have become," Zell said as he bowed his head slightly and then raised it back up proudly and continued to speak in a stern tone of voice. "In the end, after it was all said and done? My *mother*, on her *death bed* in 1939, who knew all-too-well the path I'd chosen for myself in life by then, but never gave a damn about it because she loved me unconditionally. A mother's love is never failing. Before dying, my mother, she said, she said to me, 'son, treat everybody with respect. Love those that love you, no matter their race, creed, or lifestyle. Love them, just as I have loved you, and just as much as your father loved us both'. Naomi's parents down in Alabama? They wanted the best for their offspring the same way my parents wanted the best for me and I believe that in my heart. Eileen, Rutherford and Nituna Holland didn't live long enough help Naomi, or the rest of their offspring accomplish the dream—but a man seated amongst us tonight cared enough back in 1965 to give a little black girl hope."

Kevin looked up and eyed Zell, who held total sway over the bar. People were nodding in approval and he could see Francine began to dab tears and DeeDee and Doss standing proudly along with Lucky, Fin and Mendoza as they nodded in agreement with the rest of the crowd.

Zell cleared his throat again continued speaking. "When Naomi walked into this bar in 1971 she made an impression on me. I said 'she's going to be something someday'. Today my friends, someday has come. Because a white man cared enough to not let the prejudice lowlifes in Alabama take away a little black girl's chance at life, Naomi Holland is on her way to becoming a successful lawyer here in the Windy City having graduated got damn Magna Laude! Magna Cum Laude!" he said as the crowd erupted into cheers and claps.

Zell calmed the crowd down and continued by saying, "Kevin Langley? I salute you and Serena for giving Naomi a chance. And we here today, *Naomi's* friends—we all bestow honor upon you and your wife for caring. For, for overlooking race. For overlooking creed. And for overlooking a person's lifestyle. A few minutes before my mother died, I told her, 'I'll do it ma—but I don't think no one else will be around to join me in not being prejudiced against people of different races'. My mother said I would be wrong—and she was right. Because I've been proven wrong a long time ago with the likes of Presidents John F. Kennedy and Lyndon B. Johnson, the Reverend Doctor Martin Luther King and many others. But that's the big picture. In our immediate little world, Mister and Misses Langley are two people I know of personally that cares. People do care! More than we could ever, *ever* imagine! Here's to friends! Here's to you, Naomi! And thank yous go out to Kevin, and Serena Langley!" Zell ended as he held up his glass.

"Salute!" the whole crowd yelled in unison and had a drink with Naomi.

Naomi blew kisses at Zell as she stood up and clapped with a face full of tears. She walked to the other side of the table and hugged Serena and Kevin as the music was turned back up and the celebration continued on. Naomi danced with Doss and DeeDee, and the rest of her friends, and even Serena and Kevin had danced a few times. A couple of hours later, as Naomi sat and talked with Serena and Kevin, Lucky came over and gently told her that Zell wanted to see her.

"Dad, mom, excuse me." Naomi said as she waited for a reply.

"Go on and see your friend, Naomi. Me and my trophy wife are feeling good! It's gonna be a long night for you, woman!" Kevin told Serena.

"Dad! I don't want to hear that!" Naomi said in a stunned tone of voice.

"He's a little tipsy, dear." Serena remarked as she laughed and pressed her head to Kevin's.

"And to think you didn't want to come here." Naomi said to Kevin.

"I was wrong, I admit. This is an okay place. Great speech by Zell." Kevin stated for the umpteenth time as he poured another glass of champagne. "Great speech."

Naomi smiled as she walked through the bar. She was happy

that everything had worked out between her and Kevin, who was reluctant to even go to the bar in the beginning. She stopped and chatted briefly with various mobsters as she made her way through the club towards Zell's table. When she sat down, Zell smiled as he puffed on a cigar.

"Today you've made a lot of people proud, Naomi," Zell said as he passed her a thick stack of hundred dollar bills.

"Thank you, Zell."

"Forget about it. Now, I want to know what do you plan on doing?"

"Well, me and Fin are enrolling into graduate school in September."

"I know that. But what do you plan on *doing?*" Zell asked again as he leaned forward and patted Naomi's hand.

Naomi then knew what Zell was asking. After she sat alone in Serena's lounge on New Year's Eve, six months earlier, Naomi, having made up her mind over the actions she wanted to take to pay the town of Sylacauga back for what they'd done to her family, went to *Eastside Bar* and told DeeDee, Mendoza, and Doss what she wanted to do. The men listened to Naomi and went and asked Zell's permission to do her that 'favor' he'd owed her for helping him out during the Cleveland hit on the usher the following day.

Zell gave his approval and in February of '77, Naomi began driving down to Alabama with Mendoza, DeeDee, Doss, Lucky and Fin and began scoping out the town of Sylacauga where they gathered names and remembered schedules. The five had made at least a half dozen trips to Alabama by the time Naomi graduated and Zell believed the time was getting close. The man was asking in so many words, was Naomi ready to do what she'd asked months earlier.

"Next month I want to go, Zell."

"Why so long? It's been four months already."

"Four months isn't long by my standards. And this is real big for me, Zell. I wanna make sure everything is planned out perfect."

"When have you ever known Mendoza and DeeDee to fail?

They're offering their help, why don't you take it?"

"I am—next month. I'll, I'll be ready. I promise."

Zell leaned forward, grabbed Naomi's hands and said, "When you go, don't you dare feel sorry for those mutherfuckas down there. Remember how they done her," he stated in reference to Nituna. "What kind of a coward would shoot a helpless woman in the back," he asked just before he coughed loudly, having become seriously emotional thinking about the way Nituna was killed.

Zell was a killer himself; he'd also trained killers, but he was proud to say that he never harmed a helpless woman. The old mafia figure had a loving mother, and to Zell, his mother was the sweetest woman that had ever lived. When Naomi described in detail what'd happened to her mother, Zell Verniche` wanted to kill the people who'd harmed Nituna himself. So when Naomi asked for the favor, Zell gladly offered his help. "From what I hear you speak of your mother the short time you knew her, she wouldn't want this I know," he told Naomi. "She was a sweet woman. Just like my mother by all accounts. But them racist bastards deserve what's comin' to 'em. When you're ready just say the word." Zell ended as he extended his hand, allowing Naomi to leave his table.

Naomi returned to Kevin and Serena and they enjoyed the rest of the night. Kevin had to admit that the bar was a nice place. He and Serena would go there on occasion in the days following to have a bottle of wine. They both were surprised the first time they ventured in the bar together to be asked what kind of wine they would like before they had even taken seats. They made their request, a nice Merlot, and were thankful and shocked to learn that they didn't have to pay. Kevin insisted on paying, but he was told that he was insulting Zell.

From that day forth, every time Kevin and Serena went to *Eastside Bar* they received a complimentary bottle of wine and free dinners whether Zell was present or not. The mafia Don was showing love to Kevin and Serena for what they had done for Naomi and it was fair to say that they felt honored. Kevin would always joke that Naomi had powerful friends. He never knew how right he was, however—because when it got down to it—Naomi Holland really did have powerful friends that made shit happen.

****

Naomi was riding in DeeDee's '72 four door Lincoln Continental with Mendoza and Doss on the night of June 21, 1977. The car was a pristine, long and sleek ride with chrome Mag rims and thick 'gangster' white wall tires and black tinted windows. White leather seats, and a small bar in the back floorboard and a smoke grey paint job with a white rag top capped off a true gangster's ride for all times. Naomi sat comfortably in the back of the car with Doss as DeeDee drove south on Interstate-65 with Mendoza at his side.

Lucky, Mildred, and Fin were trailing Mendoza in Lucky's two door Cadillac Eldorado. Lucky's car was black with a black rag top, black tinted windows, thin white wall tires, chrome wheels, and a fifth wheel in the back, another stylish and true gangster ride during that era.

Naomi lay in Doss's chest with a look of contentment on her face as she sipped a glass of vodka. The twenty-two year-old woman was glad she had people like Lucky and Fin, and a strong man like Doss and his father, along with Mendoza in her life as friends because they were invaluable in helping her exact revenge against those who'd wronged her and her family early on life. She then thought about Fin, who went along for the pure sake of friendship, and Mildred, who was along for the sheer adventure of it all, and would easily follow Lucky to the depths of hell because she loved him that much.

Naomi knew she was going to break the law in the worst way possible on this trip, but she had promised not only herself, but Mary and Martha as well, that she would make the town of Sylacauga pay for what they'd done to the Holland Family. She sat her glass down after finishing her drink and enjoyed the melodic sounds of Isaac Hayes's song *Walk on By*, closing her eyes and listening to the music as she lay up against Doss, hoping that what she had planned on doing would not only succeed, but also spark her sisters' memories if they were still alive.

The gang stopped in Birmingham, Alabama, just over sixty miles north of Sylacauga in order to refuel, stretch their legs and regroup. Before they left the gas station, Mendoza gathered everybody together one last time. "Okay people," he spoke lowly, "from here we on our own. Everybody already know what they're supposed to do. When you three done," he said to Lucky, Fin and Mildred, "just take off and head back this way. We all are gonna meet back here. If one or the other doesn't' show within thirty minutes, the assumption is something went wrong and the cops may be all over the place. The group that's here will head on back to Cicero and await word understand," the group all nodded and hugged one another before they got back into their cars and headed southeast towards Sylacauga.

Just over an hour later, shortly after midnight on June 22, 1977, Mendoza, DeeDee, Doss and Naomi were on the south side of town outside the home of a man by the name of George Eastman. He was now the sheriff of Sylacauga—but in 1962 he was the patrol officer who'd murdered Naomi's mother in cold blood right before her eyes.

At the same time, Lucky, Fin, and Mildred were pulling up to a lumber warehouse on the west side of town, which sat on Naomi's parents' land that they once owned. The warehouse was a huge complex. Shaped like a long gymnasium, it held long sheets of plywood, bins of dried pulp wood, and preprocessed wood that hadn't been cut to form. It was primarily a storage warehouse, but it sat on Naomi's parents' land, and for that reason, it had to be destroyed.

Lucky, Fin and Mildred drove to the back of the huge wooden structure and exited the car with Molotov cocktails and cans of gasoline to do their job. The doors to the structure were wide open with the wood in plain view and not a single soul was in sight. The three walked into the darkened structure and began walking around with flashlights, making sure the place was empty.

"They some real trusting people down here in this town," Lucky remarked as the group began spreading gasoline at the base of the stacks of plywood, which were stacked nearly to the ceiling in six rows that stretched the entire length of the warehouse. They also poured gasoline into the bins containing the dried pulp wood and doused the pretreated wood as well.

"It's a lot of treated wood in here. They must leave the doors open for ventilation." Finland remarked.

"I guess you're right. The wood does have a pretty strong smell." Lucky replied as the group continued spreading gasoline throughout the warehouse.

Meanwhile, outside the sheriff's house, Mendoza had exited his car under the starry skies with his .9mm and began placing a silencer onto the barrel of the gun as he tip-toed onto the sheriff's porch. He leaned back in his grey silk suit and peeked into the window on the first floor, and when he saw that the house was dark and quiet, he signaled for DeeDee and Doss. He'd jimmied the lock and was letting himself in by the time the two men had made it to the porch. The three men walked quietly through the house with weapons drawn.

Mendoza and DeeDee headed upstairs to search the bedrooms as Doss searched the downstairs, making sure to keep an eye on Naomi, who sitting quietly in the car awaiting her signal. Mendoza and DeeDee crept up the wooden stairs without making a sound and approached the first door on their left. They stood on either side of the threshold of the room and Mendoza pushed the slightly ajar door open. It made a creaking sound that quickly went silent, allowing him to push the door open more fully.

DeeDee looked in the room and saw a young man, younger than his son, maybe about twenty-one or so lying asleep on his back and he knew right away it was the sheriff's son. Eastman's firstborn was old enough to understand the loss of his parents. They may have even talked to him about the things that transpired with the Holland family. If so, he may tell all he knew and have heat brought down on Naomi. It was for this possibility that DeeDee and Mendoza decided the son had to go. DeeDee crept up slowly and pointed his weapon and shot the young man three times in the heart as he slept soundly, the gunshots muffled by his silencer.

Mendoza then crept towards the master bedroom while DeeDee went and checked the last bedroom. Inside that room, DeeDee saw a little girl, maybe one or two years of age. She was the sheriff's granddaughter, he knew. DeeDee eyed the baby, noticing how precious she looked before he walked towards the master bedroom where he saw Mendoza standing over the sleeping sheriff and his wife. He held up one finger to have Mendoza wait a minute and went and got Doss' attention on the first floor by snapping his fingers lowly.

Doss appeared at the bottom of the stairs and began his climb slowly and met his father halfway. "There's a baby in one of the rooms," DeeDee stated lowly. "I wanna make sure she has a couple of bottles of water and some fruit or something. It may be a day or so before they find the bodies."

DeeDee knew there would be no adults left to tend to the baby and she may go hungry before the sheriff's deputies or some other concerned citizen came by to check the family's whereabouts and he wanted the baby not to be harmed in any way when she was found. Doss headed back down the stairs towards the kitchen to search for a bottle and some fruit for the baby as DeeDee headed back towards the master bedroom.

When Mendoza saw DeeDee enter the room, he kicked the bed forcefully, causing the sheriff and his wife to awaken from their sleep. "Maggie! Gosh Jesus no cereal tonight," the sheriff's wife screamed as she sat up only to be greeted with the barrel of DeeDee's gun.

"Shut up!" DeeDee said quickly and sharply as he placed the barrel to her head.

"What the fuck is this? Who are you?" Eastman asked as he reached for his .357 magnum that lay on the night stand.

Mendoza kicked the sheriff in the face and he fell back into the mattress gagging and spitting blood from his mouth. Eastman's gun was then knocked off the night stand over to the other side of the room.

"We come to bless you and your family tonight, old man," Mendoza said as he turned on the lamp light and shoved his gun in front of Eastman's face. "We bring you the gift of redemption, mutherfucka! Get your ass up!" he commanded as he grabbed Eastman off the bed and forced him onto his knees beside the bed.

DeeDee then snapped his fingers loudly, signaling Doss to bring up Naomi. He placed three bottles of water and some fruit into the baby's crib before he left and walked down and pulled her from the car, "It's time, baby," he said as he guided

Naomi through the house and up the stairs.

When Naomi entered the bedroom, Eastman knew right away who she was and why she now stood in his home. "No, no! I'm a religious man now! I've paid for my sins! I've asked for forgiveness for you and me *both*," he said in a frantic manner as he scrambled over to his night stand and grabbed his rosary beads and began praying aloud.

Naomi had adorned a dress identical to the one her mother had worn the day she was killed, which was an ankle length pink dress and black suede boots. She had her hair platted in two thick plats just like her mother, only she was holding a baseball bat, something Nituna didn't have when she was killed.

"What do I have to forgive? You pray for me? After what you've done you pray for me? What you've taken from me— what you've done to my people can never be given back!" Naomi hissed.

"We have, we have to move past this, little girl! Dammit! That was years ago! Years! Can't you find it in your heart to forgive?"

"Where was your heart when my mother begged for mercy? Where was mercy for Ruth? And the things you and your lawmen did to my father and grandmother? You want me to forgive all of that," Naomi screamed aloud as she began to cry.

"Your father robbed the bank! What was I supposed to do?"

"Not kill him you son-of-a-bitch!"

"He broke the law!"

"And you took the law into your own hands! And so will I! I remember all that you done! And I live with it every day of my life!"

"I was just doing my job! It was a fuckin' job for Christ sake!"

"Was pointing a gun at me a part of doing your job? No it wasn't! The little girl you attempted to kill in 1962 now stands before you and she is full of anger! Unable to erase from memory what she has seen! Unable to forgive! Unable to feel sorry for what you have done to my people!"

"You said they wouldn't remember! You said they wouldn't
—"

"Rebecca shut the fuck up!" Eastman yelled towards his wife
as he sat on the floor.

"I do remember! Sam, Mary and Martha? Maybe they have
forgotten! But *I, I* didn't forget!" Naomi yelled as she began to
fill with rage. "And you," she then said to Rebecca as she
walked around to the side of the bed where the woman was
sitting upright, "you knew? And you did nothing? Said
nothing? You just went on with ya' life and said to hell with
the Holland family? But this is one member of the Holland
family that didn't forget! And she is acting on behalf of her
entire family tonight!" Naomi hissed. "*Your* flesh and blood
now lies dead here tonight! Your son now lies dead because of
what your husband has done to *my people!*"

"Not my son! Please! Not my son!" Rebecca begged.

"Now you know how the shit feels!" Naomi said as she
swung her bat and hit Rebecca in the face, knocking teeth from
the lady's mouth, her left eye out of socket and smashing her
nose flat.

Naomi then went into a rage. As she beat Eastman's wife
repeatedly she could see her mother running across the land
she once called home. She could hear Nituna pleading for
mercy, telling the officers that she had kids. "*I'm not going to
fight you! Please, you're killing me,*" could be heard in the
back of Naomi's mind as she replayed the images of her
mother being beaten and killed before her very eyes. She
screamed in an enraged manner, swinging the bat up and down
repeatedly as Rebecca's blood began splattering onto her
clothes and coating the walls and the ceiling with red slime.

"Oh God don't take her! Don't let them take her from me,
please! Rebecca! Rebecca I'm sorry!" Eastman yelled as
Naomi continued to beat his wife mercilessly.

Mendoza, DeeDee, and Doss stood back and watched as
Eastman cried and prayed aloud. The man gripped his set of
rosary beads tightly and begged and pleaded for mercy as the
thud of the bat that was taking his wife's life inside her own
bedroom constantly repeated itself over and over again. Naomi

raised the bat one last time and slammed it down into Rebecca's skull and created a sickening sound, like that of a watermelon being dropped from a high place. Eastman's wife's head had been split open completely; her brains now lay on the pillows of her bed as she lay a battered, bruised, twisted mass of expired mangled human flesh that would be unidentifiable to those who would later uncover the scene.

Naomi then walked around the bed and eyed Eastman, her bat dripping blood and brain matter of the sheriff's wife. "You have to pay! I hope you've suffered tonight the same way I suffered when you done to me, what is happening to you and your family tonight! For my people I do this!" Naomi screamed as she raised her bat.

"Forgive me! Naomi, please! Please! I beg of you! Forgive me, God Jesus, please! I wanna live! I wanna live, Naomi," would be the last words spoken by Eastman.

Naomi slammed her bat down onto the top of the man's head and caved in the top of his skull. He fell back motionless and Naomi stood over him staring with hate-filled eyes. She had so many images running through her mind. Images of Sam being taken away, images of her running trying to keep up with the car that had taken Mary and Martha away, her grandmother and father's loving arms, Nituna's hum when she worked the field. She could hear her mother and twin sister's last words echoing through her mind as well. *"Naomi help me!"* Ruth's last words before she was ran over. *"Naomi, I'm sorry!"* Nituna's last words before Eastman shot her in the back—it all came back on the angered and vengeful woman.

Naomi blacked out as she replayed some of the most terrible memories of her life and beat Eastman to a pulp. She'd flattened the man's skull completely, leaving him nearly headless, and she only continued to swing the bat. Mendoza finally had to grab her, but Naomi had turned the bat on him. Mendoza quickly grabbed Naomi's hands to prevent her from swinging the bat in his direction as DeeDee and Doss shook her back to the present. Naomi paused and looked around, slowly returning to her senses, eyeing the dead corpses as she let the bat slip from her hands and fall idly to the floor. She then turned to Doss and stared at him, blood staining her face and arms and the front side of her dress. She leaned in and hugged Doss and cried on his shoulder, clutching him tightly, yelling, "They killed them! They took my family from me!"

"We know, we know, baby. They got what they deserved tonight. We about to leave this place for good. It's over." Doss replied lovingly as he rubbed Naomi's back.

"Not until I find them. But tonight, I feel vindicated. For my people—for *my people!*" Naomi screamed as Doss hugged her around the shoulder and escorted her out of the room.

Mendoza grabbed the bat and the four exited the home with DeeDee locking the house behind him. The house looked just as calm and tranquil when the four left as it had been before they arrived.

****

"What the fuck are you doing you dingy ass red-head?" Lucky asked Mildred as she vomited onto the floor of the warehouse.

"I'm sick, ya' dumb fuck!"

"Get sick later! We got a job to do. Finish pouring that shit so we can get the fuck outta here!"

Lucky, Mildred and Fin were just finishing up dousing the bases of the stacks of the pretreated wood inside the warehouse. After finishing their task they threw the empty cans into the building and lit their cocktails and it seemed as if the flames were ignited before the bottles even broke upon impact. Mildred's hair caught afire just before she threw her cocktail. She had scratched her head while holding the flaming bottle and it ignited her hair. Lucky beat her across the head as they ran back to his car. He was beating Mildred first for being stupid, and to put out the fire second. "You dingy, red-headed, dumb—ohhh! How stupid can one broad be?" Lucky said as he drove off in a hurry.

Meanwhile, as Lucky and his crew headed north out of town, flashing lights had just forced Naomi and her bunch over to the side of the dark, tree-lined road not even a mile away from Eastman's home. The officer stepped out of his patrol car and slowly walked pass the rear of the vehicle, mindful of the Illinois license plate.

DeeDee was behind the wheel and he had his hand on his gun, preparing to fire, but the officer had racked a twelve gauge and pointed it at the driver's side window. "Driver, exit the vehicle," he commanded.

The man had the ups on DeeDee so he complied by removing his hand off his gun and easing out of the driver's seat where the officer forced him to his knees and looked back into the car briefly. "You," he said to Naomi, "step out of the back seat."

Naomi emerged from the car and the officer, as he held his gun on DeeDee, asked, "What's a bunch like you all from Illinois doing down here in my town?"

"Just passing through, mister." Naomi replied calmly as she held her hands up at shoulder length.

"You're headed north. Where ya' coming from, and where're ya' going?"

"Coming from Florida, going to, well, you see the tag. We're headed to Illinois."

"My knees ain't so good." DeeDee moaned. "And this is embarrassing."

"Shut up down there! Things could be worse."

Mendoza and Doss still had their hands on their guns as they sat inside the car. There was no way this officer could watch all four of them and they were searching for the opportune time to shoot the officer before he decided to call for back-up.

"All units we got a 73 out on highway 148, Millerville Highway eastbound at the old lumber yard. Any patrols nearby to assist fire units?"

"Sergeant Eufaula here, copy the 73. ETA eight minutes."

The officer then motioned Naomi closer, just as Doss was about to shoot from the back seat, and she now blocked his line of fire. The man stared at Naomi for a lone minute and finally said, "I always knew somebody from your family would return."

"Excuse me," Naomi said.

"I wasn't there that day. Sons of bitches had me on a bogus larceny call," the officer remarked. "Your grandmother Eileen and my father, Raymond Eufaula Senior had just formed an alliance and was ready to take on the town. I had a couple of guys I could trust that was going to look after your family until everything went through, but the day Rutherford robbed the bank worked against us. We just didn't have enough time to react."

"Who are you?"

"Just somebody who cares, Naomi. I knew your family. I know what happened. And I won't hold you in contempt for what I believe you've done tonight. Florida? Nice try. But I'd say you were about three quarters of a mile south of here at the home of George Eastman. Your mother's killer."

"What makes you think that?"

"Don't bullshit me, okay? Good men died saving you and the survivors. At least they tried. And their efforts weren't in vain because at least one of the Holland children made it I see." Eufala said as he pointed his finger at Naomi and smiled slyly.

Mendoza was beginning to ease out from the front seat with his gun. DeeDee, however, who could sense Mendoza's intent and could also hear the conversation, gave him a signal and he remained in place, easing his hand off the door handle and resting back in his seat.

"Who are you?" Naomi asked again.

"My name is Raymond Eufaula Junior. My father was a congressman the next town over in the early sixties. Your grandmother Eileen had sought him out to aide her in fighting to keep you all's land. But like I say, we didn't have enough time."

"Okay. Even if I've done what you believe, what will happen now? What is it that you want from me?"

"I want a guarantee that you are done here. I'm not gonna ask what the hell you just did down the road, but if I ever see you again? I will arrest you. Or one of your comrades will have to take me down," Eufaula said as he eyed Mendoza. "I haven't survived being on the force for over twenty-five years by being stupid. And I'm a Creek Indian myself. I understand the importance of the familial bond," he ended as he stepped aside and let Naomi pass, while at the same time helping DeeDee up from his knees.

"Thank you, Raymond," Naomi said as DeeDee got back behind the wheel.

"From here I can't help you, Naomi. You get pulled over again, you never saw me."

"There's a baby back there. She has bottles of water and fruit."

"I circle the sheriff's house every hour on the hour. Just made my round and everything seems legit. An hour from now, I expect you and your family to be long gone, Naomi."

"Raymond," Naomi then asked as she stood facing the man, "do you know where Sam, Mary and Martha are? What did they do with the—"

"The bodies of your relatives that they killed?"

"Yes."

"They burned them, Naomi. I'm sorry. Their ashes are scattered into the wind. They've become a part of the land surrounding that lumber yard that's ablaze. As far as your siblings? Haven't a clue. My search ended in Selma, Alabama where all traces of your family vanished into thin air."

Naomi extended her hand and Eufaula responded in kind. The two shook hands in admiration of one another, Naomi in admiration of the fact that this man understood the history of her family and at least tried to help and was willing to help now, and Eufaula in admiration of Naomi's courage and determination to exact revenge upon those who'd done her family wrong. Eufaula didn't condone what was done on this night, but he understood fully. Because if the shoe were on the other foot, if it had been his family that had nearly been wiped out, he would have possibly done the same thing, if only he had the courage and determination to do as much.

"When I say good men died protecting your family, two men did." Eufaula said just before Naomi climbed into the backseat.

"How'd they die? Did Eastman kill them too?"

"No. Both men spoke out against Eastman that day, but they didn't do enough and they knew it. You may be too young to remember, but as the story goes, George took you and your siblings into the living room and was preparing to shoot—"

"Us all at point blank range until one officer stopped him. 'We have a good Samaritan amongst us'. That's what George said." Naomi remarked somberly as she looked to the ground somewhat dismayed having realized just how close her family had indeed come to being wiped out completely. "If it weren't for that man I wouldn't—none of us would be alive. I'm fortunate. I'm so fortunate."

"That guy that stopped Eastman died, Naomi. And the other guy that was in the third car that ran over your twin Ruth died also."

"How'd they die, Raymond?"

"They killed themselves a year after that massacre on your family's land. Just weeks apart. Couldn't live with what they'd done and had allowed to happen. They were supposed to protect your family, but they cowered under pressure. I hope you're able to live with what you've done, Naomi."

"I'll do okay," Naomi replied before thanking Raymond Eufaula again. She then got back into the backseat of the car and told the crew it was okay to leave. DeeDee pulled away slowly and she began telling all that she and the officer had shared.

The crew finally met up at the gas station in Birmingham, refueled their cars and drove back to Illinois and made it back to Cicero on Monday afternoon. Naomi was hoping she had given her sisters hope that she was still out there and she cared. She knew Mary and Martha had the portion of her journal that said she would burn Sylacauga down if she ever got the chance. She didn't burn the entire town, but she believed sincerely that what was done in Sylacauga was enough to at least let her sisters know she was still out there if they had been reading and understood what she was conveying inside the pages of her journal.

Everything had basically gone well the night before, and the encounter with Raymond Eufaula was uplifting to Naomi. She now knew that her family wasn't alone during their fight. Fate, however, had changed their course of history. Through it all though, after talking to Raymond, Naomi had a renewed hope that she would actually find her siblings someday. She showered and changed clothes and fell onto her bed exhausted.

Before she drifted off to sleep, however, Naomi called Zell and told him she was fine. The man was proud and happy. And if Zell Verniche` had to tell it, Naomi's family had gotten their revenge.

"It's been fifteen years in the making, now, it has come to pass." Zell ended as he congratulated Naomi and hung up the phone.

Naomi sighed and laid back on the bed amidst her three Raggedly Anne and Andy dolls and went into a deep, peaceful slumber.

CHAPTER 10
THE BABY MAKING YEARS

"Mildred! Come get this mutherfucka! You been in the fuckin' crapper for over thirty minutes now! Get outta there, and come and get Junior!" twenty-nine year-old Lucky yelled aloud from the couch.

It was now August of 1983, just over six years after the massacre and mayhem in Sylacauga. Investigators in the state of Alabama had not a clue what transpired the night the sheriff and his family were killed and the lumber warehouse burned down to the ground in the fateful early morning hours of June 22, 1977. The murders of George and Rebecca Eastman, and their son Langston Eastman were cold-cased and the lumber warehouse never reopened. Naomi and her bunch had gotten away with the murder of a town sheriff and his family. The story had made the national news and nearly every newspaper across the nation.

Kevin and Serena were never told about the trip to Alabama and no one inside *Eastside Bar* besides Zell knew what Naomi and the rest of her group had done six years ago, and no one that was there with Naomi in Alabama had ever spoken about what happened down in Sylacauga, Alabama in 1977. Naomi had never heard from Raymond Eufaula Junior again, but she was grateful that it was he and not some other officer who'd stopped the car she was riding in that night. Eufaula had allowed Naomi to have her freedom after she'd exacted revenge upon the man responsible for destroying her family; and from that day forth, she and those who'd traveled to

Alabama with her had merely went on with their lives as if nothing had ever had happened.

Lucky had married twenty-nine year-old Mildred in January of 1978 just before she gave birth to his son, Faustino Cernigliaro Junior. The day after Mildred had vomited while she, Lucky and Fin burned the lumber warehouse she had learned that she was pregnant. Lucky's son was born in early February of 1978. The chubby lad was now five years old and had been given the nick-name Junior.

Lucky and Mildred was a loud and bodacious couple, often trying to one up one another. Mildred loved Lucky's proverbial sigh, "ohhh". Lucky always yelled "ohhh" when he was at a loss for words, and to hear her husband yell that word tickled Mildred a great deal. She made it a point in her life to hear him say it every day. This hot August evening in '83 was no different.

The two were alone with their son enjoying an evening as a family in their two-story, three bedroom home that Lucky had purchased in the same neighborhood where his parents and all their friends still resided.

"If I come out there I'll be naked from the waist up, and Junior doesn't need to see his mother naked from the waist up!" Mildred yelled from behind the closed bathroom door in the basement of the family's home.

"He's seen tits before! And trust me hon'—your tits ain't at the top of his wish list the way they sag now-a-days! They ain't at the top of my list either for that matter!"

"You talk to me like that, Lucky?" Mildred asked as she opened the door, her red hair all over head as she held onto a stick of lip gloss.

"Just come and get this mutherfucka here! I'm watching the game and he's making noise over the TV! I can't hear the game!"

"He might be hungry ya' lazy bum! If ya' would get off ya' lazy ass and fix dinner just for once, maybe he'll stop crying! What are we having for dinner?"

"Dinner should be the last thing on your mind! And don't you take that tone of voice and talk to me about being lazy you,

you—you haven't had a job since nineteen seventy-one and ya' ain't looking for a job in nineteen eighty-three you, you—"

"*Say it! Say it!*" Mildred said to herself as she stood in the hallway.

"Ohhh! Just come get Junior would ya' please, honey bun?" Lucky asked in mocked politeness as his legs shook rapidly over his mounting anxiety. He really wanted to watch the game this day.

Mildred laughed and clapped her hands as she emerged from the bathroom and sat on Lucky's lap.

"Now here *you* go! I'm trying to watch the Cubs game, Mildred!"

"I'm your cub. Come on and kiss momma!"

"Come on, Mildred!"

"Come on, Faustino! One kiss! You make my day every day, my love." Mildred said as she slid her tongue into Lucky's mouth and he returned the kiss with passion. "Seventh inning stretch?" she then asked.

Lucky, at age twenty-nine, was a muscular 185 pound young man standing an even six feet tall with jet black curly hair. His chiseled jaw, broad shoulders and slightly bowed muscular legs gave him a sex appeal that caught the eye of many a woman. Lucky, however, was devoted to his wife, a fact that many a woman on the street had come to resent and envy because they felt that he should have a much more eye-capturing woman accompanying him out in public than a woman of Mildred's stature.

The reason being was because Mildred was an overweight, pale-skinned red head Italian woman with thick thighs, a pudgy belly, fluffy cheeks and a double chin. Mildred, however, carried her weight well, and she had beauty in all the right places—her face with splendor unmatched, a waistline that curved inwards to put her wide hips on display, her ass round and soft, leading down to legs and calves that had a firm, sexy appeal. The woman had a body that would put many a woman half her 210 pound 5' 8" physique to shame because of the way she carried herself. Mildred's style of dress, coupled with her bubbly spirit, curvaceous figure and astonishing beauty, was a severe turn on for Lucky, who loved his wife whole-heartedly and had chosen to remain faithful towards.

"Seventh inning stretch—be naked for daddy you sexy woman you." Lucky said.

"Mildred stood up and leaned forward slightly. "You want it, daddy," she asked as she gyrated her wide, tempting ass in front of her husband's face.

Lucky reached out and rubbed Mildred's thick, soft thighs, growing hard as he caressed his way up to his wife's pussy, massaging it underneath the silk skirt she was wearing without any panties. "You know I want it, baby. Have it ready for daddy. I wanna stand behind you today, alright?"

"Alright dada!" Junior answered as he got up from in front the TV and ran and jumped into his father's lap.

"Not you! I swear I wonder about this kid sometimes! I better not ever catch you wearing your mother's clothes you son-of-a —ohhh! Get him outta here!" Lucky yelled as he sunk back into the couch. That one was a bonus for Mildred; she laughed loudly as she pulled Junior from the couch and headed towards the kitchen to prepare dinner.

****

Meanwhile, just a few blocks away from Lucky and Mildred's home, twenty-eight year-old Naomi had just made it in from work. She entered Serena's home and turned on the radio just as the piano introduction to the song *Moments in Love* by the Art of Noise began to play over the stereo. Naomi had passed the state of Illinois' bar exam a year ago and had been working for a law firm in downtown Chicago for almost eight months as a Corporate Lawyer. She'd enjoyed six years of peace and prosperity and had saved a good bit of money from the monetary gifts she often received from Doss, Zell and other mobsters inside *Eastside Bar*.

Naomi's job at the law firm was earning her $1200 dollars a week, good money for the times. She'd also received a percentage of the cases she won over the eight months she had been on the law firm's payroll and that only added to her slow but steadily maturing wealth. Some of Naomi's most notable cases had her successfully defending two major corporations,

Hadson Petroleum, and Archer Daniels Midland, (ADM), against class action lawsuits citing worker safety concerns in oil storage facilities and grain processing plants. In another case, she had successfully defended an American CFO working for Maersk Container Corporation who'd been charged with embezzlement by the company's Danish stockholders. Naomi was an excellent corporate attorney, but her main area of expertise revolved around mergers and acquisitions, contract law and tax law. She was also a proficient accountant, and was very knowledgeable in licensing and zoning.

Naomi was happy this day because she had received her first quarterly bonus check and saw that it was over $26,000 dollars. She knew, however, that she had made the law firm over five hundred thousand dollars over a six week period. All months weren't as good, but when Naomi got a good run like she had the previous six weeks she knew she could earn a good bit of extra income through her bonuses. She loved her job at the law firm, but she was beginning to think about seeking out other business opportunities to further her financial status.

Naomi briefly entertained the thought of going into practice for herself, but that would be too time consuming for the plans she had in the near future. On top of that, the competition in Chicago was fierce. Naomi knew she would have to devote many more than the fifty hours a week she was already putting in on a weekly basis in order to get her practice up and running and she wasn't ready to take on that type of commitment and she knew that opening her own law firm would be too big of a leap at this particular point in her life. She had a good paying job that allowed for other investments and the people at the law firm and throughout the business community there in Chicago knew and respected her to the highest. Many corporations requested her services, eagerly paying the twenty percent retainer fee that was required for her representation. Top CEO's of Agricultural and Technological companies kept Naomi's personal phone number in their rolodexes. She had only been at the firm for eight months and had earned $40,000 dollars in pay and another $26,000 in bonuses. With the full understanding that she was making real good money in her current job, Naomi decided against opening her own practice for the time being and stay on with the law firm. In the meantime, she would search for an investment venture for the nearly seventy thousand dollars she had managed to save over time.

Naomi and thirty-year-old Doss were still going strong as well. Doss was still working with his father and Mendoza doing 'juice loans' and contract killings right alongside Lucky. Doss was also running an after hour's lounge on the southwest side of Chicago that featured poker games, black jack tables and roulette wheels. Money was coming in on a steady and even keel for the couple.

Fifty-seven year-old Kevin and fifty-nine year-old Serena, meanwhile, were getting up in age and wanted Naomi to have kids so they could have the experience of raising grandchildren. Everybody was pressuring Naomi and Doss to have kids, but the two of them were just too caught up in each other and their careers. Kids were not in their future—so they said. Deep down inside, though, Naomi really wanted a family and she'd known years ago that she wanted Doss to be the father of her kids. The problem, however, was the timing and their hectic careers. In spite of that fact, however, Naomi and Doss still found time for one another. They often made passionate love inside Doss's condo in downtown Chicago, and even inside Naomi's corner office on the seventy-third floor of the Sears Tower.

Doss had asked Naomi how she felt about having kids a year earlier and she replied by saying that when she was ready, they would have many babies because she wanted a big family. In the meantime, she only wanted to enjoy her time alone with Doss, telling him that Kevin and Serena, and some of the friends from Eastside Bar were being selfish.

"They don't want me to have kids to start a family, Doss. Well, they do, but take Kevin and Serena. They want grandchildren, right? But they're not considering how I truly feel. All they want are grandchildren." Naomi told Doss on a sunny summer afternoon in August of 1982 after the two had shared an intense lovemaking session, one in which Doss had to cover Naomi's mouth to conceal her moans as he took her from behind over her lacquered southern Alpine Spruce desk.

"You want me all to yourself. Aren't you being selfish?" Doss asked through a smile as he gathered his shoes, silk slacks and tie off the carpeted floor of Naomi's office and walked towards the bathroom.

"It's my body. And when we start our family it'll be me and you that has to deal with our kids at all times. No one will be around when they get sick, have to receive their annual shots, and to pick them up from day care and school." Naomi responded as she sat on her chaise and lotioned her legs.

"Naomi," Doss said as he walked back and stood in the threshold of the bathroom, "you know as well as I do that Kevin and Serena, and especially Serena, will give you more help than you need with our children. When my son gets here, he'll be well loved by all."

"Your son?" Naomi asked with a wide smile. "I want daughters!"

"We can have both, baby. How many kids would you like to have, Naomi?" Doss asked as he splashed Christian Dior cologne onto his face.

"I don't know, Doss. Until I'm satisfied. That's the only way I can answer. Until I'm satisfied." Naomi responded as she placed her shoes on her feet and the two of them went and had lunch.

Naomi reflected on the conversation she had with Doss a year ago as she sat at the poker table inside Serena's home listening to the soft sounds *Moments in Love*. At the age of twenty-eight, she was a sexy 5' 8" 150 pound voluptuous woman with thick black hair, smooth, tan skin, deep, dark eyes and a beautiful smile. She was intelligent, ambitious, independent and strong.

Thirty year-old Doss Dawkins was a 5' 10" 190 pound dark-skinned man with a clean-shaven head and neatly trimmed, low cut beard and a well-toned muscular physique. He was fearless, ambitious, handsome and deadly. The two were the perfect blend of wits and treachery; a highly capable and dangerous couple they were.

As she sat at the poker table, Naomi thought about how she

and Doss were constantly being asked when they were having kids.

"Lucky got married, you two next right," was the common question asked of the two by Kevin and Serena. Naomi would only smile and say "someday".

"Before we all die, Naomi. Before we all die, woman," would always be seventy-five year-old Zell's remark when he asked the question and heard Naomi's answer which was always to say "someday".

"Ohhh! You twos is never havin' a fuckin' kid," was Lucky's reply whenever he asked and heard Naomi's standard, "someday" reply.

That "someday" was now nearing for Naomi in August of '83, but she wanted to be sure she would be able to support an unforeseen amount of kids because she meant it when she told Doss she wanted a big family. Ever since she had lost her family in Alabama, Naomi had dreamt of having lots of kids to be able to carry on the family's bloodline when she was gone. She didn't care how many children she had either; all she knew was that she wanted lots of babies, and she was planning on bringing forth as many kids as she could bear.

Twenty-nine year-old Finland Xavier, during this period of time, was working for Cook County as a public defender. He also free-lanced as a criminal defense attorney by taking on cases for various gang members throughout the city who could afford to pay the $5,000 dollar retainer fee he was charging. On top of the free-lancing, Zell Verniche`, who'd paid Fin's way through college, always had a client or two for him to represent in court Pro Bono. Fin was an excellent defense attorney and had been given the nick-name 'Salamander' by Zell, because he saw that Fin was slick-sided. The man knew how to work loop-holes, but that wasn't the only angle he used. Finland Xavier also dished out bribes and outright lied to get clients off. And in a few cases, he'd had members of 23rd wipe out witnesses before the case he was on had gone to trial. To put it plainly, Finland Xavier was a prosecutor's worst nightmare.

Fin had also shocked Lucky, Naomi, and Doss one day when

he walked into *Eastside Bar* in 1981 with a short, sexy blonde named Julianne Bixby on his arms. Lucky, Naomi and Doss had never told anyone about Fin's fetish and had always assumed he was gay. When the three pulled him aside in *Eastside Bar* and asked him about the woman, Fin stated that she worked as a clerk at the Cook County Courthouse and that he and she were intimate. He then went on and told his friends that what happened with Lester had indeed hurt him, and for a while he really was confused about his sexual identity and his dressing up in women's clothing had helped him realize that he wasn't a gay man.

"I know it helped you too, Naomi. That was another reason I did it—but we are all sane and happy and the past is behind us, right?" Fin asked that cold winter day back in 1981, as everybody nodded to say yes and raised their glass of wine in a toast to health and wealth.

As Naomi sat at the poker table reminiscing about the events that had transpired over the last few years, she noticed one of the envelopes she had taken from the mailbox was from her doctor's Nurse Practitioner. She stared at the piece of mail with the understanding that what lay inside the envelope could possibly change her life forever. She'd gone to see her doctor several days ago to take a pregnancy test and had asked him to mail the test results as she wanted to reflect on the moment when the letter arrived. Now she was regretting that decision because she would be so disappointed if the results came back negative. A smile soon spread out across Naomi's face as she stared at the letter. Thoughts of a negative test result had just solidified in her mind that she was truly ready to start a family. With a hopeful spirit, Naomi got up and poured a glass of wine before she sat back down and opened the letter. After only reading two sentences, tears began to flow down her cheeks. The test results had come back positive and she was now expecting.

"I'm having a baby!" Naomi yelled aloud inside the empty home as she raised her glass and sipped her wine. She then grabbed the letter and walked over to Kevin and Serena's home and broke the news and phone calls went out immediately.

Doss was proud. And when he learned a few months later he

was having a son, he grew even more ecstatic. Naomi broke the news to Kevin and Serena in November that she was having a baby boy, but when she told them that she was going to name her son after Doss, Kevin only sighed at her statement.

"What's wrong with that, daddy?" Naomi asked as she sat on the couch in between Kevin and Serena with her feet tucked under her body.

"Naomi, you are giving him Doss' name when you are not married. Call me old-fashioned, but I just would have liked to see that man ask you to marry him." Kevin said.

"I understand, dad. Momma?" Naomi then asked Serena.

"Well," Serena said, "you know, for a long time I've been agreeing with you. You have been very respectful of my wishes early on about not having sex in my home anymore, well, your home, you stay there now, I don't. Point is baby, why not marry? If you're married, naming the child after his father will be fine. I agree with your father on this issue."

Serena knew if Naomi had disagreed she would've said so the moment Kevin expressed himself, but she didn't. Naomi's lack of protest had led her to believe that Naomi herself didn't agree with the name chosen for her son. As they talked, Serena kept noticing the somewhat distant attitude coming from Naomi. She would ask Naomi her opinion about a matter and Naomi would merely nod. Serena knew something was on Naomi's mind so she asked her what she was thinking about.

Naomi smiled and kissed Serena's cheeks. She then kissed Kevin and got on her knees and faced them and held both their hands. "For so long," she said with a beautiful smile upon her face, "for so long I had names picked out for my kids. Native American names. Nituna and Rutherford gave us all bible names. I wanted Native American names for my kids, though, because it is a part of their heritage. When I told Doss I was having his son, he just blurted out 'Doss Dawkins the third!' The people at Eastside Bar said it too. And I just went along with them. That's not me I'm not a follower, I don't think." Naomi said as she eyed Kevin and Serena.

"You're not Naomi, what name did you have in mind?" Kevin asked as he sipped a glass of red wine.

Naomi then stood up and paced the floor as she rubbed her hands nervously. "I had Blackfoot Holland, but these are modern times so I don't want to use that. Besides, we're part Creek Indian, not Blackfoot. I decided to do some research a while back. I went to the library downtown and looked up Native American names that had a modern appeal—if it was girls I had two names, Bena and Tiva, because Holland females come out as twins." Naomi said, which cause Kevin and Serena to laugh lightly. "No, it's true," Naomi said as she stopped pacing the floor and stared at Kevin and Serena, both of whom stop smiling when they saw the seriousness in Naomi's eyes. "I told you two about my twin sister Ruth, remember? And Mary and Martha are twins. Holland females come forth as twins, identical twins," she said in a matter-of-fact tone as she went back to pacing the floor. "So I had Bena and Tiva—but when I learned this child here was to be a male I had to change it. I didn't like many of the male names in the books I read so I came up with my own. I chose Dawk—Dawk Holland. He can have part of Doss' last name as his first and it still sounds Native American. What do you think, dad?"

"Perfect. Just perfect Naomi." Kevin said lowly.

"Dawk Holland! I love it! I can't wait to hold him in my arms, Naomi. What a precious name. And it really does sound as if it derives from the Native American culture." Serena said happily.

"My only problem is breaking the news to Dawk. I mean Doss." Naomi said nervously as she stared at her parents.

"Doss loves you, Naomi. I'm sure he'll be disappointed—but if he was to deny his own son because you chose not to name the baby boy after him, that wouldn't be the Doss Dawkins Junior I know." Kevin stated.

"Yeah, but Lucky, and the friends at East—"

"This is your son," Serena said as she cut Naomi's remark short. "You name him whatever you want to. Don't worry about what they say at the bar. And Kevin's right—Doss will love him the same no matter what his name is."

Doss was indeed disappointed when Naomi told him she wasn't naming her son after him, but he understood when

Naomi told him the reasons why—she was going to give all her kids Native American names—and they would all have the last name Holland until she married.

Dawk Holland came into the world on May 29, 1984. The baby boy was darker than Naomi, but lighter than Doss. He had a light-brown colored complexion and his hair was jet black and thick like Naomi's hair. He had Doss' deep, dark eyes, but had Naomi's pouty lips and button nose. And without trying, Dawk Holland always looked angry, and Doss loved that about his son.

"He got his daddy blood running through 'em." Doss said as he held his son two days after he was born. Doss was planning on raising his son to be just like him and Naomi did nothing in protest because she wanted her son to grow up strong like his father. When Dawk was able to walk, Doss and Lucky could be seen in the neighborhood back in Cicero walking their sons together. They looked like two average fathers, but as they walked with their sons, they often discussed upcoming jobs and reminisced about old ones.

Doss was proud to have a son and would've been happy ending things right there if that's what Naomi had wanted; but he knew from past talks that the birthing of Dawk Holland was only the beginning. Doss never knew how right he was, however, and neither he nor Naomi could have predicted what was to come.

On July 10, 1985, Naomi gave birth to a set of female twins, an event that had solidified her beliefs that Holland females come forth in pairs. Naomi gave her daughters Native American names, just as she had stated to Kevin and Serena nearly two years earlier. Her oldest daughter, by only a few minutes, was named Bena (Bainyah) Holland, and the younger twin was named Tiva (Teevah) Holland.

Serena had taken early retirement shortly after Dawk was born. The woman didn't have to work as she had plenty of money saved, having spent nearly thirty years in government which was well above the time required to receive full retirement pay. Serena only had two credit card bills, credit cards that she used to buy items for Dawk before he was born; and now she was spending some of her savings on Tiva and

Bena. She'd sold her '79 Mercedes shortly after Bena and Tiva were born and had purchased a station wagon in order to have adequate room for Dawk, Tiva, and Bena. The first two years of the kids' life, Serena, Kevin, and everybody else in the neighborhood spent nearly every day with the kids.

When Zell saw Tiva and Bena for the first time, he fell in love with the babies. They were tan-skinned like Naomi, and had a birthmark under their left eye like their mother as well. Bena and Tiva's hair was short and curly and they each had a button nose and dark brown eyes. Zell had a propensity to nick-name many people he came into contact with, and his getting to know Bena and Tiva would be no different. Bena got her nick-name from Zell early on when she was only a couple of months old. The seventy-eight year-old man couldn't pronounce the name Bena, so he always called her 'Bay'—it didn't take long for that name to stick.

Tiva got the nick-name 'T-top', because Doss often drove his three kids around in his Camaro with the top back and he would always say he could hear Tiva laughing as the wind blew in her face. "She likes that T-top on that car. Little T-top is what I'll call that beautiful baby." Zell told Doss in May of '86 as he watched him pull up to Eastside Bar that day, Tiva's laughter clearly being heard by the old mobster. Doss and Naomi, along with Serena and Kevin, took to the name, and before long Tiva was going by the nick-name 'T-top'.

Naomi was receiving more help with her kids than she had ever anticipated. DeeDee had bought her a mini-van to transport his grand kids, but she rarely got to use it because the children were either with Doss, DeeDee, over to Lucky's house, Mendoza's house, at the park with Zell, Mendoza and DeeDee, or spending all day, and even spending nights with Serena and Kevin. Naomi barely had time for her own kids because everyone 'had something lined up' for Dawk, Bay, and T-top, all three of whom were growing up around mobsters.

Naomi, in 1986 had three kids and a career. She was happy the rest of that year and throughout 1987 as well; but as 1988 got underway, Naomi learned she was pregnant again with another set of twins. The friends in Cicero were happy for her and Doss, but Kevin was at his wits end with Naomi over her having so many kids out of wed-lock and he constantly asked her why Doss wouldn't marry her when they were clearly becoming a family.

Naomi would reply by telling Kevin she didn't know why Doss wouldn't marry her, all she knew was that she loved him and he loved her; these debates went on for a couple of months until things came to a head between Kevin and Naomi in February of 1988. The two were in the kitchen preparing four pound burgers when Kevin again asked Naomi why she was allowing Doss to get her pregnant without marrying her.

"Dad, Doss ain't going nowhere. He loves me." Naomi responded as she seasoned the ground beef inside the sink.

"If he loves you, Naomi, you should wait until he marries you to have more kids."

"Dad, this is my life. You don't understand." Naomi responded as she looked up from the sink.

"For almost twenty-five years I have been trying to understand, Naomi. You do so well for so long and then you just up and do something—" Kevin caught himself as he knew he was about to insult Naomi, which was not his intent by a long shot.

"What?" Naomi asked, anger beginning to emerge from within. "What? I do something stupid? That's what you were going to say, right? You think I'm stupid? Momma!" Naomi cried as she stormed out of the kitchen.

Serena was in the dining room sitting at the table preparing a salad. She'd heard the argument more than once and she, too, was somewhat disappointed in Naomi. She leapt from her seat and met her in the dining room's threshold. "You're not stupid, Naomi," she said lovingly. "Just make the man you claim love you do right by you. You deserve better than to be going around having babies for a man who refuses to marry you. That's all your father is trying to say."

"Doss is not refusing to marry me. I asked him and he said he will someday. He loves me! I know he loves me!" Naomi said with heartfelt conviction as she patted her chest.

"For once can you listen to what your father is saying?"

Serena suddenly yelled as she shook Naomi, startling her into silence. "God! I've always taken up for you, Naomi! This time you have to take up for yourself! You've grown weak, child! This is not the Naomi Holland I know! You go and *demand* that Doss marries you! And stop having his kids until he does so! *I'm* telling you now! If you won't listen to your father then you listen to *me*! You are a precious woman! Not some, not some single mother having babies in order to keep a man around! Look at yourself! Stop it! Just stop it! Before you find yourself an old unmarried woman with a bunch of kids for just a man! You hear? Be a wife and not just some man's mother to his kids!" Serena said sternly as she went and sat down at the dining room table and began shredding lettuce with her bare hands in a rapid motion. She was obviously upset over Naomi's actions and blatant stubbornness to ask Doss to marry her.

Naomi remained silent as she leaned against the threshold and looked to floor and let what Serena had said to her sink in. She knew Doss was the right man for her, but she was allowing him to get her pregnant without the obligation of being married. She went along with Doss. And subconsciously, she was making plans as if she were actually going to raise her kids alone. Naomi realized, at that moment, just how right Serena was, she had indeed grown weak. As silent tears began to roll down her cheeks, Naomi walked back into the kitchen and said, "Dad, I'm sorry. I see now what you were trying to say. I'll, I'll talk to Doss seriously about what we are going to do about our future and these kids. I don't want to raise them alone—which was my thinking. I shouldn't think like that. I know Doss loves me and he'll be here for his children. I'll talk to him."

"It's your life, Naomi." Kevin said as he rested against the sink. "But the decision you've just made is the right thing to do for all involved—especially those children. Remember your past and don't ruin your future, nor that of those precious babies. Become a family. Doss loves you and he will not let you out of his life. That I know."

Naomi then went and sat at the dining room table across from Serena, who was still fuming as she shredded lettuce. She looked over to Naomi with stern eyes, eyes that said 'you know what you have to do now'. Naomi smiled, bowed her head and said, "I always feared Nituna getting angry at me for choosing the wrong man. I guess deep inside, I was living as if you would do the same, momma."

"I don't think Doss is the wrong man, Naomi. But he's a man. Commitment isn't easy for most men." Serena replied as she added chopped onions to the salad. "Your father," she said as she wiped her hands, "when I asked how he felt about marriage? He nearly choked on his eggplant."

"Did not!" Kevin yelled from the kitchen.

Serena and Naomi laughed lowly. "Yes he did," Serena whispered through a smile. She then grabbed three tomatoes and a cucumber grown in Naomi's garden from a hand woven basket and said, "I don't know what it is with men and commitment. Sometimes you just have to pull it out of them I guess. But you won't be forcing Doss. You would make a superb wife. He'd be a fool not to marry you, Naomi."

"Dad was sort of indisposed about marrying you?" Naomi asked as she reached for a knife to help cut the tomatoes.

"Thank you, dear. I wouldn't call your father reluctant," Serena replied as she began slicing the cucumber. "Kevin was more bewildered I would say. He thought he would have to give up his Sunday football before the TV, no longer enjoy grilling during the winter or an after-work beer with his colleagues. I assured him that those things would remain intact because I wasn't giving up Bridge on Fridays and wine on Saturday nights. After that incident with Viola, things changed a little, but he still has his football, and Saturday nights we spend either at the bar, or we're here at home nuzzled before the fireplace listening to Jazz albums. Our marriage is great, Naomi. Yours will be also. You've learned a lot from us I know. I toot my horn now. Toot! Toot! That's for me and your father."

Naomi smiled and reflected on the things Serena had said. She and Kevin really did have a good marriage and had set a perfect example for her. Naomi also knew at that moment that she had to do a serious gut-check. She had the hardest time figuring where she went wrong because she felt that she was always in control her life; but as she reflected further on the matter, she'd come to understand that she didn't lose control, she'd merely given it up. She told herself her kids were all going to have the last name of Holland until Doss married her and had merely left it at that. She now understood that Doss saw no problem with what she had told him early on because he knew she was bearing his kids. What difference did it make to Doss if the children had his last name or not?

Naomi was a thirty-three year-old woman with three kids and two more on the way in February of 1988 and was under the belief that everything in her life was all right. She had a career, a good job and money in the bank—but the reality of the situation was that she was having a bunch of babies for a man who didn't or wouldn't marry her at the present time and she now understood fully that she had to make that part of her life right before she went any further.

Big plans lay ahead for Naomi. She had things lined up for the future, and if Doss didn't marry her, and her second set of twins had to receive her last name, she told herself that she and Doss would be through. An ultimatum was given to Doss the following day after Naomi's discussion with Kevin and Serena where Doss was told over lunch that if he didn't make Naomi into an honest woman, he would lose a woman who loved him more than life itself, and all five of his kids at the same time.

The law had been laid down on Doss, who'd remained silent throughout the discussion. His woman had basically given him a glimpse into the future and it was now his choice. Would he be there with his family, or leave them out in the cold? The latter was not in Doss' make-up. He would deliver his love to Naomi in a special kind of way when the time was right.

CHAPTER 11
IN SPITE OF IT ALL

"My bones ache more than they used to, Naomi." Zell said as he sat in his usual booth inside *Eastside Bar*.

"You're strong, Zell. You'll be fine."

"How are those kids?"

"Fine, Zell. They're with their grandparents at the Zoo." Naomi replied.

It was a warm sunny day in March of '88; a month after Naomi had her dispute with Kevin and Serena and she was now sitting in the bar discussing an idea with Zell, the one man she believed could help her in her endeavors. Naomi was four months pregnant now and slightly showing and in spite of being tired all the time, she kept pushing forward with her ambitions.

"That's a nice gesture right there. At the Zoo, huh? Kevin and Serena are the best, Naomi."

"They are, Zell. I'm grateful to have them in my life. They really are wonderful grandparents."

"I know, Naomi." Zell stated then asked seriously. "What did you come up with, my friend?"

Naomi had decided to buy a truck—a big rig—and put it out on the road and turn a profit. She told Zell about her idea and the old gangster was glad to help. Zell knew people, and he knew how to earn a dollar; before Naomi even had an idea formulated on how she would operate her rig, he'd already put together a business plan for her: she would run live cattle and hogs from a corporate ranch just outside of Madison, Wisconsin to a meat processing plant in Ames, Iowa. From Ames, the driver would take a refrigerated load of fresh meat to various cities throughout the Midwest and west where Zell had connections—San Francisco, Kansas City, Reno, Las Vegas, Milwaukee, St. Louis, Cleveland and Detroit.

Naomi had found a truck a few weeks back and she showed a picture to Zell as the two sat at the table inside the bar. The truck was a white Mack truck, complete with a twin-sized bed, room for a refrigerator and TV and plenty of cabinet space.

Zell looked at the picture and he quickly shook his head no. "What you need is a Peterbilt rig, Naomi," he said matter-of-factly. "Peterbilt rigs are the Cadillacs of trucks. I have this guy in Des Moines, Iowa that can set you straight. You go there tomorrow and pick out a *Peterbilt* truck. All you'll have to do is sign the papers when you get there. Make sure it's a Peterbilt rig, though. You can't go wrong with a Peterbilt truck."

"I'll need someone to deliver the truck back to the old neighborhood. I don't have a CDL."

"Don't worry about that," Zell stated as he patted Naomi's hand. "Just call me when you've chosen the truck. I'll get it home."

The next day, Naomi and Doss made the five hour drive to Des Moines, Iowa where Naomi chose a black, 1988 Peterbilt. The truck was far more lavish than the Mack truck she had chosen and it had far more amenities. The driver Naomi hired in advance to drive her truck would indeed be truly comfortable and have all the creature comforts he would ever need while he was out on the road. Naomi had set up a fuel card for the driver and had allotted the driver twenty dollars a day for meals. She had a TV and refrigerator placed in the truck, a cobra 29 CB radio, cassette player, leather and heated vibrating seats, carpet throughout, and cruise control. Naomi also installed a microwave and had a portable hibachi grill for the driver as well. The driver would have a home away from home when on the road.

A week later, Naomi was in Serena's front yard with her three kids awaiting the truck's delivery. Everybody was around this warm Saturday evening. Kevin and Serena were out in their yard with a grill full of burgers and ribs. Mendoza and Francine seemed to be busy as well; a delectable smell of sausage and tomato sauce was coming from their home. Fin was on hand with Julianne, and Lucky, Mildred and Junior were out on the block as well. Naomi had told everyone her new rig was being delivered this day, but she never expected to have a celebration.

"So, Naomi, this guy you got driving this truck? Is he stand-up?" Lucky asked as he and Naomi talked on the sidewalk in front of Serena's home.

"Lucky, I don't need a stand-up guy. I hired a driver. He is just a driver."

"You know if he fucks up, if he's late with his vig one time? One time his ass is late? We'll—"

"This isn't a racket, Lucky. My driver isn't giving me a vig."

"I know a racket when I see one. And this fits the description. I like it though. I wish I had your smarts, Naomi."

Naomi hugged Lucky quickly and thanked him for the compliment and went and sat in Serena's yard with her three kids. A game of patty-cake with Tiva was interrupted a few minutes later when she heard a rumbling sound coming down the street. Naomi got up from the grass and stepped out in the middle of the street and looked and saw the truck she had bought the week before. A maroon Cadillac was in front the truck and Naomi recognized it as being Zell's car. Everybody stopped what they were doing and watched as Zell's car rolled to halt and he slowly emerged from his car. The old mobster was handed his cane and was assisted by two of his bodyguards over towards Kevin and Serena. Naomi didn't know what was transpiring, but she knew if Zell was in the neighborhood, it had to be huge.

Zell had one of his bodyguards go over to Kevin's home and Naomi watched as the man talked to him and Serena before he produced a clip board. At that moment, Kevin laughed and shook the man's hand and Serena screamed aloud with delight. Naomi was totally confused over what was transpiring and she was more than eager to know what the gesture was about as the body guard walked back into the street and waved the truck forward.

Naomi stared at the truck in the road as she stood motionless, holding her daughter Bay, who had run out into the street to be with her mother. One of Zell's bodyguards grabbed a hold of T-top and handed her to Zell and everybody watched as the truck began rolling forward. Naomi watched with a baffled expression on her face as the truck traveled slowly, gently nudging tree branches aside as it made its way to the block. The big rig stopped before Serena's home and DeeDee exited the cab and said through a wide smile, "I have a special delivery, Naomi."

"DeeDee, you didn't have to drive this truck all the way from Des Moines. Zell had a driver scheduled to pick it up today."

"We gave him the day off! Anyways *I* had to deliver this load!" DeeDee remarked as he climbed out of the rig.

"Load? What load?" Naomi asked.

"Your husband, Naomi." DeeDee said.

Naomi went silent. She had a look of shock on her face as she held Bay in her arms. "No, DeeDee, he didn't, he not."

"He is, my sweet daughter-in-law to be. Naomi Holland, I deliver to you on this day, your future husband, Doss Dawkins Junior." DeeDee said as Kevin and Serena ran towards Naomi as her friends clapped and cheered while slowly walking forward to join her family in the middle of the street.

Doss climbed out of the truck and took to one knee in front of Serena's home and proposed. He had Kevin approve of him marrying Naomi by signing the clip board, and he delivered his love to his woman in the month of March in the year of 1988. The long-time couple married a week later with a lavish wedding on Kevin's lawn in the old neighborhood.

1988 was a great year for Naomi. She had married and given birth to her second set of identical twins on August 8, 1988. She named them Kimi (Kimmie) Dawkins, who was the oldest by several minutes, and Koko Dawkins. Right away people could see that Kimi and Koko were exact replicas of Naomi; only they had light brown eyes and brown hair. Everything else, the lips, the nose, and their thickness, was Naomi through and through, right along with the birth mark under their left eye. Doss had to admit that he didn't do much with his fourth and fifth child because they were the spitting image of his wife, miniature Naomis they were.

By the end of 1988, Naomi's trucking business was up and running and she was still doing well in her practice and was still birthing kids. She had gotten pregnant in late December of 1989 and gave birth to another son named Walee Dawkins on October 17, 1990. Walee was a slender baby, a mixture of both Doss and Naomi. He had a head full of hair, round, dark eyes, a cute nose with dark tan-skin. Right away Walee was dubbed 'pretty boy' by his father.

Naomi had her tubes tied after Walee was born, but she had regretted that she had done so as she wanted more kids. To her delight, she learned she was pregnant again in April of 1991. Her friends had repeatedly asked her to sue the hospital, but Naomi refused. She knew she was having twins before she even found out the sex of her unborn child. When her beliefs were confirmed, Naomi called them her miracle babies and she had their names picked out early on.

The friends in Cicero were waiting anxiously for Shima (Sheema) Dawkins who was to be the oldest, and Sinopa (Suhnopah) Dawkins to be brought forth, but Naomi's youngest two would not be born in Cicero. The reason being was because Naomi, while reading the *Chicago Sun Times* for lunch one day in May of 1991, had come to learn of the Oklahoma Land Restoration Act. Naomi, at two months pregnant, decided to step down from the law firm in hopes of finding her grandparents' land, which from what she could remember, was in the state of Oklahoma.

Naomi had been in Cicero for most of her life and her career, business venture, and family life were going along at a successful and rapid pace as the nineties got underway. Her kids were adapting to life in the Chicago vicinity as well, but when Naomi learned she could possibly regain her grandparents' land, she made an abrupt decision to head to Oklahoma. She had amassed some wealth, in the low six-figures, and she still had her trucking business to expand upon. Naomi knew if she found her grandparents' land, she may move away from Cicero for good and that knowledge had brought about a hard decision she had chosen for her family; but with the chance for her to have land of her own to raise her family, Naomi felt that she was making the right decision and the move would be worth it in deed. She knew she would be missed, but if her people had land in Oklahoma, Naomi felt she had to find it. And if she found it, she would bring the land back to its rightful owners by any means necessary.

People had taken from the Holland family once before and Naomi was not going to let it happen again. It took weeks of talking it over with Doss, Kevin and Serena, debating with members at the law firm, and agonizing doubt from within Naomi against her own self-doubt to make one of the biggest decisions of her life. She told Kevin and Serena, who were worried how she would fair in Oklahoma, that they themselves said it was her life. She told her friends that finding her family's land was now too strong a driving force.

"Ever since I learned of this restoration act I can't function right any more. It's on my mind constantly. I just have to go see." Naomi told Doss, Lucky, Mendoza, Fin and Zell inside *Eastside Bar* a few weeks after reading the article.

"Baby, we have a good life here in Chicago. Why disrupt it?" Doss asked.

"When they took Sam, Martha and Mary from me, Doss? I died on the inside. Kevin and Serena resurrected me and gave me a second chance at life. People have stolen from my family once and I can't let them do it again."

DeeDee leaned back in the booth and said, "You taking my grandkids to a place no one has ever been, Naomi. Aren't you worried something will happen? Like what happened back in Alabama?"

"No. I know that my friends and family here in Cicero will be there to avenge us if something like was to take place. Times have indeed changed, though, DeeDee. And this is something I have to do. I just have to do it. "

"What would be the benefit of moving away? Even if you find the land, Naomi?" Lucky asked.

"The benefit would be that what rightfully belongs to the

Holland family can be—restored. Understand, Lucky?"

"I see your point," Lucky replied. "But, you're a lawyer. What do you know about—" Lucky then caught himself when he eyed Naomi curling her lips to the side. "The garden," he said as he laughed. "The rooster."

"The one you ate!" Naomi snapped as she smiled and tapped Lucky's hand. "I know about land."

"I give you that, il mio amico," Lucky responded. "Doss? Whatever you decide my man, I'm with you. But knowing Naomi like I do? I think this may be a good thing."

"I'm thinking what would I do down there, though? All my business is here in the city." Doss remarked.

"Well, son," DeeDee chimed in, "you can always return and do business. And now that I think about it, this move may be to your benefit."

"How, dad?"

"Still learnin'," Mendoza said. "If what Naomi is sayin' is true. Doss? You'd be at an advantage."

"Mendoza's right, Doss," Naomi said as she stared into her husband's eyes. "I know what and who you are. And I love the life we have here in Cicero—but ever since I read that article, I been dreaming of having land. My own land. *Our* own land. We have Serena's house and your condo, but wouldn't it be beautiful to raise kids on a wide-open ranch? Get in touch with the land?"

Doss laughed to himself. He was a killer for hire in Chicago, not a rancher 'in touch with the land' in Oklahoma, but he would support his wife's dreams. And the more Doss thought about it, the more he let sink in what Mendoza had said about him having an advantage. If Naomi really did have land in Oklahoma, he would love to have his kids raised far away, in a safer environment where enemies couldn't get to them. With those thoughts in mind, Doss agreed to make the trip with Naomi to at the very least, find out if the land even existed. Within a month, he and Naomi had made arrangements to drive to Oklahoma and search for her parents' land.

CHAPTER 12
THEY WERE HERE ONCE

It was now late June of 1991, and thirty-six year-old Naomi was sitting in the last booth inside *Eastside Bar* with eighty-three year-old Zell Verniche`, who wanted to talk to her alone before she left town. Zell's chauffeur poured them both a glass of wine and backed away from the table and the two friends talked a little while longer.

"Do you have any regrets, Naomi?"

"None whatsoever, Zell. In fact, I wish I could've done more."

"Like what, il mio amico?"

"Like find my brother and sisters before I left here. This new move will have me putting on hold my search for them. That was supposed to be the next phase of my life. I was supposed to begin looking for them again. But now I'm married and have six kids and two more on the way."

"You started a family by choice, Naomi. That has nothing to do with you finding your blood. All these years I've known you, I've never known you to not be able to handle two or more major tasks at a single time."

"Thank you, Zell. I just wish, well, a lot of good has been going on in my life these past few years. I often wonder how my family is doing. Are they okay? Alive even? Are they struggling? Do they know who I am? Those questions haunt me constantly. And knowing I have to put that search on hold only adds to my anxiety over them and prolongs what I hope to be a happy reunion."

"Things happen for a reason, Naomi. You've heard me say that before. I see you going down there and building something beautiful. This just feels right all of a sudden."

"You were adamant about me not going. Now you offer?"

"My blessings, Naomi," Zell replied as he sat his cigar down and looked her directly in the eyes. "The first day I laid eyes on you back in nineteen seventy-one I had a feeling you were going to do great things and you have. But this? This here is by far the greatest moment of your life. Seize it and make it yours. Go down there and claim what's rightfully yours. Find that land, and from there, I have this, this gut feeling that what you've longed for for so long will come to pass."

Naomi's eyes watered at that moment because Zell had spoken aloud what she'd been thinking ever since she'd made the decision to move her family to Oklahoma. She believed in his words. She felt herself, that if she earned her grandparents' land, that all the ills that her family had suffered early on would be washed away. Not from memory, however, but washed away in the sense that the family could have a new start.

"Zell," Naomi said as she reached out and grabbed the man's hands, "you've been more than a friend to me. I love you, old man. I'll never forget what you've done for me."

"What happened back in nineteen seventy-six was just the start, Naomi. You now have all the tools you need mentally to take on this challenge. The tools needed to find your family, to earn back that land, and to become one of the most successful people I've ever known. You and Doss? You two are by far amongst some of the best to come out of this thing of ours," Zell said as he handed Naomi an envelope stuffed with hundred dollar bills. "A little something to help you get started down there in Oklahoma. And if you need help, like what happened in your past before you met Kevin? Don't hesitate to call. We're all hoping for the best outcome in you and Doss' plan, Naomi."

Naomi got up and went to the other side of the table and hugged Zell tightly. She then whispered in his ear, "Thank you,

Santa. But the gift you bring, for some reason, I feel it will not be needed. It'll be very peaceful down there. My heart says so. But I'll keep your number close just in case."

"Be safe, Naomi. And look after those babies." Zell ended as he relinquished his grip on Naomi and leaned back in his seat. "Salute."

"Salute." Naomi replied as she wiped a few tears, turned away and headed towards the front of the bar where the rest of the friends were hanging out.

Everybody from the old neighborhood was on hand to see the Holland-Dawkins family off and to wish them a safe trip. Kevin and Serena wanted to join the family at the start, but Naomi wasn't sure if she would be able to find the land; but if she did, she would send for them both so they could have a lengthy visit. She had left Fin in charge of her trucking company, *Holland Express, LLC* and everything was set in place.

Mildred took hold of Naomi's hand the moment she stepped outside and walked her to the Winnebago that Doss had leased. She was standing to Naomi's left, shielding her as Serena and Kevin walked towards the family's car to retrieve precious items for Naomi.

"You have a safe trip, Naomi. I can't wait to see what the land looks like."

"Thanks, Mildred. The only thing is…you will have to listen to Lucky—"

"Complain about why you took Dawk away from his big brother Junior? He's already started." Mildred said as she and Naomi laughed lightly and began to strap the children into their car seats.

Doss, meanwhile, was talking to his father and Lucky. "You gonna look over the gambling room while I'm down there, right," he asked Lucky as they stood just outside the bar with several other mobsters.

"Yeah. I got it covered. Me and a couple of guys headed that way tonight. DeeDee's setting up the new arrangement. You ever had any problems over to that place?"

"Nah. Those are working people coming through.

Remember, no loans or tabs. Except on the liquor, we get that for little or nothing anyway." Doss replied.

"Okay. But I'm still bringing in extra muscle just in case." Lucky remarked.

"I always carried when over there. By the way, if any contracts come down I'm up for it. Just give me a couple of days to travel back." Doss stated.

"Okay you're in, il mio amico. Be sure to take plenty pictures." Lucky replied.

"Why?" DeeDee asked. "It's flat and dry out there. You'll be back when you get thirsty down in that wasteland, son."

Doss laughed and said, "For all we know, we could be going to the promised land. Naomi hasn't slept in two days she's so excited about this trip."

"Lotta steak down that way." Mendoza said as he exited the bar and stood amongst the men. "Make sure, make sure you eat a nice steak while you're down there."

"Eat a steak? That's the best advice you can give, Mendoza?" DeeDee asked through laughter.

"What? I hope Naomi does find her parents' land. That way, when Francine and I visit, we can have a nice hearty steak in the steak capitol of the world."

"That's why you spreading now." Francine said to her husband.

"What do you know about it?"

"I know plenty about it." Francine replied as she patted Mendoza's round belly. "You're gonna catch up to Zell if you don't slow down." she stated as the group chuckled.

Fin was on hand to see Naomi off as well. "Have a safe trip, Naomi. I'm gonna miss you. We had, we had some fun times," he said as he picked Kimi up from her stroller and passed her to Mildred.

"We did, Fin." Naomi replied as she strapped Walee into his car seat. "Times that I'll never forget. Thank you for looking after the trucking company. Call me if you need anything."

"Will do, but this is a cake walk. I like the business. I'm learning a lot."

"That's good. Take care of yourself." Naomi replied as she hugged Fin tightly and returned to strapping her children in for the trip.

All the friends were gathered out front now watching Naomi as Doss went and got behind the wheel. Francine was about to speak aloud when she saw Serena approaching, but Serena silenced her and tip-toed towards Naomi.

"You forgot something." Serena said with a smile as she stood directly behind Naomi.

"What, momma?" Naomi asked as she buckled Koko into her car seat.

"Your sisters and brother. They want to see what Oklahoma looks like too."

Naomi turned around and saw Serena holding her three raggedly Anne dolls and her eyes grew wide. "Oh God. How could I? Momma, believe me I—"

"It's okay, Naomi," Serena said lowly. The two women then embraced, clutching the dolls as Kevin soon joined in and hugged Naomi.

"Your siblings are still out there. I believe you helped them when you went to Alabama." Kevin whispered into Naomi's ear.

Naomi drew back and looked Kevin in the eyes. "You knew about that, dad?" she asked in disbelief.

"We both knew," Kevin answered. "But we don't judge you. Not for marrying Doss. Not for what you've done. You're ours, understand? Our only child. When I read about that big fire in Alabama and the other thing with those people, I knew it was you, Naomi. You did what I didn't have the courage to do from the sixties up until now—seek justice. I don't agree with what you've done, but, I understand. I understand."

"Dad? I'm lucky you worked at that home. You saved my life. You literally saved my life. And this, this is hard for me, but I have to do it. When, when I find our land, I'll—"

"We'll be here, Naomi—waiting, hoping, and praying that all goes well. Now go, before we hold you hostage here in Cicero." Kevin stated as Serena handed Naomi the three dolls.

With a face full of tears, Naomi stepped back and turned and got into the Winnebago and slowly, Doss merged with the traffic. "I love you! I love you all!" Naomi screamed from behind the window as she watched her parents, and her friends disappear into the background.

****

It took two days to reach Oklahoma City, the state capitol of Oklahoma. Naomi's plan was to look at state records and see if she saw her mother's name anywhere because she didn't remember her grandparents' names. Nituna spoke of them occasionally, but Naomi just couldn't remember.

Naomi and Doss, with kids in tow, walked towards the state capitol building and entered and found the office that held landowners' records. Naomi was delighted to see a staff of mostly Native Americans working inside the office because she felt that the workers would be receptive to her inquiries. She walked up to the counter and a young Native American approached and said, "Good morning ma'am. Are you here to participate in the Oklahoma Land Restoration Act?"

"Yes. But we're not sure where the land is located and we only have my mother's name. Nothing more."

"That's okay. What's your mother's name?" the young woman asked with a smile.

"Holland. Nituna Holland."

"Okay, Nituna Holland. I'm Siloam, by the way."

"I'm Naomi Holland."

The young woman smiled and sat down at a computer. She entered Nituna's name into a data base system, but Nituna's name didn't come up. "Did she go by any other name?" the woman asked.

"I can't remember."

"Well, where did she come from?"

"We all were from Sylacauga, Alabama." Naomi replied.

The woman typed in Sylacauga, Alabama and found a host of Native American names. Finally, after scrolling down the list, she came across the name Nituna, with the last name being Grunion. "There's a Nituna Grunion. Sound familiar?" the young woman asked as she looked up from her computer screen.

"No, I can't remember the name Grunion. I'm sorry." Naomi replied sadly.

"That's okay. Let's cross reference the name Grunion and see what we can come up with."

Naomi watched the woman work as she held onto Walee, the rest of the kids sitting in small wagons eating cookies and being jolly with their father.

"Well," the young woman said a few minutes later, "there's a Grunion family in the registrar. The land is in Kay County near a town called Ponca City. The original owners were Apollo and Sapphire Grunion, but the state owns it now."

Naomi believed she would now have to fight for the land. She placed her free hand to her forehead in frustration and began thinking of lawyers she could contact back in Chicago. Siloam, however, noticed her distress and told her that she could help. "It's really not that difficult to reclaim the land, Naomi," she said. "All we have to do is find proof that your family was actually there. Believe me, the federal government doesn't want a law suit, and after all that our people have been through? They aren't making it hard to reclaim what's rightfully ours. Now, the land is north east of Ponca City, about an hour and a half, maybe two hours north of here. Why don't you find a place to stay tonight and meet me here tomorrow morning around eight and we'll drive there and find the land and see if we can locate documents, pictures, or anything else that proves your family was there."

"That's all we have to do?" Naomi asked somewhat unsure of the woman's over-eagerness.

"Naomi, trust me, if your family was there once, the land is yours. The federal government is being bombarded with lawsuits by Native Americans claiming land and money was swindled from their predecessors and they are winning those cases. Most are being settled. But before you file a lawsuit, I know for a fact that it's worth a look because something may be there to prevent litigation."

The next day, Naomi, Doss, their six kids and the young

woman drove north to Ponca City. Naomi and Doss learned during the trip that the young woman was named Siloam Bovina (Boveenya). She was a full-bloodied Cherokee Indian that lived alone, orphaned early in life and was now an eighteen year-old volunteer worker at the state building. Siloam was a thick woman like Naomi; she had high cheek bones and coarse, dark brown hair with tan skin and hazel eyes and stood about 5' 8", the same height as Naomi coincidently. Siloam had what seemed to be a permanent smile on her face. Her hazel eyes radiated joy and optimism, as if something good lay just around the corner and she knew exactly where the prize lay and was heading directly towards it. Despite her somewhat turbulent past, Siloam Bovina seemed to be at peace with herself and with life in general. She was a very pleasant person to be around because she just simply radiated positivity, even when she wasn't speaking.

Naomi felt an instant connection with Siloam and Doss and the kids liked her as well. As they rode, Naomi allowed the young woman to feed Walee, listening in as Siloam fed her youngest son with a smile on her face while humming lyrics to a song that she was familiar with.

"What's that song's title?" Naomi asked.

"It's by Elton John, Naomi. One of my favorite songs."

"I noticed you have a guitar. Can you play?" Naomi asked.

"I most certainly can. Would you like to hear?"

"Sure."

"Okay. I'll play Elton's song and I'll sing it for you." Siloam said lowly she wiped Walee's mouth clean and grabbed her guitar.

As Doss drove the RV north up Highway 177, Siloam began stringing her guitar. Dawk, Bena, Tiva, Kimi and Koko were playing amongst themselves, but they grew quiet when they heard the melodic music in their little ears. Doss reached over and grabbed his wife's hand just as Siloam began to sing..."*It's a little bit funny...this feeling inside...I'm not one of those who could...easily hide...I don't have much money...but, boy if I did...I'd buy big a big house where...we both could live...*"

"How wonderful life is!" Naomi said aloud, remembering the

name of the song.

"No, Naomi. The actual title is Your Song. A lot of people make that mistake so you're not alone. Aren't the lyrics the coolest?" Siloam replied.

"You have a lovely voice, Siloam."

"Thank you," Siloam replied as she continued to sing, looking into the big, round, brown eyes of Kimi and Koko..."*So excuse for forgetting...but these things I do...you see I've forgotten...if they're green or blue...Anyway the thing is...what I really mean...those are the sweetest eyes...I've ever seen...*"

Naomi enjoyed the peaceful and melodic voice coming from Siloam as she and her family rode towards Ponca City and she soon joined in on the chorus..."*And you can tell everybody... this is your song...it may be quite simple but now that it's done...I hope you don't mind...I hope you don't mind...that I put down in words...how wonderful life is...while you're in the world...*" Naomi laughed aloud as she and Siloam brought the song to an end. She couldn't help but notice how good the young woman was with children and she especially admired her demeanor. It was fair to say that Naomi was growing fond of Siloam as they rode towards Ponca City.

The group reached the town after an hour and a half ride and Siloam, who'd directed the family to Ponca City without having to use a map, guided them east through town onto U.S. Highway 60 and over a lake to a road that headed north for a few miles. She had Doss make a left turn when the road t-boned into another four-lane road, and after another mile or so, Siloam had found the location that may contain Naomi's grandparents' land, which sat on the left side of the road.

Doss turned off the main road and stopped before a rotted wooden fence that had a rusted chain around it. Just before the fence was a freshly-painted side that read: *213 Acres of unclaimed but previously developed property. Acreage claimed by the state of Oklahoma on said date of February 22, 1961. All unclaimed property and items therein are for sale upon closure of the Oklahoma Land Restoration Act at $3,000 per acre.*

Siloam and Naomi exited the vehicle and Naomi wrote down the names of the contactees within the state while Doss removed the rusted chain and pushed open the wooden gate leading on to the property. The group then climbed back into the vehicle and Doss began a slow drive down a winding dirt road that lay in between a thick row of trees that lined either side of the road for several hundred yards. The road ended where the trees cleared, and it was at that point that a vast expansion of hilly, lush green land came into view.

Doss, Naomi and Siloam stared in awe at the countryside. The property was like one huge garden, hidden away from the road by the trees, and had the three feeling as if they'd stepped into another world. As far as one could see there was nothing but land—grassy, hilly land that featured a thick, dark green canopy of trees on both sides—and the beauty that their eyes were feasting on, they all knew, was only what they could see on the surface and at first glance. What else lay hidden remained to be seen, and all three wanted to explore further because the land, in a word, was captivating.

Doss went and opened the door on the Winnebago to let the kids out and immediately, seven year-old Dawk, and five year-olds Bay and T-top emerged and took off running into the open field with two year-olds Kimi and Koko following, their short legs barely able to keep up. Naomi watched as her kids ran and jumped about in the grass asking aloud was this place going to be their new home.

"I hope so, kids. I really do hope it is." Naomi replied as she looked over the land.

Naomi saw tree-lined hills in the distance on either side extending southwards for about a half mile. The trees surrounded the land, creating a natural border to the east and west around the lush, green field. There was a huge barn that sat atop a mound off to the left with three silos beside it and two stage coaches out front. She walked a bit of ways into the grass and quickly discovered that she was at the beginning of a narrow dirt road that was nearly overgrown with vegetation. The city, or maybe the state, had maintained the road leading fully onto the property, but they went no further. The barn was what was grasping Naomi's attention and she had made up her mind that she began searching for proof of ownership there; she began walking that way as she gathered her oldest three. The kids had just made it back to their mother when a snake emerged from underneath a fallen piece of wood and slithered into the grass. Naomi grabbed for her kids, but Dawk, Bay and T-top merely took off running in the opposite direction, believing their mother was chasing them in order to play.

"There's snakes out there!" Naomi yelled as Doss and Siloam followed her.

Upon hearing the word 'snake', the horseplay and laughter amongst the children ceased. Dawk scooped up Kimi, Bay snatched up Koko, and the two, along with T-top, ran back towards their mother. The look on their faces was priceless. Eyes wide, mouths open screaming, Kimi and Koko bouncing like rag dolls in their siblings' arms and laughing hysterically as the gang of five ran pass Naomi, back to the Winnebago where T-top opened the door to let her siblings in and slammed the door shut behind herself once she climbed aboard.

Five little heads soon emerged in the windshield and passenger side window of the Winnebago. "We good right here, momma," Dawk said on behalf of everybody.

Naomi stood laughing as Siloam chuckled and said, "That snake was a timber rattlesnake, Naomi. It's a poisonous one. They usually steer clear of humans and you never really encounter them. If that snake is moving about like that then that means that there is a great source of food around. The land may be infested with rodents. When you clear the land, you must remove the rodents and rubbish piles and the snakes will leave naturally."

"Yes. We will definitely have to do that. The kids like to get out and play and I don't need a medical emergency."

"I know. But snakes are easy to control so long as the land is tended to."

Doss was holding onto Walee as he looked over the field that seemed to go on forever. He also kept jumping at the slightest movement of wind-blown grass. Doss didn't' want to get bit either; if this was truly Naomi's land, he would make certain that the land was cleared of snakes at all costs. He held onto

Walee and walked very cautiously, constantly eyeing the ground around him.

"You okay back there, Doss?" Naomi asked when she saw Doss standing in one place looking around at the land.

"Yeah. I'm fine, baby. I'm umm, I'm just taking it all in."

"It is breathtaking isn't it?" Naomi asked as she resumed walking.

"Yes it is." Doss answered lowly as he stared at the land without blinking.

Doss saw so much potential in the land. The family had plenty of room to build a house and he could play out in the field with his kids and wouldn't have to worry about them getting hit by cars, which was a serious probability in Cicero. The man was hoping that the land belonged to Naomi because this was truly the American dream. What every man wants for his family. It was what Doss wanted for his family. The land was fit for life. The kids would have timeless fun exploring the field and the surrounding woods. There was a creek that flowed through the land where the kids could swim, if the water wasn't too deep, and maybe even fish.

Doss had come to see what his wife had being saying all along: that they could raise their kids on their own land and give them a life that many people could only dream of giving their children. Here they would be safe, far removed from the violence of Chicago. He returned to the family's vehicle and stood outside with Walee and watched Naomi and Siloam's figures get smaller and smaller as they walked off into the distance headed towards the barn.

"Daddy, we wanna see more." Bay said as she and Tiva stuck their heads out the window.

"They have snakes out there, Bay. It's a little dangerous."

"Not if you put us the wagons." Bay remarked.

"Who's gonna pull the wagons? Because I'm climbing inside myself."

"Daddy, you too big to fit in!" T-top said through laughter.

"You kids really wanna go up there?"

"Yeah, but only in the wagons!" Bay answered.

"Okay. It'll take a while because I'll have to pull both wagons myself. But if I see another snake we turning around, okay?"

"Yayyyyyy! Let's go everybody!" T-top yelled aloud as she and Dawk grabbed the two red wagons.

Doss placed his kids into the red wagons, plump Kimi and Koko along with Bay in one, and T-top, Dawk and Walee in the other and began trudging across the land. Uphill was the hardest, and the kids were adamant about not walking. Downhill was a lot easier, though. Doss was having a hard time in some areas pulling the kids in their wagons, but he continued on. Halfway towards the barn, Doss was ascending a small hill when he lost his grip and slowly, the wagon containing Kimi, Koko and Bay began to roll back down the slightly sloping hill.

"Here we go!" Bay exclaimed happily as she turned around and faced downhill with a wide smile on her face. She'd been wishing for this to happen the whole time.

Doss tried to grab hold the wagon, but he'd just missed the side rails. It seemed like it happened in slow motion when the wagon began rolling downhill. Kimi and Koko were facing their father with wide smiles on their faces, totally oblivious to what was about to happen, but blissfully joyful at the same time.

"We 'bouta go onna roller coaster ride, daddy!" Bay yelled excitedly as the wagon rolled away.

"Bay! Bay!" Doss yelled.

"Wheeeeee!" Bay yelled aloud with her hands in the air as the wagon began moving downhill.

Two year-olds Kimi and Koko fell back against Bay and held on to the sides of the wagon and were laughing uncontrollably as the wagon bounced up and down while rolling downhill. A hump in the land forced the red wagon into the air, tilting it over onto its right side before it landed on all four wheels and continued rolling until it came to a stop in a small valley in between the hills.

Bay, Kimi and Koko were crying laughing. All three siblings wanted to do it again so Bay got out to push the wagon back uphill. She hadn't set foot on the land all but a few seconds when she remembered the snakes and quickly climbed back into the wagon. "Daddy! We need help down here," she yelled.

"We wanna go on the roller coaster!" Dawk then yelled. "Daddy, let our wagon go so we can we roll downhill!"

Doss looked and saw that Bay and her younger sisters were okay. They were just waiting on him to finish pulling them towards the barn. He was worried that they would get hurt, believing he'd erred when he lost his grip, but the hillside's land was basically smooth and the ride did seem fun and the kids had obviously enjoyed it.

"We coming down, Bay. Y'all stay put." Doss yelled downhill as he picked Walee up and sat sideways in the wagon. What Bay and her sisters had done seemed like innocent fun and now Doss wanted to try it with his other three kids.

T-top made room for her father and together, the four rode downhill. A little slower than the ride Bay, Kimi and Koko had seconds earlier, but it was still a real rush for the kids. Doss spent a lot of time with his offspring back in Illinois and his work never interfered with his home life. The gangster cared about his family tremendously and was never one to not show love to his kids, nor was he the type of father who was hands off. To the contrary, whenever Doss spent time with his kids, he made sure to make the best of it and gave them something to remember and talk about. Time shared with his kids was always utilized to the fullest and given out of genuine love. Already, memories were being created in Oklahoma that would last a lifetime, and Doss knew it-all-too-well.

"God, I hope this is ours." Doss said to himself as he climbed out of the wagon laughing right along with his kids. "Alright gang," Doss then said, "let's go find momma."

Doss and the kids reached the barn a short while later where Naomi and Siloam were searching. The barn sat atop a hill so the dirt floor had a slight slope to it. Hay was strewn about the ground floors inside the barn and the place was emanating a pungent smell.

Dawk, Bay, T-top, Kimi and Koko were now out of their wagons and standing outside the barn kicking up dust and turning over rocks. "Daddy we saw a snake. He crawled under that hole." Dawk said as he ran up and tugged on Doss' pant leg and pointed to a hole that led back into the barn.

"Naomi, they—"

"I know, Doss. Siloam says the snakes are just as afraid of us as we are them. You and the kids stay outside the barn. We saw several snakes in here too and we'll be out in a minute." Naomi remarked.

Naomi and Siloam found nothing of value in the barn, which was filled with nothing but old clothes and rusted farm tools. Rotten hay bales were scattered throughout and the wooden rafters appeared to be dry-rotted in some spots. The ladies emerged from the barn and Doss and the kids followed them as they walked around the left side of the wooden structure through knee-length grass, all the while looking out for snakes as they approached the crest of the hill. When they reached the backside of the barn they saw a herd of about thirty or so cattle casually traversing the land that lay in the wide valley below.

"Someone left behind cattle." Siloam said.

"How could they survive without humans around?" Doss asked.

"They are adaptable," Siloam answered as she pointed to the bottom of the tree-lined hill to her right. "There's a stream over there to the west that flows south and curves back east into the woods, and the grass throughout this land is lush. There's plenty to eat and plenty to drink here. I'm surprised there aren't more cattle."

Naomi stood looking over the valley, swaying gently from side to side with a look of contentment on her face as she watched the herd of cattle lumber gently across the land, headed towards the stream to drink. In her mind, even if the land wasn't hers, she had enough money to buy at least twenty acres of land, but twenty acres could never compare to the 213 acres that may possibly belong to her family. Naomi wanted it all now, and she was in agreement with Doss and Siloam also when they said that the land was awe-inspiring, but paradisiac would be a more fitting description for the area in her eyes. The land was exquisite, tranquil and pristine, even in its run down state if Naomi had to tell it. The cattle marched on westward across the land, clearing the group's line of vision and unwittingly allowing a small log cabin to come into view.

"There's the home!" Siloam yelled excitedly as she descended into the low land behind the barn.

The group followed Siloam downhill and enjoyed a long, leisurely walk that took nearly fifteen minutes across lush green grass that was now becoming heavily sprinkled with patches of cow dung. "You could grow *excellent* crops here, Naomi," Siloam said in near amazement. "This place here is very fertile. You can build a fence halfway across the land to separate the cattle and have a place to do farming. Awesome land your grandparents have."

"It's not ours yet. We may not even be in the right location." Naomi remarked.

"I think we are in the right place, Naomi. I have a real good feeling. This place is beautiful!" Siloam exclaimed before she giggled like a little girl and began to race Dawk, Bay, T-top, Kimi and Koko across the land towards the log cabin.

Naomi couldn't help but to smile as she watched Siloam, who was a naturally optimistic and fun-loving person, run behind her children. When they reached the log cabin, Naomi's kids, out of breath and full of joyous laughter, sat down on the dry rotted wooden steps of the log cabin and called for their father and younger brother. Doss walked up and sat Walee down and went into a bag and began giving juice to the kids while Naomi and Siloam entered the log cabin and began another search.

"Hmm, not too sturdy. The barn is *much* sturdier than this place. Your grandfather passed away before your grandmother." Siloam stated sadly.

"How do you know that? I mean, just by looking at the two buildings how could you tell, Siloam?" Naomi asked.

"Because the barn seems to have been under renovation once upon a time. You can tell by the tools and the saw horses inside the building. Some of the rafters look newer in certain areas too. Progress was halted there and it seems as if no other men were around to carry on the renovating process. I hope I'm not dampening the mood, Naomi. I'm just trying to give you an idea of what may have possibly happened."

"No, no, I'm intrigued by your insight, Siloam."

"Thank you. My best guess is your grandfather got sick and could no longer tend the land. He died suddenly and your mother passed away without securing the proper paperwork to preserve the land for the family's heirs, which is you and your family, Naomi."

"Is that good or bad?"

"That's a hard question. Bad the way it ended a long time back—but it could be real good for your family today."

"How so?"

"Because what we need has to be here because the barn is desolate. If your people were indeed here, what we need is hidden somewhere inside this cabin. If your grandmother did nothing else, I believe she at least left proof that they were here once." Siloam said as she pressed her boots to the floor heavily.

Naomi walked around the cabin following Siloam as she watched her tap the floor with the heel of her boot, making sure not to miss a spot. "What are you doing now?" Naomi asked inquisitively.

"A lot of people here in Oklahoma have either a cellar or a sunken safe built into the floor to protect their important possessions and documents from storms and tornadoes." Siloam said as she continued to tap the floor with her heel. She tapped one place in particular and it produced a hollow sound which caused her to get down on her knees and knock around on the floor. Siloam then ran her hands across the wooden floor and found a crease and pulled hard and a door popped open. "Okay," she said with a wide smile, excited over the discovery, "if this really is your people's land, Naomi, something should be here to *prove* that it is your family's land."

Naomi helped Siloam pull up a trunk and the two pried it open with a switch blade. There inside the trunk, Naomi saw a pile of hand woven, faded-tan wool blankets. She grabbed one and opened it and saw Mary and Martha's name inscribed into the blanket along with a letter that was dated July 9, 1959,

"*Mother,*" the letter read, "*Now I have four! Mary and Martha are just the most precious things! My suspicions were right. Holland females really do come forth as twins. I wish poppa was around to hear the news. Samson is doing well. He doesn't talk much, but he has the cutest dimple in his little chin. My shadows, Naomi and Ruth are very active, quite busy they are. The three of us work the field together almost every day and they're becoming quite the little horticulturists. Momma, I love my family, and I love you too. I pray for poppa in heaven and although the town's people here aren't really nice to me and Rutherford at times, we are doing okay. I miss you, and love you always, Nituna.*"

Naomi held the letter close to her heart as she began to shed tears. These were her mother's words. Nituna's handwritten letters to Naomi's grandparents; people whom she'd never gotten to know in life. History, however, was coming back to life this day—Holland History. Naomi placed the blanket and letter aside and grabbed the next blanket and opened it and saw Samson's name inscribed into the cloth. Another letter fell out that was dated May 4, 1957, "*Mother, I now have a son! Samson Holland is his name. Tell poppa that he has a grandson to carry on after he's gone. Naomi and Ruth now have a little brother and they're more than happy. Both are doing good with their schooling, and the harvests are bountiful. We are doing really, really well, mother. And our family is growing. I love you both, Nituna.*"

Naomi, her face covered in tears, sat the blanket and letter down and picked up the third blanket and slowly unfolded it, knowing what was inside. Just as she expected, when the blanket was opened, a letter fell out. Naomi stared at the letter on the floor in total silence.

"You're going to read it, Naomi? It's your birth she's talking about, I believe." Siloam said as she knelt down beside Naomi.

Naomi looked at the blanket and saw the names Ruth and Naomi inscribed; she held onto it tightly and looked at the letter that lay on the floor in front of her. "Please, can you read it for me, Siloam?"

"Okay, Naomi," Siloam said lowly as she picked up the letter that was dated December 12, 1954.

Naomi held the blanket tightly and closed her eyes as Siloam began to read, "It says, 'Apollo, Sapphire, your daughter has given birth to two precious daughters. I named them Naomi and Ruth, after the bible characters. I shall name all of my children after characters in the bible. Naomi is strong and healthy, but Ruth is sick often. Tell Apollo to send some remedies in the next care package as my supplies are getting low. I must do all I can to save Ruth, I'm scared she'll die mother. I don't want that to happen. I'm crying now as I write because of this feeling of powerlessness as I watch my daughter get sicker by the day. I'll write again soon. Goodbye for now mother, love always, Nituna'." Siloam ended as she gently placed the letter back in front of Naomi.

Siloam was staring straight ahead, tears running down her face as she imaged in her mind what Nituna was feeling at the time she was writing this particular letter. "Nituna was a very loving mother, Naomi. I wish I had a mother like her," she said as she wiped her eyes. "Welcome home," she ended.

Naomi picked up the letter and held it tightly. "My mother's words. I never knew Ruth was sick early on, you know? She was always active, more active than all of us. Never knew she'd fought illness early on. These are priceless, Siloam. This is my family's history I'm holding in my hands. Thank you for helping my family find our land," she said as she rubbed Siloam's shoulder.

"Glad to help, Naomi." Siloam said lowly, tears steadily filling her eyes. "Glad to help."

Naomi would cherish the items Siloam had discovered forever; and she now had the proof that her people really did own the land. They were there once. Naomi found a picture of her grandparents, Apollo and Sapphire Grunion, dressed in full Indian garb and wearing head feathers. They looked like royalty. There was a picture of a young woman inside the trunk that was dated November 1942. It was Nituna shortly after she met Rutherford Holland. Nituna was nineteen then and had the name Nituna Grunion at the time. Naomi was staring at a treasure trove of Holland history including many pictures and scores of hand-written letters from Nituna and several from Eileen. She would hold onto those items for all times as they were crucial documents that bore witness to a life that once was, and days long gone.

Just to see her mother's face again, to see her mother's handwriting, to hear Nituna express delight over her family was heart-warming to Naomi. It also hurt the woman because she missed her mother more than anything. Seeing the warm disposition she surmised her mother had just from reading the letters, Naomi wished she could go back and relieve the short period of time she'd spent with her mother. The trunk containing the letters, pictures and blankets would have to suffice for now, however, and the items contained within would remain a permanent part of the Holland family history.

Siloam searched the remaining items in the trunk, as Naomi read letter after letter with tear stained cheeks, and had come across the deed which had Naomi's grandparents' name on it and a map of the land, which contained two streams, one on either side of the property marking the borders, and a line drawn halfway down the stream at the southern portion of the land marking the southern border. The highway to the north marked the northern border. All the tools needed to reclaim the land and begin life in Oklahoma had been unearthed on this day. There was also a business deed titled *Grunion Farms* inside the trunk. Naomi's grandparents on her mother's side were farmers. They owned a third square mile of land, or 213 acres of property. To put it in perspective, Naomi knew that one acre of land was equivalent to the size of a football field with the end zones removed. Her grandparents had 213 such football fields and were very prosperous people. At the time of their death in 1961, the Grunions were worth just over $290,000 dollars according to old bank statements found inside the trunk.

Siloam took the papers and returned to Oklahoma City with Naomi and her family and went to work. It took a week for her to put the information together, but Naomi was awarded the land a week after Siloam had filed the petition. The land had a tax lien on it, but it was forgiven by the state. Naomi would lose the family fortune, however, because the bank where the account was kept had become defunct during the Savings and Loan Scandal in 1986. Naomi didn't care about the money.

And fighting for dividends she'd never seen when she had plenty of her own was a battle she cared not to divulge herself into. In Naomi's eyes, she'd won already. She was expecting a serious battle and years of litigation but when it got down to it, she didn't have to fight for the land at all. Reclaiming the land was the easy part if Naomi had to tell it, but now the hard part, that of developing the land and making it thrive once more begins. Those were the thoughts that were running through Naomi's mind as the family rode north out of Oklahoma City towards Ponca City with deeds to land that would allow them to start life anew.

CHAPTER 13
LIVING OFF THE LAND

Ponca City, Oklahoma was now about to become the Holland-Dawkins family's new place of residence. A brochure picked up by Doss during the family's return trip from Oklahoma City had given them a little information on their new place of residence. Ponca City had a population of just under 26,000 people and sat in the north central part of the state. The city was named after the Ponca Indian tribe, but was now over 80% white, with African Americans making up another 4%, Hispanics 7% and a mixture of other races, including Asians and Pacific Islanders making up the rest. The city was fifteen miles east of Interstate-15 and only eighteen miles from the Kansas border to the north. The small town held two lakes, Kaw Lake, which was south of the family's land, and Ponca Lake to the north. The nearby Arkansas River kept much of the land in the county irrigated, thereby making it ripe for agriculture. After reading the brochure herself, Naomi had come to the conclusion that her grandparents had chosen a pristine place to call home.

Siloam had ridden with Naomi back to Ponca City once she'd received the deeds and had helped her set up the Winnebago by the stream. "Now the real work begins, Naomi," she remarked as she stood beside Naomi on a warm late summer evening in the month of July.

"I can't wait to get started. This is a huge undertaking, Siloam—but if done right this place can be transformed into something beautiful."

"It already is beautiful, Naomi. Just look at it."

As Siloam stared eastward over the vast, hilly land that lay before their eyes, Naomi stood beside her with the realization of just how big the task was that lay before her and the family. The first chore was for the land, which totaled a third of a square mile, to be cleared of the overgrown grass and the removal of the rats and snakes around the barn. A barrier also had to be set up to keep the cattle from wandering out of the pasture and into the area Naomi had planned on using for agriculture. The herd would have to be fed as well. A permanent place to sleep would be needed also because the Winnebago was becoming tight and cramped.

When Doss walked over and asked Naomi was she ready to head to town to get a couple of motel rooms, she replied by saying, "We're going to stay here, Doss."

"What? You kiddin' me right, Naomi?"

"No. I'm serious, Doss. We will live off the land."

"Baby, we don't have a place to bathe, to use the bathroom. We can't cook. How will we survive out here?"

"We'll get one hotel room so we can all bathe, and we can get some coolers and ice for drinks and a box of chicken to eat. Doss, I really want to spend the first night here on our land. Let's do it." Naomi said as she kissed Doss' lips softly.

Doss really didn't want to stay on the property as it had not the necessities of life; but his wife had just reclaimed it back from the state and she was overjoyed. He fully understood how she felt so he agreed. "If that's really what you to do, baby, we'll do it," Doss said lovingly as he ran his hands through Naomi's hair and rubbed her cheeks gently.

Siloam then asked Naomi could she drop her off at the bus station so she could return to Oklahoma City and the family climbed into the Winnebago and rode into town where Doss rented a room and began to bathe the kids while Naomi drove Siloam to the bus station. As they rode in the Winnebago, Naomi mentioned some her plans. "I want to rent two trailer homes," she told Siloam. "And I imagine I would need to rent some farming equipment and hire a few workers to help cut the grass and rid the land of snakes."

"Getting rid of the snakes should be job one. Those things are deadly. And Doss will never feel safe walking around. Not to mention the danger the kids would face should they encounter one." Siloam stated.

"I'll make sure to find the best exterminators. The snakes must go or else my family will stage a revolt." Naomi said as she and Siloam laughed lightly.

"Transforming the land will be a tremendous task, Naomi, but it'll be fun. I wish I could see it when it's completed."

Naomi said nothing as she continued driving towards the bus station. She was thinking real hard at this moment. Siloam had helped her a great deal, and the truth was, Naomi didn't want her to leave. She thought about asking Siloam to stay, but she decided against doing so because for all she knew, Siloam may have very well had a life of her own and was happy in Oklahoma City. They arrived at the town's bus station, which was no bigger than a small post office, and lucky for Siloam, a bus passing through Ponca City on its way to Houston, Texas was scheduled to arrive within the hour. It was nearing seven 'o' clock in the evening and the bus station was closing so Siloam would have to wait outside. Naomi paid for Siloam's ticket and sat out in front in silence for over twenty minutes. The question she'd been wanting to ask Siloam was right on the tip of her tongue, but she just couldn't force herself to do it. Naomi was never really the type of person to be at a loss for words, but she didn't want her offer to be turned down by Siloam as it would crush her spirit so she kept silent.

"The bus is here. It's early." Siloam suddenly said as she stood up and grabbed her ticket out of her purse.

"Siloam," Naomi said as she stood up just as the bus came to a halt in the small dirt parking lot, "I wanna thank you for all you've done."

"It was my pleasure, Naomi. Take care of those kids. When they are out in the field, be mindful of the snakes. I don't want them to get bit."

"We will. Me and Doss, we'll, we'll be fine. Thank you." Naomi said.

Siloam stared at Naomi with that beautiful smile, her hazel

eyes gleaming proudly. She removed some of her hair from her face and smiled one last time before she turned and walked towards the bus.

Watching Siloam leave was painful for Naomi. She felt as if she was watching one of her own children take off on a journey for the last time, never to be seen again. "Siloam!" Naomi called out just before Siloam stepped onto the bus.

Siloam stopped and turned around and Naomi saw right away that she was crying. "Yes, Naomi?"

"Stay. I want you to stay with us." Naomi said as she walked towards Siloam and hugged her tightly. "Stay with us."

"You going or you staying," the driver of the bus asked in an agitated manner.

"I'm going." Siloam remarked.

"Siloam, why won't you stay?" Naomi asked in disbelief.

"I will. I'll return tomorrow. I have to let the office know what my intentions are and I have to gather some things."

"You won't have to worry about anything. We'll look after you."

"Thanks, Naomi. But I still have some personal possessions I would like to retrieve."

"Will you be back? Really?" Naomi asked in an unsure tone of voice.

"Yes. I'll return tomorrow. Thank you for wanting me around. This is the nicest thing anyone has ever done for me."

"I'll see you tomorrow, Siloam."

"Good-bye for now." Siloam replied before she gave Naomi another hug and boarded the bus.

The family rode back to their land after bathing and Doss parked the Winnebago by the stream. After the family ate, the kids were tucked into three of the four twin beds inside the Winnebago and they quickly went to sleep as Doss and Naomi sat up in the two front seats of the vehicle under the darkness of night talking about their future.

"I estimate I would have to spend close to one hundred thousand dollars getting this place up and running, Doss. I'll have just under thirty thousand dollars left after that. We still have the truck running and Fin is doing real good with that for me. That'll generate at least fifteen hundred dollars a week."

"Lucky been running the gambling house on the south side for me since my main man Eddie got locked up on a murder charge. It's slowing down though; I'm lucky to make two thousand a week. Twenty third ain't been having any contracts lately, either."

"You sound worried, Doss."

"I'm not worried, baby. I just want this to work one hundred percent. I know for a fact that with eight kids, and with all this land, we're gonna have to do better than one Winnebago, one semi and a gambling house. Hospital bills, the cattle, taxes on the land, it's a lot on the table we have to deal with."

"You're right. But together, baby? We can do anything. And I know you won't let us go without. Neither would I. I love you, Doss. Thank you for all that you have done." Naomi said as leaned over and kissed her husband.

"I haven't done much yet," Doss replied as he stroked Naomi's hair. "It was your idea to come down here. Siloam helped find the material you needed to reclaim your grandparents' land. I'm just a city boy along for the ride right now."

Naomi laughed lightly and turned the headlights of the Winnebago off for a minute and a silvery hue encompassed everything around her and Doss. Only the sounds of nature— croaking frogs, screeching owls, crickets, and the occasional rattle of a timber rattlesnake's tail could be heard. "This is nature in its purest form, Doss." Naomi said with a wide smile as she enjoyed the melodic sounds created by the non-human inhabitants of the land.

"I would much rather hear the El passing and police sirens." Doss replied as he opened two bottles of beer for him and Naomi.

"I know you would, city boy." Naomi said jokingly as she grabbed a flashlight and stepped out of the Winnebago. "My God," she said nearly out of breath a few seconds after stepping out into the darkness.

"What is it?" Doss asked as he emerged from the

Winnebago. "Wowww," he then said lowly.

Naomi and Doss were staring up into the night sky. Back in Chicago, only a few stars could be seen on a clear night, if any at all. Husband and wife were staring up at hundreds, literally thousands of twinkling stars over their land in Oklahoma, however; some of the light emanating from the stars was as big as silver dollars and falling stars appeared often. Some stars were sparkling green and many others twinkled, changing from light green to red and back again. There was a purple hue in the sky towards the south east portion of the land and it had numerous blue and purple twinkling stars hidden in the light dust. Doss wrapped an arm around Naomi's mid-section from behind, removed her thick black hair from her neck and kissed her softly.

Naomi closed her eyes and sighed. "What are you doing, Mister Dawkins?" she asked lowly.

"I'm taking you behind the woodshed, Misses Dawkins. Let's go make out like some crazy teenagers in love."

Naomi laughed. "The kids are asleep. Sounds like a plan Mister Dawkins," she said as she pulled away from Doss and walked behind the Winnebago, making sure to sway her hips sexily to further entice her husband.

Doss sipped his beer and continued looking up at the stars as Naomi disappeared from sight. A minute or so later, she peeked back around the side of the Winnebago and held her sweat pants out before Doss and shook them slowly. Doss walked over to Naomi and when he got there, he saw his wife leaning forward against the side of the Winnebago with her rear poking out. He removed his slacks and pressed into Naomi and kissed her neck and earlobes before entering her slowly and before long, the moans emanating from the two were intertwined with the sounds of the nature surrounding them. The two climaxed together and washed themselves with a gallon of water and sat out under the stars and held one another in sweet serenity while the kids slept.

****

The following morning, the kids were up and active. Naomi was tending to Kimi and Koko, who were crying to be fed, and

Walee was entertaining himself with a box of animal crackers as he sat in the front seat of the Winnebago. Dawk, Bay and T-top, meanwhile, were outside behind the home with their father by the creek.

Doss was walking in the water with Bay following his every step. Dawk and T-top had walked across the three foot deep creek and were running around the mini forest, but Doss had to call them back for fear of snakes while making sure the water was safe to wade around in. Upon seeing that the creek had a hard, sandy bottom and wasn't too deep, Doss let the kids splash around as he sat with his feet in the water watching closely.

Naomi had just finished feeding Kimi and Koko and was about to tend to Walee when she heard a horn blowing off in the distance. She opened the door on the Winnebago and saw a seventies style white Volkswagen bus riding across the land along the fence through the high grass headed towards the creek. "It's Siloam, Doss. She came back like she said she would." Naomi remarked as she smiled pleasantly.

The family greeted Siloam as she pulled up to the edge of the creek and exited her van. Dawk, Bay and T-top ran up and hugged her and tugged at her dress, eager to show her the creek they were swimming in while begging her to sing another song.

Siloam greeted the family and pulled open the door on her bus and pulled out a huge pot. "I brought some items I thought we may need, y'all," she said. "I have a pot to boil water, two tents, insect repellent, extra blankets and a compass. I have other items, too, flashlight, matches—"

"Siloam," Doss said, "you didn't have to buy those things for us. We can manage."

"I know. I didn't buy these though, Doss. I been had them. See, I, I live here. This bus has been my home for two years now." Siloam replied with a smile.

Doss didn't know what to say. Siloam had basically told him she was homeless and it didn't seem to bother her in the least. She seemed content with her lot in life.

Naomi placed her hand over her heart, walked over to Siloam

and asked, "You haven't a place to stay, Siloam?"

"I do. I live like you and your family are living now—off the land. It's quite a peaceful existence." Siloam remarked as she handed the blankets to Naomi. "The kids can cover with these at night. I'll boil some water and make us all breakfast. I have," Siloam said as she pulled open the door on a small refrigerator in her bus, "I have grits, three rolls of sausage, two dozen eggs and a gallon of milk. Do you have paper plates? If not I can travel back to town and pick us up some. Some cups, too, if we haven't any."

The kids were too young to understand what was transpiring; but Doss and Naomi understood fully and they were moved, touched in fact. Siloam had very few worldly possessions, but she was willing to share all that she had with people she had met just days before, and barely even knew. Her friendship was genuine and she really cared and wanted to help. It would be for those touching reasons that eighteen year-old Siloam Bovina would be welcomed into the family with open arms by Doss and Naomi in July of 1991.

Siloam made breakfast for the family using water from the creek once it was boiled clean. They then traveled into town and Naomi purchased a two bedroom trailer and a one bedroom trailer home and both would be delivered within a week's time. Progress was being made. By the beginning of October of 1991, the family had Siloam's bus, the Winnebago and two trailer homes to live out of while on the land. Two portable showers were behind the trailers for the family to bathe and Naomi had also rented a dumpster and four portable toilets so the family could have a place to dump their trash and relieve themselves until a sewer line was installed. The northwest portion of the land, which was to one's right when he or she first entered the property, had become the Holland-Dawkins family's temporary home at the out-set.

A clothes line ran from Siloam's bus to a nearby tree. Clothes were washed at a Laundromat in town and taken back to the land to be hung and dried. Doss was over that job and he loved it. He often took Dawk, Bay and T-top with him to help out and to teach them responsibility. The killer-for-hire and career criminal who'd spent all of his life on the streets of Chicago was adjusting well to life in Oklahoma. Doss was an excellent father as well. He spent most of his days walking along the creek with his oldest five and pointing out different birds with the aid of binoculars and an Oklahoma Bird Watcher's guide book he'd purchased from a bookstore in town. The kids would always find small crickets and turtles and play with them for a while before exploring other areas along the long, winding creek.

Naomi meanwhile, was eager to build a home for her family. The trailers were okay for the time being, but she didn't want to become complacent and find herself living under the same conditions five years down the road. Naomi was ambitious and wanted more comfortable surroundings for the family. She often talked to Siloam in confidence about building a home, but she and Doss' finances were getting low. Naomi didn't have enough money to build a home and it bothered her a great deal.

"Maybe I can take out a loan." Naomi said as she and Siloam watched Doss hand out candy to the kids on Halloween evening. "My credit is excellent. The only problem is, I will need tractors to maintain the grass, wood for the new fence to contain the cattle, which I haven't been tending to at all, and the biggest problem would be the payroll I would create once the plans for the home is drawn up. I think I'm in over my head, Siloam."

"Naomi, you are in need. I know of this program that the federal government is sponsoring for the state that may be able to help. It's a part of the Land Act."

"What program, Siloam?"

"It's a grant program. You won't have to pay it back. With eight kids and little income, because Doss hasn't a job, well, a legal, job, we can—"

"Wait, what do you mean 'Doss hasn't a legal job'? What are you sayin' about my husband, Siloam?" Naomi asked as she eyed Siloam cautiously.

"Doss looks like a dangerous man. What does he do for a living, Naomi?" Siloam asked meekly.

Naomi didn't reply right away. She had never been asked

that question before by anybody outside of Kevin and Serena; but she was glad Siloam had asked, because if people back in town were to pose this particular question to her, what would she say concerning Doss' occupation? "He was a warehouseman in Chicago," Naomi replied. "He quit his job to move down here, but his heart is in Chicago. He was in the process of buying his own warehouse until we abruptly gave up our life in Chicago and moved here. Doss wants to return to doing business in Chicago after we are established, but as of right now, he hasn't the finances to do so. This grant, do you think I would qualify?"

"There isn't a doubt in my mind, Naomi. Next week we can travel back to Oklahoma City and fill out the paperwork. We could do it here in Ponca City, but they will only forward it to the state capitol anyway. Besides, my former coworkers will be glad to put your application on top of the pile at my request. It's worth a shot. What do you think?"

"Let's take your bus when we go. We'll leave Doss with the kids and have a girl's day out." Naomi said as she smiled at Siloam.

"Okay. If the grant comes through, you will be well on your way, Naomi."

"*We*, Siloam. *We* will be well on *our* way."

Siloam smiled and laid her headscarf-covered head on Naomi's shoulder and sighed happily when Naomi hugged her tightly and began rocking the two of them. Naomi knew she had just lied to Siloam about Doss's occupation, but she felt Siloam didn't need to know what her husband actually did for a living at the time, if ever at all. Doss was a gangster; but that wasn't a side of Naomi's husband that she wanted neither Siloam nor the kids to know. And Siloam actually saw Doss as a father figure and a man that loved his family more than life itself; Naomi would always uphold Doss in his criminal endeavors, and she would always shine light upon him as being a loving father and a good man, which he was towards his family and friends, including Siloam Bovina.

Taking Siloam's advice, Naomi traveled to Oklahoma City the following week and applied for a federal grant and was awarded $55,000 dollars six weeks after she'd applied.

Towards the end of 1991, she began to hire workers from a labor pool in Ponca City to not only build a home for the family, but to tend to the land as well as the money she was afforded was more than enough to not only finance the home, but to simultaneously transform the land from an open, unattended prairie, into a productive farm land rich with life and livestock when coupled with the twenty-seven thousand dollars she had remaining. The grant was a true blessing for the family and Naomi was now on her way to building a home. Moving to Oklahoma was by far the best decision thirty-seven year-old Naomi Holland Dawkins had ever made in her life thus far.

CHAPTER 14
THE FIRST HOME

It was now April of 1992. After an unusually warm winter, and giving birth in late December of '91 to Shima Dawkins, who Siloam nick-named 'Spoonie', because she was practically feeding herself with a plastic toddler spoon at only four months, and her identical twin Sinopa Dawkins, who earned the nick-name 'Tyke' by all because she was the youngest in family, Naomi's dream of building a home for her family had come to pass.

Nineteen year-old Siloam Bovina had become Naomi's best friend and surrogate daughter as the two had been real close since the day they had first met. She now paid Siloam a weekly salary and together with workers from the labor pool, they slowly began to pull the land together. The grass was cut and the barn had been freed of rodents and stabilized. The snakes were cleared out and the cattle were kept behind a newly erected fence on the southernmost portion of the land near the southern stream.

With Siloam around, Doss was able to travel back and forth to Chicago and conduct business with 23rd Street. He was now receiving a contract every month from 23rd as a drug war had erupted between two rival gangs, one from Chicago, the other from Detroit. Doss was putting in a lot of work for the Chicago gang during this period of time, but the day the family was scheduled to move into their new home, the gangster was there on the ranch with his family.

Doss, Naomi and Siloam were up bright and early on this late

April morning and were busy preparing breakfast for Doss and the kids inside the two bedroom trailer home. The trailers were to be vacated this day, but Naomi had forgotten to buy cooking utensils to cook inside the new home, so the family would eat breakfast inside the trailers before touring their new place of residence. Naomi was glad to not have to spend another night inside the trailers because the storms in Oklahoma seemed to produce tornadoes that devastated trailer homes. She grew scared every time a storm passed and feared for the lives of her kids during those times; but all was well with the completion of the new home which was a huge five bedroom brick and steel structure with six baths and a storm cellar.

As Naomi and Siloam prepared breakfast inside the two bedroom trailer, Doss was in the one bedroom trailer home dressing the kids. A lot of noise was being made inside the cramped tin structure. The kids were running around, yelling at one another, wrestling and slamming doors. Doss was glad the family had a new home as well because the trailers were just too small for a family of eleven. Even with two homes side by side, a Winnebago and a small bus, there still wasn't enough room. Doss was changing the pampers on four month olds Spoonie and Tyke as they lay on the bed when three year-olds Kimi and Koko ran into the room. Koko was screaming to the top of her lungs.

"What's wrong with you, Koko?" Doss asked.

"Bay, Bay got my baby doll and won't give it back." she whined.

"That's no reason to cry, Koko. Bena give your sister her doll! Your mother and I have both told you not to irritate her!" Doss yelled down the hall as he wiped Spoonie's bottom clean with a baby wipe.

"She gave it to me last night!" six year-old Bena snapped back from the front of the trailer.

"No I ain't. You took it from me just now!" Koko yelled as she and Kimi ran out of the room.

"No I ain't ain't a proper sen—no I ain't is not a proper sentence, Koko! Bena give your sister her doll back before I take off my belt!"

Doss heard rumbling coming from the hallway so he peeked down the hall and saw Bena holding Koko in the headlock just as Kimi jumped on Bena's back in an attempt to help her twin. Bena took Kimi and Koko down to the floor with her and the three wrestled. Kimi was soon laughing, but Koko really wanted her doll back from Bena. She swung and hit Bena in the mouth and Bena stood up and threw the doll at Koko and it hit her in the face. The three year-old screamed aloud and began kicking at Bena as she lay on the floor twisting herself around in a circle.

Doss stood up and reached for his belt at that moment and Bena took off running out the front door of the trailer home. "I'm a whip your behind when I catch up with you, Bay!" Doss yelled out the front door.

Just then the smoke alarm went off in the kitchen and Doss ran that way. As he did so, seven year-old Dawk and six year-old T-top ran out the kitchen and down the hall. Doss went into the kitchen and saw a pot on the stove that was smoking as one year-old Walee sat by himself on the floor smiling up at him. He turned the stove off and grabbed the pot and when he did, he grimaced and sat it back on the stove when he saw what was inside. Dawk and T-top had placed a pile of crickets into the pot of water and were attempting to boil them. They succeeded, but when the water boiled off, the crickets had burned to a crisp. It wasn't the first time Doss had caught the two boiling crickets, but this time around, they had set off the smoke detector and the smell inside the trailer was becoming nauseating.

Doss then remembered Spoonie and Tyke were alone on the bed so he scooped Walee up and trotted back to bedroom just in time to prevent Spoonie from rolling onto the floor. Doss wasn't new to this routine; but when left alone with the kids, it seemed as if they did every conceivable thing they could think of to get under their father's skin. The man had gained new respect for what Naomi was doing while he was away in Chicago, but he wouldn't trade it for the world. His kids misbehaved and agitated one another constantly, but they were just that, kids. And the things they got into on the ranch were typical to kids growing up on a farm, at least that's what Doss thought. Kimi and Koko had soon settled down, and Dawk, Bay and T-top were now outside running around in the field. Doss dressed his youngest daughters and son went and had breakfast with his family.

After they ate, the family walked over to the new home. They were walking the short distance when Doss caught up to Dawk, Bay and T-top. "I have something for you, Bena," he said as he held an open bag of M and M's on display before his oldest daughter.

Dawk and T-top's eyes lit up. "Candy," they yelled in unison.

"I want some candy, daddy." Kimi and Koko remarked simultaneously.

"No!" Bena said. "You selfish with your doll." she ended as she poked out her tongue at Kimi and Koko.

"Give Dawk and T-top some of your candy, Bena. Kimi and Koko, I'll give you your candy later. You two had candy earlier, anyway." Dawk answered.

Dawk and T-top held their hands out and waited on Bay to pour them some M and M's, but when she tilted the bag the dead crickets that Dawk and T-top had in the pot earlier landed in T-top's hands. She screamed aloud, dropped the crickets and rubbed her hands clean on Dawk's shirt.

Dawk jumped back and looked at the black spot on his shirt and said, "You got bug juice on me, Tiva," as he charged at his sister.

T-top laughed and she and Bay took off running towards the new house with Dawk giving chase. Doss laughed aloud. He'd gotten his oldest three back for their mischief earlier. Kimi and Koko laughed with their father as they trailed him towards the new home. Upon their arrival, the entire family stood outside of the new home and just stared in admiration at the brown bricked two story home with a huge, pecan wood covered porch that stretched from end to end.

"This place is jumungous!" Dawk yelled.

"The word is humongous, Dawk." Naomi replied. "You kids like it?"

Naomi's oldest five all gave a resounding yes and climbed the stairs as their mother held the door open. "No running." Naomi said to her kids as they entered the pristine furnished home.

Doss followed and he stared with proud eyes over what he and Naomi had designed and built. The home opened into a living room that had white wooden rails on either side. An opening was halfway down. On the left side of the aisle was the family room. Here, Naomi had placed all the artifacts, her Raggedly Ann and Andy dolls, a refurbished portrait of her grandparents, Nituna's hand-woven blankets and the silver box that held her mother's and Eileen's letters into a four foot wide, ten foot tall double door pecan wood curio cabinet. Two elongated leather sofas were in the room facing one another with a circular wooden table in the center. A fireplace was sunk in the wall and two leather chairs were on either side. It was a room that was designed to have a calming effect come over any and everybody that entered the area. Naomi had plans on gathering her kids there from time to time to read to them from her mother's letters and tell them of their family history.

On the right side of the aisle was a library. Naomi had a desk near the front window and a short couch before the desk. On the wall was a book shelf filled with Naomi's law books and two sets of encyclopedias. This would be Naomi's office and a place for the kids to read and study. The family walked past the two rooms and climbed three wooden stairs at the end of the aisle and stepped onto lacquered cherry wood floors. A small over look with a railing ran along both sides of the aisle; allowing an elevated, open view of the family room and library from the kitchen area. To the right past the library was a long hallway that led to two bedrooms and a bathroom. To the left was another hall that led to a music room and the dining room. Straight ahead was the kitchen. The kitchen was a wide open area that featured an island counter and stainless steel appliances all the way around the wall. The wall to the back of the kitchen led out to the back of the home where a wooden deck that over-looked the stream was located.

Just to the left of the kitchen was another set of stairs that descended into the den. The den featured a bathroom, a big screen TV and sofas throughout. To the right of the kitchen was a flight of stairs that led to the basement which was where the wash room and storm cellar was located. A winding staircase that crossed over the kitchen was near the door leading to the storm cellar and another smaller staircase was inside the den.

The upstairs portion of the home was the sleeping area. Doss and Naomi's bedroom, which featured a private bath, was to the right at the end of the hall and the room where Spoonie, Tyke, Kimi and Koko would sleep was just outside. To the left were the remaining three bedrooms and two more baths. The rooms inside the home were huge and there was plenty of space for everyone. No longer would the family have to be cramped into two small trailers.

Naomi was happy with her new home, but she knew she would need a bigger place as the kids got older; and maybe, if ever she found her siblings, they would need a place to stay as well. The ambitious woman was already planning to build a bigger home someday; and she now had the assets to do so. It would be a dream home; an estate for the entire family that could be passed down from generation to generation.

The family settled into their new home and Naomi and Doss went to work building up their wealth to further prosper the family's income through Doss' criminal endeavors and Naomi's farming and livestock. Life was good in Ponca City, and after such hard work restoring the land, Naomi thought it to be time to invite the family and friends from Chicago down and welcome them to the newly erected ranch.

CHAPTER 15
WELCOME TO THE HOLLAND RANCH

"Momma, how long before they come?" Bena asked her mother as she helped her and Siloam hang a banner over the wooden gateway leading onto the ranch.

It was a warm sunny Saturday morning, July 4th, 1992 and on this day, Naomi's family and friends from up north were coming down to celebrate the holiday and see the land for the first time up close and in person. Bay and T-top's seventh birthday, which was several days away, would also be celebrated on this day.

Thirty-seven year-old Naomi Holland-Dawkins had been on the land for just over a year now and had adapted well. She now had a work crew that consisted of Siloam and four ranch hands. She was homeschooling Dawk, Bay, T-top, Kimi and Koko and they, too, along with Walee, had adapted well to their new home. Naomi's eight kids were all the benefactors of their mother and father's prosperity. They were being raised by parents who were financially well-off.

"They should be here any minute now, Bena. Hand me the hammer please, baby." Naomi requested as she climbed a tall ladder.

As Naomi tacked the banner, which read: *Welcome To The Holland Ranch*, DeeDee's sleek, elongated Lincoln Town Car emerged from the woods that encompassed the dirt road leading to the ranch's entrance. Lucky's El Dorado followed, and Kevin and Serena trailed them in Kevin's brand new Jeep

Cherokee.

Bena ran up to her grandfather's car, and we he exited, she jumped into his arms. "Welcome to our home, Grandpa!"

"How you been, sugar?" DeeDee asked as he kissed Bena's cheeks.

"Been good, papa!"

"You still boiling crickets?" DeeDee asked through laughter.

"Dawk and T-top boil crickets."

"That's right. You like to fight with Kimi and Koko. They gone pay you back when they get older."

"They can't 'cause by then I'll be older!" Bena replied.

DeeDee laughed and placed Bena back on her feet and she ran and greeted Serena and Kevin. "Little Bena, how are you, cutie pie?" sixty-eight year-old Serena asked as she knelt down and gave Bena a tight hug.

"I been good, grandma."

"Are you sure? I heard about you picking on your sisters. Why do antagonize Kimi and Koko?"

"You don't be seeing everything, grandma. Those two? They're impossible to deal with some days." Bena replied as Serena laughed aloud.

"How you been, Naomi," sixty-one year-old Kevin asked. "We've missed you so much back in Cicero. Zell even sends his love," he said as he handed Naomi an envelope stuffed with hundred dollar bills. "He says to buy more cattle."

"Thank you, dad. Zell is such a sweet man. I'll have to call and thank him. Would you all like to come with us to Oklahoma City while you're down here and see what it's like to attend a cattle auction?" Naomi asked aloud as she hugged sixty-one year-olds Mendoza and Francine.

"Can we eat what we buy?" Mendoza asked.

"You won't get to eat my new cattle, Mendoza. But I have fresh steaks ready to grill for you. I never forgot what you said the day I left. You will get your Oklahoma steak today, but let me show the lay of the land first."

"Okay, Naomi. I told you DeeDee, wait until you savor the

beef down here. You'll never look at a Chicago steak the same." Mendoza remarked as he walked back to his car.

The group was all preparing to get back into their cars until Naomi stopped them and said, "We're walking."

Lucky and Mildred and their son, fourteen year-old Junior, were standing just inside the gate talking to Siloam and they'd heard Naomi's remark. Everybody did. DeeDee walked underneath the wooden gate and stared out at the land. "I'm not messing up my new gator shoes walking across this land, Naomi!" he quipped.

"I told you all to dress casual." Naomi said as she placed her hands on her hips and smiled at DeeDee.

"Silk slacks and gator shoes are casual where I'm from. I'm not wearing a suit jacket, neither a tie." DeeDee replied.

"Here we wear denim. Denim jeans." Siloam stated shyly.

DeeDee looked down at Siloam and smiled. The sixty-one year-old man loved women—young women to be exact—and he thought Siloam was just the cutest thing ever. He grabbed her hand and said, "For you sweetie I'll wear only my—"

"Dad, she's only nineteen," Naomi replied as she removed DeeDee's hand from Siloam's and got in between the two.

DeeDee chuckled slightly and looked back out at the land and saw Dawk, T-top, Kimi and Koko playfully running his way with Doss following behind pulling Walee, Spoonie and Tyke in a huge red wagon. "Look at that," he said as he placed his right hand over his eyes to block the sun. "Is, is that my son dressed in jeans and a flannel shirt?"

"Yes, dad. Doesn't he look nice?" Naomi asked.

DeeDee, Mendoza, Lucky, and even Junior, Mildred and Francine burst into laughter when they noticed Doss' attire. The males, with the exception of Kevin, who'd taken Naomi's advice and wore jeans and tennis shoes, were all dressed in silk slacks and shirts and wore dress shoes. DeeDee didn't even own a pair of jeans, nor tennis shoes for that matter. When Naomi said to dress casual, he only thought she meant not to wear a suit—everybody did.

"Where's he getting his clothes from now, Naomi? The

Frontier Outlet?" DeeDee asked through laughter.

"Don't mock my man, DeeDee. He looks nice. And he is dressed for the occasion just like mom and dad. You hoodlums have to learn that there's more to life than just a suit and tie. Look at you all—dressed as if you're going to Carnegie Hall to see an opera."

"Speaking of music, my stomach is singing real loud. Can we go eat?" Junior asked.

"No hello how you doing my name is...just 'where's the kitchen' huh, ya' knuckle head? Be polite!" Lucky said to his son. Junior shoved Lucky and two began slap boxing as the grand kids ran up and greeted their grandparents and the rest of the friends.

"Okay, everybody," Naomi said as she clapped her hands together to get everyone's attention, "we'll start the tour here with a walk to the barn on the hill. From there we'll visit the log cabin my grandparents once lived in and the cattle and horses to the south."

"A walk?" DeeDee asked as he eyed the barn on the hill off in the distance. "You don't have a golf cart or something we can ride in, Naomi? This is a lot of land. That barn looks like a tent from here."

"I have a bus we can use." Siloam remarked.

"Yeah," DeeDee said, "a bus would be perfect. Go get if you don't mind, sweetie pie." When DeeDee saw the small white Volkswagen bus headed his way, he looked over to Naomi and said, "This ain't gone work, now. What kind of bus is this? I'm thinking she—"

"You thought she had a bus like the ones back in Chicago?" Naomi asked through laughter. "What would we be doing with a massive machine like that here on the ranch? And quit whining about everything, old man!" she chided.

Siloam rolled her bus to a halt before the group and Dawk, Bay, T-top, Kimi and Koko climbed in first. "Come on grandpa, you can ride first with us." Bena said as she slid over on the carpeted floor.

DeeDee was well over six feet tall so he had to bow his head and hunch over as he climbed inside. He tried to sit on the carpeted floor, but he just couldn't get comfortable. "Wait a minute, now," he whined as he climbed back out of the bus and rubbed his knees. "I'm a tall man. I can't sit on that floor. What time does the next bus come? Maybe that one will have more seats." he remarked as he looked at his watch and then looked up and down the dirt road as if he were searching for a city bus.

"I'm sorry, Mister DeeDee," Siloam said from the driver's seat through laughter, "the next bus will be by in five minutes."

"This ain't no different from the big city, Siloam. I guess I'll just have to wait. And don't you go to break on us. We have somewhere to be today." DeeDee remarked.

The group laughed at DeeDee's remarks and was really getting their kicks for a short while. After four trips from the entrance of the ranch back to the barn, the family had begun their tour on foot. It was a delightful expedition that lasted for nearly two hours. They were leaving the cattle pen, their last stop along their journey when DeeDee paused in the middle of a field of cabbage and said aloud, "This place is beautiful, Naomi. I never knew Oklahoma could be so beautiful. I thought it would be a flat, barren place like Kansas or Nevada. But the stream, the little canyon down yonder, the forest, cattle, this place is a slice of paradise."

"Down yonder, dad? You gone fit right in." Doss chuckled.

All the friends and family from Chicago were amazed over the land. Naomi had often sent pictures of the progress being made, but the photographs didn't do the Holland Ranch justice; one had to see it to really appreciate it. Now that they had, everybody had every intention on coming down to the ranch whenever they could get away from the city.

The family had grilled steaks, steamed cabbage and homemade cornbread and had eaten to satisfaction. A celebration for Bena and Tiva was then held beside the creek behind the house with a huge cake, birthday hats and ice cream and everybody was now sitting around relaxing just as the sun began to set. Naomi and the rest of the females were on the patio watching the kids play in the creek with Junior and Siloam while Doss, DeeDee, Mendoza, and Lucky sat in lounge chairs beside Siloam's bus that was parked near the creek as they, too, watched the kids splash around.

The men were smoking cigars and sipping brandy as they updated Doss on how things were going back in Chicago. A few months back, just before the start of spring, Doss and Lucky, on Zell's orders, had killed a man from Milwaukee that was trying to set up a cocaine operation. They'd buried the man behind an old abandoned warehouse in Racine, Wisconsin, just south of Milwaukee, but the body was found by an engineering crew that was searching for a new sewer line locale.

"It's a cold case as far as the law is concerned, son." DeeDee said to Doss. "But his men had no doubt that the hit came from Chicago."

"Me and DeeDee went back to Milwaukee and eliminated his two partners before they put the pieces together completely, Doss." Mendoza replied.

"Thanks you guys. Zell asked them nicely not to set up in his city but they disobeyed. They basically asked for what they received." Doss said.

"Shit's crazy. People just don't listen." Mendoza said before he took a puff of his cigar. "That other thing, the gambling room? The young kid, Eddie, the guy who use to run the place's son? He said his father told him to ask you if you could look after him for keeping quiet on that murder he went upstate for."

"I been taking care of that for you, Doss." Lucky responded. "But gambling,"

"I know," Doss said, cutting Lucky's remark short, "me and Naomi talked about that a while back. We need a new venture —or new contracts. The Milwaukee job was supposed to be the last hit to make the peace with the boys from Detroit. Outside of gambling, I have no other income as of now."

DeeDee poured another glass of brandy for himself and said, "The war is over, son. Zell knows things are tight and he's looking for a new racket. Me and Mendoza told him about your idea—the cocaine? He says no drugs."

"What you think, dad?" Doss asked.

"It's not my call, son."

"But if it was," Mendoza said, "DeeDee and I both would agree to it. So long as it doesn't get put out on the streets of Chicago. They killing one another behind that shit up there. Our friends in Milwaukee, Saint Louis, Detroit and Cleveland are from the old school—from the day when a man's word actually meant something."

"That's who we would like you two to deal with," DeeDee said, "but there's no one like that left in Chicago that we can really trust. The old timers are retiring or not interested. Besides, Zell gave the order and it stands until he changes his mind or dies, whichever comes first."

"Times are changing, men." Doss said. "We can't just sit by and let this opportunity pass us by. We getting pushed out and it's not by force. The new trend is white powder and we should have our share. We're missing out on some serious money."

"Zell's from the old school," Mendoza said. "The man grew up with the likes of Capone, Giancana, and Lansky, and for him, it's about respect, not money."

"Dad, in this line of work it's always about the money." Lucky said. "All those guys you just named sold drugs at one time or another. Luciano ran a heroin ring from Sicily when he got deported. I mean, don't get me wrong, Zell's the man. I learned a lot from him, but Doss is right, times are changing and we need to change with them."

"You're right, son," Mendoza replied before he took a sip of his brandy. "But so long as Zell says not to sell drugs we have to follow orders—unless something were to happen to 'em."

DeeDee, Doss, Lucky and Mendoza all grew quiet at that moment because the thoughts running through their minds was a thought neither man wanted to express openly. "Are we all thinking the same thing?" Mendoza asked, breaking the silence.

"If we keep on the route we're traveling, we're going to lose all we worked for and there won't be nothing left. We have to wet our feet with this white powder and Zell's standing in the way." Lucky remarked.

"We take down Zell," Mendoza said. "We take down the Boss, we have to take down his body guards and anybody not in agreement with what we're contemplating."

"The only people who won't go along with us on this is his guards. Everybody's itching to sell product. Zell's chauffeur had even asked me about dabbling in the business and I told 'em I would talk to you guys first. One thing's for certain, dad —with Zell out the way, it'll be that much easier for us to move ahead with that racket."

"Whacking the boss," Mendoza said lowly. "Not since Gotti hit Paul Castellano has this move been made. Fortunate for us, Chicago answers to no one. Our business is our business. What we forge today is never to be spoken about—ever!"

"It's the right move, dad." Lucky said before sipping his drink.

"We'll see, son. And if we do it, it remains our secret."

The four men shook hands and sealed the deal, and by the time the family from up north had left the ranch a week later, a plan was set in motion to remove Zell from his position as Boss of 23rd Street Mafia and replace him with Mendoza Cernigliaro, another mafia figurehead that would guide the family through their next racket—the cocaine drug trade.

CHAPTER 16
THE CALL

Mendoza had just showered and dressed after the long drive back from Oklahoma. He and Francine were about to prepare tea and sit out on the front porch when the phone rang. He tightened his diamond cuff link and picked up the phone. "Cernigliaro residence. Mendoza speaking," he said as he checked his appearance in the dresser mirror.

"The Boss says for you to come to headquarters—alone." the voice on the other end stated dryly.

"What? Now?"

"Not now. In two hours. When the sun goes down."

"Okay, umm. Okay, I'll be there."

"You have no choice," the man said before he hung up the phone abruptly.

Mendoza had an immediate sinking feeling in his stomach as he set the phone back down into its port and headed downstairs knowing he'd seen this move a time or two.

Sam Giancana, Sonny Black, Roy DeMeo, "Mad Sam" DeStefano—all were powerful mafia figures that had received 'the call' in one form or another and they never saw the light of day again. Mendoza had even made 'the call' a few times in his career, but on this day, he'd just gotten the call and it unnerved him greatly because he knew it was a strong chance that he may not leave *Eastside Bar* alive. Right away he knew that somehow, Zell must have found about the hit against him and was aiming to strike first.

"Everything okay, baby?" Francine asked as she walked into the living room holding a tray with a tea kettle and two ceramic cups.

"Yeah. Every, everything is fine. Look," Mendoza said as he removed his wedding ring and placed it on the table, he then removed his wallet and pulled out his driver's license, "I have to look into something for a minute. I'll be back tonight."

"What about the tea?"

"Save it." Mendoza said as he put on a pretentious smile.

Francine wasn't fooled in the least, however; she knew something was going on with her husband and she wanted answers. "Mendoza who was that on the phone? What's going on?" she asked anxiously.

"Nothing I can talk about. I have to go and see DeeDee."

"Are you coming back?" Francine asked worriedly.

Mendoza, as he reached for the door knob, looked down towards the floor and said lowly, "I honestly don't know, Francine."

"Mendoza," Francine cried as she set the tray down and ran and grabbed her husband. "Mendoza what happened?"

"Nothing I can't fix. I'll be okay. If you don't hear from me in a couple of day's time," Mendoza paused at that moment and thought about how sudden lives could change in the business. "I never thought I'd be betrayed by one of my own."

"Who betrayed you?"

"DeeDee."

"You're wrong! Mendoza, you're wrong! Doss is your friend!"

"You know as well as I do Francine, that in this business, friends are the ones who do you in. If I'm not heard from in two day's time, you have Lucky and Junior go after Doss. He'll come looking for me when he finds out I'm the one who killed his father." Mendoza said as he walked out the door, leaving behind a stunned Francine.

****

Mendoza climbed into his brown two door Cadillac coup de' Ville, merged onto I-290 and headed eastbound. As he drove down the highway with the sun at his back, he kept thinking over and over again, wondering how and why DeeDee would have betrayed him. The two had been partners in crime for over thirty years and trust was never an issue. He checked his watch and saw that he had just over an hour to make it over to *Eastside Bar* for his meeting with Zell, so he had to take care of DeeDee right away.

Mendoza shook his head repeatedly in disbelief over his possible upcoming actions as he pulled up to DeeDee's condominium and slid into a parking spot in the underground garage where he sat in silence for a minute and thought about what it was that he was about to do. He soon climbed out of his car imaging in his mind how things would go down, unable to believe that he would have to kill his closest ally. Before exiting the elevator, Mendoza placed a .38 revolver in the back of his waistband and walked down to the corner suite and tapped on the door.

DeeDee's place sat on Lake Shore Drive overlooking Lake Michigan. His condo was a luxurious three bedroom two story layout on the thirtieth floor of a high-rise. It contained a private balcony with a Jacuzzi and fireplace and a garden patio with an outdoor grill and was worth over a half million dollars.

DeeDee opened his door, smiled and immediately walked back into his home and right away, Mendoza knew he was wrong in his assumptions. He was also happy he didn't jump-the-gun so to speak because his closest friend had turned his back on him and had shown no hesitation when he laid eyes on him. Mendoza had been a killer all his life and he knew all the angles. He knew that even a hardened and experienced killer like DeeDee and many others, when confronted with the same fate they'd dished out to so many for so long, even those hardened killers would hesitate for a split second when caught off guard. Mendoza knew if DeeDee had set him up, he would've been surprised to see him over to his place because DeeDee would've been under the impression that he was already dead, or in the process of being killed. He would also have not turned his back on Mendoza if he had been a part of what was going down and felt that his life was in danger.

Mendoza stepped in and closed the door and locked it,

watching DeeDee as he flipped through the channels on his TV, his back still turned towards him as he stepped off into the living room of the luxurious condominium.

"I just ordered a pizza and I got a twelve pack cooling in the fridge. I'm gettin' ready to watch this Cubs game. What brings you over this way? Surprised you and Francine not having tea on this lovely Sunday evening," DeeDee said as he went onto his balcony and lit his fireplace.

"It's the middle of July. What the hell you turnin' that thing on for?" Mendoza asked as he stepped out onto the balcony.

"I like having my balcony doors open when I'm up relaxing. The sun goes down it gets a bit nippy up this high. And I just like the ambiance."

"Ambiance," Mendoza said lowly as he looked out over the orange-hued waters of Lake Michigan, which held a reflection of the setting sun on its surface. "I never get tired of this view."

"Me neither. Man, the chicks love it, too. Done stood behind many a woman right here on this balcony, my friend."

"I'm, I'm not your friend, Doss."

Upon hearing Mendoza's remark, DeeDee poked the wood in his fireplace one last time and stood up and faced Mendoza, who now had his back turned to him. He eyed Mendoza with a cautious look and gripped the iron poker tighter and asked, "What's that statement supposed to mean?"

"What it means is I'm ashamed to be called your friend after what I've thought about doing today."

"You talking in riddles, man. What's on your mind?"

"I got the call today." Mendoza said as he turned and faced DeeDee.

DeeDee knew about 'the call' himself; it was amongst the Italians, but he knew of several instances where men were called down to *Eastside Bar* and taken off to be killed. In a mere matter of seconds, DeeDee had surmised what Mendoza's visit was all about. He sat the poker down, spread his arms slightly and said, "You think it was me who gave you up for wanting to kill Zell, don't you?"

"That was my first reaction. But all the way over here I kept thinking that it didn't fit."

"But you had to see for yourself."

"I did. And I feel like shit about it because out of all people, you and I, you and I are more like brothers than just a couple of guys that do hits, you know?"

"I'm not your problem. What is the problem is what are you going to do? You still have to meet Zell."

"I know. I know. And it may not even be what we're thinking. The only person who would've really sold me out would be Zell's chauffeur because he asked my son about selling drugs and Lucky told him he'd talk to me. This is a big misunderstanding, Doss. My fuck up," Mendoza said as he turned and headed for the door.

"I know what it is and I know who it's on. And we gone talk about that when this is all over so we can get some shit straightened out. Now, with that aside, my question to you is, are you just gonna go down there and let Zell kill you? Let's just hit all those mutherfuckas and take over like we planned!"

"I would love to. But the pact we made on the ranch had consequences going in and I knew it. Zell was always a smart man. Hell, he trained me for Christ's sake. The son-of-a bitch sent his chauffeur at my son to get a feel for what was circulating in my crew so he could know what to do with us."

"Well, what's your orders?"

"If you don't hear from me by midnight tonight, I want you to ride over to Lucky's place, put a team together and take Zell down. Those are my final orders shall this be my last day." Mendoza said as he dialed Francine and told her everything was okay between him and DeeDee before he headed out the door.

****

The drive back to Cicero was the longest drive of Mendoza's life. Over and over again he kept thinking about how the conversation on the ranch, and the one statement made by his son regarding Zell's chauffeur, had turned into a catalyst that would possibly end his life. Getting called to your own funeral was not an everyday occurrence in the lives of the vast majority of mankind was Mendoza's thinking; and many in everyday life would not even answer, or show up for that matter. Mendoza was true Mafioso, however; and he lived and died by the Mafia creed of "this thing of ours" and he obeyed all mafia laws. His plan, his going along with and certifying a hit on the Boss had backfired and now, he had to face whatever consequences lay ahead like the man he was at the time of his planning to kill Zell Verniche` down in Oklahoma. Mendoza lived every bit of his life like a man, and he'd made up his mind that he would die like one on this day shall it be his last.

The elegant brown Cadillac rolled to a halt just before the vacated entrance to *Eastside Bar* under the now moonlit sky and before Mendoza could even climb out of his car, he was greeted by Zell's body guards. The three men frisked him outside the entrance, removing his revolver before escorting him inside and locking the doors. The bar was dead silent on the inside and empty of patrons. Sunday nights were huge in *Eastside Bar*, but on this night, it was as empty as an arid desert. Tumble weeds might as well have rolled through to garner a more full effect.

"I guess this is it, huh, fellas?" Mendoza asked as he removed his black canvas b-bop cap.

"Your guess is as good as mines, il mio amico," one of Zell's bodyguards replied as he nudged Mendoza forward.

"Care to share what the reasoning is behind all this?"

"I think you already know. But if you must, the Boss said no drugs on his watch. The rest? He'll explain. He's in his booth."

Mendoza walked through the dimly lit bar, his gator shoes pressing hard against the wooden floors as he traversed the lounge. When he reached the end of the bar he peered over to his left and saw Zell sitting in his booth with his back facing the rest of the bar. Zell sipped his glass of wine and said, "For the first time ever, I sit with my back to the door. But I always trust the men around me so I'm not worried about a damn thing tonight."

Mendoza said nothing as he approached Zell. He rounded the booth and made eye contact with the man and could see nothing but disappointment in his eyes. Zell poured another glass of wine and extended his hand, allowing Mendoza to sit.

"What do you have to say for yourself, Mendoza?"

"Well, Boss. I—"

"That was a rhetorical question. Rhetorical, meaning I ask, but I need no reply." Mendoza nodded and Zell continued speaking. "You know, when Capone, when Capone got involved in bootlegging, the lawmen here, they said, they said in secret, 'it hurts no one'. If people back then wanted to poison their bodies with the devil's juice so be it. The government turned their heads the other way because they could be bought, and they, too, drank the devil's juice and viewed it as harmless fun. But this new devil, this white powder, is even more powerful than the devil himself. So much so, that it has caused a rift in this thing of ours."

Zell paused in his talks and eyed Mendoza, who discerned that he was now allowed to speak. "Boss," Mendoza said lowly, "the government allows this white powder to enter this country."

"Certain men do," Zell replied. "But I have no affiliation with those men. Nor do I care to do business with those men. Drug dealing is a snake business."

"A snake business that leaks money through its pores."

"Right you are, my friend. Right you are. And it is for that reason that I can no longer lead this outfit."

"What are you saying, Boss?"

"This outfit's indulgence in white powder will drive me into a war that I'm no longer able to manage, Mendoza. I haven't the strength to wage another battle with younger, fiercer adversaries that I know will come with the business. But I also have other reasons."

"Those reasons being?"

"I went to the doctor while you were down visiting Naomi and he told me, he told me I have only six months to live."

"Why? How?"

"Pancreatic cancer. My back is killing me as we speak and I can't take a fucking shit in peace. My days are numbered, Mendoza. But before I leave here, I wanted to pass along the hat. When you leave here today, you will be Boss."

"I don't know what to say. I'm, I'm—"

"I am glad you didn't kill me today is what the fuck you were going to say to me, right?" Zell said as he eyed Mendoza coldly. "I know you and your crew was contemplating on moving that shit behind my back. And for that, I have every legal right to wipe you and your entire crew off the fucking map. This, this drug thing, though? It's too much of a temptation for everybody. Even my chauffer and bodyguards want in on the business."

"Why are you letting me live? Why are you putting me in charge knowing I will only do what you've denied for so long?"

"Because I feel it's time. Plain and simple. And I don't wanna make the same mistakes other Bosses before me have done, which was to hang on too long, get murdered, and have the whole organization fall to pieces. I don't know if you had it in for me, but someone may have. Before I lay in a pool of blood I choose to leave standing up right and die with dignity. I love this thing of ours, Mendoza. This thing of ours has made us all money. And before we all turn into cannibals and start eliminating each other, I choose to step aside. Whatever happens here once I'm gone is none of my business."

"I can lead this outfit, Zell. You know that. But until you're —when you're no longer apart of this outfit, until that day, your order will stand firm."

Zell laughed lowly, his massive, broad shoulders bouncing up and down underneath his white silk suit jacket as he eyed Mendoza and said, "Fuck you asshole. And I mean that not in a disrespectful manner, but in a laughable manner because you're grateful to me for allowing you to do something that I feel may very well destroy not only your crew, who I love so much mind you, but your whole fuckin' family. And understand that if this was ten, even five years ago your ass would be going into a meat grinder balls first while your ass is still breathing. So don't give me that grateful attitude shit. Just view this gesture for what it's worth. It's a business decision attributed to my ill-health—nothing more. Understand me?"

"I understand fully, Boss."

"As you should. You take your chance with this drug business. But I worry about your future, Mendoza. And that of your family's. I'm, I'm not going to be around to see what tragedy befalls you and your crew if ever that perceived tragedy happens. I'm moving down to my home in Florida and I'm going to enjoy what time I have remaining with my family. The job of Boss is now yours, understand? You run twenty-third as you see fit, Mendoza. I've made millions off the rackets and my family, my grandkids and grandchildren? They will never have to work a day in their lives. Slaving for the government or some other rich, arrogant prick is not in my family's future. I've done the hard work for everybody. Learn from me."

"You've taught me everything I need to know to run this business with a level head. Whoever gets in the way of twenty-third on this next move will be dealt with. This new racket is something my crew can more than handle."

"That I believe in my heart. That's why I chose you, Mendoza. You're a gangster by nature. What you do is in your blood. It's in Lucky and Junior's blood. DeeDee and Doss's blood. Your entire crew is built for that racket and that's why I chose you." Zell said as he extended his hand.

The two men shook hands and Mendoza was made for a third time on this night, and Zell, within two week's time, had moved down to Florida. The old Mafioso didn't last two months let alone six; he died alongside his family in his sleep in late August. Everybody from Chicago had flown into the city of Naples, Florida to attend Zell's funeral. Naomi was even on hand to see the old gangster who'd been her friend for over two decades lay in his final resting place.

With Zell's passing, 23rd had come under the complete control of Mendoza Cernigliaro and his crew and with new guidance came new business. Contract killings had resumed in the Midwest because just as Zell had told Mendoza shortly before his passing, a war had erupted. Four hits on drug dealers in Cleveland, Cincinnati and Indianapolis had earned profits and 23rd Street had garnered new respect as they looked for ways to enter into the drug trade. The crew didn't know it at the time, but it would be during their searching for ways to invest into the white powder they were so eager to distribute, that a chance meeting involving Finland Xavier in the month of September of 1992 would lead to a business deal that would forge a bond that would last for years to come.

CHAPTER 17
THE PROPOSITION

A shiny, black, stretched Cadillac limousine with dark tinted windows had just made a right turn off of Michigan Avenue onto Washington Street in downtown Chicago carrying five occupants. The driver paid his four passengers no mind as he guided the vehicle through the bustling streets of the Windy City. Three of the limousine driver's four passengers, who were teenagers, began to act as if they were in a band when the introduction to Tears for Fears' song *Everybody Wants To Rule The World* came across the stereo as the limousine's only adult passenger gazed in awe over the world famous city's architecture.

The four Asian passengers had just traversed the Miracle Mile and were now cruising through the city's legal district at a slow pace through all the traffic. The teenagers sat facing the rear of the limousine on a long, black, soft leather seat that was more like a couch. The two young males acted as if they were playing instruments, their eyes closed and heads tilted back as they tapped their feet in rhythm to the music and slapped their hands on their knees as if they were playing actual keyboards and drums.

The young Asian female held her left hand before her round face as if she was holding a microphone. She began snapping her fingers and sang first verse of the song…*"Welcome to your life…there's no turning back…even while you sleep…we will find you…acting on your best behavior turn your back on mother nature…everybody wants to rule the world…"*

The adult male smiled and reached out and touched the young female's cheek as she sang and said, "Your mother and father should be alive to see what a beautiful young woman you've become. You have such a lovely voice."

Thirty-nine year-old Finland Xavier, meanwhile, was walking briskly up the stairs to the Cook County Courthouse in downtown Chicago to sign in as he was to be in court all day today. Finland hadn't been in a good mood as of late. The man was becoming tired of representing penniless petty crooks who had no resources and multiple convictions. The most he could do for many of his defendants was to plea bargain for a lesser sentence. His freelance endeavors paid well, but the clients were few and far between, and ever since Zell had died, many of the old mobsters had retired, so work coming from 23rd Street Mafia was scarce. Fin was trotting up the stairs lost in his thoughts when he heard someone yell aloud, "Salamander!"

Fin looked around and saw a young Asian man standing at the bottom of the stairs with three Asian kids with him, two young boys, and a little Asian girl, all of whom appeared to be in their teens. He walked back down the stairs and stared at the man with apprehension. "Do I know you, sir," he asked cautiously.

"No you don't—but I know you, Salamander," the man replied in a curt and confident manner.

"How do you know the name Salamander?"

"A friend of yours told me about you last evening here outside the court building. I have a problem, and she said you can help."

"What's your problem, young man?"

"Well, I need representation. Are you available?"

"Who told you of me?"

"A blonde lady. Short in stature with blue eyes. Her name was Julianne Bixby."

"Ohh, yes," Fin stated as he smiled and reminisced about the many sexual escapades he and Julianne had shared in the past. "Well, how can I help you?"

"Let's not talk out here. It is a very important and private matter."

"I have court today. All day today."

"I understand. I'll just wait for you in the lobby. Please, when you're done, find me there."

Fin nodded and turned and went into the court building. All day he thought about the Asian man and what kind of problem he had. When court convened for the day he went and searched for the neatly dressed young man under the belief that he was probably looking for an immigration lawyer and was prepared to direct the man to the I.N.S. once he found him. When he found the man in the lobby, Fin began to speak on immigration, but the man quickly interrupted him by saying, "I'm a naturalized citizen, Salamander. So is my son Philip Tran here, my god son Grover Kobayashi, and my god daughter, Xiang Nyguen. Say hello to the counselor, children."

The three kids spoke and the man then introduced himself. "My name is JunJie Maruyama and I've heard that you can make problems go away. My limousine's right outside, let's go and talk right out front."

Fin and JunJie walked to his limousine and climbed inside the car. "I come from Nagano, Japan," JunJie began, "I came here in 1983 at the age of twenty-five with my partner and his son, which is Grover out there. Together we got into shipping and real estate in Seattle, Washington. Grover's father was killed in Japan. Now, nine years later, it is only me and the three young ones," thirty-four year-old JunJie Maruyama stated.

"What does that have to do with me, Mister Maruyama?"

"Nothing. Not that part anyhow. Let me lay it out for you, my man," JunJie said as he turned and faced Fin head on. "My partner, you see? He was into other things. I'm a legitimate business man and I will always consider myself a legitimate business man. From time to time, though, I move a certain kind of product here or there, understand?"

"What kind of product?"

"My partner was an excellent drug smuggler. I tried to keep that side of the business going, but I've come to the realization that I'm not a drug dealer."

"Mister JunJie? I may be from the streets, I may be black, but I'm a lawyer, not a drug dealer. And frankly I'm insulted that you would—"

"You're right. I'm totally out of line." JunJie said as he waved his hands from side to side. "Here's the deal. I was busted with two kilograms of cocaine last month and I now run the serious risk of having the kids taken away and also being deported. I love America because this country has made me rich beyond compare and I now consider it my homeland. What I offer today and today only is a business proposition. If you're not interested, say so and you'll never see me again."

Fin was intrigued all of sudden. The manner in which JunJie spoke, which was emphatic and to the point, led him to believe that he was all about business—serious business. "What kind of business proposal are you talking about, Mister Maruyama?" Finland asked.

"One that involves a lot of money, my man." JunJie replied as he leaned back in his seat and crossed his legs. "Right along with murder," he added as he eyed Finland with a serious stare.

"Murder? I'm sorry, but I don't kill people, Mister Maruyama."

"But you know people that do. I want you to find three witnesses that are scheduled to testify against me next month. They turned state's evidence on me and now I run the risk of being sent away. I'm not known here in Chicago, but if my colleagues back in the state of Washington find out that I'm a pusher I'll be ruined back home in Nagano, and in Seattle. I'm a business man first and foremost, Salamander. And this job I need done is a part of the business I have chosen for myself. I also have this new venture that I believe can make us a lot of money, but that's for later. The pressing issue as of now is that I have to have those witnesses eliminated. You know people that can do it and you've had this kind of work done for clients before me. Julianne said so. Tell your contacts that there's one-million dollars to be paid for this job."

"Really?" Fin asked as he rubbed his chin. "Who are these people you speak of, Mister JunJie?"

JunJie opened a briefcase and produced a manila folder and

handed it to Fin, who opened the folder and saw a single sheet with three names on it: Clementine Green, Kyle Desmond, and Trenton Years. JunJie leaned forward and pointed to the names on the sheet Fin held in his hands and said, "These three people here had me set up. They bought one kilogram and when I came back here to sell the other two, they had the police waiting. They must die for betraying my trust."

"How did you get way out here in Chicago?"

"I own a warehouse here in Chicago just off of Interstate-55 near the rail yard. I had a shipment of white powder delivered and took it upon myself to find a dealer here in town. Dumb move for a smart man I know—but if done right, this proposal could net you and your friends a lot of money in the long run. This murder-for-hire job is just for starters."

"All you have is names. How will I find these people?" Fin asked.

"You have contacts, right? I can describe them to you, but you have to track them down. That's why I offer a million dollars. This is very important to me, Salamander."

Fin held onto the file and pointed to JunJie and said, "You know how to contact me. How do I contact you once I find these marks?"

"Mister, what's your real name, Salamander?"

"Finland Xavier."

"Okay, Finland. I know a good outfit when I see one. And from what I've learned about your friends from 23rd Street, they are damn good. A legendary outfit by all accounts. This is a great opportunity for you and your friends. What do you say?"

Fin thought for a minute. The offer from JunJie was too tempting to pass up, and he was right in everything that he was saying. Twenty-third was indeed a legendary outfit; but before he could put this offer on the table before his friends, Fin had to find out if JunJie was for real. "I'll need half that money up front," he told JunJie. "That way I'll know you serious. You'll deliver the other half when the job is done. And we can no longer meet here understand?"

"Understood. I have to be on my way back to Seattle." JunJie replied as he checked the time on his platinum Rolex. "Here's my contact information," he then said as he went into the inside pocket of his silk suit jacket and handed Fin a business card with a phone number and an office address in Seattle. "I can be reached here in the morning hours. You have a month to do the job because my court date is five weeks away. Set up a bank account here and I'll drop the first half of the payment," he ended as he began to exit his limousine.

"What if I say nothing and just keep the half a million dollars for myself?" Fin asked.

JunJie slowly sat back down in his seat, closed the door and looked Fin squarely in his eyes. "You can run off with my money if you want to," he said, his dark, slender eyes giving off a cold appearance, "but you will lose far much more, Finland Xavier. If I believed that giving a complete stranger five-hundred thousand dollars knowing he may very well run off with it would hurt me financially, trust me, I would not do it."

"You got a point." Finland replied. "But let me ask you something, Mister Maruyama."

"Go right ahead, my friend."

"Just exactly what is this new venture you speak of?"

"Well, that remains to be seen now doesn't it? You do this job first. Set up a bank account here, take care of those witnesses, and we'll talk about our next venture when the smoke clears. If you want to continue to do business with me upon hearing my proposal, then we'll do business. If not, we'll go our separate ways and toast to a successful hit."

"If you put it on the table, and the price and plan is right, we'll do further business. But as you say, let's deal with this job first and see what we have left when the smoke clears."

"We have a deal, my man." JunJie replied as he and Finland shook hands inside the limousine.

Fin exited and smiled at the young Asians as they climbed back into the limousine with JunJie. The car pulled away from the curb and merged into the traffic of downtown Chicago and slowly blended in with the surrounding vehicles before disappearing from sight. On this day, in September of 1992,

Finland Xavier and a man by the name of JunJie Maruyama had unwittingly forged an association that would lead to the formation of one of the most violent and formidable criminal organizations the Midwest had ever seen.

CHAPTER 18
THE THREE FOR ONE JOB

Fin was now sitting in the *Eastside Bar* with Mendoza, DeeDee, Lucky and Doss talking about the chance meeting he had with JunJie Maruyama just a couple of hours earlier. Mendoza and DeeDee were reluctant upon hearing the story, but Fin had gone to his small office near the courtroom and checked the man out as thoroughly as possible with the resources he had on hand. JunJie, just as he said, dealt in real estate. Some of his transactions took place in Vegas and San Francisco and involved well-known real estate moguls from New York, London and Hong Kong. The man was legit in the eyes of the law, but he also had a dark side. A dark side Finland had seen up close and personal. His legit status, however, didn't prevent the crew from *Eastside Bar* from asking questions pertaining to this sudden and seemingly unbelievable offer that had derived from a total stranger.

"What kind of man would ask a lawyer—one whom he doesn't know mind you—to kill a few low level drug dealers for a million dollars," sixty-one year-old Mendoza asked.

"I asked myself the same thing the whole ride over here," Finland answered. "But this man is who he says he is and he guarantees half up front. I can set up a bank account and we'll see what happens."

"We should form a business of some sort with this new-found wealth if it proves true. A new racket you know, fellas? Take our game and move it towards legitimate businesses." Doss said.

"Now that there," DeeDee chimed in, "that there would be an unprecedented move on our part."

"For good or bad?" Lucky asked.

"For the good, Lucky," DeeDee replied. "That's the one thing Zell never brought to the table—legitimate assets."

"Zell's dying, and I mean no disrespect to the man," Mendoza said, "but his dying has led to new doors being opened. Had he been alive today? We wouldn't even be having this discussion. A legit business is the way to go."

"With that being said, pop—what'll we do? I mean, we still livin' outside the law. And I have a feeling that this other venture Finland mentioned to us that this JunJie guy has on the back burner isn't lawful." Lucky said.

"I don't think it is either," Finland remarked. "He said he moves a product or two. Sounds like drugs to me. Don't know what kind, though."

"That guy could be involved in anything," Doss chimed in. "It could be stolen merchandise from Asia. Heroin. Cocaine. Marijuana. Whatever it is, judging by his portfolio, it has to be worth a lot of money—legal or illegal. I think we can learn something from this man. To me, it looks as if he's a criminal with a legitimate front that he uses to wash dollars clean. Sort of like the way my wife does with my proceeds. We need to start ourselves a business to get on level with this guy."

"The question still stands," Lucky said. "What kind of business shall we operate?"

"Guys," Fin said, "I'm handling Naomi's trucking company and I know the ins and outs of running the business. Maybe a trucking company, our own trucking company would be the perfect front."

"That's a damn good idea." Mendoza stated. "Trucking would be the perfect front. Families have been engaged in that business for decades and still are. This trucking company, what shall we call it?"

"How about J.J. Lines?" Fin stated.

"J.J. Lines?" Doss said. "That'll be—dynamite," he quipped as he stood up and slapped his hands together. The crew laughed and Doss spoke again once he sat back down in his seat. "J.J. Lines is too superficial. Let's go with Midwest Express," he then said seriously.

"Midwest Express sounds good. Real good. Fin, you draw up the papers and open a business account under that name. We still have that connect down in Des Moines where we can get a rig for cheap. Let's all put up seven grand if and when that guy drops that loot, get us a truck and trailer and go to work. Fin you handle the logistics." Mendoza said as Junior placed a glass of wine in front of each of the five men as they continued to talk.

"Okay," Fin said as he raised his glass, "today, we form Midwest Express with the intent of becoming partners with Mister JunJie Maruyama in Seattle," he ended as the men all touched rims and sipped their wine.

Two days later, Fin called JunJie and told him the account was open and gave him the routing number. It would take a month or so for the company to be registered with the state, but Fin had used the papers he filed for the license to open a business account. The Monday following the weekend, Fin went and checked the bank account during lunch and saw a statement balance of $500,000 dollars. He took off early that day and emptied the account except for $5000 dollars, money he would use to keep the account active. He entered *Eastside Bar* with five checks, each worth $99,000 dollars, and a small celebration ensued as the men began to plot on their marks.

****

Two weeks later on a Tuesday night in the later part of September 1992, Mendoza, DeeDee, Doss, Lucky, and Junior, after having their marks' identifications confirmed through pictures that were supplied by Finland and verified by JunJie, were inside the *Eastside Bar* having a drink at the counter before they headed out. On this night, they were planning to execute Clementine Green, Kyle Desmond, and Trenton Years, all of whom were in their mid to late twenties.

The men thought they would have been completed the job; but Clementine and Kyle didn't have a record and had gone underground. Trenton, on the other hand, was easy to find. He resided in his own home in Gary, Indiana. Fin had obtained his address and mug shots via Cook County court records because he'd been arrested numerous times for armed robbery and had various assault charges. Mendoza and DeeDee spied the address and began tailing a 1993 convertible red BMW 3 Series that Trenton drove. He rode around in the car with the top down during the day time and perused strip clubs there in the city during the night. Mendoza and DeeDee were looking to kill twenty-nine year-old Trenton Years in his car the first chance they received.

Twenty-six year-olds Clementine Green and Kyle Desmond were long time lovers who were only looking for a way out of a jam. Kyle had caught a drug charge after he and Trenton scored the first kilogram from JunJie and he'd decided to cooperate in order to avoid jail time. Trenton and Clementine were cousins, so it was nothing for him to go along with Clementine and help her keep her man out of jail. The three, however, had crossed the wrong man. A man who'd called upon a specific kind of person to help him solve a mounting problem. Negotiations were off the table and there was no amount of money one could offer that would change the outcome for these three unfortunate souls.

Clementine and Kyle was a little harder to track down because they had no jacket and the men on 23rd Street were all thinking one of two things—that both Clementine and Kyle had skipped town—or were just laying low until the heat cooled down. Playing the latter, Doss began asking around and soon learned that Clementine and Kyle were hiding out in the Cabrini Green projects with their baby daughter. Fin had gotten pictures of Clementine from the Social Services Office so Doss could show his contacts on the streets. One of Doss's young and trusted soldiers confirmed for him that the woman in the picture was the same woman who was living in an apartment in Cabrini Green Projects. He also told Doss that the young man with her was indeed Kyle because he'd shot dice with him a number of times. Satisfied that they had all the information needed, the men finished their drinks and set out to their jobs.

"Okay, gentlemen," Mendoza said. "As of now we're on the clock. Any trouble comes along everybody's on their own until morning. Check in time should everything go right like I know it will, is four this morning."

"Got it, pops," Lucky replied as he, Doss and Junior exited the bar and hopped into his ride.

"Hey, Lucky," Doss said as Mendoza pulled away from the curb in his El Dorado, "remind me to pick up some new Jordan's for my kids before I head back down to Ponca City tomorrow."

"Okay, Doss. How you getting back home? You driving?" Lucky asked as he merged onto Interstate-290.

"I'm gone fly out this time to see how it works out. The drive home takes twelve hours. A flight down to Oklahoma City is only two and a half hours. Naomi and the kids can pick me up, we'll spend a day down in OKC and head back to the old fort."

"Flyin' is cool. I gotta say this, though—it sure feels good to be back in business, you know? I got a feeling that what we about to get involved in with this guy from Seattle is gonna reap huge dividends."

"So do I. That's why I wanna see how these flights will run. Driving back and forth twelve hours each way will grow old fast. I gotta feeling things are about to pick up too, brother. Feels good."

"Right it does," Lucky said as he turned up the radio. "That's a jam right there," he said upon hearing the music.

"Why do I feel like I'm in a time machine, dad?" Junior asked his father from the backseat as "*Diamond in the back*", being sung by William Devaughn, played on the radio.

Lucky turned up the radio and snapped his fingers as he sang along with the song, "*Diamond in the back, sunroof top... diggin' the scene with a gangster lean...diamond in the back, sunroof top...diggin' the scene with a gangster lean oh, ooh, oooh...*"

"Son, this here is a classic car, and that's real music right there as well. It's better than that be-boppity bop 'comin through the front door leavin' brains on the floor, I need money bitch give me some more' shit you listen to at home." Lucky said as Doss and Junior laughed aloud.

Junior continued laughing aloud and said, "That was cool,

dad. But this car is still ancient."

Lucky looked over to thirty-nine year-old Doss, who was laughing right along with Junior, and said, "You with him? You sidin' with that mutherfucka back there in the backseat?"

"Hey, man? It is about time for a new ride. This car is like seventeen years old. But that rap was crazy—brains on the floor, mutherfuckin' money give me some more. Where you hear that, Lucky?"

"That mutherfucka in that backseat right there plays that rap shit all day. He even has Mildred, his own mother, his fuckin' mother, listening to that shit."

"All rap ain't bad, pops. It's just new times. The new school is comin' in now. Not ta' mention chicks dig rap music." Junior replied.

"Hey, I'm old school. Old school car. Old school music—and chicks still dig me. DeeDee still rides the big Lincoln, or the, or the Millenia, Milllumina—"

"The Millennium Falcon. Han solo's ride from Star Wars," Doss chimed in.

"There ya' go," Lucky yelled aloud through laughter. "The first time Naomi called DeeDee's ride that shit all I could hear was the theme from Star Wars. I see it every time DeeDee pulls up in that thing. Naomi nailed that one. That's a long ass ride your pops has, Doss. And he still gets action with that machine as old as it is. Speaking of Naomi, how's my wife doing down there in Oklahoma?"

"*My wife*—is doing just fine. She has this dream of building a huge mansion down there on the ranch and buying another truck." Doss stated as the group rode through the streets of Chicago on this cold, clear night.

"Well, with this kind of money we gettin' for these marks she'll at least get her truck right away, right?" Lucky asked seriously.

"Yeah, but I would love to see my wife and kids with a bigger house. The house we have now is fine. But with all that land, we can design a house the way we want it and build that sucker from the ground up."

"I would love to see you do it, Doss," Lucky replied. "The ranch really is like a paradise. A lovely, two or three story mansion would be the icing on the cake for that land. And you and Naomi deserve it. We'll get there my friend—we'll get there. That girl, Siloam—she datin' anybody down there?"

"Siloam is real busy helping Naomi with the kids and the farming when I'm not around. When I'm home, she goes out on the weekends, but I can't actually say that she's datin' someone."

"She's datin' me, pops."

"Junior? You call me pops one more time you, you—Ohhh! Shut the fuck up back there! Check and see if you put the bullets in the gun the right way you Mildred-looking mutherfucka!"

Junior and Lucky loved to chide one another; and even though they were on their way to murder two people, the mood in the car was light and jovial. Lucky and Doss behaved in the same manner in which Mendoza and DeeDee behaved around the two of them when they were training them to become killers-for-hire back in the day. Lucky and Doss were merely passing on what they'd learned to Junior, which was to always keep the mood light and calm, it's just a job that needs doing.

"Hey, hey, pops, calm down. You gettin' a little too feisty. Don't give yourself a heart attack tonight." Junior stated as Doss laughed.

"I swear, when we done? I'm leaving his ass tied up in the bathroom with a note telling everybody he did it—and the fuckin' pistol will be lying right there on his fuckin lap! I'll send your ass, you, you—Ohhh! Alright! Alright now! Here we go. Enough of the dumb shit." Lucky stated seriously as he turned into the projects on Chicago's North East side.

Doss carefully guided Lucky through Cabrini Green and a lot of people waved at him as he rode by. Doss was well known in this part of Chicago. He once ran a gambling house here back in the day before he moved his operation closer to Cicero. He also loaned people money back in the day and sometimes paid peoples' rent and never asked for the money back. Doss Dawkins, and his father DeeDee were well-respected gangsters in not only Cabrini Green, but in just about all of Chicago's housing developments. This was one of the reasons why Doss and his father were so close to 23rd Street. They had access to areas of Chicago that members of 23rd could not travel into on their own without repercussions from Black Gangsters.

Lucky parked the car before two tall buildings that had scores of people out in front. The men checked their weapons and then exited the car and began their walk through the swift, cool, blowing wind headed towards Clementine's building. Lucky had on a pair of dark grey silk slacks black leather shoes with a buttoned up black leather blazer and black fedora. Doss was wearing a black silk suit and black leather trench coat with a pair of black gator shoes, while Junior had on a dark grey silk jogging suit and a pair of black suede shoes with a black b-bop Kangol.

Junior was a little suspect of the area. He'd never been in this particular project before and he found the place to be unfit for human habitation. The wary-eyed youngster had a bigger thought on his mind also—there was no telling who Clementine and Kyle knew back in this area. People were everywhere. Cabrini Green looked more like a small downtown city as the numerous project buildings, at least fifteen stories, could easily pass for downtown offices in many cities.

Lucky puffed on a cigarette as he walked with Doss and Junior and he'd noticed how quiet his son had become the moment the trio had entered the projects. "Son, you okay back there," Lucky asked.

"I'm cool, dad." Junior replied. Junior was thinking that his father surely would not walk into a place as wild as this without being sure that the people he were going to kill were not being protected by, nor related to anyone in the area.

"Don't worry, son," Lucky said. "Doss and I wouldn't be here if we didn't think we could pull this job off."

"I know, dad." Junior responded as he continued eyeing the people that were out, all of them going about their business of ushering kids into buildings, toting plastic bags of groceries and hanging out doing things that the law wouldn't approve of;

but who was Junior to judge anyone back here? He was out to kill someone after all.

As Junior walked up the sidewalk trialing his father and Doss, Lucky took a puff off his cigarette and coughed loudly and spat onto the concrete. "Them cigarettes are gonna kill your ass one day, Lucky." Doss said. "Why you pick up that stupid habit anyway?"

"I tried one a year ago when I didn't have a joint to smoke. I thought it would get me high but I was dead wrong. Now the shit's just been gettin' outta control. And not to mention this mutherfucka behind me constantly gets on my fuckin' last nerves." Lucky answered, forcing Doss into a chuckle.

"Why not just blow your brains out on the floor, head for the door, but leave the cash on the floor." Junior said as the three laughed and continued their walk through the projects.

The three walked towards Clementine's building and came across a group of about eight or nine males, some in their teens, some in their twenties, playing dice out front. The young men, all dressed in high-end baggy jeans and brand new rugged boots, some with hooded sweatshirts and some wearing expensive leather jackets, paused the game and stood up and spoke to Doss as he approached. The well-respected gangster shook a few hands as he walked in between the group and asked, "Who got the hot hands tonight?"

"Right here! I been sticking these niggas all night," a husky young man with a smooth, baby-like face and braided hair called out to Doss as he grabbed the crotch of his baggy, navy blue Girbaud jeans and held out his left wrist. "I done took one watch—this a Rollie, too! Plus I got two diamond rings out these busters! I'm hot tonight."

Doss knew the brown-skinned young male that spoke to him very well. His name was Eddie Cottonwood. Eddie's father ran Doss' poker room back in the late eighties, but he was now locked up in Rockville State Prison and serving a twenty-five to life sentence for killing a man who owed Doss money. Doss never ordered the hit, but Eddie's father did it anyway; and he never mentioned Doss' name when he was sent away.

Doss always looked out for Eddie by giving him money to

take care of himself, and it was understood by all around that Eddie was indeed a good hustler. He'd been taking the money given to him by Doss to sell cocaine and was using some of the profits to take care of his newborn daughter, Nancy, and his younger brothers Jason David and Donnell. Doss made it a point to look after Eddie and his people whenever he could on the strength of Eddie's father, and he also had work for the seventeen year-old from time to time. This night was one of those times.

Doss and Eddie walked a few steps away from the game and spoke in near whispers. "You double checked it right?" Doss asked as he pulled out a money clip.

"Yeah, Doss. They don't fuck with nobody back here, man. They don't have no people stay back here either, and dude not affiliated. Look like they just hidin' out and laying low like you thought."

Doss gave Eddie a hundred dollar bill and said, "Work with that until I get back, young brother."

Eddie looked at the hundred dollar bill and frowned, his gold grill coming into view under the lights in front of the building. "You said I get a G."

Doss didn't want Eddie to leave the dice game. He wanted everything to continue on as it would have before he showed, and it he wanted it the same way when he left. "Anybody ask you something, all I did was give you money to play dice, alright?"

"Yeah. But the—"

"You know I'm solid." Doss said lowly. "I want you to stay out here, and if you see anything suspicious, or if you see the police riding through, you let me know."

"How I'm gone do that? By the time I run up there the law gone be all over the place."

Doss handed Eddie a cell phone and he looked at it like it was from outer space. It looked like a small loaf of bread with a thick black wire coming out of the top. "You use this like a house phone. If the police come through all you gotta do is hit the green button, my pager number already set." Doss said.

"Okay, but you be back through, right?"

Doss laughed to himself. Eddie was just like Junior—every detail had to be explained in order for him to get the big picture; but that was a good thing because Doss knew once Eddie understood fully, he could be counted on to do what was asked of him without fail, just like Junior.

"Yeah I be back through." Doss answered. "But just in case," he added as he called Lucky and Junior over.

Lucky walked over and handed Eddie the keys to his car and said, "If either of us don't come back down here, you take my car and keep it. It's worth ten grand at least on the streets."

Seventeen year-old Eddie Cottonwood now had Doss's cell phone and the keys to Lucky's car. He now got the full picture —these men were here to kill someone and they were willing to pay him for his help. He nodded seriously, gave Doss a pound and said, "Handle your business, Doss. I got you. And I'm a look after your ride," he told Lucky as he opened his black, red and white leather Chicago Bulls jacket and put a chrome handgun on display. "I got ya' car, dog. We good. And I'm a been flipped this bill you gave me, too, Doss," he ended as he turned and headed back to the dice game.

"Who was that," another male from the group asked Eddie upon his return.

"A gambler I deal with that owe me money. He gave me a hundred of what he owe so I can break y'all niggas again. What's hatnin'? Somebody fade Mister Benjamin Franklin."

"Damn, nigga! You gettin' money all kinds of ways tonight, huh? I fade," one of the young men out the group was heard saying as Doss, Lucky and Junior walked into the building.

It was after midnight when the men began traversing the stairs. The elevators inside the projects rarely worked and when they did, it was a good chance when you got on, they would break down while you were in them. Clementine resided on the fourteenth floor; it would be a long walk, but the stairs were safer than the elevator. Doss, Lucky and Junior walked leisurely up the stairs, lightly chatting as they did so. Doss often walked the land in Oklahoma with his kids and had no problem walking the stairs as the long walks and time spent running around the ranch kept him in excellent shape and physically fit. Junior was fit as well; but Lucky, because of the lack of exercise and smoking cigarettes, grew tired half way up.

"Hey Junior," Lucky said out as he paused and sat on the stairs to catch his breath, "go up there, and tell that bitch and her old man, to walk down here for a minute, so we can kill 'em both here on the stairs."

Junior laughed lowly and said, "They would be real nice to walk down here and let you put a couple slugs in them, dad."

"Hey," Lucky responded as he got up and the men continued on, "I've killed nice people before, son. Back in Cleveland. Hey Doss remember that job?"

"Right in her screaming mouth." Doss stated matter-of-factly as he traveled up the stairs.

"Right in her big, screamin', pastor-dick-suckin' mouth." Lucky stated through laughter as he reminisced about the woman he'd killed back in 1976.

When the men reached the 14th floor, their handguns were drawn and their entire demeanor had changed. Hand signals were now being used. Doss pointed to Lucky, signaling that Clementine's apartment was at the end of the hall on the right, about twelve doors down. The hall t-boned into another hall that had an iron screen covering the front windows in order to prevent residents from being thrown over the sides, like in times past. Lucky and Junior walked down the dimly lit corridor and stood in the hall just outside of Clementine's apartment.

Doss waited near the stairwell for Lucky and Junior. When they were in place, Lucky nodded back down the hall towards Doss and he tripped the switch in Clementine's apartment and quickly ducked back into the stairwell. A few minutes later, Kyle walked out of the apartment to check the circuit breaker. He opened the box and upon seeing that the circuit had been tripped, he reset it and walked back towards the apartment. When he passed the stairwell, Doss emerged and asked in a cool and calm manner, "Hey man, you know where a young lady name Tina stay on this floor?"

"I don't know no Tina, man." Kyle replied as he continued

on to his apartment.

"Damn. Maybe she stay out front. Let me head down that way." Doss said as he followed Kyle down the hall.

Just before Kyle entered his home he was greeted with two . 9mm hand guns that held silencers over the barrels. He stared at the guns that had been shoved into his face just as a gloved hand was wrapped around his mouth from behind. Kyle was guided into his apartment in silence and Junior closed the door and locked it.

Clementine came out the room holding her baby and when she saw the three men shoving Kyle towards the sofa, she took off running back into the bedroom and locked the door and hid her baby.

"Do your job, son." Lucky said in a clam manner.

Junior ran towards the bedroom and kicked the door open and aimed his weapon on Clementine. The frightened young woman screamed when her assailant kicked the door in, but she was quickly silenced by a bullet that had entered her chest and exited her back. Junior then walked over and saw that Clementine was still alive as she lay on the floor beside the bed. She was reaching for her baby as she eyed her assailant standing over her with his gun aimed squarely at her head. Junior said nothing as he looked Clementine square in the eyes and shot her two times in the face. She died on her bedroom floor right beside her crying baby. Clementine Green was Junior's first kill. And he felt no remorse for killing the mother of a new born child—to him—it was just a job that needed doing.

Doss and Lucky, meanwhile, were preparing to take care of Kyle, having tied him up and sat him down on the sofa. Kyle was breathing hard at this moment, unable to believe he was about check out. He asked Doss through panted breath why he was being killed.

"You been hiding out for a reason—because you snitched on your man after you got busted with his drugs. He sent us so you can pay him back with your life." Doss replied in a cool, calm and collective manner as he screwed a silencer onto the barrel of his .9mm.

"I swear! I swear man! That was all Trenton idea! All we was supposed to do was hold the drugs?"

"You got the drugs here?" Doss asked.

"Trent kept everything. He played us! Tell, tell that Asian man I ain't had shit ta' do with him gettin' ripped off and I'm sorry."

"I'll give him your message," Doss replied as he and Lucky took aim and shot Kyle in the head and torso a total of twelve times.

As the three men turned to leave the apartment, Doss, remembering he had seen Clementine holding a baby, turned to Junior and said, "You didn't kill that baby did you?"

"No. She won't even remember this shit." Junior replied.

"I know. But we have to take care of her. We can't leave her in this house for long either." Doss responded as he walked to the kitchen.

"So you're not a monster after all." Lucky replied as he congratulated Junior on his first kill and headed for the hall leading to the bedroom.

Junior watched in wonderment as Doss opened the refrigerator and looked inside while his father went into the bedroom. Lucky reappeared with the baby, which could not be more than a few months old, inside a clothes basket. He walked into the kitchen toting the little girl and stood beside Doss as he rocked the baby in the basket.

"What's going on?" Junior asked inquisitively.

"It's feeding time." Doss replied.

"We gonna take her with us?" Junior asked in perplexed manner.

"What are we gonna do with a new baby? I can barely support your ass." Lucky stated to Junior.

Doss laughed as he placed a pot of water on the lighted stove and grabbed a bottle of formula from the refrigerator with his glove-clad hands and placed the bottle into the water. He and Lucky stood by the stove quietly and patiently inside the kitchen, Lucky gently rocking the baby, who made not a sound.

"I'll have Fin make an anonymous call and report the bodies. The last thing I want is to be labeled as a monster that left a baby to die." Doss said as Lucky nodded in agreement.

Doss remembered the night in Sylacauga, Alabama when his father had ceased all activity to make sure that a baby would not starve to death inside a home once all the adults were killed and he'd never forgotten the experience. As he eyed the baby, he couldn't help but to think that she would grow up without a mother and father and he wondered how she would fair in life. Doss ended his thoughts there, though; the baby's parents may have been dead, but she would live. At least she would have a chance at life. The killer-for-hire then thought about his family and how much he loved them, and how much he missed them when he was away from the ranch working. "I can't wait to see my family later on," he finally said as he smiled at the baby girl and rubbed his fingers gently across her cheeks.

The water began to sizzle and Lucky grabbed the bottle and dabbed Doss' wrist. Junior was laughing to himself. He and his father and Doss had just murdered two people, now his father and Doss were caring for the child belonging to the people they had just killed as if she were their own. Lucky and Doss may have been cold-bloodied killers, but only when necessary in Junior's eyes. The manner in which his father and Doss were catering to this baby would become a lesson Junior would never forget.

"It's ready." Doss stated as he placed the bottle into the baby's mouth.

Lucky sat the clothes basket containing the baby in the center of the living room and covered her with a thick sheet. The three men then left the apartment, headed down the stairs and out the building. They walked pass the dice game and Doss called out to Eddie, who stood up and handed Lucky his keys and showed Doss four hundred dollars. Doss gave Eddie another nine hundred dollars and the teen dapped him and went back to the game. Nothing would be said about the double murder committed in Cabrini Green. Doss, Lucky and Junior's job had been a success and their work was now done for the night.

****

275

"...but we could never see...tomorrow...no one...no one told us...about the sorrow...so...how can you mend a broken heart...how can you stop the rain from falling down..."

Mendoza and DeeDee had been following Trenton Years through the streets of Gary, Indiana for almost two hours, but Mendoza, who was driving, could never find the opportune time to pull up alongside Trenton's car to allow DeeDee to pull the hit. When he did have an opportunity, there were always witnesses around. Mendoza and DeeDee weren't for walking, and they hated to trail a mark. They had planned on killing Trenton from the front seat of DeeDee's Lincoln Town Car, but not being able to tail him into an isolated location was seriously aggravating the men. Trenton was going from strip club to strip club on this night, and each club had people out front and in the parking lots. Mendoza and DeeDee were both getting sleepy now. The two men were in their sixties, old vets to homicide that went to bed early most nights, and they were pissed to high heaven that Trenton had them out past their bed time waiting for them to kill him.

The two men sat outside a strip club waiting for Trenton to emerge as Al Green's song *How Can You Men a Broken Heart* played on the radio, both of them dozing off on occasion as the song played. Mendoza quickly raised his head after nodding off, thinking he'd been out for several minutes, but when he saw Trenton's car still parked on the street and heard the same Al Green song on the radio, he knew he'd blacked out for only a few seconds. He looked over to DeeDee, who was sound asleep, and coughed lightly to rouse him.

DeeDee quickly raised his head and Mendoza asked him, "How's the family on the ranch?"

DeeDee knew he had blacked out and it was a good chance Mendoza had nodded off too. The two men knew they had to stay awake so they began conversing. "Naomi's always talking about building this big house," DeeDee replied as he yawned and rubbed his burning eyes. "She wants to build a mansion down on the ranch and I wanna see her do it. To see my grandkids living in all that luxury would be all I could ask for. My entire life of crime would have been worth it."

"Yeah. That would be nice. I would like to see that, too.

Naomi deserves it." Mendoza replied. "Now that's a song," he then said as he turned the volume up on Barry White's song *Can't Get Enough of Your Love*.

Barry White's song now had DeeDee reflecting on Sharona Benson, the twenty-four year-old woman he was sleeping with that now lived in the condo he owned on Lake Shore Drive. Sharona was a fine, dark-skinned female with a curvaceous ass who adored DeeDee and catered to his every need. She cooked for DeeDee. Served him breakfast in bed and ironed his slacks and shirts. The woman also had a head on her shoulders. She was a commercial advertiser for a major marketing firm in downtown Chicago. DeeDee had met her almost a year ago when he was trying to have several billboards designed to advertise around the city for a bar-b-cue and fundraiser he and the mayor was putting together for impoverished inner city kids. DeeDee thought she was the most precious thing he had ever seen and couldn't help but to ask the woman out to dinner. When she accepted, DeeDee swept her off her feet by flying her on a private jet to the Virgin Islands to have dinner the next day. She had been with DeeDee ever since.

"What you know about that music?" DeeDee asked Mendoza as he reflected on Sharona.

"Plenty much." Mendoza replied. "Francine and I don't just sip tea all day, you know?"

"That song makes me want to go see my baby." DeeDee said as he shifted in his seat.

"Makes me want to my baby, too. My baby of forty years."

"A lifetime." DeeDee replied as he gazed down at the wedding band he'd never removed. "I miss Shelia. My son's mother was the sweetest woman I knew and she was all I ever wanted. After she was killed, I never found another like her."

"You know, a lot of the young gals you deal with—"

"Look just like Shelia?" DeeDee asked, cutting Mendoza short.

"Yeah. Not all, but some. Is that on purpose?" Mendoza asked as he looked over to DeeDee.

"I'm not stuck in the past, Mendoza. It just works out that way sometimes. I like young women. They're full of life and they do things in life. That's all to it. I wish I could find a woman my age that's active and excites me. If I do, I'll settle down."

"You ain't settling down ever. You don't want a woman your age. You love young women and that's all to it. At least you fuckin' young women in your old age, though—unlike this guy Trenton we been tailing. How many pieces of pussy can you look at in one night and not fuck neither one? I mean, this guy here is spending all his money—and he ain't fuckin' nothin'—young or old."

"I know. They have a lot of young females out there and I know for certain that it's some good pussy over there." DeeDee said as he eyed the entrance of the club, which held many teenage female patrons in tight jeans and skirts standing under the canopy talking to various young men that were out front.

"You say good pussy over there?"

"Yeah. Good pussy is over there." DeeDee said as he eyed Mendoza.

Mendoza looked out the driver's side window and smiled before he turned back to DeeDee. "Good pussy is everywhere. Matter of fact, I know of some good pussy that comes through the bar. But you gotta pay for it."

"I know every female that comes through that bar. If there was a female that done came through there that I hadn't fucked or tried to fuck I would've known who you were talking about." DeeDee said as he began nodding his head to the music.

"You haven't been looking hard enough. This gal that hangs around the bar back in Cicero comes around only on occasion. She's a, a umm, a sorta blonde haired gal. Slightly graying on the edges with green eyes, real nice-looking. She's a hot momma. But you gotta pay for it."

"She got grey hair? What? She a hundred?" DeeDee asked as he righted himself in the seat.

"No. She's hot. You would wanna pay just to see her naked. Gray hair and all."

DeeDee leaned back as he eyed the club, he was now vaguely

paying attention to Mendoza as the woman's perceived age had turned him off. "I may pay for pussy, but I pay for young pussy," he told Mendoza. DeeDee then began thinking; he'd never seen the woman, maybe she would be someone his age that he could settle down with. "I do need a woman close to my age. You was right about that," he said. "This older woman you talking about, show her to me the next time she enters the bar. If she's got some spunk I'll lay down my game and sweep her off her feet just like I do the younger ones."

"Alright, I'll show you to her next time. She comes, she comes in with this old retired professor from Northwestern from time to time."

"Is that right?" DeeDee asked as he rubbed his neatly-trimmed beard. "You know Kevin used to work over to North —" DeeDee paused mid-sentence and thought about the description of the woman Mendoza had described to him and he laughed aloud. "Mutherfucka," he yelled as he erupted into laughter. "You better stop playing with Naomi's mother before she comes back here and, hey," DeeDee couldn't help himself, he laughed hard at Mendoza. "You son of a bitch! You gone, you gone stop playing around with Serena and Kevin like that! And you definitely gone stop fuckin' with me!"

Mendoza was laughing himself. "Kevin lucky I love 'em," he said. "When I first *saw* Serena I wanted to fuck that broad but she never gave me the time of day! And when she went over to Kevin's house that Christmas Day in '66 I said, 'well, there goes my shot at *that* piece of ass'! I'm glad thems two got together, though. Boy I tell ya', they did a helluva job with Naomi."

"I know. My daughter-in-law is as strong as ever—can't wait to see her and my grandkids later this week."

About an hour later the strip club had finally closed. Mendoza and DeeDee quickly spotted Trenton when he exited the building and their eyes trailed the man as he walked to his car and slid in behind the steering wheel. Trenton left the parking lot and began heading north out of Gary towards Interstate-90. He cruised under an overpass and stopped at a red light and finally, Mendoza and DeeDee were able to pull off their job. Mendoza pulled alongside Trenton's car on the driver's side and DeeDee stuck a .357 magnum out the passenger side window and fired four shots. Trenton immediately slumped over the front seat and DeeDee slowly and casually stepped out of the car underneath the overpass amidst the sounds of cars and trucks rumbling across Interstate-90 up above and fired two more rounds into Trenton's skull.

"He dead?" Mendoza asked.

"Well, if he can pick his brains up off the front seat and put 'em back in his skull he'll live." DeeDee answered nonchalantly as he got back into his Lincoln Town car's passenger seat just as Marvin Gaye and Tammi Terrell's song *"Your Precious Love"* began to play. "Hey, that's a classic right there. Reminds me of my baby, Sharona." DeeDee stated as he and Mendoza made a right turn and rounded the on-ramp and headed back to Chicago.

CHAPTER 19
THE BAD HOUSE

"How's everything back home, baby?" Doss asked Naomi over the phone.

It was a cool Saturday morning in Mid-March of 1993. Naomi was in the kitchen eating breakfast and was waiting on Siloam to come down and mind the kids so she could tend to the land with her four ranch hands.

Naomi and Doss was doing real well financially now. After Doss got paid completely for the job he and his crew did back in Chicago and Gary, Indiana for JunJie six months ago, he returned home to his family in late September of 1992 with his new-found wealth. When he handed the two checks to Naomi, that totaled just under $200,000 shortly after his arrival, Naomi knew right away what she was going to do: she would take the money her husband had given her and reinvest it into the ranch.

The first thing Naomi did was buy two Suburban SUV's to transport the kids safely in one group. She then bought more livestock from the auctions in Oklahoma City. She bought four steers for mating, a dozen heifers, eight calves, one hundred chickens, a dozen roosters, two hogs for mating and a dozen piglets. The family now had close to one hundred heads of cattle because the thirty-two cattle that were roaming the farm had produced calves themselves after Naomi began caring for them. She was now planning on sending some of the cattle to market in a couple of years. Cattle could earn up to $2,000 dollars per head when brought to the slaughter house, and by then, Naomi knew she would have enough chickens and hogs to send to market as well.

Naomi also bought another semi-truck. She now had two trucks running livestock to Ames, Iowa, and frozen meat throughout the west and Midwest and was earning about $4,700 dollars a week after all expenses were paid. The drivers and ranch hands were all paid well and everybody was happy and healthy. Everything was going smooth by March of 1993.

"Everything's going good, my love. Really, really good. When are you coming home again? You've been gone since late January and the kids all miss you. So do I." Naomi said as she exited the back door of the home and sat on her patio to converse with her husband.

"I'm waiting on Fin to return to Chicago. He's meeting with JunJie today. That thing we discussed? It's about to unfold. Your financial prowess will be needed once more, baby. When Fin gets back, I'll be on my way."

"Momma! Bay got grandpa baby doll he gave me for Christmas and she won't give it back!" four year-old Koko yelled aloud from deep inside the home.

"Exactly what do you need me to do?" Naomi asked, ignoring her daughter.

"The money that'll be made will need to be invested. You have any ideas off the top of your head?"

"Trucking." Naomi replied. "We're generating good dollars with the two trucks we have. The more trucks, the more freight we can move. There's plenty room to expand there."

"Okay. And maybe we can begin planning that dream home we been discussing."

"That would be wonderful, Doss."

"Momma! I said Bay got my baby doll and she won't give it back!" Koko yelled again.

"Doss, we'll finish this conversation tonight. Call me then okay? Let me deal with these kids and get them situated for Siloam so I can go to work." Naomi said as she sighed in disgust.

"Okay. I love you, Naomi."

"I love you too, Doss." Naomi replied before she ended the

call and got up and entered the home to address Koko's situation.

"What is it now, Koko?" Naomi asked aloud as she walked into the kitchen.

"The same thing! Bay took my baby doll that grandpa Kevin had gave me for Christmas and she won't give it back!" Koko yelled as she ran up to her mother and hugged her legs. "She always take it and keep it, momma."

"Bena get in here right now!" Naomi shouted.

"Naomi," Siloam then said as she entered the front door, "Flacco said there are several bales of hay out by the canal and he needs a new pair of wire cutters to cut the barbed wire."

"Okay, Siloam. We need more feed for the chickens, too. I'll grab a pair of wire cutters from the feed store for Flacco." Naomi replied as Bay walked into the kitchen from the den with her arms folded and apologizing repeatedly to her mother.

"Why do you agitate your sister in that manner, Bena?" Naomi asked as she rested her arm on the counter top.

"I don't know, momma." Bena replied as she watched her mother grab a set of keys from the key rack at the end of the island counter.

"Come on with me, Bena." Naomi remarked as she headed for the front door.

Bay began crying as she followed her mother to the front door. "Momma, I'm sorry. Please don't do this," she pleaded lowly.

Dawk and Kimi walked out of the den holding Spoonie and Tyke respectively, with Walee, trailing behind sucking on a bottle of orange juice. They all surrounded Bena in the kitchen. "Where y'all going?" Dawk asked Bena lowly.

"Bena, I said come with me." Naomi said as she neared the front door.

Bena looked at her siblings for a few seconds and then hugged them all. "You know where it's at. Don't forget me. Send, send Siloam or somebody. Send daddy to get me when he gets back," she said as she wiped her tears and walked down the stairs and up the aisle leading to the front door where her mother was standing. Bena held her head down and was crying freely as she approached her mother. "Momma, please," she pleaded one last time.

"We've been here before with this problem, Bena. You're going to have to learn to listen to what your father and I have to say." Naomi replied as she held the front door open to allow Bena to exit the home.

Naomi had been having problems with Bay harassing Koko and confiscating her younger sister's toys. Bay meant no harm; she just really liked the doll and teasing Koko at the same time. Naomi was only planning on taking Bay along for the ride to the feed store in town in order to talk to the six year-old, but Bay and her siblings were under the impression that something more drastic was about to go down.

The reason being was because Naomi often threatened to take her children to what she termed 'the bad house', which was actually a small orphanage. The children passed it every time they went into town. Dawk saw kids playing outside in the front yard of the one story white wooden structure several weeks back and asked what it was, and Naomi replied by telling Dawk and the rest of the kids that the house was a house for bad kids and she would take them there if they were ever bad. It immediately became known as "the bad house" to the kids.

It was a terrible thing for Naomi to say to her kids considering her plight once upon a time, but Naomi's eight could drive any sane person to the brink of insanity when they got on a roll. Walee, Spoonie, and Tyke were too young to understand what Naomi meant when she spoke of 'the bad house', but Koko, Kimi, Bena, Tiva, and Dawk knew full well what the "bad house" was; and they all feared being 'dropped off at the bad house', as their mother often said to them. Siloam often suggested that Naomi not to say such things to the kids because it was having a negative effect, but Naomi never believed Siloam words. This day, however, Naomi would see firsthand the impact her words were having on five of her kids.

Bay, dressed in blue jeans and a white t-shirt and white sneakers, walked down the stairs towards the suburban and

Naomi opened the door. "Sit in that back seat and remain quiet until I speak," she said in a stern voice.

Bay climbed in, shivering and sniffling, and when Naomi slammed the door and got behind the wheel and started the SUV and pulled away from the house, Bay started crying hysterically, believing she was going to the 'bad house'. "I don't wanna go! I don't wanna go!" Bay screamed.

"Well, you're coming, anyway. I warned you before, Bena. You shouldn't irritate your sister. You should be her protector, not her bully." Naomi replied. "Now shut it!"

As Naomi drove away, she suddenly heard screams coming from the house. She looked in her rearview mirror and saw the top half of four year-old Kimi's body. The frantic four year-old was yelling hysterically as she ran behind the suburban. "Momma, no!" Kimi screamed repeatedly. "Momma, no!"

Eight year-old Dawk was holding one year-old Spoonie as he ran and tried to keep up with Kimi. "Momma, stop the car!" Dawk yelled.

Four year-old Koko was crying along with two year-old Walee and one year-old Tyke on the porch. "She can have it! Kimi! Tell momma Bay can have it!" Koko yelled aloud as she cried and held onto her younger brother and sister, both crying to the top of their lungs as they, too, had sensed something was wrong.

"Momma! She said Bay can have it!" Kimi yelled aloud as she ran behind the suburban.

"Momma, she not gone be bad no more!" Tiva yelled as he ran behind Dawk and Kimi.

"Momma, don't take Bay to the bad house!" Kimi screamed as she caught up with the SUV.

Naomi stopped the suburban and stared back at Kimi as she ran up to the driver's side door and pleaded mercilessly. "Momma please! She can, she can have the baby doll! Koko said Bay can have the baby doll so you won't have to take her to the bad house!" Kimi yelled as she looked her mother square in the eyes.

Dawk and Tiva joined Kimi and pleaded with their mother not to take Bay to the bad house. "She was just playing! Bay was just playing," they said repeatedly.

"What is all this talk about the bad house?" Naomi asked in a dumbfounded manner as she exited her vehicle and knelt down and scooped Kimi into her arms.

"You said if we ever be bad you gone take us to the bad house! Don't take Bay to the bad house! Don't take nobody to the bad house! Say no! Say no momma!" Kimi pleaded as she placed her hands on her mother's cheeks and tried to twist Naomi's face from side to side to get her mother to say no. "Don't take Bay to the bad house! We don't wanna lose Bay ever!" Kimi cried as she hugged her mother's neck tightly.

Naomi could now see fully what Siloam had been trying to tell her: she was scaring her kids terribly with the threat of taking them to the bad house. *God, how could I be so stupid? I come from that. And I threaten to send my own children to a place worse than hell?* Naomi asked herself. "I would never take any of you to a place like that, Kimi." Naomi said softly as she held her tightly and rocked her slightly to comfort the frightened child.

"You promise?" Kimi asked as she hid her face in her mother's neck. "Because I don't want nobody to go there ever."

"And you never will." Naomi replied as she reached down and opened the door to allow Bena to exit the vehicle.

Bena hugged her mother and said, "I'm sorry, momma. I was just playing."

"I know that." Naomi replied as she placed Kimi back onto the ground and knelt down before Bena. "I'm sorry for saying that. And I will never say it again. It's just that, sometimes, sometimes, you all drive momma up the wall." Naomi replied through a smile and tear-stained cheeks as her six remaining kids approached the SUV. When her kids got nearer the vehicle, Naomi reiterated to them what she had said to Bena and Kimi. "No bad house okay? Momma was wrong. She was wrong for saying that and she's sorry. I'll never take any of you to the bad house," she said lovingly as she gently stroked the cheeks of each of her kids.

The kids stopped crying after they heard their mother speak

and felt the gentle touch of her loving hands and they all grew happy when they saw their mother hug Bena tightly. "I'm sorry, Bay. You know I love you and will never take you to that place, right?" Naomi asked in a near whisper.

Bena shrugged her shoulders as if she was unsure and said in a low tone, "I been behaving badly with my sister. I wanna tell her I'm sorry."

"Well, let her know how you feel, Bena." Naomi replied lovingly as she pulled Koko forward and hugged her two daughters around their waists simultaneously.

Bena looked Koko in the eyes and said, "I'm sorry. I just like that doll because it's a black one with pretty brown eyes and hair."

"I like this doll, too. But if you really want it you can have it. I have some more dolls I can play with if you really want this one." Koko replied as she held the doll out before Bay.

"I can have it?" Bena asked in amazement as she stared at the doll.

"It's yours, Bena. And I won't ask for it back ever." Koko replied as she extended her arms and handed Bay the baby doll.

"Thank you, Koko. I have candy corn in my drawer. I'll give you some. I'll give you all of it if you want it." Bena said as she took the doll from Koko and held it close to her body.

"I'll just take some. We can play with the dolls together and eat the candy."

"Okay. Thank you, Koko." Bena replied as she reached out and hugged her sister.

Naomi smiled proudly through her tears. She wished she had a camcorder to record this special moment as she had just watched two of her kids resolve their own dilemma, a dilemma that had been instigated by unprincipled and deceitful threats that were bestowed upon them by their mother. Naomi told herself that she would never again make that mistake.

"Come on," Naomi said to her children, "we all going to the feed store. To the feed store and back here, back home to our land, okay? No more bad house. Momma promises you all," she ended as she loaded her kids in the vehicle, some still in their night cloths.

Siloam had watched the whole event transpire from inside the front door, but she wanted to stay out the way and let the family work things out for themselves, which they did. And Naomi had finally gotten the point concerning her threats to take the kids to 'the bad house'. A few minutes after Naomi had left the ranch with her kids, Siloam noticed dark clouds rolling in from the northwest. She went inside and placed two bags of powdered doughnuts onto the island counter so the kids could have something to eat when they got back and went and sat and waited on the front porch for Naomi and the kids' return. She'd waited for over an hour as dark gray clouds continued rolling across the land, darkening what was once a bright sunny day. Worried about the threatening weather, Siloam got up and ran up the hill beside the home and turned towards the northwest and stared at the dark grey clouds that were steadily rolling in. *"It's going to rain real bad real soon,"* she thought to herself. "Naomi, y'all hurry back," she then said aloud as she ran back down the hill towards the home and waited for Naomi and her kids.

After another hour had nearly gone by, Siloam, worried sick about Naomi and the kids, walked out onto the porch with hopes of seeing the suburban riding back on to the land. She stomped her foot on the porch in aggravation when she saw no sight of Naomi and the kids. *"Naomi had to have seen the clouds rolling in,"* she said to herself as she ran down the stairs towards the hill once more.

As she ascended the hill, Siloam looked and saw that Naomi had indeed made it back, only she was at the log cabin. Naomi had parked her suburban by the barn and had taken her kids to her grandparents' old home to the far south portion of the land where the cows grazed to let them pet the calves and feed the chickens when it began to drizzle.

"Come on kids, let's get out the rain. We'll stay in the cabin until the storm passes." Naomi said.

"We gone run back to the house by Siloam." Kimi said as she and Koko took off hand in hand and ran home.

"Okay. Let Siloam know we are at the cabin. Tell her Flacco and the boys went to get lunch for themselves." Naomi yelled as she ushered her remaining six kids towards the cabin.

Siloam noticed Kimi and Koko running down a small hill in the middle of the field and she ran out and grabbed them both. "Where's everybody else?" she asked.

"Momma said she gone stay at the cabin until the rain stop. Flacco gettin' lunch she said to tell you." Koko replied as the rain began to pick up.

"They should have all come!" Siloam said in disbelief as she took hold of Kimi and Koko's hands.

Siloam knew danger was in the air and she was now taking it upon herself to get everybody to safety. Since Kimi and Koko were closer to the house, she took them home and placed the twins inside the storm cellar. Kimi and Koko caught sight of the powder doughnuts on the island counter as they walked through the kitchen towards the utility room entrance to be placed in the storm cellar and they wanted them—badly.

"Let me get some doughnuts before we go downstairs." Kimi said.

"Not right now, Kimi. You and your sister hide here and don't move!" Siloam stated as she guided the kids down the stairs into the cellar.

"I want a doughnut!" Kimi yelled back as the wind outside began to pick up and thunder that rattled the house, ensued.

"Kimi, please. We'll all eat together after the storm, alright? Just stay here." Siloam said through heavy breathing before she climbed the stairs and closed the steel door and locked it.

Naomi and six of her kids were inside the log home when it started to rain tremendously. The lightening also picked up, turning the darkened sky a bright white each time a bolt sprung forth from the black clouds above.

"This is a storm the likes of one I haven't seen since my childhood days in Sylacauga." Naomi thought to herself as she looked out of the front window of the cabin.

The rain was coming down sideways because of the strong winds. Thunder was rumbling, vibrating the log cabin as if it had springs underneath. Runoff from the rain was streaming towards the cabin and meandering around the porch and emptying into the small canyon behind the log cabin. Naomi began thinking that she should have taken all of her kids home the moment Kimi and Koko headed that way, but she didn't think that the storm would be so fierce. She went and sat with her kids, who were all sitting on the floor, Bena playing with her doll, and the rest nuzzling up against their mother slowly drifting off to sleep.

Siloam, meanwhile, had run to the hilltop beside the home and saw that the cows were headed away from the log cabin and headed up the tree-lined hillside and over the top and down the other side to the creek. The area behind the hill was like a small valley where one could take shelter and it seemed as if the cattle knew what was coming.

"Tornado!" Siloam said to herself as she took off running towards the log cabin.

By now, the storm had picked up tremendously and Naomi began sensing danger as the house began to vibrate more and more from the incessant thunder. Wood began to blow away from the home and Naomi, remembering that Siloam had told her that the cellar was a protection from thunder storms, decided to place her kids in the cellar inside the floor of the log cabin. There wasn't enough room for Naomi and Dawk inside the cellar, and as Bay and Tiva held onto Walee, Spoonie and Tyke, the five of them crying, Naomi slammed the cellar shut and slid the bolt across it before she and Dawk went and huddled in the small bedroom closet.

Strong gusts of wind rocked the house. Quaking thunder shook the ground. And before long, pelts of ice began to pound the rusted tin roof. Naomi and Dawk huddled in the bedroom closet as the storm swept about. Naomi soon began humming as she rubbed Dawk's head to soothe her son, but she was just as scared as he. It was while she was humming to Dawk that Naomi suddenly remembered that Kimi and Koko had run towards the home. Worried that her middle daughters may have gotten trapped in the open field, she took Dawk by the hand and headed for the door. The storm was so loud now, Naomi had to bend down and holler into Dawk's ear. "We're going to look for Kimi and Koko!" she yelled aloud.

Dawk nodded eagerly. He was scared Kimi and Koko were

going to die this day and he was going with his mother to save them; only Naomi and Dawk didn't know that everyone that was inside the log cabin needed to be saved. Naomi reached the door and she was met by a soaking wet, heavy-breathing Siloam.

"You, you all have to get away from this house!" Siloam said as the door flew off the hinges, having been caught up by the strong winds.

"Where's Kimi and Koko?" Naomi screamed over the howling wind.

"They're safe! We have to leave this house!" Siloam stated as she looked around, "Where's the rest of the children?"

"In the cellar! They're safe there!"

"Nooo! This is a bad place to be!" Siloam yelled as she ran to the cellar, released the bolt and opened it.

"Leave them alone! They're safe there!" Naomi screamed as Siloam began to pull the kids from the cellar.

"Momma, they can't stay in there! This house is going to fall and crush them!" Siloam yelled.

Both Naomi and Siloam stared at one another as the wind whipped about and ice pelted the roof and water blew through the log cabin. "Siloam!" Naomi yelled.

"Never mind! I'm sorry I said that!" Siloam screamed as she removed the kids from the cellar.

"I am! You hear? I am!" Naomi yelled over the howling wind and pounding rain and ice as she grabbed Spoonie.

Siloam grabbed Tyke, Dawk held Walee, and Bena and Tiva followed closely as the group sprinted from the house with Siloam leading the way. "We don't have enough time to make it back to the house! We're going to where the cows are! We'll be safe there!" Siloam yelled.

"What about Kimi and Koko?"

"Momma, they're safe. They're safe believe me, please! We have to get to the valley on the other side of the hill!"

"Okay, I trust you Siloam!" Naomi yelled as she held onto Spoonie.

The group ran across the land, hail pelting their heads,

blowing raindrops stinging their skin, and thunder and lightning shaking and striking the ground. Naomi, Siloam and Dawk covered Spoonie, Tyke and Walee's heads and took the blows as Tiva and Bay, who were following closely behind, fought off the falling ice as best they could. They cried aloud from the stinging ice as they ran across the open field with their family. Bay, who was the last one trailing Tiva, fell down when a lightning bolt struck the log cabin, which had been vacated just seconds before.

Naomi heard the explosion and she turned around and saw that the log cabin was now in flames. She also saw Tiva struggling to help Bay up from the ground, all the while being pelted by hailstones the size of golf balls, and constantly slipping on the loose and muddy soil. Naomi turned and ran back with Spoonie in her arms and pulled her two daughters up from the muddy soil.

"My doll! I dropped my doll!" Bena yelled.

"Run! Just run to the hill and don't stop!" Naomi yelled as she shoved Bena and Tiva forward.

Naomi ran and grabbed Bena's doll, but as she turned to run, she slipped in the mud. She caught her fall with one arm as she held onto Spoonie and Bena's doll, regained her balance and got up and took off running again just as the pile of loose mud where Bay and Tiva were just seconds earlier had gave way and washed down towards the canyon behind the log cabin. Naomi knew that if she hadn't gone back for her oldest two daughters, they would have both been swept away towards the canyon and the canal that was beginning to fill with water and debris. She gave thanks to God as she caught up with the group, knowing she, too, was lucky to escape having gone back for Bena's doll.

The family ran through the blinding rain, stinging ice and crackling lightning screaming in terror; afraid for their lives. They crossed the hill and made it to the area where the cows were and walked slowly in between the animals. The cows sniffed and huffed, blowing fresh water from their noses as Siloam guided the family to the center of the cows, which were standing inside a stone embankment beside the flooded creek.

The adult cattle had surrounded the younger calves in order

to protect them and they seem to shift and make room when the humans entered the circle. The group knelt on the ground inside the embankment behind the cattle and it grew eerily calm inside the stone crevice as the rain began to come down harder and the skies grew black. The surrounding cattle merely stood as if they were waiting for the finale to arrive.

"The stream is overflowing but it won't cover our heads!" Siloam yelled to Naomi over the loud storm as the family knelt down in ankle deep water that overflowed from the creek. "Hold on tight and close your eyes, momma! Kids close your eyes! Dawk cover Tyke's eyes!" Siloam yelled.

The family closed their eyes and huddled amidst the cows and waited for the storm to pass and suddenly, what sounded like a freight train could be heard approaching in the distance; ears were popping and the cows mooed loudly. The noise was so loud neither family member could hear the other's scream even though they were all hugging one another in tight circle. Water began spraying the family and a frightening sound, that of trees being snapped in half was repeated over and over again. The family remained motionless in the rock crevice as wood splinters and debris from anybody's guess crashed all around them. It seemed like an eternity, but after only a few seconds, the tornado had passed and minutes later, just as quickly as it had come up, the storm had cleared the land.

Naomi and her children, Siloam included, checked themselves over. They were all muddy and soaking wet, but free of injuries. After brief hugs and reassurances, the group made their way through the ankle deep water beside the overflowing creek and crossed back over the hill to search for Kimi and Koko. Naomi and Siloam ran to the home. Once inside, Naomi sat Spoonie down in the family room and called out for her two remaining kids. Dawk, still holding onto Walee, ran out into the field to search whilst Tiva and Bena ran upstairs to search for their younger siblings.

Siloam, still holding Tyke had went to the cellar and opened it and walked down the stairs and yelled aloud, "Momma! They're here!"

Naomi went into the utility room and walked down the stairs and entered the cellar and screamed aloud as she held her hand chest. There, lying on two Minnie Mouse blankets with a white powdery substance around their lips, were four year-olds Kimi and Koko.

"What happened to them? My, my babies!" Naomi screamed as she ran and knelt beside her daughters and began shaking them rapidly. When Kimi and Koko stirred awake, Naomi sighed in relief. "I thought—never mind. I can't imagine," she said, nearly out of breath.

"That's sugar from the powdered doughnuts I placed on the counter, Naomi. They're fine." Siloam remarked with a smile.

In spite of being told to remain in the cellar, four year-olds Kimi and Koko dared to exit the side door of the utility room and venture back into the home and retrieve the powder doughnuts that Siloam had placed on the island counter. Not only that, they ran upstairs to their room and grabbed their favorite blankets and they still, at their young age, had sense enough to return to the safety of the cellar.

"I believe they knew about the storm before it even hit," Siloam said to Naomi. "I believe that's why they came home. True survivors they are. Smart children you have, Naomi."

"That was a wild ride!" Dawk said while wiping his body free of mud.

"Yes it was, son." Naomi remarked. "Siloam, you mentioned the storms, but this storm was epic. Weather, spring weather, has to be paid closer attention. We now know what to expect. This can't happen again. We can't get caught outdoors."

"Besides the lightning and ice, that was fun. It was like a big shower." Tiva remarked as she removed her muddy tennis shoes.

"We coulda got struck by lightning, T-top." Bay said as she wiped her doll free of mud.

"Moo. Moo." Spoonie then said in imitation of the cattle as she patted the mud on her mother's face.

"Yes," Naomi replied as she smiled at her daughter, "Cows say moo."

"Speaking of cows, what happened to Kimi and Koko?" Dawk asked as he looked at his sisters lying on the blankets rubbing their eyes.

"Dawk don't you say that about your sisters!" Naomi replied as she tapped Dawk's arms lightly.

"What's that white stuff around their lips?" Dawk asked.

"Powdered doughnuts, son. They are fine, though. We all are fine. You saved the family today, Siloam. To have Doss come home to such a tragic loss would have left him a broken man. Thank you. You are truly an angel."

"You're my angel, Naomi. The mother I never had."

"If that's what you feel in your heart, who am I to deny you? I will never do that to my own children." Naomi replied as she hugged Siloam tightly. "I love you like you were my own and I always will."

Siloam gripped Naomi's back and heaved heavily. Finally, someone deemed her precious enough to call her 'daughter'. Words could not express the gratitude that coursed through Siloam's heart at this moment. She was happy to have the one thing she never had in life—a mother who cared. She was grateful to be able to call Naomi 'momma', but even more, Naomi was honored to have Siloam respect and love her enough to want to do so. Naomi would give to Siloam, from this day forth, the very same thing that Kevin and Serena had given her early on: unconditional love.

****

While Naomi and the rest of the family in Ponca City were surveying the damage from the storm, Fin was in Seattle meeting with JunJie with intentions on setting up a drug distribution network. The two men were locked inside JunJie's office on the fifteenth floor of the Park Place building just off Interstate-5 discussing their new venture as they played a game of chess.

"The hits were successful. Now, I did mention a new venture and I believe you know what it is I was referring to, Finland." JunJie said as he moved a solid gold pawn two paces forward.

"I do. I did some price checking. The going rate is twenty-two per back home." Finland replied as he moved a white diamond knight to the center for defense.

"I offer a much better price. Seven off of the going rate of twenty-two." JunJie replied as he moved one of his golden knights to the center to counteract Finland's move.

"You trying to corner the market?" Fin asked as he sipped a glass of red wine and moved a pawn two paces forward.

"The lower the price, the faster the sale. Especially if you have a low wholesale cost and plenty to move." JunJie replied as he moved another pawn to paces forward.

"May I ask who's behind the sale?" Finland asked as he slid one of his bishops into position to take JunJie's knight.

"You may. But that doesn't mean I have to answer." JunJie replied as he slid a pawn forward one pace to block Finland's move.

"I wanna know who I'm working for, Mister JunJie. If I put myself and my friends on the line for this move the least you could do is explain to me how this thing will work from the top down." Finland replied as he moved his second knight to the center of the platinum board.

JunJie leaned back in his chair and rubbed his chin as he eyed the board. His next move would be crucial. Finland could remove a major piece from his side if he made an error. It was also ironic to JunJie because in the same manner in which he was calculating his next move on the chess board, he also had to calculate just how much he was going to reveal to Finland. To give up too much information would tip the scales; to give not enough information would undoubtedly crash the new venture before it even got off the ground. JunJie liked Finland and had been respecting the man ever since he'd made his problem back in Chicago go away. To lie would be detrimental to the Cause so JunJie decided to tell Fin as much as he could without letting him know everything. "The Colombians charge a fair price," he said as he slid a pawn forward to counteract Finland's advance. "Three thousand per kilo is what they're charging. I supply the route to America and from there I am who you work for. My money, our venture, our deal. You will answer to me and no one else. I set the price."

"Will this be stepped on?" Finland asked as he slid his bishop across the board and took one of JunJie's pawns.

"No shake on the product. It's one hundred percent." JunJie replied as he moved his knight into position and took Finland's bishop.

"That sounds good. But I'm overseeing the distribution. My city. My product. Once it's in my hands you have no power or no say so over anything that happens, unless you're missing money." Finland replied as he moved his knight into position and took JunJie's knight.

JunJie leaned back and thought as he stared at the board. Fin was asking for complete control of the drugs once they were in his hands. JunJie, however, had no intentions on giving Fin control of the product completely because he wanted a say so in all matters. The cunning Asian was a versatile business man that knew how to make a deal, however; on top of that, he trusted Finland. "I was willing to split everything fifty-fifty with you and your friends. But if you want complete control, that drops to sixty-forty." JunJie said as he moved his queen forward and took JunJie's knight.

Finland wasn't in agreement with JunJie's deal, but he knew of another way to recoup the ten percent disadvantage and then some. Not wanting to reveal his hand, Finland decided to play hard ball. "Mister Maruyama, I have to get that load back to Chicago from here. My transport. My risk," he said as he moved his second knight towards the center of the board.

"My money. My product." JunJie said as he slid his queen forward and took Finland's knight.

"What we now have is a stale mate, my friend." Finland replied as he used his second knight to take JunJie's queen, which was the major piece on the board.

JunJie laughed aloud and said, "No stale mate, Finland. Set the price at eighteen. That's still four below wholesale on the streets and fifteen net. We split it even. I wanted the price lower, but this way we both win," he ended as he knocked over his own king. "This game is over, my friend."

Fin sat his glass of wine down as he thought briefly. He knew he'd just won the game as JunJie had forfeited the moment he knocked his king over. Fin also knew he'd won the negotiation. His intent at the outset was to drive the price per kilo up and still keep it under twenty-two, and he had just succeeded. Eighteen thousand per kilogram was the perfect price. It was four grand cheaper and was pure Colombian uncut. Finland knew the product could be cut, at least to eighty percent, and it would still be more potent than anything on the streets of the Midwest.

"We have a deal, Mister Maruyama." Fin said as he stood up and shook JunJie's hand.

"Good. I'll have my limousine driver take you to the airport. Call me tomorrow. It's important we keep in touch." JunJie remarked as he dialed his chauffeur's number and requested that he pick Finland up from in front of the building.

****

Finland made his flight and landed at O'Hare International Airport back in Chicago three hours later just before seven p.m. and was greeted by Doss and Lucky. The men shook hands and walked towards the front doors.

"How'd the meeting go?" Lucky asked.

"Silky smooth, brothers. Silky smooth."

"Good," Doss replied. "You can fill us in on the way back to Cicero. My father and Mendoza are waiting on us outside. After we discuss the new arrangements, I have to get back to Oklahoma immediately."

"Everything okay?" Finland asked.

"The ranch was hit by a tornado this morning." Lucky said.

Finland stopped in his tracks and stared at Doss and Lucky. "Is everybody okay," he asked worriedly.

"They're fine. We took a big hit though. Nearly all of the poultry was wiped out. The farm equipment, Naomi's grandparents' log cabin was burned completely and the barn was destroyed. But none of the family was hurt."

"That's a blessing in itself." Finland replied.

"It is. Insurance will cover the farm equipment and the poultry. The cleanup will hurt more than anything else." Doss replied.

"You want me to come down and help?"

Doss nodded to say no. He knew and trusted Finland, but he

was now about to become deeply involved in the drug game with JunJie Maruyama, a man the crew barely knew. Finland knew more about JunJie than anyone, and Doss didn't feel right having Finland know his family's whereabouts. It wasn't anything personal against Fin, Doss was just keeping his family safe; and he felt that the safest move was to not let Finland know his exact location down in Oklahoma.

The men continued walking in silence towards the main entrance and spotted DeeDee's car parked across the street from the main doors. DeeDee and Mendoza were standing outside the car and they greeted Finland as the men all hopped into the ride where Finland began giving up the details concerning the deal he'd made with JunJie. After listening to Fin, everybody was in agreement that money could be made; all they had to do now was wait for Finland to set up the distribution channel.

CHAPTER 20

PONDEROSA

It was two days after the storm had passed. Naomi and Siloam went and surveyed the damage the storm had left behind the day of after witnessing nature's fury firsthand and saw that the log cabin in which Naomi had placed five of her kids had burned to the ground. The cellar where the kids were had caved in and was covered with burnt logs and other debris. Siloam was right; Naomi would have lost five of her kids that day. Naomi also saw that the old barn had been obliterated by the tornado that swept across the land and she had decided on the day the storm had swept across the land that she would begin working on a dream home for the family.

Four days after the storm, Kevin, Serena, DeeDee, Mendoza, Lucky, Junior, Francine and Mildred all came down to the ranch to help Naomi, Doss and Siloam clean up. It was a welcomed sight for Naomi's kids to see their grandfather DeeDee's long, slick, four door grey Lincoln rolling up the dirt road leading to the guest house. DeeDee always bought gifts when he came to town, as well as Kevin and Serena.

A week into their stay, DeeDee and Mendoza had went into town and purchased some new jeans and tennis. They had spent the first week walking around in slacks and shoes, but they finally caved in when they realized how ridiculous they looked picking up loose boards and debris while dressed as if they were going out on the town. When they emerged from the house in their un-ironed black wrangler jeans and grey and white flannel short sleeved shirts, and black cowboy boots, everybody laughed.

"It's official." Doss said. "You two have just been broken in down here."

"How I look everybody?" DeeDee asked from the front porch as he looked himself over.

"You look like Boxcar Willie." Naomi replied through laughter as she stood at the foot of the stairs with her husband and kids and took a picture.

Mendoza began laughing at Naomi's remark, and DeeDee looked over to him and said, "That's funny, Mendoza? I wouldn't be laughing if I were you. I may look like Boxcar Willie, but can you explain to me why you look exactly like Uncle Jessie from the Dukes of Hazzard in that get up you wearing?"

Mendoza laughed hard right along with everybody else. "I can't believe I'm dressed like this. Naomi don't you tell no one about this," he said just as Siloam took a picture of him in his jeans and flannel shirt.

"Can you imagine if that were to get out? Can you hear the laughter inside the bar back in Cicero?" Serena asked Mendoza through laughter.

DeeDee was laughing aloud. He looked at Mendoza and said, "Now I got something I can hold over your head."

"Don't get too comfortable with yourself. Remember, Naomi took your picture first with that camera. Whatever pictures are taken down here, I'm making sure there's double prints so I'll have something to hold back over your head."

"My daughter-in-law wouldn't do me like that now would she?" DeeDee asked as he smiled lovingly towards Naomi.

"Don't be surprised if there's an eight by ten of both of you all sitting on the bar one day when you walk in." Naomi replied as the family all laughed.

"You and your bright ideas." Mendoza then said to DeeDee. "All we had to do was pick up two plastic bats, three balls and two mitts for Spoonie and Tyke. Now look at us! We look like farmers from the eighteen hundreds," he ended as he walked down the stairs and grabbed Spoonie and Tyke's hand. "We goin' play ball," he ended.

The trips to Oklahoma were always fun for the family from Cicero. They never knew what to expect, but they knew it would be a wonderful experience, especially with the kids on hand. Two days before the gang from Cicero left, the land having been cleaned free of storm debris, Naomi had told them all about her plans on building a dream home for the family. Everyone was supportive; no one more than DeeDee, who wanted more than anything to have his grandchildren grow up and live in a lap of luxury. He wrote a check out on the spot, contributing $45,000 dollars towards the down payment on the materials.

Serena and Kevin at that point, had decided to stay on the ranch the rest of the year and beyond until the house was completed. The spring of 1993 was a fantastic year for Naomi despite the harrowing experience the family had gone through with the storm. The kids had two of their grandparents on hand full-time and Naomi just loved having Kevin and Serena around.

Over a year later, in May of 1994, after much rain and a few tornadoes that swept across the land leaving behind little or no damage, the family's second home was ninety percent complete. The fixtures were all in place and the plumbing and electricity was up and running. All that remained was the pouring of concrete for the storm cellar and the huge patio out back, and to replace the rotted wooden fence that led to the home with new, white-painted wood.

Naomi spared no expense in financing the home, which cost her $580,000 dollars to build; but was appraised and valued at $1.3 million dollars at its inception. She had taken out a second mortgage on the family's first home to help cover the expenses on the second home after Doss kicked in another $80,000 dollars to push the dream towards its completion. By the end of May 1994, Naomi had finally built the dream house she had so desired for her family. She named it Ponderosa because the home had Ponderosa wood covering seventy-five percent of its interior, including portions of the ceilings, the bedroom floors and hallways.

Ponderosa was a two story, ten bedroom, eight full bath,

steel, vanilla marble and caramel brown brick home complete with a movie theater, exercise gym, playroom, several study rooms, a music room and two huge gourmet kitchens. Ponderosa wooden floors ran throughout, ceramic, granite and marble was everywhere. Four huge vanilla marble columns, each seven feet in diameter, and caramel-colored marble stairs encompassed the entire front portion of the home, which sat atop the hill where the barn once sat and faced the entrance to the land. Thick Ponderosa wood double doors, eight feet tall and featuring gold door knobs led into the home's interior. The foyer was the size of a small apartment and the downstairs living room was the size of a large condominium.

Doss and Naomi both had private offices and the home had a lovely library filled with law books and encyclopedias. The most beautiful room in the home, though, was the Great Room on the second floor. The Great Room encompassed the entire center of the home from front to back and featured a water fountain that sat at the top of the stairs and separated the living room area from the grand marble staircase that led up to the room. Vaulted Ponderosa wood ceilings and soft, caramel-colored hand sewn carpet imported from Bangladesh left one speechless. There was a kitchen near the back of the room that held French doors that led to a second floor balcony that overlooked the back portion of the land and the patio below. The Great Room also included a huge marble fireplace, six feet in height in the center of the back wall. Two sets of French doors on either side of the fireplace gave way to a balcony that overlooked the back portion of the land. It was real peaceful and quiet on the balcony, which shaded the home's huge patio perfectly. Ponderosa, in all, was over 14, 000 square feet. The downstairs patio would be complete in a week's time, and from there, the family would begin to furnish their ten bedroom sprawling mansion that had been custom designed and built from the ground up.

CHAPTER 21
DO US A FAVOR

By late September of 1994, a few months after the family had moved into Ponderosa, Fin, Doss and Lucky had finally organized a network of drug dealers to distribute JunJie's cocaine to four cities: Milwaukee, Cleveland, St. Louis and Detroit. Lucky and Doss had obeyed Mendoza and DeeDee's order not to put cocaine on the streets of Chicago. They did, however, have solid connections in other parts of the Midwest with gangsters from back in the day who readily bought the cocaine at a wholesale price of $18,000 dollars a kilogram.

Fin would schedule the shipment and would notify Doss and Lucky of the product's predetermined date of arrival ahead of time. Doss would leave his ranch and meet up with Lucky in Cicero and from there they would head over to JunJie's warehouse in Bedford Park located on West 71st Street on Chicago's south side. There inside the warehouse, the men would cut, mix, and distribute the cocaine and the profits would then be split evenly. The network had been up and running since August of 1993 and it was going along smoothly.

A lot of activity went on in JunJie's 50,000 square foot warehouse during the day as it did legitimate business with numerous trucking firms that hauled loads pulled from the many CSX trains that were destined for the Windy City. Lucky and Doss were never seen, however; they made their deals at three or four in the morning and were gone before the sun arose. The only time they went to the warehouse was to mix product and make an exchange.

Fin, at the same time had become the front man for Midwest Express, the trucking company that ran the cocaine shipments from Seattle to Chicago three times a month. He had a small office inside JunJie's warehouse to monitor legitimate freight he set up for Naomi, but his office was mainly used to run the cocaine shipments. Most of the time, the truck driver, who was out-of-the-loop concerning the cocaine shipments, drove another route; but when he ran what was termed "the Seattle run", it was a different story.

During the Seattle run, the driver, a middle-aged white man, would take a refrigerated trailer loaded up with pallets from JunJie's warehouse in Chicago to the ports of Seattle. The trailer would be unloaded at one of JunJie's docks and the refrigerated trailer would then be reloaded with pallets of frozen produce from the same door. It was a "gravy run" to the driver, who was paid what he knew to be better than the trips were worth. But unbeknownst to the driver, mixed in with the load of frozen produce would be a pallet containing eight kilograms of uncut Colombian cocaine.

From Seattle the truck driver headed back to JunJie's warehouse in Chicago on what was labeled a JIT (just in time) run and the shipment would be unloaded personally by Fin. The hidden pallet of cocaine would then be broken down, cut and repackaged. Eight kilograms of uncut white powder would be turned into twelve kilograms by Lucky and Doss the same night and was distributed over a four or five day period. The cocaine was never in Chicago for more than a week.

Fin, Lucky and Doss were running a mid-level cocaine operation and were making a good bit of money and operating under the radar. Doss and Lucky only worked a couple of hours of month which allowed them to remain focused and on top of any potential threats to their business, and to spend quality time with their families. It would be fair to say that the crew from Cicero was on top of their game; but a problem in the realm of competition would arrive in late September and the crew would have to let their reputation and strength be known to all those who felt bold enough to dare to impede upon their operations.

****

In the latter part of September of 1994, 55 year-olds Coban Benito and Humphrey Gaggi exited their black 1994 four door BMW 7 series and walked up onto the docks of the warehouse in Chicago and tapped lightly on the door that held Fin's office.

Lucky opened with an Uzi in his right hand and extended his left hand and said, "Benvenuti I miei amici. Come va la vita a Saint Louis?" (Welcome my friends. How's life in Saint Louis?) Lucky rarely spoke Italian as he wasn't too proficient; but he knew the proper things to say to Coban and Humphrey, who spoke fluent Italian, and viewed any Sicilian that didn't speak the language at all as being too Americanized. It wasn't a slight against Lucky, though; Benito and Gaggi were just from the old school Italian Mafia.

Coban shook Lucky's hand and replied by saying, "Buona. Ma puo' essere migliore. Abbiamo un problema." (Good., but it could be better. We have a problem.)

Lucky greeted Humphrey and the three men entered the small four-cornered white walled office that held one large wooden desk, a CB radio that sat atop a tin cabinet file and a map of Illinois hanging on the wall behind the desk. "Doss," Lucky said, "our friends have a problem on their home turf."

Doss was sitting behind the desk using a sharpie to write the coded names of the purchasers on the neatly wrapped kilograms. He looked up and peered over his eyeglasses and asked, "Is it a big problem, or a little problem?"

Coban nodded to Doss and removed his dark grey silk suit jacket, brushed the lent off the sleeves and hung it up on the coat rack in the corner and sat his black felt fedora on top of the file cabinet. Lucky and Doss smiled to themselves. Coban and Humphrey were truly from back in the day. Even though they were purchasing kilograms at three in the morning on the south side of Chicago, the men weren't in a rush to do so. Most dealers would buy and split; but Coban and Humphrey conducted their business without the least bit of haste or concern.

"Is there coffee around? It's been a long trip?" Coban asked as he sat down before Doss.

"Sorry, Coban. Next time, give us a heads up and we'll have a fresh pot brewing when you get here." Lucky replied with a hint of apprehension as he tightened his grip on the Uzi.

"We have Scotch on hand." Doss replied as he marked the last of the six remaining kilograms he had left and sat back in his chair. He then crossed his legs and eased his hand around the rubber handle on the pistol-grip twelve gauge shotgun he had laying on the floor to his right, ready to scoop it up and blast if the deal went sour.

Doss and Lucky were always on alert for a set up. Coban and Humphrey rarely hung around long. The men were trusted, but Doss and Lucky both knew and understood, however, that they were dealing cocaine in large amounts; and in the line of work they were involved in one could never be too careful. Even one's purported friends could turn into an enemy in a split second.

"Scotch makes me drowsy. Forget about it," Coban said as he ran his hands through his frost-white, thinning hair. "Faustino, remember I told you about the guys that were moving in from California?"

"I thought you said they had left, Coban." Lucky replied.

"Well, they didn't." Humphrey chimed as he pulled out three pictures of three black males and pulled a thick pair of bifocals from his suit jacket. "They moved into this house on the west side near Jefferson Street and they putting their shit out on the streets and charging thirty per kilogram," he said.

"We only charge eighteen. You can sell wholesale between twenty-five and twenty-eight or you could break it down into ounces and you'll still have them beat." Doss remarked.

"That's the problem." Coban stated. "They're selling ounces too. Our price is twelve hundred per ounce. These guys are charging two thousand an ounce and they are demanding that the street level dealers purchase their product. Two of our customers have been murdered for not doing business with these guys. The ones standing strong are getting afraid and considering the offer."

"If something isn't done," Humphrey said, "we will be forced out. Which means—"

"We will be forced out." Doss remarked, cutting Humphrey's statement short. "That's a big problem, gentlemen. How will you handle the situation," he asked as he eased up on the twelve gauge.

Coban opened a briefcase and poured out stacks of hundred dollar bills onto the desk top and Doss and Lucky stared at the money and then eyed the two men. "That is eighty-one thousand dollars," Coban said. "The buy money for two kilograms and fifteen thousand dollars per head on those three guys from Los Angeles. We need you to do us a favor."

Lucky looked down at the Uzi he was holding, and then looked over to Doss, who was already formulating a plan to take the men down.

"How much product are they moving?" Doss asked.

"One of our customers told us that the men have at least twenty kilograms on hand at all times stashed away in a car wash somewhere in town." Coban replied.

"You don't know the location?" Lucky asked.

"No." Coban remarked. "All we know is that they hang at this club downtown. They're there every weekend."

Lucky shrugged his shoulders and looked over to Doss and said, "We can kidnap one of 'em and have 'em take us to it before we kill 'em all."

"I was thinking the same thing." Doss replied. "We gone need some help on this one."

"I got my people." Lucky said.

"So do I." Doss replied. "Don't worry gentlemen," he then said to Coban and Humphrey, "give us a few days to put it all together. Sit on these two for now," he said in reference to the two kilograms he slid across the desk. "Make them think you're done—and we'll get the job done."

Coban and Humphrey shook hands with Doss and Lucky, took their cocaine, and left the premises. Doss and Lucky remained at the warehouse for another hour where they made a deal with two mobsters from Cleveland and left around 4:30 in the morning. As they rode towards Cicero, the men discussed the job they had been given.

"We should use a lure." Lucky said as he drove his Eldorado down the Dan Ryan Expressway.

"That's what I was thinking—but she has to be good."

"You got somebody in mind?"

"My main man Eddie know a few females, but his girls are undisciplined. I have someone in mind who has control over his women and could maybe supply us with another good lure."

"What time you wanna go and see DeeDee?" Lucky asked.

Doss looked over to Lucky and smiled. "How'd you know?" he asked.

"Your dad's a slick pimp if I ever saw one. I'll let my dad and Junior know tonight so we can all meet up tomorrow and get this shit mapped out." Lucky said.

****

The following evening, Junior and Mendoza were on their way to meet Doss and Lucky over to DeeDee's place to discuss the hit. Junior was driving his grandfather's new four door black Cadillac Brougham this day, and since he was behind the wheel, he felt as if the car was his. The car was laced out with black leather seats and dark tinted windows and had a suspension that made riders feel as if they were floating on clouds.

Mendoza had just gotten a grocery list from Francine and had entered the car. Junior backed out and turned the radio up as loud as it could go, blasting Notorious B.I.G.'s song *Big Poppa*. Mendoza sighed and looked out the passenger window, shaking his head slowly in disgust as he listened to the song…"*I love it when you call me big poppa…to the honies gettin' money playing niggas like dummies…I love it when you call me big poppa…if you got a gun up ya' waist please don't shoot up the place…'cause I see some ladies tonight who should be havin' my baby…baby…*"

"What the hell are we listening to?" Mendoza finally asked.

"That's Biggie Smalls granddad. You don't know him?" Junior asked as he cruised past *Eastside Bar* and blew the horn at a few females he knew as he bobbed his head to the music.

Junior was making money right along with his father and grandfather, and at the age of eighteen, he was enamored with rap music. He jammed the latest jams, dated numerous women and considered himself to be a player to the highest degree. Junior was a fun-loving lad and loved to have a good time, but he had a swagger about himself that often annoyed his grandfather.

"Look, Junior, I don't care to hear Mister Smalls elaborate on the women who should be havin' his kids. Where's my Barry Manilow CD?" Mendoza asked as he turned the volume down.

Junior burst into laughter and yelled aloud, "Another time machine! You and pops are just alike!"

"What do you mean time machine? Barry White's music is timeless." Mendoza replied.

"You didn't say the Maestro! You asked for Barry Manilow, granddad."

"No I, no I didn't! I said, I said, 'where's my Barry Mani—I said 'where's my Barry White CD'."

"See there? You almost said it again!" Junior said as he laughed aloud. "That's what you and grandma listen to? Barry Manilow's greatest hits?"

"No! I don't listen to Manilow. I listen to the Maestro. The real Barry."

"Oh yea? Well, what's this here in the console?" Junior asked as he grabbed several CDs. "This is, this is Barry Manilow—This One's for You! Neil Diamond—On the Way to the Sky! John Denver—good ole Johnny boy—Rocky Mountain Holiday is the name of this one! What the hell are *you* listening to is the question!" Junior said as he laughed uncontrollably. The Cadillac nearly swerved into the next lane on the freeway he was laughing so hard. Tears were running down Junior's face at this moment.

Mendoza had grown slightly embarrassed. He liked those CDs and the artists, but that was his little secret and Junior had just uncovered it. "You just don't know good music, boy," was all Mendoza could say. "I do have Barry White's Greatest Hits. See? It's right here in the glove box. And that is what I meant to say! And this is what I want to hear. Now let's go on and have this meeting," he ended as he ejected B.I.G.'s CD and replaced it with Barry White's CD and selected the song *Secret Garden.*

Mendoza and Junior made it over to DeeDee's condo forty minutes later and after a few drinks the men all sat around and began discussing their options concerning the hit. "Now," DeeDee asked as he turned down the volume on the upcoming Bears game, "you need a female to go down to Saint Louis and be a lure you say, son?"

"Yeah, dad. Eddie and Junior can fit in at this club, but we need a female to lure one of the men away from his crew."

"Well, what kind of a female are you looking for?"

"One with a head on her shoulders. Trustworthy, and knows how to use a gun." Lucky responded just as a brown-skinned woman with cropped hair and wearing an all-in-one tight-fitting dark blue dress and orange three-inch heeled ankle boots descended the stairs.

"DeeDee, have you seen my car keys? I hate to leave so soon but I promised my daddy I would take him to the Bears game. I'm a little behind but his lazy ass will just have to—oh! Hello everybody! Excuse my rant. DeeDee, have you seen the keys to my Porsche, baby?"

DeeDee looked over to Doss, Mendoza, Lucky and Junior and smiled as he sipped his drink. "I think we can work that out, gentlemen," he said with a sly smile. "Sharona? Come over here and sit with us men for a minute, baby. We need you to do us a favor."

CHAPTER 22
THE SAINT LOUIS HIT

Three days after their meeting in Chicago, Mendoza, DeeDee, Doss, Lucky, Junior and Eddie Cottonwood were eating dinner inside the restaurant adjacent to The Millennium Hotel in downtown Saint Louis. The plan was for Eddie and DeeDee's female companion, Sharona, who'd flown into town the same day, to strike up a conversation with one of the men inside the reggae club located on 14th Street, which wasn't too far from the hotel. From there, Sharona would lure the man into a secluded area and Lucky and Eddie would pounce on him, kidnap him and take him to a predetermined location where they would force him to give up his stash locale. His counterparts would then be exterminated and the cocaine would be split evenly.

The men ate steak and grilled shrimp to satisfaction and when done, DeeDee and Mendoza went and climbed into a cargo van supplied by Benito and Gaggi. Doss, Lucky and Eddie rode in one of the men's old Mercedes 190s and the group headed towards the club where the men were known to hang out. Eddie and Junior went in whilst Doss and Lucky stayed behind in the car and DeeDee and Mendoza sat parked a little ways down the block in the van.

"You think this shit's gonna work, Doss?" Lucky asked.

"I really don't know, Lucky. If the lure is as good as my father says she is it should. We can count on Junior and Eddie. Sharona is the key."

"You right about that. It was a good idea to have the boys dress down. That reggae joint is sure to be full of young hip-hoppers."

Meanwhile, inside the club, Sharona Benson, the crew's lure who'd arrived by taxi, was tapping the counter repeatedly trying to get the bartender's attention. Sharona was a twenty-six year-old Black/Puerto Rican. She was tan-skinned with short black hair, a soft, shapely ass and huge breasts. She had been with DeeDee for three years now, having fallen in love with him the day he'd flown her to the Virgin Islands for an impromptu dinner. DeeDee had Sharona by thirty-seven years, but he looked years younger, was fit and more active than many a man her age. She'd been DeeDee's loyal companion and ally ever since that trip to the Virgin Islands.

Sharona's father was a retired member of the El Rukn Gang. He'd planned on teaching his daughter the ways of the streets early on, but Sharona was more of a book worm. She took an abrupt detour after receiving an academic scholarship to attend Missouri State University where she earned a degree in Commercial Advertising. Sharona's father never acknowledged the fact that his daughter wanted better in life because he was determined to have her follow in his steps and join the gang he ran; but she was a strong-willed female and saw the streets and gang-banging as a dead end road.

When Sharona met DeeDee, however, she saw up-close and firsthand what a real gangster's lifestyle was all about, and it was highly different from the life her father had led and had tried to force on her. Living from day to day and fighting for scraps in a dilapidated neighborhood was not a life worth living if you were going to be an outlaw in Sharona's eyes. DeeDee on the other hand, although being a gangster, had money, lived with class, carried himself with respect and knew how to enjoy the finer things life; be it a quick flight to Maine in the month of May to have a seafood lunch before they made love in a rustic mansion over-looking the Atlantic Ocean, or a jump flight to Vegas to watch the Mike Tyson fight from the front row, DeeDee kept Sharona intrigued and pleased, in and out of the bed. She had learned more from DeeDee than her father could have ever tried to teach her and truth-be-told,

Sharona somewhat viewed DeeDee as a father; but she had the privilege of sleeping with this 'daddy' and loved him more than the man who'd seeded her. Sharona may have been a part of corporate America, but she was just as down as the women who'd been living the street life for years on end; maybe even more so because of the man she loved and whose tutelage she'd been under for the last three years or so.

The tight-fitting white silk dress Sharona wore, and the white stilettos with straps that hugged her thick calves had many of the men's eyes, and even a few women inside the large club looking her way from time to time. Sliding into her role with ease and coming off as a damsel in distress at the bar counter, Sharona began waving her hand in mocked frustration. She could have easily gotten the bartender's attention, but she was trying her best to lure one of the men she knew to be from California into a conversation. DeeDee had shown the pictures to Sharona the day she agreed to help him out and she'd been studying the pictures for the past three days. She knew exactly what she was doing and whose attention she was trying to draw.

Tired of hearing Sharona pleading for the bartender's attention, the young man next to her yelled aloud, "Hey, homie? Can't you see my girl need a drink?"

"Your girl?" Sharona said as she eyed the man with her slender, sexy eyes while bobbing her head and snapping her fingers to Third World's song *Try Jah Love*. "As far as I can remember, I came here by myself."

"What you drinking on, baby?"

"Gin. On the rocks."

"Okay. You go at it hard huh, mami?"

Sharona laughed and said, "I'm not Spanish. My name is Sharona."

"They call me Cool D," the man replied.

"Like the rapper Kool Moe Dee? He was whack back in the day." Sharona said.

Cool D laughed and said, "Nah, baby, I'm west coast. You know niggas out there 'bout that money. That's why I'm here in the Lou, to make money."

"That's supposed to impress me?"

Cool D laughed at Sharona's remark as he lit a cigarette. She had attitude, and he liked it. The twenty-two year-old considered himself a lady's man and had been a Rolling Sixty's Crip for as long as he could remember. He had a few bodies under his belt and felt as if he had the world in his hands. He and his affiliates had been in Saint Louis for six months or so, and being that they were from the much bigger Los Angeles, Cool D and his boys felt as if the city belonged to them. Saint Louis was country in their eyes. They had killed two mid-level dealers and hadn't been retaliated on and now had the other dealers buying their product at nearly twice the going rate out of fear. Saint Louis was theirs for the taking from their standpoint and whatever Cool D and his boys wanted, they usually got—or else they took it by force. "Look," Cool D said as he blew smoke into the air, "I'm not tryin' to impress you. I'm tryin' to get with you."

"You cool—D." Sharona said before she smiled sexily at the young man.

The bartender came over a few seconds later and Cool D ordered a gin on the rocks for Sharona and a triple shot of rum for himself. Ten minutes into their conversation, Cool D was asking Sharona if she would like to take a ride in his new Lexus. Sharona ran her hands through her hair at that point to signal Eddie and Junior. Junior got up and left the club, Eddie, however, walked over to the bar where she was sitting and jumped into his role. "Hey, sis, it's time to stab out. I gotta be at work in the mornin'."

"Damn, Johnny we just got here!" Sharona snapped towards Eddie.

"Whoa, whoa, homie." Cool D said. "This your sister?"

"Yeah. And I'm her ride. She knew when we got here I wasn't tryna stay long!"

"You always do that shit! You always wanna go out but then you wanna fuckin' leave early! You a ole mark ass nigga!"

Cool D, who was trying to keep the peace, got between the two upon noticing the tears that were beginning to flow down Sharona's cheeks. He stepped in front of the young lady and said, "Hey, homie, my name Devin. Look, umm, if your sister wanna hang I'll drop her back at the crib no problem."

Eddie looked at Cool D and frowned and drew closer to him and said, "What you think my sister a hoe or something? What you gone drop her back when you done fuckin' her? That's what you meant to say right?"

Cool D dropped his cool demeanor at that moment and replied, "Cuz, she ain't ready ta' go 'cause she kicking it with a real nigga—something you could never be ole bitch ass Lou nigga."

Eddie lunged at Cool D, but Sharona stopped him just as Cool D's two boys began heading their way. "Johnny, just go! Go 'head home! You always wanna fight! People ain't 'bout that shit no more they just tryna have a good time!"

"You wanna stay, stay! Fuck it I'm gone." Eddie retorted before he turned and walked out the club.

"Your brother a real asshole." Cool D remarked as he and Sharona stood by the bar.

"He can be at times. He just broke up with his girl. She left him for another dude so he got that male ego thang going on. Anyway, what about that ride you promised me?"

Cool D looked over to his boys and pointed to Sharona and they nodded. One of the males made a motion for Cool D to call him and he nodded before he grabbed Sharona's hand and escorted her out of the club. The two walked hand in hand down the quiet street towards Cool D's 1994 navy blue, four door Lexus with gold Daytona rims underneath. As he approached his car, Cool D eyed a white male walking his way trying to light a cigarette. The man was obviously drunk as he kept staggering whilst trying to light his smoke. Cool D and Sharona stepped aside, but it didn't prevent the man from bumping into Sharona.

"Hey, baby, how you doing? You, you got a light?" the man asked.

"I don't smoke, mister." Sharona replied lowly.

"What about you, my friend? You got a light for a drunk?"

"Look man, take your drunk, cracker ass up the—"

Cool D was silenced when he felt the barrel of a gun sticking in his back. "What's up with that bitch ass Lou nigga now, huh, mutherfucka?" Eddie hissed as he went into Cool D's pockets and grabbed his car keys.

"Take the car, homie. All this behind your sister wanting to chill with a real nigga?"

Eddie didn't answer, and Cool D still hadn't realized he'd just been set up. DeeDee pulled up in the van with the side door open and Cool D was thrown into the back and flanked by Mendoza and Lucky, who was pretending be to be drunk and asking for a light. Cool D began screaming for help just as the door was pulled shut.

"Shut 'em up." DeeDee requested calmly from the driver's seat. Lucky hit his victim across the head repeatedly as the van pulled off and he was knocked into a semi-conscious state.

Eddie and Sharona, meanwhile, had hopped into Cool D's car, and Doss and Junior followed, both parties trailing the van over to a garage over in Saint Charles, Missouri, a small suburb west of the city, which was owned by Benito and Gaggi.

Cool D was toted inside and stripped of his clothes and tied to a chair in the middle of the concrete floor. A small light illuminated the damp, empty room and Cool D was awakened with a hard slap across his face. When he focused, he realized that he was now staring at his captors. Lucky, DeeDee and Mendoza were all dressed neatly in silk suits and gators, looking more like businessmen than killers. DeeDee took over the situation while Lucky and Mendoza stood off in the distance.

"Fuck you niggas want from me?" Cool D asked as he tried to shake off his drowsiness.

"Where's the stash?" DeeDee asked calmly as he tapped the side of Cool D's head, irritating the wounds he'd received from the butt of the gun during the ride to Saint Charles.

"What stash? What the fuck you talkin' 'bout, old man? You and the resta these Corleone-looking fake ass gangsters?"

DeeDee had no time for games. The crew had to learn the locale of Cool D and his crew's stash so they could hit it before his boys began to question his whereabouts. As Cool D continued to act tough and play dumb, DeeDee merely nodded and casually walked behind his chair and grabbed an item off one of the work benches. When he returned, he was holding a Black and Decker drill in his right hand. He squeezed the trigger on the power tool and placed it to Cool D's knee and asked again, "Where's the stash?"

"I said fuck you, old man!"

"You better talk if you wanna leave here upright," Sharona said as she stepped into view with Eddie trailing behind her.

"You set me up, bitch? You dead when I get out this mutherfucka!"

Sharona laughed and went over to DeeDee and stood on her tip-toes and kissed his lips. "You need anything else, daddy," she asked.

"Y'all niggas is dead! Dead!" Cool D hissed.

"You doing a lot of shit-talking given the position you in, guy." Sharona said. "I'll be out front. Good luck...Cool D," she said in a sexy voice as she ran her hands through Cool D's Jehri-curled hair.

DeeDee watched Sharona leave the room with a pleasant smile on his face. He then turned back to Cool D and said, "She got your ass good didn't she? Thought you had some grade-A pussy coming your way, but you done slid down a razor blade and landed your ass in an alcohol river, son."

"Bitch wasn't shit! Ain't none of y'all shit!"

"Look, son," DeeDee said calmly as he stood before Cool D, "you wasting my time. Just tell us where the stash is."

"It's in ya' ass, old man! Fuck everybody in here with a sick dick!"

"Okay, you wanna be a hard ass." DeeDee said as he squeezed the trigger and casually drove the drill bit into Cool D's right knee cap, raising and lowering the steel bit until it penetrated the backside of his leg.

Cool D screamed aloud and nearly knocked over the chair. The pain was excruciating. Cold steel penetrating bone and tearing flesh, muscle, and tendon had given him a new perspective all of a sudden. "Fuck, man! Enough! Enough!" he cried out in agony.

"You ready to tell me where the shit at now, hard ass?" DeeDee asked in an angry tone as he slowly pulled the drill tip from Cool D's knee. "I guess you know now that I ain't fuckin' around with your young ass!"

Cool D nodded and immediately gave up an address in south Saint Louis. DeeDee then looked over to Mendoza, Lucky and Eddie, who left the garage while DeeDee remained with a now terrified Cool D. Thirty minutes later, Lucky, Mendoza and Eddie were bagging up twenty-two kilograms and preparing to leave a rundown car wash just south of I-44. Cool D had given up the stash, which was located in a locked shed that had been unlocked with the aide of bolt cutters.

While Mendoza, Lucky and Eddie were headed back over to Saint Charles, Doss and Junior had just began stalking Cool D's two comrades. The men had just left the club and walked down to where Cool D's car was parked and when they saw that it was gone, Doss watched as they went to a payphone.

"They must be paging their homie." Doss chuckled towards Junior, who was in the backseat with a Chicago Piano, commonly known as a Tommy Gun, draped across his lap.

"I think they're a little too late," Junior replied calmly.

Doss checked the time on his watch and saw that it was now after one in the morning. He and Junior had been waiting for Cool D's counterparts to emerge from the club for almost two hours. The men were still at the payphone, obviously awaiting Cool D's callback, but it never came. After ten minutes, the men began walking in Doss and Junior's direction. The two slid down in their seats and watched the men go by and jump into a white Corvette. When they pulled off, Doss followed.

"When I give the signal, you let 'em have it, Junior." Doss said as he tailed the two men onto Interstate-70.

"No problem, Doss," Junior replied calmly as he stared at the tail lights of the Corvette from the backseat whilst pulling a black ski mask over his head.

Doss trailed the two young men for about five miles until they exited onto Jefferson Street. "They must be going back to their old neighborhood," Doss said. "Coban said they hang in an area off Jefferson Street."

Junior sat upright and Doss, knowing he had to hit the men before they reached their home turf, pulled up alongside their car at the red-light on the cars passenger side. "Hit 'em," he said.

Junior opened the back door on the BMW, stepped into the night air with the ski mask covering his face and dressed in all black, and sprayed the Corvette's interior before Cool D's partners ever knew what hit them. Their bodies flailed about in the interior that had quickly been blotted with blood and burnt flesh. Two cars behind Doss and Junior's ride began backing up the ramp when their occupants witnessed what was transpiring and the riders ducked for cover. By the time they arose, the shooters were gone, and all that remained was a bullet-riddled pristine white Corvette that had become the final resting place for two lone men.

Doss and Junior drove the car over to East Saint Louis and met up with Benito, who would dispose of the car and the gun used in the homicides, and returned to the garage an hour later and after being dropped off by Gaggi. Once the group was all back together, they ran down what they'd all done and were satisfied with the hits and had come to the conclusion that their work in Saint Louis was all but complete.

"What about this guy?" Lucky asked DeeDee as he lit a cigarette. Cool D was no longer of any value to the crew now because they'd gotten what they'd come for and had also taken care of his partners.

"We're done with that guy. No further use for him. You wanna do the honors, Junior?" DeeDee asked as he held out the drill.

Cool D was shaking his head from side to side and begging for mercy. "Shut up hard ass," DeeDee said.

"I'll do it, dad," Doss replied. "Junior took care of his boys a while ago. Your son did damn good on his second hit, Lucky. He's coming along just fine in my eyes."

"Like I knew he would, Doss. Put that drill right in top of that guy's skull." Lucky remarked as he patted Junior on the back to congratulate him.

Cool D had pissed his pants the moment he heard Lucky speak. His boys had been killed, and he was now the lone survivor. Suddenly, the new venture to Saint Louis, the overtaking of other drug sets, and the murders of two rival dealers didn't seem as bold as it once had been. Cool D thought he and his crew were untouchable, thought they were the biggest dealers on hand in Saint Louis, but he now realized that his previous actions had awakened a sleeping giant, a sleeping giant that had come through like a runaway freight train and was intent on wiping everything off the map. Cool D also knew he was in for some serious pain, and the casual attitude of his killers only added to his horror. He began pleading for mercy—telling everybody in the room that he was on the next flight back to L.A. if he were to be let go.

"My dad says you're a hard ass. You hard, mutherfucka?" Doss asked as he held the drill tightly in his left hand, squeezing the trigger every now and then to let loose that whizzing sound the drill produced.

"Come on man! I got, I got money, dog! I can, I can get you anything you want! Anything! I got hoes, we got more drugs back home! Man—man I'll suck your dick! Don't kill me please, mister!"

Doss looked back at his team and shook his head in disgust. This was a new one for the Chicago gang all together. The men they'd killed in the past were just that—men—even with death on the horizon, the marks that saw it coming died like men. Cool D, however, had pissed his pants, tried to plea bargain, and when that didn't work, he'd turned into a broad.

"You young cats today," Doss said, bringing about a monologue that he felt needed to be told. "You li'l boys is gangsters when you with your crew. You go around flaunting your money, intimidating the weak and thinking you the shit because you lay down with a different female every other night and got a body or two under your belt. You was a man a minute ago. Now you wanna suck dick. I wish I had a tape recorder, because I'd damn sure send this back to your clan in L.A., but they won't give a fuck. They sent your punk ass down here to the test the waters and guess what? You failed."

Doss said calmly as he walked over to Cool D, grabbed his head and held it in place as he drove the drill bit down into the top of his skull.

The cracking sounds of Cool D's cranium, coupled with the gurgling sounds he emitted were stomach churning. The chair shook furiously, Cool D defecated his jeans, blood ran out the seams of the tape and brain matter began seeping from the hole in his skull the moment Doss removed the drill bit. Neither of the men flinched. They merely stared at the lifeless corpse for several minutes until they decided to leave. The men left the garage, but not before Mendoza called Coban to send a cleanup crew to chop up and dispose of the body.

It took less than a week for Doss and the crew to eradicate the streets of Saint Louis of what was sure to become a problem. Twenty-two kilograms were split evenly amongst all —three kilograms each. The L.A. boys would never return to Saint Louis and try to set up shop again when they learned that two of their men were shot dead and one was now a missing person's case. Rumor soon spread that the Italian Mafia had knocked off the gangbangers, and for the L.A. Crips, a war with the mafia was not a battle they wanted to engage. Coban and Humphrey returned to their business and were able to keep the price low and the streets of Saint Louis were once again free and clear of competition thanks to the gang from Chicago.

Doss and the crew had pulled a highly successful hit; but the prices the boys from L.A. were charging were actually legit. They were only trying to get ahead of the game. They knew what Doss and the gang from Chicago didn't know at the time; but Finland Xavier would set that matter straight for the crew without any repercussions in a matter of weeks.

****

In mid-October of 1994, JunJie had called Fin and asked him to fly out to Seattle for a meeting. Two days later, Fin was sitting in an office in downtown Seattle. JunJie often requested that the entire crew from Chicago join Fin, but Fin always told JunJie that the rest of the family would like to remain behind the scenes. Fin was the only face JunJie knew back in Chicago, and on this day, he asked Fin about Fin's associates again. "Just who do you have doing your handy work, Finland?"

"I told you Mister Maruyama, the family prefers to remain unseen. They have done lots of jobs for lots of people and they believe it's safer for everyone if they remain behind closed doors." Fin said as he bit into an apple as he sat in a chair facing JunJie.

JunJie swayed back and forth in his chair, the Seattle skyline at his back as he twirled a pen in his hands. "I really am impressed with their work. They took care of my problem all in one night. Who are these people? Really?"

Fin smiled and leaned back in the chair. "Do you like their work?"

"Of course I do. I just want to know who I'm supplying. These guys are smooth. I can learn from them."

"Trust me Mister Maruyama, they're learning more from you than you could ever learn from them. You yourself are a smooth operator. Trust me, you have nothing to worry about. The family is at your beck and call, leave them be. In the meantime, I'm your man, your go-to-guy. Let's leave the rest of the family where they are, okay?"

"I trust you Fin, and I like you as well. If you want to keep your friend or friends hidden, fine. If ever I have another job, I'll contact you and you can contact your people. Maybe, maybe you are doing this all by yourself and there really is no one besides you." JunJie then stated.

"I'm just a lawyer." Fin stated through laughter.

"You have outside interests though, right? Like the hit on those boys from L.A.?"

"Does that bother you?"

"Not in the least. But they were right for charging what they were charging."

"What do you mean, JunJie?"

"You'll come to understand why those L.A. boys were asking what they were asking after I explain to you this move we have to make." JunJie replied as he buzzed his front office.

"What move?" Fin asked as Grover Kobayashi and JunJie's son, Phillip Tran, entered the office with a bottle of champagne.

Fin turned and spoke to the two young teens. He knew them somewhat and had seen them on the many trips he had taken to Seattle. When he didn't see the young girl, named Xiang Nyguen, however, he asked JunJie her whereabouts.

"Xiang Nyguen in Vegas now with a man named Asa Spade." JunJie replied.

"Asa Spade? What? Is he a card dealer?"

"No. He's a pimp."

"You turned that sweet little girl into a whore?" Fin asked in disbelief.

"I turned you into a crooked lawyer, Finland."

"You didn't turn me into anything." Fin stated as he and JunJie laughed. "If anything, I made you the man you are today when I accepted your proposition that day."

"You row, I steer, and the boat goes right where we want it to go." JunJie said as he sipped his champagne.

"What does that mean?"

"What I mean is, we need each other my friend. It doesn't matter, I row, you steer—you steer, I row. All I know is, you and I go hand in hand. Without you, it wouldn't work—without me, it wouldn't work. Don't take what I say personal, and maybe that was a bad metaphor to use. I didn't turn Xiang into a whore, Finland. She fell in love with this guy Asa, whom I owed a debt, and she decided to stay. She's happy in Vegas, lots of pretty lights, big lights. Xiang is in good hands."

"So you introduced her to a pimp?"

"If you wanna look at it that way. But to me it was just a debt paid."

"That's all she was to you then? Collateral?"

"Don't see me that way Finland. I care about Xiang and I always will. I just knew she would be much happier in Vegas, okay? Besides, Asa's a good guy. If we expand the network I aim to do business with him. Enough about Xiang, here's the reason you visit me—the Medellin cartel has fallen."

"And Pablo?"

"Escobar has been killed by the U. S. government. With him now dead I had to make a new connection out of Venezuela.

The prices went up. Tell your people the new price is twenty-two." JunJie stated as he turned to face Fin once more.

"Twenty-two is what everybody else is charging." Finland remarked.

"Was charging, Finland. Was charging. With the Medellin cartel now defunct, prices are going to go up drastically. I'm now paying seven per—not the three I once was. The Cali cartel seems strong—but there's a war in South America. Until it ends, thirty per is the new going rate almost everywhere."

"Ahh," Finland said. "That's why those L.A. boys were charging thirty."

"Right. They saw it coming. Only they set up in the wrong city. Their demise there has worked in our favor, though. We are still eight under wholesale and by raising the price, we still gain fifteen per. What I'm doing is—."

"Passing the cost on to the customer." Finland said, cutting JunJie's reply short.

"Correct. It's no different than what goes on in the petroleum industry, real estate, or any other form of business. We are in this to make a profit. No need to be greedy and charge thirty. We can move it faster at a cheaper price and have much bigger clientele."

"I understand fully, Mister Maruyama. I'll notify the family of the price change when I return to Chicago." Finland ended as he stood up and was escorted out of JunJie's office to a waiting limousine.

CHAPTER 23
HOME FOR THE HOLIDAYS

1994 was closing out with the completion of the Holland-Dawkins family's mansion and a new deal between JunJie and Fin. Naomi's trucks were still pulling in revenue and the kids were still being home schooled by Siloam, Kevin and Serena. DeeDee and Mendoza and his family had joined Doss and Lucky on the ranch for Christmas and it was a loving family atmosphere. Lots of laughter and talking abounded. The kids were a delight, just a pure delight to be around. Growing up together with siblings close in age gave Doss and Naomi's progeny of eight many an adventure, and the holidays were always special. All the family from Chicago was on the ranch and food was always being cooked or prepared and there was much fun to be had.

On Christmas Eve, most of the family was all sitting in the Great Room. The Great Room didn't have a TV. This was the place for the family to interact with one another without any distractions. Stories were told, songs were sung, and food was cooked inside the second floor kitchen. Siloam was beginning to learn to play the guitar superbly and she often had a song to sing; something that brought great delight to the family.

As the family kicked back in the huge room, Naomi's middle daughters, six year-olds Kimi and Koko, begged continuously to open their gifts that were under the huge eight foot tall pine Christmas tree that was adorned with gold balls and a platinum star mounted on the top. The fireplace was going and The Temptation's song *Silent Night* played over the sound system mounted in the walls.

"Momma, can me and Koko open our gifts?" Kimi asked, her big, round, beautiful brown eyes displaying a pleading look.

Naomi was talking to Serena and Francine, telling them about her upcoming growing season as she sipped a glass of wine. "Not now, Kimi," she said as she smiled down at her daughter and ran her hands through Kimi's thick mane of silky brown hair. "When you go to sleep and wake up we'll all open our gifts, okay?"

"But, I counted. I have fourteen gifts. Grandma's name is on four of them. One is a doll I already know. Can I open that one?"

"Kimi," Serena chimed in, "your mother said when you wake up. It'll be there tomorrow, baby. Let the grownups talk."

Kimi sulked and walked away and was quickly joined by Koko and the two walked into the kitchen were their grandfathers were. "Grandpa DeeDee, can we open one gift? The one with grandma's name on it? It's a doll." Koko asked.

"Well," DeeDee, who was a little tipsy from the gin he'd consumed said, "from the looks of things, you've already been denied. But I tell you what, if you manage to sneak it out we'll open it," he ended as he knelt down and hugged his granddaughters.

"Really?" Kimi and Koko asked simultaneously as their eyes lit up with glee.

"Really. This is Christmas and you two have plenty. They'll be more gifts to open tomorrow. Grab one and come back. But if you're caught. It wasn't my idea."

"Grandpa DeeDee you the best!" Kimi said as she kissed her grandfather's cheek before she and Koko ran back into the Great Room to accomplish their mission.

"Naomi's going to blow her top if she finds out." Kevin said as he rinsed of a huge butcher's knife.

"Hey, Kevin" Doss chimed in as he sat a watermelon that Naomi had grown in the home's indoor garden onto the counter, "I could've over-ridden that. Kimi and Koko are real savvy, but remember, those are Naomi's kids. She gave birth to them, and she knows each and every one of them like the back of her hand. Kimi and Koko will not return with a gift."

"I wouldn't be surprised if they did, though. Those two can melt butter just by staring." Mendoza said.

"Alright, fellas," Lucky said, "what are we going with, the gin or the vodka?"

"Vodka." DeeDee said.

"No, no." Mendoza said. "Vodka will shrink it. The gin is what we need. It'll soak in better."

"Grandpa Kevin when we gone eat that watermelon," nine year-old Bena asked as she ran into the kitchen.

"This here is for the adults, Bena." Kevin replied.

"All you got is one? Where the melon for us little people?" Bena inquired as the men all burst into laughter.

"Hey, there's pie on the counter. A kiwi pie. You like kiwi don't you, Bay?" DeeDee asked.

"It's really good. Siloam used a kiwi to make my canker sore go away one day. She gave me a kiwi to suck on and I ate the whole thing. I never had a kiwi pie, though. Can I have a slice?"

"You sure can." Mendoza replied as he grabbed a saucer for Bena.

"Siloam is real good with home remedies." Doss replied.

"Who you telling?" Lucky responded. "Remember, remember I caught that Charlie horse back when this place was being built?"

"Yeah, I remember that." DeeDee said as he held the melon so Kevin could slice it.

While he was cutting a hole into the center of the melon, Kevin said to Lucky, "You thought she was crazy when she told you to suck on those mustard packs."

Doss laughed aloud and said, "He told Siloam, 'hey, I ain't sucking on nothin'!'"

The men all laughed again. Kevin then said, "He was up all night crying like a baby. Me and Serena left the guest house and went slept in the Winnebago."

"What he said, again that night, dad?" Doss then asked through laughter.

DeeDee grabbed his leg and mocked Lucky. "Son, he said, he said, he was sitting on the sofa in the den at the time and he yelled out, 'if Siloam don't get in here with that mustard I'm gonna cut this son-of-a you know what off at the knee cap!" the men erupted into laughter at that moment as they mocked Lucky, who laughed himself.

The men were having a ball on this day. Never mind they'd committed a heinous attack on rival dealers a couple of months earlier; that was just their line of work. DeeDee, Doss, Mendoza, Lucky and Junior were chameleons of the sort. They could turn their gangster and killer instinct on and off like a light switch. And when they were on the ranch one could never even imagine the horrible things they were doing to people; but no one outside of Naomi and Francine knew what actually went down when the men were conducting business back in Illinois and elsewhere so they were revered by all in the family, especially the children.

"Alright, she's ready. Bring on the gin, gentlemen." Kevin said happily.

Bena sat at the island counter and ate her slice of pie as she watched her grandfather DeeDee pour gin into the circle Kevin had cut into the melon. She knew they were pouring liquor into the melon, but she didn't know why. She was going to ask for a slice, but when she saw what was happening, she frowned, jumped from her stool, and walked out of the room and went in Dawk's room to watch TV with him and Walee. Liquor would only ruin the taste if Bena had to tell it.

****

Early on Christmas morning, while the adults were still asleep, Kimi and Koko were sitting up in their queen-sized canopy beds staring at one another from opposite ends of the room. "You ready?" Koko asked as she opened her silk screen and jumped from her bed and grabbed her skates.

"Yeah. You sure we won't get in trouble?" Kimi asked as she reached into her toy chest and grabbed her skates.

"Momma said whenever the man comes to clean the floors,

the day before we can skate."

"But it's Christmas. Nobody works on Christmas."

"Momma said he coming tomorrow, which will be after Christmas. We can do it today." Koko remarked as she headed for the door.

The twins tip toed from their bedroom and ran towards T-top's room where they saw her and Bena playing a shooting game on their Super Nintendo system.

"I thought I heard y'all comin'. Y'all 'bouta skate?" Bena asked as she fired at the screen.

"Yeah. We thought y'all was still sleep." Kimi replied.

"On Christmas Day? With all those gifts under the tree? We been up!" Tiva remarked as she lowered her toy gun. "I wanna skate, too, now."

"Me too. Let me get my skates." Bena said as she ran back to her room.

Bena returned and saw T-top doing Kimi and Koko's hair. Naomi's middle twins had long, silky brown hair that flowed to their necks and T-top loved to style it for her sisters. She was tying Koko's hair into a pony tail and Bena assisted by doing the same for Kimi. T-top then went into her armoire and pulled out two pairs of her shorts. "It'll be hard to skate in those night gowns. Put these shorts on," she told Kimi and Koko while handing them the pairs of denim jean shorts. Kimi and Koko were big for six years of age, plump little girls they were and they could easily fit Bena and Tiva's shorts and shirts.

Several minutes later, Bena, T-top, Kimi and Koko were all at the foot of the front hall holding on to the wall giggling uncontrollably. The girls rarely got to skate, but their mother had told them whenever the floor crew was scheduled to come and polish the wooden floors, which was usually once a month, they could skate the day before. The hall in the front of the home on the second floor was ten feet wide with fifteen foot ceilings. The kids could literally race down the long hall, through the music room towards the opposite end of the hall. From there they would bank left and skate down another narrower long hall and bank left again and would emerge from the hall that crossed the middle of Ponderosa and ran through the center of the Great Room. Ponderosa was so spacious the kids could literally use the second floor of the home as their own personal skating rink. They were truly living the good life.

"Ready?" Bena asked aloud as she turned on her headphones.

"Go!" T-top yelled.

The sisters all pushed off the wall and began skating down the wide open hall. They passed a study on their left, a huge walk-in closet and the upstairs library before emerging before the wooden rails that bordered the Grand Staircase, which was modeled after the stair case on the Titanic, complete with a crystal chandelier. They then entered the music room where they paused for a minute and strummed a few keys on the Grand piano. The music room also held Siloam's guitar and amplifier, Kimi and Koko's violin and a karaoke machine the family often used during the warmer months on the back patio. They left the music room and skated past their classroom, which held a dozen wooden desks, a chalk board on the back wall and a TV mounted in the right corner near the ceiling.

The sisters made a left turn and formed a single file line. This narrow hall contained many paintings and portraits created by Siloam and the kids. They then passed the art room on the right, which featured numerous wall-mounted finger paintings created by three year-olds Spoonie and Tyke, along with drawings by four-year-old Walee and oil paintings created by the oldest five. This portion of the home belonged mainly to the kids.

Banking left again at the end of the narrow hall, the girls entered the hall leading back towards the Great Room. The hall was the same size as the front hall and held many Native American oil paintings created by artists in around Ponca City. The four had skated past the water fountain in the Great Room and entered the opposite hall and rounded the bend for a second time when Bena turned around and began skating backwards.

"Bena the best skater ever!" Koko said.

The four sisters had a flow going as they lapped around the top floor of Ponderosa. They passed the Grand Staircase a third time and Naomi, having just walked into the Great Room, ran and retrieved her camera off the mantle above the fireplace when she saw her daughters cruising by on their skates and disappearing into the music room.

"I told you we weren't going to get into trouble, Kimi!" Koko yelled as the girls skated through the Great Room and waved at their mother as she filmed them.

The family had enjoyed a wonderful Christmas. And the week leading up to New Year's Day was joyful as well. On New Year's Eve, Doss took his kids outside once the sun went down and they let off fireworks in the snow. Naomi had taken many pictures and had filmed hours of footage over the holiday period and the memories would never be forgotten. While the family was on the balcony counting down New Years and waiting in anticipation for Doss, DeeDee, Mendoza and Junior to fire off weapons at midnight, Naomi adjoined to her bedroom and sat quietly at her desk with her hands resting underneath her chin, closed her eyes and began praying silently.

"Lord, I know I do many a wrong thing in my life, but if you hear me, if I'm worthy of your ear, make sure Martha, Mary and Samson are doing as well as I am. My family is my life. I miss my brother and sisters. Please, if it is in your will, let me find them someday. Amen."

Naomi opened her eyes just as gunshots began to ring out from the balcony outside the Great Room and she shook her head sadly. The "many a wrong thing" she was referring to was the fact that unlike tonight, when her husband fired a gun, more times than not, a person was on the opposite end to catch the bullets. She always told herself, though, that the will of God supersedes even that of her own sins, and it was for this reason that she believed her prayers would be answered. Naomi was hoping, longing for the day when she would find her siblings. She believed in a God. She believed He could give her what she was asking for, but she never knew just how high a price she would have to pay for those prayers to be answered, because the road leading towards the first unification between Naomi and a portion of her lost family members would come at high cost not only to Naomi, but to several people she held dear in her life.

CHAPTER 24
AN UNFORESEEABLE OCCURENCE

Six year-olds Kimi and Koko had awakened shortly after midnight on a cold, snowy night in February of 1995. Both were in need of a snack, so they leapt from their beds, adorned their pink silk robes and pink fur bunny slippers and walked towards the upstairs kitchen. They searched the counter for the carrot cake their grandmother Serena had baked, but it had been eaten. They then remembered the watermelon they saw their grandfather Kevin slicing and they went and opened the refrigerator door and took several slices and laid them on saucers.

Bay, meanwhile, was lying in T-top's bed listening to her headphones while she watched Dawk and T-top play the Super Nintendo game when Dawk and T-top decided they needed a drink. They sat the controllers down and left the room and when they walked into the kitchen, they saw Kimi and Koko sitting on the floor eating the watermelon while playing with their dolls, and they, too, grabbed a slice of watermelon.

"This melon taste funny." T-top said as she savored the taste.

"It does. But it's good ain't it? Shoot! I need another slice." Koko said.

When Koko got up from the kitchen floor, she stumbled a bit. "Why the room spinning?" she asked as she wobbled to the refrigerator. Koko opened one of the refrigerator doors and fell on her rear end and started laughing as she held onto the door's handle.

T-top stood up to help her sister, but she herself fell forward. She caught herself with her hands and righted herself and immediately started crying. "What kind of watermelon that was?" she asked through tears as she sat down on the kitchen floor.

Dawk was feeling so good he felt like dancing. He ran into the Great Room with his slice of watermelon and began to act as if he was playing a guitar.

Kimi and Koko, meanwhile, had eaten their second slice of melon and could not stop laughing. They would stand up and wobble and let themselves fall to floor, bracing their fall with their hands.

T-top soon got up and went and sat next to Dawk in the Great Room and she still could not stop crying. She listened as Dawk strung the strings on the violin. "Sing, sing that song y'all sung on the patio the day grandpa DeeDee and Mendilozoza had them funny clothes on," she said to Dawk.

Dawk stood up, wobbled a bit and caught himself and asked, "Who, who is Mendilozoza? You mean, Menzoza?"

"Not, Menzoza. Mendizoza. Daddy 'nem friend from Illilinois."

"Mendoza," Dawk said slowly as he began singing The Marshall Tucker Band's song titled Can't You See. *"Can't you see…what that wom, woman, Lord, she been doin' me…"*

T-top was becoming more emotional listening to Dawk, even though he was messing up the lyrics to the song, and she cried louder. "That is such a sad song," she said through her tears.

Bena, in search of Dawk and Tiva, soon entered the Great Room and saw the watermelon her siblings were eating on the kitchen floor. "Oh, man! Grandpa put liquor in that melon!" she exclaimed.

"That's why I feel good!" Dawk snapped as he began stripping his clothes off.

"Boy! Put your clothes back on! Momma gone kill y'all!" Bena said as she ran and picked up the uneaten slices of watermelon off the kitchen floor.

While Bena was picking up the watermelon, Naomi emerged

from the hall. She was going to check and make sure the kids weren't up at this hour being that they had class early in the morning. She entered the Great Room and had stumbled upon what could only be described as a hot mess. Dawk was now butt naked stringing the violin and dancing like Chuck Berry, one leg out in front of his body as he scooted across the floor.

"Momma, they ate grandpa Kevin's watermelon." Bena said as she picked up the last two slices and ran into the kitchen.

Naomi was furious. "Put your clothes back on before I lit it up!" she yelled as she walked towards Dawk, who quickly dropped the violin and took off running to his bedroom.

Just then, Kimi and Koko emerged from the kitchen. The two were staring at their mother and running sideways whilst laughing, headed directly towards an expensive clay vase, about to knock it down. "Exit stage left!" Koko yelled aloud as she and her twin picked up momentum.

Naomi had to run and catch Kimi and Koko in order to prevent them from ruining the area and hurting themselves in the process. At that moment, she wanted to whip her kids senseless, but she knew they weren't at fault. She had requested that Kevin place the watermelon, which he'd once again filled with gin, in the downstairs kitchen before he went to sleep because she knew her kids often awoke during the middle of the night to have a snack. She calmed them down and gave them water and sat with them in the Great Room and placed biscuits in the oven to put something on their stomachs before she put them back to bed.

Later that morning, John Hiatt's song, titled *Blue Telescope,* played low and soft on Naomi's radio inside her overly large downstairs kitchen. Kevin and Serena, both unaware of what had transpired with five of Naomi's kids the night before, were preparing breakfast for their grandchildren whilst Naomi and Siloam tidied up the theater room inside the mansion. Serena had discovered John Hiatt's CD via Siloam when the family went to town the week before and the woman fell in love with the man's music and simply adored his song *Blue Telescope.* That song was heard every morning for over a week and Naomi's kids, Naomi herself, Siloam and Kevin all knew the lyrics.

"Grandma why you like that song so much?" Bena asked Serena, who was now in her early seventies.

"Well sweetie, the lyrics are just superb. He loved that woman so much, but she went away."

"Why she left, grandma," Dawk asked.

"They just went their separate ways, okay?"

"Then that's a sad song." Tiva stated.

"Every song to you is a sad song. Just like that song last night." Dawk replied.

"Every song ain't a sad song. I was crying last night because I was, I was, what was that word momma used, Bay?"

"Inebriated." Bena replied.

Kevin and Serena both paused and stared at one another after hearing Bena's reply. Serena eyed Kevin with a look of disappointment as she held two plates of grits and eggs and said, "Tell me you moved that watermelon from the second floor to the first floor last night before you came to bed, dear."

"I completely forgot, Serena. Did you kids eat any watermelon last night?"

"Sure did!" Koko snapped.

"And we had a funky good time!" Kimi remarked as she clapped her hands and began gyrating in her seat.

"Ohh my Lord. Let me go and find Naomi. No wonder she's been distant all this morning. She's upset." Serena remarked as she sat the plates down. "Kevin look after your grandkids—and make sure they don't consume any more liquor will you please?"

"Very funny, Serena." Kevin replied, embarrassed over his actions.

Back in the theater room, Siloam was conversing with Naomi as they wiped the wooden furniture on the seats. "Momma, I been thinking about going to college. How does that sound?" Siloam asked.

"Okay." Naomi remarked, vaguely paying attention to Siloam.

"Yeah. I been thinking—since I been homeschooling the kids

here on the ranch, I can enter the field of education or maybe music since I love it so much. I'd like to be a rock star, but I'll settle on becoming a teacher."

"That's fine Siloam."

"Also, I wanna explore active volcanoes in the Pacific. I can climb down and scoop up the hot lava with my bare hands and bring it back to the lab for volcanologists to study."

"Okay." Naomi replied.

"Momma, you haven't heard a word I've said to you. Are you okay?"

Naomi looked up at Siloam before she took a seat. "I'm sorry," she said dejectedly. "College would be fine. I'll support you, even if you wanna be a rock star, baby. It's just, last night, Dawk, T-top, Kimi and Koko all got a buzz from Kevin's watermelon. He left it in the upstairs kitchen after I specifically requested that he move the thing to the downstairs kitchen. He knows the kids get up in the middle of the night looking for a snack."

"Are they okay?" Siloam asked as she sat beside Naomi.

"Amazingly, they are fine. I thought they would be sick this morning and unable to have class, but they are fine."

"I'm sure Kevin is sorry. If he even knows what happened. Did you talk to him?"

"Not yet, but I most certainly will. I can't have my kids getting drunk. I mean, Dawk was dancing naked, Tiva was crying nonstop and Koko and Kimi nearly knocked over that Aztec vase." Naomi said.

Siloam chuckled and said, "Sounds like a big fiasco."

"It was. And it's not funny. The kids could've really hurt themselves, Siloam." Naomi said as she got up and left the theater room.

"I'm sorry, Naomi." Siloam said just as Naomi pulled the door shut tightly.

Meanwhile, back in the kitchen, six year-olds Kimi and Koko were nodding off at the table, having grown sleepy from listening to Serena's favorite song over and over again. Kimi dozed off and quickly raised her head and asked over the music, "Grandpa? When we gone eat? And when you gonna play something else?"

"When I get good and ready, Kimi."

"That's the answer to the question for the song, or when we're gonna eat?" Koko asked.

"She gonna slop y'all down in a minute." Dawk blurted out as Bena and Tiva laughed.

"Hey! Don't say that to them, Dawk! What's wrong with you, son?" Kevin asked.

"Yeah, what's wrong with you, son?" four year-old Walee stated in imitation of Kevin.

"Walee, please be quiet." Kevin said.

"But I'm on your side, grandpa."

"I don't need back up for Dawk. Dawk apologize to your sisters!"

"I'm sorry—big and bigger." Dawk stated as Bena and Tiva laughed again.

"So, look at you! You got hair like a girl!" Kimi stated.

"Leave him alone!" Tiva said to Kimi.

"And you leave her alone!" Koko then said to Tiva.

Before long Naomi's oldest five were arguing at the table as Walee stood in his seat instigating the event. The four year-old, as Spoonie and Tyke cheered him on, slid his chair across the floor and placed it beside Bay and took sides with her and Tiva. "That's your big sister you don't talk to her like that! Y'all two is flip by the mouth!" he yelled towards Kimi and Koko.

"Shut up, Walee! This not even none of your business!" Kimi yelled.

"Don't say nothin' to him!" Spoonie yelled.

"Shut up talkin' to us over there! Tiny self!" Koko yelled.

"It's a lot of hatred in this family." Dawk said lowly.

"You don't know what you talkin' about. You can have a fight and still like somebody." Koko replied.

"What kind of liking is that? I never seen momma and daddy fight and they like each other a lot."

340

"Momma and daddy love each other. I hear them say that all the time. I love you, but that won't stop me from knocking you out today." Koko told Dawk as she balled up her fists and dotted her eyes and lips.

"I'm a pull all your hair out you touch me."

"Oooh! You ain't, you better not touch her! How you gone fight a girl, Dawk?" Kimi asked.

"The same way I would fight a boy—to win! Let her step over here!" Dawk replied.

Walee, at that moment, decided he would now side with Kimi and Koko. He slid his chair around the table next to his middle sisters, climbed into the chair and said, "Say, Dawk? Now, we share the same room, but hitting a girl ain't right. Apologize to Kimi and Koko."

Dawk looked over to Bay and T-top and the three burst into laughter. "You heard your boss," Tiva said. "Apologize to your sisters."

"The day I say I'm sorry will be the day those two lose weight."

"Forget you, Dawk! You just mad 'cause we got more muscle than you!" Kimi said as she raised her arms and tried to produce muscles.

"That ain't muscle that's fat on y'all two." Bay said through laughter.

"That's it! You gone leave, leave big and bigger alone!" Walee snapped.

"You tryna be funny!" Koko said as she slapped Walee's arm.

"Don't touch me!" Walee said as he shoved Koko's shoulder.

"Don't touch her!" Kimi replied as she shoved Walee.

"Leave Walee alone!" T-top yelled towards Koko.

"Leave Koko alone!" Kimi yelled to Tiva.

Walee and the oldest five were back yelling at each other whilst Spoonie and Tyke laughed aloud. The ruckus was ear-deafening. Serena, unable to find Naomi, heard the commotion as she descended the stairs and ran into the kitchen in order to calm the kids down. "Shut up! Shut up! Shut up! Shut up!

God! Just one time can you all sit together at the table and not argue?"

"Yeah man, y'all kin! What's wrong with y'all savages?" Walee snapped as three year-olds Spoonie and Tyke laughed and tried to repeat his remarks.

Naomi's oldest five went silent after hearing Walee say the word 'savage' just as Naomi entered the kitchen. They all placed their hands in their laps and looked down at the table. Walee, Spoonie and Tyke, however, were still going at it. "That's right," Walee said as he stood in his chair, "savages is what y'all acting like this morning," he said.

Dawk was shaking his head at Walee trying to silence him, but Walee kept going on and on, repeatedly saying the word savage as Spoonie and Tyke cheered him on. The oldest five were eyeing their mother standing in the threshold, and Walee, Spoonie and Tyke, once they noticed how quiet everyone at the table had gotten, all turned around slowly. When they saw their mother staring them down, all three grew scared. Walee, Spoonie and Tyke, just like the rest of the children, knew the word 'savage' was never to be said by anyone in the family because their mother had told them to never say the word, stating that it was worse than cursing.

Spoonie and Tyke began fidgeting their hands rapidly as their mother began walking towards them. She went over to Walee and slapped his legs hard as he stood in his chair. She then grabbed him by his shirt collar and forced him into his chair and shoved him in front of the table. She then grabbed Shima and Sinopa's hands and swatted them while yelling at them to never say the word 'savage' again. All three were crying incessantly when Kevin went over to comfort them.

"Daddy, let them be! They know better than to call each other names!" Naomi yelled.

"Baby, they're just kids! They mean no harm!" Serena stated as she entered the dining room.

"Momma, don't tell me what to do with my children!"

"Naomi, I'm just saying—"

"I said don't tell me what to do, momma!" Naomi yelled.

Kevin stared at Naomi and said, "Why are you so hostile all

of a sudden? Serena meant no harm in what she was saying."

"Fine! Do whatever you want! But when they get drunk again, you deal with them!"

"I was aiming to talk to you about that, Naomi!" Kevin remarked as Naomi stormed out of the kitchen.

Naomi walked back into the kitchen and said, "What happened last night should have never happened! You let them get drunk of your stupid watermelon! Don't you ever do that again!"

"It was a mistake, Naomi! A mistake! Unlike you, I'm not perfect."

"Now you are being facetious! It's not about perfection. It's about responsibility. I could be sitting in the hospital now had I not gotten up, dad!"

"And I would be right there with you. Feeling just as sorry and responsible for the whole mishap just as I am at this very moment."

"That's supposed to make me feel better? Well it doesn't, dad. It doesn't." Naomi hissed as she walked out of the kitchen.

Naomi went and sat in the observation room for over thirty minutes, thinking hard about the way she talked to Serena and had downed Kevin. She knew she was wrong, and she came to the conclusion that she had overreacted. She was preparing to apologize when Siloam walked in and said, "Momma, I need to get new markers and crepe paper for the kids."

"Okay, we'll go in a minute. The kids do have to get their day started. I want to dress Spoonie and Tyke before we leave."

"That's okay, momma, I'll dress them when I return. You should relax. Look, what happened last night was just a mistake. A mistake, momma. You know Kevin would never intentionally put the kids in harm's way. Don't you?" Siloam asked in an unsure manner.

"Of course I do, Siloam. I overreacted. I'll go apologize right now and let them know I'm over the entire thing."

"They're in the Suburban waiting on me, momma. Kevin

needs a prescription filled and Serena wants fresh zucchini and beef chunks. You three can talk when we get back while I get the kids ready for their assignments. Don't worry, everything well be fine. Mistakes happen."

"Thank you, Siloam. But can I at least get the kids ready while you all are away?"

Siloam laughed and said, "Sure, momma. See you when we get back," before she kissed Naomi's cheek and headed towards the back patio.

"Is Naomi okay?" Kevin asked Siloam worriedly the moment she hopped behind the wheel of the suburban.

"She's fine. She wants to apologize to you both when we return."

"I should be the one apologizing. I remembered the watermelon just as I laid down, but I was so tired after all the cooking we'd done I just didn't feel like climbing the stairs to move it back to the first floor. It's my fault."

"It was a mistake, Kevin. A mistake. Naomi understands that." Serena said as she kissed Kevin's cheeks.

"Still, I have to let her know how sorry I am. We have to talk when I get back."

"We will. We will. And I'll do a nice pot of beef stew for supper and we could relax in one of the studies and play a board game with the kids after their schooling is done. It'll be okay." Serena said as Siloam, who was constantly nodding her head in agreement over Serena's remarks, drove off the ranch.

Naomi walked into the dining room shortly after Siloam, Kevin and Serena had left to tend to her kids, who were sitting quietly and being served plates of grits and bacon by Dawk, Bena and Tiva. After reflecting on the matter, Naomi had come to the full conclusion that she had overreacted. She would be sure to apologize to her parents, who she knew would do no harm to the kids in away way shape or fashion, upon their immediate return.

After getting the kids fed, dressed, and situated in the classroom to begin their assignments, Naomi checked her watch and saw that nearly two hours had passed. The snow had stopped falling shortly after Serena, Kevin and Siloam had left and she figured they should have been back by now as the roads would have been clear. She went to the front door of the home and opened it, expecting to see the two women along with Kevin coming up the long road leading to the home; instead she saw a state trooper's patrol car headed to the house. The police had never been to the ranch, and the moment she saw the car, Naomi ran down the stairs and met the patrol car at the end of the road in front the home.

"What happened?" Naomi asked in a panicked state as she eyed Siloam exiting the passenger side of the patrol car. "Where are my parents?"

"Momma, I didn't mean to! We was on side the road and this truck just came from nowhere and—"

"Where's Kevin and Serena?" Naomi asked again.

"She, she's dead momma! She and Kevin are both dead!" Siloam said as she went to hug Naomi.

"What did you do? What did you do?" Naomi asked as she brushed Siloam away from her. "What did she do to my parents?" she asked the officer as he exited the driver's side of the car.

"Ma'am, Siloam here had gotten a flat tire. She pulled over, put out the road flares and she and Kevin proceeded to change the tire. While standing outside the car, an eighteen wheeler skidded out of control and hit the front of the SUV. Siloam was able to dodge the on-coming truck, but Kevin was pinned against the SUV and Serena, she was crushed inside the car. I'm sorry."

Naomi stared into empty space at that moment. She had a blank look on her face, one of disbelief. She slowly turned and faced Siloam with a disappointed look, shook her head from side to side and merely walked away, headed back towards the stairs leading into the home. The kids were all standing in the doorway and they watched as their mother dropped to her knees and fell forward into the snow. Siloam and the kids ran to Naomi's aide and the officer called for an ambulance before he ran to help Naomi.

Siloam was ushering the kids back to the stairs when Naomi, having regained her composure, but still lying on her belly in

345

the snow, yelled aloud, "Siloam you get away from them!"

Siloam looked back at Naomi and knelt at her side and said, "Momma, they don't need to see you like this!"

"You get away from *me* as well!" Naomi said as she was helped from the snow by the officer. "Don't touch me, Siloam! You and your art supplies! They didn't have to go with you! This is all—" Naomi caught herself before she went any further, but it was too late. Siloam knew right away what she was about to say.

Siloam was already feeling responsible for Serena and Kevin being dead, but hearing Naomi almost say it was her fault had hurt the young woman's heart deeply. She took off running into the snow-covered field as Naomi called out to her. "I'm sorry!" Naomi yelled as she watched Siloam run away.

Paramedics and another patrol car came onto the ranch after ten minutes, but Naomi had only fainted from the shock. She refused treatment and had the state troopers watch her kids as she began heading in the direction in which Siloam had taken off running several minutes earlier. After a short search, Naomi found Siloam down by the guest house. She could see her standing beside the home before a small fire burning in the snow. Naomi yelled Siloam's name and ran her way and Siloam began discarding items into the fire at a furious pace. The closer she got to the flames, Naomi could clearly see that Siloam was burning pictures of she and Naomi. She grabbed Siloam and hugged her tightly and said through tears, "Siloam, I'm sorry! It's not your fault! It's wasn't your fault!"

"You don't mean that, Naomi! You hate me now! I never meant for this to happen!" Siloam yelled as she broke free of Naomi's grip and ran across the frozen creek, nearly slipping on the ice as she made her way into the woods behind the guest home.

Siloam had called Naomi by her name for the first time in almost two years and she knew right away that the relationship between her and Siloam had been severely damaged. It would be up to her to amend the relationship, but burying Serena and Kevin was most important as of now for Naomi. Siloam would be okay after they talked the matter over was Naomi's thinking as she walked back to Ponderosa and tended to her kids for over two hours, explaining to them what'd happened to their grandmother and grandfather. The kids were saddened by the loss and would feel the impact of their grandparents' death for a long time.

It took Naomi two weeks to make the arrangements. Kevin and Serena were buried in Cicero, side by side. DeeDee and Doss were there as well as the Cernigliaro family, and everyone was saddened by the untimely death of the Langleys, who were nothing more than a sweet and caring couple who dared to do right by an orphaned child. Naomi sat alone by her surrogate parents' graves in twenty degree weather in a state of total shock. She was also heart-broken that Siloam had run away the same day of the accident after she caught her beside the guest house burning pictures that were supposed to be a permanent part of the family. Twenty-one year-old Siloam Bovina had vanished into thin air, leaving behind all of her personal possessions, and never even phoning to let Naomi know she was okay. Naomi had argued with Serena the day she died and she had basically blamed Siloam for Serena and Kevin being dead. It was a bitter pill to swallow. Everything that could have been done wrong the day Serena and Kevin died had been done by Naomi. And the thing that was paining her the most was the fact that she never got to apologize to Kevin for disrespecting him so harshly. Sitting along in the light snowfall, Naomi stared at Kevin and Serena's graves and said in a low voice, "Momma, daddy, I'm so sorry. I wasn't the best daughter I could've been. I always wanted things to go my way. I was spoiled I know, but please, please," Naomi cried as she leaned forward and placed her hands over her face and heaved heavily. "You two were my benefactors, and you left me so suddenly. We had so much to look forward to. So much more to share. I'm, I'm really sorry that this happened to you."

"They will miss you more than you miss them, baby."

Naomi turned and saw Doss standing behind her. She stood up and eyed him and said, "I really believe that, Doss. They loved me, more than I loved them."

"Don't say that, Naomi," Doss replied as he hugged his wife. "Your past, what happened in Alabama? It changed you, baby —but you did the best you could in spite of, understand? You are a magnificent woman, a great woman."

"You really mean that, Doss? Am I?"

"Naomi, you are my angel. For all the bad things I do out here, you are wholesome. You, my love, are my light in the darkness that I travel through out here in the darkness of these streets."

"That's the sweetest thing you ever said to me, Doss."

"I meant every word. Look at our beautiful kids, our friends, our life. The pain will heal, and we'll still be here to share in your wonderful memories."

"You know, I wonder why people like Zell live into their eighties and both my mothers and fathers, Nituna and Rutherford especially, had their life snatched away. Why?" Naomi asked as she stared at Doss, her eyes searching for a sincere answer from her husband.

"No one really knows why God allows bad things to happen to good people. Maybe this is part of some big plan."

Naomi, at that very moment, was unable to accept her husband's rationalization. As sincere as Doss was with his words of comfort, his speaking on God had triggered a volatile reaction within Naomi, who for so long, held a form of animosity towards the higher Being.

"Was it in God's plan to let what happen to Nituna happen," Naomi asked angrily. "Was it God's plan to have Ruth run over and my brother and sisters taken away? What kind of plan is that, Doss? You keep saying God! I keep *asking* God! Everybody keeps saying God! God, God, God! Where is God? There can't be a God! Because if there was a God, a real God, He would not let people like Zell live a long time and die in their sleep—but take my parents in the flash of an eye! I never got say what I wanted to say to them! And then Siloam! She left me! I never got to fix *that* part of my life! When will it all come to pass, Doss? I've been asking God for someday for so long and this is what I get from God?" Naomi said as she extended her hand towards Kevin and Serena's graves before she took off running through the cemetery.

Doss ran after his wife and cornered her beside a mausoleum that was hidden from view. "You can't stop believing in God,

Naomi," he said with conviction. "As much wrong as I do, I still believe in a higher power. Look at all God has given you. Don't you dare blame Him for this!"

"I take it back, okay? I take it back, Doss," Naomi said in defeat. "But it's hard to understand what kind of plan, what kind of future God has in store for me. This is one of the worst times of my life! The people I love keep getting taken away. God gives us what we can bear, but this," Naomi said as she bowed her head and waved her hands side to side, "this here is too much. And Siloam. That girl never complained about nothing. Wouldn't hurt a soul, and never once raised her voice. I hurt her, Doss. Hurt her so bad she ran away. Left her van behind along with all her clothes. She was burning pictures of her and me when I found her. She's outta my life for good— just like Kevin and Serena. I lost three people I loved dearly." Naomi said as she reached out and wrapped her arms around Doss' neck and screamed loudly. Soon all of Naomi's friends and her kids were surrounding her, giving hugs and words of comfort.

Naomi, Doss and her kids returned to Oklahoma a week after the funerals and Naomi spent the rest of the winter with her husband and kids. Doss had taken a semi-hiatus from his criminal activities to be with his family full-time in February of '95 and his constant presence was of great reassurance to Naomi, who still hurt inside from time to time. And as the spring season came in, Naomi, still unable to let go of the day she lost Kevin, Serena and Siloam, had entered a state of great depression. If she didn't get over losing her surrogate parents and Siloam, Naomi knew she would never be of any value to her family once more. What to do to remedy the situation, however, had left the grieving woman perplexed.

CHAPTER 25
TAKE TO THE OPEN ROAD

Naomi sat alone on her patio in the early morning hours in June of 1995, four months to the day she had lost three very important people in her life. Several things were troubling the thirty-nine year-old woman during this period of time. For one, Naomi believed that Siloam would have returned when she got back after Serena and Kevin's funeral, but Siloam was nowhere to be found. On top of that, she missed her parents and her lost siblings greatly. Everything in Naomi's life had been turned upside down the day Kevin and Serena died. Her health was also in jeopardy. Several times she had collapsed while working in the cabbage patch. Farmhands assisted her and notified Doss each time. She was given a prescription for Prozac in the month of April to combat her depression, but she had never bothered to take the medication. She believed she needed to get away, if only for a short time, in order to regain her senses. Medication was not the answer.

Tired of listening to doctors' advice, and seeing herself falling ever deeper into depression, Naomi began to take action to get herself out of her funk. A few weeks earlier she'd purchased another Peterbilt truck for herself. She sat on her patio eyeing the massive black vehicle that had just been delivered an hour earlier and a certain kind of calmness, a spiritual sort of calmness overcame her. She felt that getting away may be the very thing she needed to get herself back on track. Naomi eyed the vehicle with adulation. This would be her cure for depression. She already had her first run planned

351

—a load of canned tomatoes from Oklahoma City to Chicago, Illinois. Once there, she would visit Kevin and Serena's gravesites, make her final peace, and take to the open road for a short period of time.

As she contemplated the future, Naomi's eight kids walked out onto to the patio. The kids knew why their mother had bought the truck for herself and they were worried that she was leaving forever. Doss had sat in the Great Room and reassured his kids, but they were still scared their mother was leaving them behind. The kids had gotten accustomed to their father leaving for a few days or weeks, and returning at a later date, but their mother had never left them alone for any amount of time. This was new to everyone. The kids slowly approached their mother from behind, eyeing her sadly as they walked in a spaced-out group, each remaining close to the sibling they felt the most comfortable with at the time. Dawk led the way with T-top at his side. Walee followed with Spoonie and Tyke on his heels and Bena brought up the rear, walking in between Kimi and Koko, holding their hands tightly for comfort and reassurance. Doss, meanwhile, stood back in the French doors watching in silence. He'd encouraged his kids to tell their mother how they felt and what they thought, promising them that their mother would not tell them she was going away forever.

The kids walked across the patio towards their mother and approached from the rear. Naomi was so caught up in her thoughts, she never noticed her kids approaching until they rounded her lounge chair. She was startled briefly, but regained her composure and sat upright.

"Hey my beautiful babies." Naomi said lovingly with a wide smile on her face.

"Hey, momma." Dawk replied. "We, dad said it was okay if we ask you something."

"Sure. You all can ask me anything. It doesn't mean you will always get an answer." Naomi said as she smiled and laughed lightly.

None of Naomi's kids laughed. Kimi and Koko looked as if they were going to burst into tears. Spoonie and Tyke were fidgety with their hands, and it was because of their actions and behavior that Naomi, at that moment, knew something was troubling her children. The reason being was because whenever Spoonie and Tyke were anxious, their round eyes would widen and they would rub their hands together in frustration while staring at their mother. Naomi sensed her kids' distress. "What's wrong with you all? What is it you want to ask me?" she inquired as she straightened up and pulled Spoonie and Tyke close.

"You brought that new truck for yourself. Dad said you not leaving us. If you not leaving, why you got that truck for yourself?" Dawk asked.

Naomi looked over to Dawk as she rubbed Spoonie and Tyke's back. She knew and understood right away how her kids were feeling because she was wondering how she would maintain her composure on the road without being around them for an extended period of time. Now that she knew for certain this move would upset her kids, she decided she wouldn't stay out as long as she had planned at the outset. Still, Naomi had to get away in order to return to her old self. The family needed a fully focused and functional Naomi, not a woman who was beside herself with guilt and regret. Those things had to be removed from Naomi's psyche; and in order to remove those unwanted emotions, the open road was the cure the grieving mother had deemed right for herself. She beckoned all of her kids close, and they eagerly approached their mother, jockeying for position to stand before their rock.

"You kids," Naomi said lovingly, "you are dealing with the loss of your grandparents like the big boys and girls you are and I'm proud of you all. Momma just has to clear her head for a minute in order to be able to take care of you all the way you need to be taken care of and to look after the family's businesses."

The children all looked at their mother in a confused manner. To them, they had always been taken care of; they couldn't fully grasp what their mother was implying, and Naomi knew it. "Your father and I have a lot of responsibility," Naomi said as the children stood in a huddle before her. "The houses, the land, the animals, our workers, they all have to be tended to, paid weekly, and you all have to be taken care of. You will understand what I mean someday, but right now, I just want you to know that momma can't do all those things because she misses your grandmother and grandfather too, too much right now. A few days behind the wheel of my new truck will make momma happy again. Can I ride in my new truck for a few days? And when I get back, I promise not to be sad anymore."

"Where you gonna ride to?" Kimi asked meekly.

"I'm going to Chicago. To where your grandparents were buried. I have some things I want to say to them. That's what this is all about, me missing you all's grandparents. It has nothing to do with me wanting to leave you all."

"What will you say to grandma and grandpa?" T-top asked.

Naomi looked at her second oldest daughter, smiled and said, "I want to tell them what I tell you all every day of my life— that I love them. They were, well, I was angry with them the day they passed. Remember?"

"At the table, Walee said a bad word." Koko said lowly.

"I didn't mean for them to die, Koko. I always tell them I'm sorry in my prayers," four year-old Walee remarked as he placed his hands inside his jean pockets and looked to the ground in shame.

Naomi gently lifted her youngest son's chin and said lovingly, "You did nothing wrong, Walee. What you said and did that day did not cause your grandparents to pass away. What did the doctors and I tell you concerning what happened that day?"

"That it was an unforeseeable occurrence that had nothing to do with me and it wasn't my fault," Walee replied lowly as he stared his mother in the eyes, tears running down his cheeks in the process.

"That's right. Grandma and grandpa hear your prayers. And they don't blame you. They don't blame any of us. You remember that okay, son?"

"Yes, ma'am." Walee replied as he smiled and stepped forward and hugged his mother. "Thank you, momma."

Walee, for a short while after the funeral, thought it was his fault Kevin and Serena had died. Even at his young age, he was able to discern that his actions had caused an argument between his mother and grandparents. The next thing Walee knew, Kevin and Serena were dead. Walee had nightmares over his actions, and Naomi had to have several counseling sessions with him over a two week period. The kids all received counseling and were doing okay now. Naomi's depression had come about because she was so preoccupied with making certain her kids weren't grief-stricken, she had neglected her own mental well-being. Now that the kids were better, Naomi was seeking time for herself so that she could heal. That was her sole reason for purchasing the new truck.

"You know what," Naomi said as she smiled at her kids, "Spoonie and Tyke have never fed—"

"Fed the goats!" Bena yelled happily, cutting her mother's remarks short. "Koko, I told you Shima and Sinopa never fed the goats!"

Doss walked onto the patio at that moment. "You kids are okay I see." he said aloud.

The children ran back to their father and grabbed at him. "You was right," Koko said with a smile, "momma said she not leaving ever!"

"That's what I been trying to tell you all. Now, let's take Spoonie and Tyke down in the field so they can feed the goats for the very first time."

Feeding the goats was like a passage of right for the children. They had all done it before and it so much fun. Everything about the event was to be enjoyed, none more enjoyable than the walk towards the stockyard. Dawk, Bay, T-top, Kimi and Koko ran down the theatrical stairs of the patio and climbed the fence leading into the open field and began doing cart wheels as they laughed aloud and made their way towards the stockyards to mingle amongst the animals.

****

Naomi took to the open road in June of 1995 with her first run and things inside Ponderosa were good the first week out. The only thing Doss really had to contend with was the kids' constant questioning him regarding their mother's return. When Naomi finally returned on Friday evening, just four days later, the kids never let her out of their sight. Naomi and Doss had to wait until the early morning hours to make love because Naomi just couldn't get away from the kids for a split second until they all went to bed.

Doss was enjoying the time he spent alone with his kids. The first week may have been trouble free for the attentive father, but anarchy was on the horizon, however; because once the children knew for certain their mother was not abandoning them, their behaviors changed entirely, especially for the big three. The second time around when their mother left it was open season on mischief for the children, namely Dawk, Bena and Tiva; and Doss would indeed have his full with his oldest three, but plenty good would come out of it—at least if forty-one year-old Doss Dawkins had to tell the story.

CHAPTER 26
TRAINING DAY

"Well we got no class...and we got no principals...and we've got no innocence...we can't even think of a word that rhymes...school's...out...for...summer..." Alice Cooper's song *School's Out* was blasting loudly inside of Siloam's white Volkswagen bus just after three in the morning on a warm, arid night in the middle of the field behind Ponderosa in late-June of 1995.

All would have been fine except for one thing—eleven year-old Dawk was driving the bus. And from here, things would only descend downhill—figuratively and literally speaking. For months now, Dawk, Bay and T-top had been using Siloam's bus as their personal hideout. On weekends during the time they were being homeschooled, the three would sneak out early morning and take sodas, chips, sliced deli meat and bread, milk and cereal over to the van, which had been parked beside the guest house, and sit inside and watch Saturday morning cartoons on the TV Siloam had inside the van. They would return home before being missed under the belief that no one knew what the three of them had been up to; but when the TV went out one Saturday morning in late May, Dawk searched the downstairs kitchen drawers until he found the key. He went and started the van and charged the battery.

"We should take it for a spin." T-top said with a devilish grin.

Dawk refused on that day; but when the battery went low again this early summer morning, he went and grabbed the keys to start the van once more. When he did, Alice Cooper's song was just starting. Having done away with their homeschooling for the summer, Dawk, Bay and T-top all grew happy and the song only added to their delight. Dawk got behind the wheel and put the van in drive and thus began a ride of rebellion. He drove the van towards the front gate and turned onto the road leading to Ponderosa and sped past the left side of the home and drove down the dirt road leading the cattle pens and made a wide right turn into the open middle field. Bay and T-top were being thrown throughout the interior of the van, but they didn't care because they were too busy laughing to the top of their lungs as they thrashed about inside the van.

Dawk, Bay and T-top were treating Siloam's van as if it was their own personal ride at Disney World, and each were determined to have their turn in the driver's seat. Dawk reached the guest house and he and Bay switched seats. Bay cruised around the land in the van, much to Dawk and T-top's disdain.

"What we sight-seeing? Punch this thang, Bay!" Dawk yelled aloud.

"We have to be careful not to hit anything." Bay replied as she slowly approached the cattle pens once more and cruised back towards the guest house where T-top got behind the wheel.

T-top was hyper by the time she got into the driver's seat. Bay hadn't even taken a seat before her twin mashed the gas. Dawk was okay with his driving, and Bena did just fine during her cruise, but T-top was downright reckless as she made a beeline for the cattle pens.

"Why you going this way? You gone roll over momma cabbage patch!" Dawk yelled from the back of the van.

"Shut up, boy! I know what I'm doing!" T-top yelled over the music. No soon as she had spoken, T-top slammed into her mother's cabbage patch. "Oh, shit!" she yelled as she swerved the van to the right.

"You gone run into the hill!" Bay yelled as she held onto the dash board.

T-top swerved the van back to the left and numerous heads of cabbage began crashing into the windshield. By now, the joyride was over, and T-top was ruining her mother's cabbage patch. She tried to hit the brakes, but mashed the gas instead and the van sped up. Cabbage was being shredded, Bay was screaming, Dawk was cussing, and T-top was crying, repeatedly saying she was sorry. All the fun had been taken out of the ride all of a sudden. And things got worse when T-top crashed through the gate separating the middle field from the harvest field.

Dawk was trying to get to the front of the van, but he was constantly being thrown backwards as the van bounced across the hilly land. Bay tried to turn off the ignition but it was on the opposite side of T-top, she couldn't reach the switch because she, too, was being bounced around furiously.

"Which one is the brake? I wanna stop!" T-top yelled though her tears as she approached the cow pens.

"Just hit the one opposite of the one that you hit to make it go fast!" Dawk yelled from the back of the van.

T-top had grown confused. She tried to remember, but she guessed wrong. Tiva hit the gas pedal again and when the van sped up even more she let out a terrifying scream as she let go of the steering wheel and covered her face.

"Oh no! Oh no!" Bay screamed as she pulled T-top down with her and shielded her from the upcoming impact. "Dawk get down!" Bay yelled aloud.

"What's happening?" Dawk asked as he righted himself and looked out the front windshield. "Aww shit!" he yelled once he caught site of the impending doom as he lay down on the floor of the van.

Siloam's bus crashed through the gate holding back the cattle and tore through the chicken coop. Poultry flew into the air and the windshield was now covered with shattered eggs, dead bird feathers and two live chickens that had been wedged inside of the windshield wipers. The van then tore through two bales of hay, completely out of control. The family's numerous head of cattle began mooing loudly and scattering as the van ripped through their rest haven. The bus bounced into the air with force, having rolled over a calf that was a little too slow, taking him out of the game completely. A large heifer was sideswiped as the van whizzed by, headed directly for the canal towards the back portion of the land, narrowly missing the pig sty before it careened off the eight foot embankment and landed flat into the two foot deep canal.

Doss, meanwhile, was running out onto the patio. For a long time he'd known about his oldest three's venturing out to sit inside Siloam's bus, but when he caught sight of the van whizzing through Naomi's cabbage patch, he scrambled to unlock the gate blocking the stairs on the second floor and hurried out onto the patio to get the kids out of the van. Dawk, Bay and T-top never even knew their father was outside watching them now. He took off after the van screaming aloud, trying to get the kids to stop the vehicle, but he was too late. After witnessing the van crash through the stockyard area, he made a bee-line for the canal.

Dawk, Bay and T-top, meanwhile, were scrambling around trying to get out of the van when they heard their father's voice off in the distance. "We gotta get outta here! Dad gone skin us alive!" Dawk said as he pulled the side door open, jumped out and ran down the middle of the canal. T-top and Bay followed their older brother, the three sloshing through the two deep channel and laughing aloud before jumping up onto the bank, climbing the hill and running towards the thick forest towards the east.

When Doss made it to the van, he slid down the hill and ran towards the vehicle, worried that his children were hurt. Instead, he heard their laughter echoing across the land. He climbed back up the embankment and saw three silhouettes disappearing into the woods. "Get y'all behinds back here right now!" Doss yelled aloud.

"So you can whip us? I think not, daddy!" Bay's voice echoed out across the land just before she disappeared into the woods with her siblings.

"Okay," Doss said lowly, realizing that his kids weren't harmed. "You three wanna play games now, huh? Okay," he ended as he jogged back to Ponderosa in his pajamas.

When Doss entered the home and made it back to the second

level, Kimi and Koko were jumping up and down in the middle of the floor in the Great Room. They'd seen what their oldest brother and sisters had done and they just knew Dawk, Bay and T-top were in trouble. "You whipped them? You whipped them, daddy?" they asked repeatedly.

"What are you two doing up? It's only after five in the morning."

"We heard the noise outside like you," Koko replied.

"We saw it all, daddy! They ran in the woods! They took Siloam's bus and went varooooom! Right into the water back there!" Kimi said as she held her hand out like a car careening off a cliff.

Doss chuckled slightly at his middle daughters. "Hey," he said as he knelt down and pulled them close, "you wanna help me catch those three?"

"Do we!" Kimi and Koko replied in unison.

"What you need us to do, daddy?" Koko asked as Walee, Spoonie and Tyke entered the Great Room.

"People tryna sleep, yeah?" Walee snapped. "What's all this racket?"

"Yeah! What's all this ratchet?" Tyke imitated.

"It's racket you copy cat! Can't even talk right!" Koko snapped.

Tyke poked her tongue out at Koko and ran and hid behind Walee.

"That li'l runt can't save you!" Koko snapped as she ran towards Walee.

Tyke took off running and stood behind her father. "Daddy can stop you! Nah, nah, na nah nahhhhh!" she sang whilst poking her tongue out at Koko.

"Daddy, can I hit her just one time, please?" Koko asked in all sincerity.

"No fighting, Koko. Don't ever fight your sisters. Now, what we all are about to do is have a search party."

"Yayyy," Walee screamed. "We havin' a party early in the morning! Already! We got some cake? Let me see if we got some cake in the kitchen!" he quipped as he walked off towards the upstairs kitchen.

"It ain't that kind of party, mighty mouse!" Kimi snapped.

"A party is a party. And where there's a party? There's cake!"

"Walee," Doss said, "a search party is when you go looking for somebody or something. Like how Flacco and the ranch hands sometimes have to do when the cows or the chickens get out."

"You mean to tell me we going look for some chickens at this hour?" Walee asked as he folded his arms in disgust. "We don't need no cake for that! And I ain't going look for no chickens this early in the morning!"

Doss couldn't help but to laugh at Walee as he gathered his youngest five, dressed them all up in green camouflage outfits and fixed them breakfast, all-the-while explaining to them what they were going to do exactly. He was using his binoculars to see if he could spot Dawk, Bay and T-top while the young five ate, but it was to no avail. The oldest three, wherever they were, had every intention on making their father find them before they received their punishment.

Doss and the young five were standing out on the patio when Flacco, the family's twenty-four year-old Hispanic ranch hand approached. Flacco had just arrived on the ranch to start the day, but he quickly noticed the destruction and reported back to Doss. He removed his ten gallon hat, scratched his head and said somberly from the bottom of the patio stairs, "Doss? There's, there's been an accident. Someone has crashed Siloam's van through the stockyards. It's in the creek. I think we have vandals, senor."

Doss explained the events that had unfolded just before Flacco's arrival and had him bring the family's three bloodhounds back to the patio. When Flacco left to retrieve the dogs, Doss turned to his kids, placed a ten gallon hat onto his head, buttoned up his camouflage jacket and said, "Atten-hut!"

The kids all knew what to do. Their father had explained to them that they were a platoon on the hunt for three villains, and whoever spotted the three villains first would receive a hefty reward. They all stood at attention in a single file line from the smallest to the tallest while saluting, Tyke out in front and Kimi and Koko bringing up the rear.

"Okay, ladies and gentleman," Doss said as he walked back and forth before his young five, pretending to be a drill sergeant, "what we have on our hands is a pack of marauders! They need capturing! Are you up for the job!"

"Yes, sir!" Kimi yelled aloud.

"Here ya' go trooper!" Doss said as he handed Kimi a whistle. "When I say blow your whistle Captain Dawkins, I want you to blow the whistle as hard as you can, okay?"

"Got it, dad!"

"Captain, Koko?"

"Yes, sir?"

"When Captain Dawkins blows the whistle, I want you to yell aloud 'release the hounds', okay?"

"High yi!" Koko replied.

"What are me, Spoonie and Tyke gonna be doing?" Walee asked.

"You three comrades will remain next to your General. Which is I! General Dawkins!"

"Why we comrades? I wanna be a Captain like Koko and Kimi!" Walee complained.

"How old are you comrade, Dawkins?"

"Four! What that gotta do with it?"

"You have to be at least six to be a Captain. Sorry, comrade."

"And you be sure to call us both Captain Dawkins when we out there," Koko snapped.

"Some things about this family just ain't right with me," Walee said just as Flacco returned with the bloodhounds.

"Here you go, Senor Doss. Me and the guys will start the repairs as soon as possible," he said before jumping back onto a small tractor and returning to his duties.

Doss took the dog leashes and handed a plastic bag to Walee and he and the young five began walking through the middle field. He caravanned across the land on foot with his kids following close behind; Walee doing cartwheels, Kimi and

Koko skipping along happily, stopping every now and then to break out in dance, while Spoonie and Tyke kept running in order to keep up whilst laughing aloud and playing a game of tag with their father. Times like these were cherished by the kids. Their father, the man they knew, was fun to be around at all times. He made them laugh, piqued their brains, taught them many things about life and kept their curiosities on edge at all times. Doss Dawkins may have been a merciless killer and drug dealer, but his kids had never seen, nor did they know that side of their father. To them, he was their hero and their protector, and not only that, he was very much their best friend.

The group walked casually across the sprawling land, the five singing and skipping along happily behind their father across the field and through the stockyards until they reached the van in the canal. From there, Doss walked down along the banks of the water until he came upon the spot where he'd seen Dawk, Bay and T-top emerge from the water and run towards the woods. Doss knew about the little hangout his oldest three had erected near a big hickory tree in the bend of the canal about a hundred yards inside the woods and he was willing to bet that they would be hiding there inside a small canvas tent they'd set up and often camped out in on some days.

Walee opened the plastic bag and pulled out one of Dawk's shirts and waved it in front of the dogs' noses at his father's request and within seconds, the three bloodhounds climbed the embankment and began trotting towards the woods with their noses planted firmly to the ground. Doss pulled the dogs back at that moment and said, "Captain Kimi Dawkins? Report to the front lines and blow your whistle!"

Kimi ran to the front of the group and blew hard on the whistle. At the same time, Koko ran ahead of the group. This was Koko's crowning moment. She was now in control of the animals that would run in and find her older brother and sisters and deliver them up to her father. Koko couldn't contain her joy. To see Bena and Tiva get a butt-whipping had her floating on clouds. Bena and Tiva, and especially Bena, always found a way to make Kimi and Koko cry—be it hiding their favorite baby dolls, snatching the covers off their beds, or be it the despicable Bena headlock—whatever they could think of to do to make their younger sisters cry, Bena and Tiva would do it; now, however, if Koko had to tell it, today was Bay and T-top's day to cry and she and Kimi would be able to throw it back in their faces for all times. The joy rising within Koko was bursting through her veins; she was laughing uncontrollably and couldn't help but to do a little dance, bouncing slightly as she snapped her fingers and said, nearly in tears from the joy within her heart over the thought of Bena and Tiva getting the belt, "Release the hounds!"

Doss let go of the leash and the three bloodhounds made a beeline for the woods, entering the forest in the exact same spot that Dawk, Bay, and T-top had passed through. The group followed the dogs into the woods and before long they came upon the small tent the oldest three often camped out in. The dogs were in and around the tent, but they would go no further. Doss assumed his oldest three were nearby so he began yelling for them to come on out.

"Might as well face the music you three!" Doss yelled, his voice echoing through the dense forest. "We got y'all surrounded."

"Come on out!" Koko yelled. "Daddy got his belt!"

Walee placed Spoonie and Tyke behind him and said, "I think we made a mistake."

"How?" Kimi asked.

"They not in the tent and the dogs ain't moving. Where they at?"

Doss went and checked the tent and saw that it was empty. He guided one of the dogs around the area and the dog walked to the edge of the canal and stopped. Just then, faint taps began to be heard. One of the dogs yelped allowed and took off running back towards the field. A second dog was hit and it, too, took off running out of the forest. The third dog was standing right beside Doss and it was hit as well. The dog took off running just as another tap was heard. That tap landed next to the big hickory tree beside Doss. He looked at the tree and saw that it was a paint ball shot. More shots began hitting the trees around him so he grabbed the kids and lay down in the grass.

Peeking up over the tall grass, Doss scanned the area until he spotted Bena and Tiva across the canal. The twins each had a paint ball gun and were firing off shots at their father and siblings, the shots landing about eight feet up, but clearly hitting their targets, which were the trees directly behind Doss and his young five.

Kimi began blowing the whistle repeatedly, Koko began screaming, and Spoonie and Tyke were now crying. Suddenly, that butt-whipping Koko had hoped to see her oldest sisters get was out of her mind. Being shot at was not a part of the deal and they wanted out immediately.

Walee was dumbfounded. "I told you something ain't right with this family, General Dawkins," he yelled. "Why you got us out here in the open, General Dawkins? Me and Dawk share the same room and he shootin' at *me* General Dawkins? What's wrong with this family, General Dawkins," he asked as he lay flat on his back looking up at the sky.

Doss, however, was in awe. He watched from a crouched position as Bena and Tiva fired off shots, not at random, but aiming at specific targets and hitting them repeatedly. He also eyed Dawk, who seemed to be in control of the situation and telling his sisters where to shoot. It was during this time, while he was being pinned down by his oldest two daughters that Doss had an epiphany he was willing to at least consider for future benefits. By no means did he ask for it, but on this day, the day Doss Dawkins would always remember as 'training day', had become the catalyst that he would use to steer his oldest three kids' energy into a more productive line of work.

CHAPTER 27
IT'S IN THE MAKING

"Hello everybody and welcome back to Fresh Air. I am your host Terry Gross and I'm, I'm sitting here today with Melissa and Melanie Abernathy. For those unfamiliar with this story, if you've missed the first half of the show, Melanie and Melissa are identical twins separated at birth and found one another nearly three decades later. The first half of the show described their journey through life and their never knowing of the other's existence until they met one another on a subway train in New York City. But as it turns out, these two sisters worked in the same career field, which is, which is the field of architecture, and worked at competing firms. It is a miraculous story and if you've missed it, this show will air again later today. Be sure to check your local NPR listings for the times as they may vary. Now, Melissa and Melanie both resigned from their professions and started The Lost Orphan Committee and they've been helpful in finding lost relatives."

Naomi was rolling down Interstate-80, one hundred miles west of Cheyenne, Wyoming headed towards Portland, Oregon the day following Dawk, Bena and Tiva's misadventure when her country radio station's signal began fading out. She began searching for another station when she stumbled upon a show on National Public Radio, (NPR), which piqued her curiosity. She listened as two identical twins related their experiences of growing up not knowing of one another's existence. She set her cruise control, placed her shades over her eyes and listened intently to the identical twins' heart-warming and triumphant story. When she learned of The Lost Orphan Committee, she'd decided to call the organization and see if they could help her with the finding of her siblings, but as she listened more closely, Naomi realized she had the same resources within her grasps. The show on NPR, however, did give keen insight on how to do a proper search for missing relatives. The host of the show was asking all the right questions, and Naomi was soaking it in as she drove her rig down the highway.

"So, what was The Orphan Committee's first successful endeavor," the host asked the twins.

"Well," one of the sisters replied. "There was this guy over in New Jersey who believed he had a brother, but he couldn't quite remember his age or his name. So we did a back search at the hospital in which he was born and discovered that there was another birth four years earlier—a boy with the same last name, same mother, but different father," she said enthusiastically.

"Right," the other sister chimed in, "that was a real easy case and it actually gave us a false sense of optimism because we believed all cases would be just as easy."

"Okay," the host remarked. "And you write about that in your book, Searching For Answers—How to Find Those You Love in Today's Tech Savvy World. Good book by the way. Very informative. So this guy and his brother, they lived just a few miles apart, right?"

"Right," one of the sisters replied. "We found him by searching elementary school records. From there we got high school records and moved on to college transcripts and got a list of jobs he'd applied for through the college's job program. We found him working as a manager for a beer distributor center over in Newark, New Jersey near Meadowland Stadium."

"But all searches weren't as fruitful, right?"

"That's correct. And some of our findings ended in not such a good way. We found relatives who were deceased, didn't care that they had lost family members, and some were never found. But the joy of reuniting lost family members who truly love one another is worth the temporary agony of defeat and the anguish that sometimes arises when family members are reunited."

"Good stuff here, guys, or ladies," the host said through light laughter. "So in the short time we have left, can you give those that are listening and maybe faced with this same conundrum a few pointers that may be helpful to them in their searches should they not contact your organization?"

"Sure," one of the sisters replied, "but we encourage everybody who's facing this plight to at least give us a try. We want to help, and we'll do everything we can to try and give those people the answers they seek. With that being said, what advice I have, what I'm about to say, is a little, a little ominous? If that's the right word to use? But our searches into many cases that are over twenty years don't always end well. From those past experiences we've learned to start with obituaries in the last known place of a missing loved one if it's known."

Naomi drove down the road with a cold stare as she listened to the woman speak. She knew she was right in what she was saying, because she herself had done the exact same thing years ago, but what the woman said next would give Naomi a newfound hope because it was an area in which she'd never even considered looking.

"Once we've completed our search of the obituaries, and by the way, most of the libraries now have newspaper archives dating back to the 1800's, so if they've made those obituaries, it is there, you just have to keep searching. But once we've completed what Melanie calls the death search, we began looking at prison records. Several of our case members have been found behind bars, and those were some of the best reunions ever," the woman ended.

"I just want to say that this has been a wonderful interview," the host said. "The book is out now at Walden, K-Mart and many other outlets and it is a valuable asset to those searching for lost family members. The Lost Orphan Committee is a non-profit that works on donations, so those wanting to support Melissa and Melanie's endeavors can do so by calling 1-800-MY-FAMILY, or you can send a check to P.O. Box 77114, New York, New York and request a free brochure by again calling 1-800-MY-FAMILY."

Naomi began thinking hard as she rode down the highway. The information she'd heard had given her renewed vigor. She'd never even considered looking into jailhouse records for either of her siblings. Anxiety was coursing through her veins as she headed further west, wishing she was headed back home instead to begin another search for her long-lost siblings. Four and a half hours later, Naomi was pulling into the parking lot of a mall just outside of Salt Lake City, Utah that had a bookstore. She went in and purchased the sisters' book and read the remainder of the day. The following morning, she called Fin back in Chicago.

"Xavier Law Firm, how can I help you?"

"Finland, it's Naomi."

"Naomi. How are you doing out there on the road?"

"I'm great, Finland," Naomi replied in a heavy voice.

"You okay," Finland asked. "You're getting homesick aren't you? Missing Doss and the kids I bet."

"I am. But I have something I need you to do if you'd be so kind."

"Anything. What is it?" Finland asked as he closed his office door.

"I want you to begin a search for Sam, Mary and Martha Holland."

"Naomi? Where would I start? I don't even know where to begin. I'd love to help, but I don't know what to do."

"I didn't either. I guess I was hoping for a miracle, Fin. But those things don't always happen. I heard a wonderful story yesterday and read this fascinating book on how to find lost family members. I mailed you a copy. I think, I think this will work."

"What are we doing exactly?"

"State by state, starting in Alabama, I need for you to get the prison records of every prison and county jail in the state and look for the names Samson Holland, Mary Holland, and Martha Holland. I know it's a long shot, but the authors of this book said they've found lost members that way. I know they may be married, Mary and Martha, but Samson would still have the last name Holland. Can you do it?"

"I can. It'll take time to compile all that information. And then we're only talking about one state. An undertaking of this caliber could take years, Naomi."

"I've been without them all this time—what's a few more? Alabama. Start there, and then move to Mississippi, Georgia, all the southern states before expanding outwards. What's your fee for doing this?"

"Naomi? To be able to help you find your family? I can't put a price on that. We'll do this together, and I look forward to reading that book if you believe it'll help us out. How old would they all be now?" Naomi gave Fin the necessary information regarding her siblings and he immediately made an inquiry into the names of the state prisons in Alabama and began making calls, using his credentials as a Criminal Defense Attorney to obtain the names of past and present detainees going back fifteen years. The path to finding Naomi's siblings, with the aide of her life-long friend, Finland Xavier, was now in the making. The only thing that stood before Naomi, unknowingly, was time.

****

A week later, Naomi had returned home from her trip to Portland, Oregon. She'd called when she was about three hours out and requested that Doss take out some ribs and steaks so she can grill for the family and share the news that a new search was underway for Sam, Mary and Martha. When she arrived on the ranch, Naomi was expecting to see her kids running out of the house to meet her on the patio, instead, she was greeted with complete silence. It was after six in the evening and Flacco and the other ranch hands had already left. The Suburbans were all beside the home so Naomi knew the family was on the land, only she didn't know where. She ascended the patio stairs and called out to the family as she entered the kitchen, but she got no response. She then went over to the sink and saw that Doss hadn't taken out the ribs and steaks as she'd requested. "Forgetful man," Naomi said lowly just as gunshots began ringing out in the woods on the southeast portion of the land.

Naomi walked out onto the patio and heard several more gunshots. She climbed into a golf cart and rode to where the gunfire was emanating and upon stepping into the woods, she saw Dawk, Bena and T-top kneeling behind a log, each of them holding a .22 caliber rifle and firing at large cans on the opposite side of the creek.

Doss saw his wife walking his way and he went to greet her, but the young five all beat him out. They ran up and grabbed their mother, Spoonie and Tyke jumping at her legs with their arms stretched out, Kimi and Koko telling everything Bena and Tiva did wrong in life, and Walee trying to calm everybody down. Naomi gathered her kids, kissed her husband and then eyed Dawk, Bena and Tiva, who seemed preoccupied with shooting the rifles.

"When did this start?" Naomi asked as she pointed towards her oldest three.

"I told you what they did last week. Punished them good by taking their TV and games away. This here, this here is training."

Naomi tilted her head to the side and eyed Doss. "Training for what?" she asked.

"We'll talk later. After we return from dinner. But come check them out. They pretty good. Especially Bay and T-top."

Naomi walked over to where her kids were shooting, the loud sounds echoing through the forest as she stood behind her oldest three.

"Momma," Bena yelled out aloud, "momma watch me aim and hit that can over there!"

Naomi watched as Bay hit her target dead on. She was a good shot. All three were good shots she had to admit. Thirty minutes later, the family went into town and had dinner and returned home to relax for the night. After settling the kids into the theater room with a good movie, Naomi met Doss over in his private room on the first floor. He closed and locked the door, poured Naomi a glass of wine and sat her down on the couch and removed her boots and began massaging her feet.

"What's all this?" Naomi asked before sipping her wine.

"I can't be nice to my wife? I missed you, baby."

"Don't baby me," Naomi chided. "What are you up to?"

"Okay, here's the deal," Doss said as he stood up. "My main man Eddie been doing real good taking care of things back in Chicago."

"But?"

"But he can't know all that I do. He doesn't know about the ranch or anything outside of the business and that's how I want it to stay. But if something were to happen to Eddie, Junior, or Lucky, who would I have behind me? My father and Mendoza are getting up in age and new enemies may arise." Doss said as he eyed Naomi.

There was no further explanation needed. Naomi knew what Doss was saying and asking indirectly—he wanted to train his oldest three kids to follow in his footsteps.

"What do you plan on doing exactly?" Naomi asked as she sat her glass down and moved to the edge of the leather sofa.

"You've seen for yourself how good Bena and Tiva are. I mean they like little snipers. It's a natural gift they have. With the right training? The opposition won't even see us coming. We can hit 'em from a distance."

"Doss?"

"I know what you're thinking. You're wondering why put them out like that, and truth be told, it may not even get to that point. But if ever the day arises, should I need help in this line of work? Who better than my own flesh and blood? People I know for certain will never backstab me?"

"I always knew it would come to this. The day Dawk was born I knew. If we do this, we have to be careful. And it stops with the oldest three. The young five will not have a part in that life."

"So you agree? You okay with this?"

"I am. It'll be years before the big three reach that point and by then all this may have concluded. Everybody retires at one point or another. You may not even need them, but if you do? Make sure you know what the hell you're doing with them. Make sure they're ready, Doss."

"Thank you, baby. I swear, I'll give them all they need to

know to be the best at what they do."

"That is the very thing that worries me, my love."

"What you mean?"

"Ever since they were younger I saw in our oldest three your father and you, Doss. They're just like you and DeeDee. The life is in their blood."

Doss scratched his nose and looked to the ground proudly as he placed his hands inside his jean pockets. He knew himself that Dawk, Bena and Tiva had true killer instinct. Under his guidance, they could surely hone in on their skills and become a formidable crew that would be hard to deal with. At age eleven, Dawk Holland was fearless, observant, and had a quiet strength about himself—he was a natural born leader in Doss's eyes. Nine year-olds Bena and Tiva were fearless as well, and they had the natural gift of prowess, coupled with an uncanny ability to hit targets precisely from a distance—a deadly duel in Doss's eyes.

"We may be on to something big, you know, Mister Dawkins?" Naomi said as she got up from the couch and walked up behind her husband and hugged him from behind.

"I really want to see what this will become, baby. See what all we can accomplish. With my kids by my side? It's no telling how far we'll go in this line of work."

"It's years of from now."

"But it's already in the making, baby. It's already in the making." Doss ended as he turned around and kissed Naomi fully on the lips.

CHAPTER 28
I WON'T BE HOME FOR DINNER

Naomi, after agreeing with her husband to allow him to begin training Dawk, Bena and Tiva to walk in his footsteps, returned to the road a couple of weeks later after celebrating Bena and Tiva's tenth birthday. She would return home every couple of weeks or so until she came off the road in November of 1995 to spend the winter holidays with her family. Doss was back and forth to Chicago during this time and the crew from up north was gaining a serious foothold on the drug trade in several cities throughout the Midwest. The violence had subsided on the streets, and as spring of 1996 came in, Doss returned home a couple hundred thousand dollars richer and the money was invested back into the family on the ranch through the purchasing of livestock, another semi, and the hiring of two more ranch hands.

Things were going along real well for the family. Naomi was back on track, having overcome her depression, money was being made and the children were all doing well in their homeschooling. The only thing missing in Naomi's eyes was her siblings. Fin had come through with several names of black females with the first name of Mary and Martha just after New Year's, females the twins' age, which were locked away in Alabama. Naomi made calls down to a couple of the facilities and talked to two of the women at separate facilities, but neither of them were her sisters. She'd also made three trips to Alabama to visit the jailhouses that she couldn't contact in person and came up short there as well with her search.

Naomi returned to the road in April of '96, shortly after Doss's arrival back on the ranch. The man resumed his role as father, all-the-while giving steady guidance to his oldest three, who were taking to the handling of guns like fish to water. Naomi returned home every other week or so, joyful to see her kids, but still a little disappointed that neither of her siblings had been found as of yet. Fin was working hard on the project, though; he often called with information relating to the search, but each time, things just didn't pan out for him and Naomi, who was beginning to get down-hearted over the fact that neither of her siblings could be found.

During the early part of May, Naomi once again climbed into her rig and fired up the engine. She had a trailer load of livestock that she was transporting to Ames, Iowa, and from there, she would pick up one of her refrigerated trailers and run a load of frozen corn down to Dallas, Texas after spending the night at home. She would only be out for four days this go around, much shorter than normal, but the joy of driving had begun to run its course in her eyes. She'd started driving as therapy to overcome the pain of losing Kevin and Serena, but along the way, the drives had morphed into a search for her lost siblings. Each time Naomi left the ranch, she always believed in her heart that she would return home with at least one of her siblings, but her dream had never come to pass.

Closing the steel doors on her trailer and placing a seal onto the handle was the last step for Naomi. She'd made up her mind that this would be her last run for a while, a good while, because once again she felt herself getting into a funk over not finding her siblings and would rather be home, which was now the place where she gained the most joy. She climbed into her massive rig and prepared herself for the eight hour drive down to Ponca City, intent on making it home in time for dinner. When she left ConAgra Foods, Naomi got on her cellphone and called home.

"Hello! Hello! I said hello!" the squeaky little voice on the other end answered.

"Who's this? Sinopa is that you?" Naomi asked.

"Momma," Tyke whined. "Bay, Bay said me and Shima was an accident!"

"Where's Bena, Tyke?"

"I wekon she in the mobie moom. The wovie—she back there."

"Hello? Naomi?" Doss said through slight laughter once he took the phone from Tyke.

"What's going on now, love?" Naomi asked, still laughing over Tyke's inability to correctly pronounce the words 'reckon', 'movie' and 'room' right along with her husband.

"It's like WWE around here, baby. The kids found a bowl of Snickers in your private room and now? They're just bouncin' off the walls," Doss replied matter-of-factly amidst a spat involving Walee, Kimi and Koko.

"You ain't old enough to tell me what to do!" Walee yelled.

"I ain't telling you what to do! I said stop running through the house like a wild bull! You wanna run you go outside and run around like the rest of the horses!" Koko was heard yelling.

"Ain't nobody even messing with you! Leave me 'lone!" Walee snapped back.

"Just a regular day down here, baby," Doss said through light laughter. "How you doing out there?"

"I'm fine. I'm headed home now. It's nine now, so I figure I'll be back between five and six this evening. What do you want for dinner?"

"Gone light up the grill, baby!" Doss exclaimed. "Flacco and the boys skinned a long horn yesterday and I have had these thick T-bones marinating in a butter and garlic sauce that will have you wanting to fight somebody."

"We got enough fighting going on at Ponderosa."

"Nahh, I got it under control. I already talked to Bena and she apologized, but Sinopa still a little plagued by it all. A game of soft ball will ease her mind."

"It always does. Sinopa and Shima are really taking a liking to that sport thanks to their grandfather and Mendoza. How are the big three coming along?"

"Remarkably. I'm not worried in the least about their aptitude. They got it in 'em, baby. It's in them."

"Okay. Umm, I think tomorrow, I'll take Kimi and Koko

with me down to Dallas so I can talk to those two. This older sister thing is getting out of control. Those two wanna run every aspect of their younger brother and sisters' lives."

"They only doing to them what Bena does to them sometimes."

"I know, but you know them my bunchkins. I just miss them. I miss all of y'all."

"And we all miss you, baby. Me and the big three going do a little shooting before I—"

"Hold on, Doss. I got another call," Naomi replied and clicked over. "Hello?"

"Can I speak to a, a Naomi Holland-Dawkins, please?"

"Speaking?"

"This is Melissa Abernathy from The Lost Orphan Committee? I was asked to contact you on behalf of a Finland Xavier?"

"Oh my! Miss Abernathy how are you? I've read your book and it has inspired me to look for my lost siblings!"

The lady laughed and said, "Thank you Naomi! I only wish you would've contacted me a long time ago. Mister Xavier told me all about you."

"We've been searching. I've called prisons in Alabama and I've even made trips to Alabama without any success. Fin was working on—"

"The state of Georgia, I know," Melissa said, cutting Naomi's remark short. "He contacted us a couple of months back, though, and told us about the case. Your story fascinated us! Me and Melanie didn't know of one another, but you, Naomi, you had a wealth of information."

"Finland never told me he contacted you all."

"To be honest, and it's not a slight against Fin, but the man was overwhelmed. Name after name, call after call, state by state. He was looking at the time factor. He saw that he needed help and had us join in the search. He called us his 'silent partners'. Naomi," Melissa then said, barely able to hold back her joy, "I found a Martha Holland in the Pearl County Women's Correctional Facility in Pearl, Mississippi!"

Naomi exhaled at that moment. Her heart was telling her that the day she'd been waiting on for so long had arrived at that very second. May 13th 1996 would be a day forever remembered by forty-one year-old Naomi Holland-Dawkins.

"Naomi? You there?"

With tears streaming down her face, Naomi, as she pulled over the shoulder of Interstate-29, could only speak towards, "Thank you," she said.

"Me and Melanie just want you to know that this may not be the end, Naomi. I called you personally because Finland said that all the women who had the first name of Mary and Martha didn't have the last name of Holland. But, as we speak, there's a Martha Holland behind bars in Pearl, Mississippi."

"That's her! That's my sister!" Naomi cried.

"I only wish you the best. And, and we'll keep on searching those records in Mississippi for you. But maybe this'll help end your search."

"I owe you all so much! Thank you!"

"If anything else comes down the line I'll be sure to contact you. Be sure to thank your friend Finland. You're blessed to have a friend like that in your life."

"I'll be sure to do that. And I'll be sure to let you all know the end result." Naomi replied.

"We're looking forward to hearing back from you. Take care, Naomi."

Naomi hung up the phone in order to call Fin, but she remembered she'd left Doss on the other line. He'd hung up so she called her husband back and shared the news with him, replaying the conversation she'd just had with a lady by the name of Melissa Abernathy.

"I'm on my way to Mississippi today! I won't be home for dinner, Doss! I found Martha! I found her!"

Doss was laughing uncontrollably. The man was overjoyed for his wife. "Take all the time you need, baby!" he said happily. "Let me know when you meet her! Take pictures if you can and we gone throw down when you get back!"

"Okay," Naomi replied. The woman was giddy beyond

words. "Let me call, Fin and talk to him, Doss! Call Lucky and tell him the news! God! Serena and Kevin! Siloam! They should all be here to see this! This is a happy day, Doss! A happy day! Tell the kids I found one of their aunts! And it's a good chance Martha knows!" Naomi couldn't help but to cry and laugh aloud simultaneously. "Martha may know where Mary and Sam are! Doss," she screamed emphatically as she jumped up and down in her seat, "I found my sisters! I found my sisters! Thank you God in the heavens above! Oh my, God! Oh my, God!" Naomi hung up the phone and screamed to the top of her lungs inside her rig. The produce company in Dallas would now have to wait for their load of frozen corn because Naomi Holland-Dawkins now had a new run to make. She had to go and see her long lost sister Martha Holland.

****

The following day, May 14th 1996, Naomi was emerging from a taxi that had taken her to The Pearl County Women's Correctional Facility located just outside of Jackson, Mississippi. She went in and talked to administrators, explaining her story and using her credentials as an attorney to garner an impromptu visit to see Martha Holland. The administrators, however, explained that Martha Holland had been moved to Grenada County Jail, about a hundred miles north of Jackson. Before she left, administrators gave Naomi the last known address of Martha Holland, which was 2213 Casper Drive.

Naomi caught a taxi back to her rig. She was a little downhearted at this moment, believing that maybe she'd gotten her hopes up way too high. She should've known things just seemed too good to be true was her thinking, but she couldn't turn back now. She felt that she was so close to finding her sisters that she was willing to chase after a possible dream, a mere fantasy that would only lead to heartache. Disappointment would crush her, no doubt, but she'd come this far, she felt that she might as well continue on with the journey, even if it did turn out to be a futile waste of time.

Naomi drew out a map towards Casper Drive, popped in Michael Jackson's *Bad* CD and let her truck forward out of its parking spot. She found the street ten minutes later and her heart began pounding as Michael Jackson's song, *You Are Not Alone* played lowly on her stereo.

"Just the other night...I thought I heard you cry...asking me to come...and hold you in my arms...I can hear your prayers... your burdens I will bear...but first I need your hand...then forever can begin..."

The neighborhood Naomi had traveled into reminded her of a lot of parts of Cicero and certain rundown areas on the south side of Chicago. She was unable to believe that people, let alone her people, her family, were living in such a dilapidated area. Knowing how rough and callous people back in Cicero and Chicago could be, Naomi reached into her overhead compartment and pulled out her .44 magnum and sat it on the dash because for all she knew, the people who resided at 2213 Casper Drive could be a bunch of crazies that had never even heard of a Martha Holland. She reached the home on Casper Drive and saw that the place was boarded up. She exited her rig and looked around for a minute in stunned silence. This neighborhood, in her eyes, was in the process of being torn down. Saddened, but optimistic because she still had the hope that the Martha Holland in Grenada, Mississippi was indeed her long lost sister, Naomi hopped back into her truck and made a left turn onto a street named Friendly Lane. By now, Michael Jackson's song was reaching its crescendo. It was Naomi's favorite part of the song because Michael Jackson was indeed singing from the heart. She couldn't help but to sing along with the man as she cruised down Friendly Lane.

"You are not alone...you're not alone...I am here with you...I am here with you...Although we're far apart...You're always in my heart..."

Naomi's rig cruised pass the home on the corners of Casper Drive and Friendly Lane and it was there, upon clearing the home on the corner, that a woman sitting in a wheelchair came into view and Naomi's eyes widened. Right away, she knew her search was over. She exited her rig and yelled aloud, "Mary!"

****

Naomi Holland-Dawkins had found her long lost sisters,

Mary and Martha Holland, on May 14th 1996, nearly thirty-one years after they'd been separated. The reunion, however, was bittersweet because Naomi had learned through Mary that their brother Samson Holland had been killed in 1984 and that Mary had lost one of her twin daughters, Rene "Ne`Ne`" Holland, and she was now paralyzed from the waist down from a gunshot wound to the back. Martha Holland was indeed locked up in jail in Grenada, Mississippi; but she was okay and would be released in 2001…

…"Naomi!" forty-two year-old Martha called out to her sister as she walked up Ne`Ne`s hill holding a plate of food wrapped in plastic and gripping a bottle of iced-tea.

Naomi emerged from her thoughts and looked around. She'd been thinking about days long gone for so long and so hard, it was if she'd walked them all over again. Martha had interrupted her thoughts just as she was beginning to reflect on the events that had taken place in the years following Mary's rehabilitation.

"I didn't even hear you approaching, Martha. How'd you get way over here?" Naomi asked.

"Well, I damn sure didn't walk that's for sure. I drove a golf cart," Martha replied as she laughed lightly. "Doss said you might be hungry up here and he asked me to bring you some ribs along with this letter. And I wanna know when you coming down from here to join the party. I been locked up for over seven years, been missing you for over thirty years and you up here all alone. What? You don't love me?" Martha joked.

Naomi laughed and said, "You know that could never be possible, Martha."

"I know, sis. You still thinking about back in the day?"

"Yes. I tell ya', Mary and Dimples? When they first got here? It was a little hard for the two of them." Naomi said as she opened the letter. "Oh," she said happily. "How wonderful. The Abernathy twins received their donation."

"Abernathy," Martha said. "Those the ladies that helped you find me and Mary, right?"

"Umm, hmm. I send them a ten-thousand dollar donation

every year around this time to help them out."

"That's what's up! So you coming down?"

"In a little bit. Our sister really had it hard when she first got here, Martha."

"I know. Mary was still depressed over Ne`Ne` and was blaming Regina for Ne`Ne` being dead."

"Those were some tough times, but we got through it. You wanna stick around? Hear some more about the things that happened after Mary started walking again?"

"Nahh," Martha replied. "I'm having so much fun talking to Dawk and tripping off Walee crazy behind. I talked to Siloam, too, she told me about her return and all. I never knew she ran away. You told us a lot, but I love hearing stories from the rest of the family. I'm going back to talk to the divas, Kimi and Koko."

Naomi laughed and said, "Those two, there? Child, please. They be in their own little world."

"And I plan on digging into it. Here's your food. See you after while. Don't take too long or I'm gone send your mini-mes to get you next time. It's a long ride over here," Martha ended as she kissed Naomi's cheek and ran back down the hill.

Naomi smiled as Martha disappeared from sight as she began reflecting on the events that transpired after Mary's rehabilitation.

"Those were really some fun times," she thought aloud as she drifted back off into her thoughts.

CHAPTER 29
SHE CAME BACK

It was a sunny morning in the month of July in the year of 1997, a month or so after Mary had regained her ability to walk and run and the bulk of the family was out working the ranch on this warm, sunny morning. Mary was learning to ride a horse during this period of time. Dawk, Bena, Tiva, Kimi and Koko had all learned to ride horses via Flacco and several other ranch hands, and Walee, Spoonie and Tyke were learning to ride ponies. Thirty-eight year-old Mary, however, was slow in catching on so she would sometimes ride with Naomi in the early morning hours as she and a couple of ranch hands led herds of cattle over to the stream on the western portion of the land in order to water them down.

As Mary sat behind Naomi atop a beautiful Clydesdale horse, she told her of an idea she had in mind. "What would you like to do at this stage of your life, Mary? What's your idea, sister?" Naomi asked as the horse walked gently across the land, two dozen or so cattle trotting behind it, Naomi, and Mary with their heads to the ground in a gentle stroll as two of the family's blood hounds ran ahead of the entire group, barking loudly in the air.

"If you don't mind, Naomi, I can see myself growing a crop of strawberries, cucumbers, and cabbage in the open field out in front the guest house, maybe some onions too. All kinds of produce. And I can have pumpkins in the fall. I wanted to ask you because I'm not sure what you want to do with that part of the land. Even if you wanted to grow anything there," Mary replied as she held onto Naomi.

"You wanna open a business, Mary?" Naomi asked proudly.

"Something small. A little produce stand. There's an old wooden shack right by the bridge over Kaw Lake on the side of the road heading back into town? I was thinking that it would be the perfect place to set up because a lot of traffic passes through that area."

"I used to grow cabbage up there myself. When Tiva ran over it, I salvaged what I could and let it return to its natural state. Sure, you can grow anything you want to grow there as you see fit."

"Thank you. You know, back in Ghost Town, I used to have Ne`Ne` and Dimples help me in my little garden out back a lot. I wonder what Ne`Ne` would want to do now."

"Knowing her the way I do from your stories, she would be over in the stockyards with Dimples and my oldest five slopping pigs and feeding chickens and horses. That's what I believe Ne`Ne` would have chosen to do. She would've been really happy here. She was highly-spirited."

"You're right. I miss my baby. I wonder, I wonder if Dimples will want to return to gardening with me, though. Because this will be on a much bigger scale than the garden I had under my kitchen window and I'll need her help."

"Ask her. She loves working the stockyard, but you two are very close."

"I'll ask her later. What steps will I have to take to buy that building if it's up for sale?"

"Don't worry about the logistics. I'll get to work on that for you, Mary. I'll get the paperwork done, and whatever tools you need also. And we can get Siloam to—dammit!" Naomi then said under her breath, remembering Siloam was no longer apart of the family.

"You miss her don't you?" Mary asked.

"Yes. In spite of all that has happened, I still miss that young woman," Naomi said sadly. "Well enough of that. My sister is opening a business!" Naomi said as she continued guiding the cattle towards the stream.

A week later, Mary, with the aide of Dimples, and one of Naomi's workers, began to plow the land out in front of the guest house with a small tractor. She was only planning to upturn the soil and irrigate the land this year, and she'd successfully completed the task. By the fall of '97, the land was ready for planting. Mary would have to wait until spring to do so, however, because she didn't have all the proper tools needed to start a crop on five acres of land.

Naomi wasn't new to farming by a long shot. She knew exactly what Mary would need in order to raise a successful crop. So for Christmas of '97, she bought Mary a brand new 1998 Ford F-150 pick-up. It was black with chrome wheels and an extended four door cab. Naomi also bought her sister a wide assortment of tools and her own tractor and four-wheeler. Mary was overcome with emotion as she stood out in the snow before the guest house eyeing all of her new equipment right along with the friends and family from up north. The holidays were always special for the Holland-Dawkins family, and the '97 holiday season had completely solidified Mary. She was truly were she belonged and was about to embark on what had subconsciously been her dream job—that of a farmer.

****

The harvest season of 1998 had finally arrived and Mary was the first one up on this cool morning in the latter part of the month of March and she was eager to get to work. She was planning on planting onion, strawberry, and cabbage and tomato seeds along with mustard, turnip and collard greens. Each of Mary's planted crops was separated into neat squares. Their orderliness enabled her to ride freely through the huge field on her four-wheeler in order to check her produce, and it also allowed the irrigation system she had set up using the creek behind the guest house to better water the food.

Naomi had purchased the old wooden stand beside Kaw Lake that Mary had mentioned to her early on, which sat just inside the city limits, back in January. The location was on busy U.S. Highway 60 leading into town and had plenty of parking in the gravel lot out front. Mary couldn't wait for harvest time, which was late August, but on this sunny morning in March of 1998, the happy thirty-nine year-old was out preparing to seed and water her land.

Fourteen year-old Dawk, and twelve year-olds Bay and T-top were preparing to water down the cows, and twenty-one year-old Dimples and nine year-olds Koko and Kimi were preparing to slop the hogs and feed the horses and chickens. The entire family was busy this morning, except for a select few.

Naomi was in bed with Doss while the bulk of the family and the ranch hands were out working. She was scheduled to help her big three take the cows out to pasture, but she and Doss were in the mood for some raunchy sex. Forty-two year-old Naomi sat astride her husband wearing a cowgirl hat and boots, breathing heavily as she rode Doss towards a deliciously anticipated orgasm, but her loud moans and the slapping of flesh upon flesh had awakened six year-olds Spoonie and Tyke.

The twins were outside their parents' door crying because they thought their father was hurting their mother. Naomi heard her daughters crying; she had been through this once before with Spoonie and Tyke and she had to stop on that occasion, but on this day, Naomi was so enthralled in the pleasure she couldn't stop. Neither could Doss. Just then there was a hard kick on the wooden double doors that led into the pleasure palace. "Hey! Spoonie and Tyke crying out here! And I'm hungry!" seven year-old Walee yelled as he repeatedly kicked the door.

Naomi and Doss were hard at it now; they couldn't stop even if they wanted to. The moans grew louder. Naomi, with sweat beading down her back, planted her hands on Doss' sweaty chest and placed her boot-clad feet on either side of her husband and began bouncing up and down at a furious pace. Doss, in turn, was thrusting up into his wife like a man possessed as he gripped Naomi's wide, luscious ass tightly. Spoonie and Tyke were crying. Walee was banging on the door. The parents were going at it nonstop.

"Get away from that door!" Naomi yelled aloud, as she bounced on Doss's rigid pole.

The crying and constant banging on the door quickly came to an end just as Naomi's body quivered from the orgasm and she slowly rolled off her husband. The two kissed passionately before Doss got up and put on a robe and went and cracked the door and peeked out into the hall and saw Walee sitting on the floor with Spoonie and Tyke beside him. "What did we tell you three about getting up and knocking on this door when you hear me and your mother talking," he asked his youngest three kids.

"We hungry!" Walee snapped as he stood up.

"It's just after six in the morning. You three should still be sleep."

"You and momma mating woke us up." Walee said.

"We wasn't mating. We were talking, son." Doss stated calmly, trying to hold back his laughter.

"Come on man! Talking dad? That's the best you can come up with?" Walee asked as he folded his arms and looked up at his father with a look on face that said, "*You really want me to believe that shit?*"

Doss couldn't help but to smirk at his son's expression before he asked, "What we were doing then, son?"

"I'm not going to talk like that in front of the young ones," Walee replied as he pointed towards Spoonie and Tyke.

Doss couldn't help but to laugh at that moment. Walee truly had the gift of gab. His manner of speech could be aggravating at times, but also funny, as it was to Doss on this morning. "Okay, and keep it clean, what do you think me and your mother doing, son?"

"Y'all doing like the cows do when they make babies—mating! It's eight of us already! How many more of us do you need?" Walee said as he held out his hands to plead his case.

Doss laughed again and looked back at Naomi who was now wearing a gown and robe as she shook her head. "He got a mouth on him, Doss," she stated as she walked out the room to tend to her youngest three.

As the sun broke over the horizon, Dawk, Bay and T-top had just finished count on the cattle before they set out to water them and saw that a dozen of the two hundred head of cattle were missing. They walked behind the slaughter house, which was built in the same spot of Naomi's grandparents' home that was destroyed by the tornado in 1993, and headed towards the canyon that was at the southernmost part of the land where the cows had free access to graze, mate and defecate. Sometimes, however, a few of the young cattle would walk down a small embankment that led into the canyon to gain access to the canal to drink. Unable to climb back up the embankment, the adolescent steers would get stuck and began to panic as they mooed loudly in frustration. This day was no different.

Dawk, Bay and T-top sighed when they saw the cattle pacing back and forth in the canyon, mooing as if they were calling for help, all the while searching for a way out by clawing at the sides of the canyon with their front hooves.

"Stop walking down there, stupid animal," twelve year-old T-top yelled at the cows.

"They can't understand you," a voice spoke out from the opposite side the canal.

"What happened?" T-top asked.

"They can't understand you."

The big three looked over and saw a slender white man with a grey beard standing behind a white fence. They'd seen the man on several occasions and he really didn't have any kind words to say. He'd once called Flacco a wetback and the two men argued. He'd even had a word or two with Naomi about slaughtering bulls, calling her a murderer. None of the Holland-Dawkins family liked the white man, whose name they never even bothered to know, nor did they care to know. He'd been on the land opposite the Holland Ranch for two years or so, arriving shortly before Mary and Dimples arrived on the ranch, but he was a constant nuisance. Always butting into the family's business and trying to tell them how to run their operation.

"We not stupid, man! We know animals can't talk!" Bay said in a disgusted manner.

"Well, if ya' can't keep ya' damn cattle out this here canal, you need not be farming," the man said as he threw a hose into the canal and turned on a water pump.

"We know how ta' get 'em out this here ditch. That ain't the problem. What is a problem is that water hose you just threw down there. You gone have ta' take that hose out our canal," thirteen year-old Dawk snapped.

"This canal belongs to the city." The old man replied.

"It's on our land! Your fence sits way back there on the other side this canyon, dude. So we not only own this here canyon, we own the canal, and the land on the other side the canyon up to your fence." Dawk replied from atop his horse.

Dawk believed he was right, but the old man was actually correct. The city owned the land on ten feet of either side of the canal. Dawk didn't see it that way, however; he believed that since the man's fence was ten feet away from the canal on the other side, the land leading up to the fence *and* the canal belonged to the Holland-Dawkins family.

"Where this fool come from anyway?" T-top asked from atop her horse.

"Momma say he got that land from the city. She tried to get it but she said he beat her to it." Dawk answered. "He shouldn't even be on that land. That should be our land. His old white ass fucked it up for us." Dawk ended as he hopped down from his horse and grabbed a rope in order to begin lassoing the cattle to pull them back up from the canyon.

Just then, nine year-olds Kimi and Koko ran up to the group, eyed the scene, and then looked directly at the man's pond across the canyon. "Catfish!" they said in unison.

"Mister, can we have one of your catfish?" Koko asked with enthusiasm.

"No you can't! They are not for sale."

"We don't wanna buy any! We won't you to give us one so we can eat it! Just one, mister! Please?" Kimi pleaded.

"No! And stay the hell away from my fish! I catch any of you over here it's gonna be gunfire!"

Dawk ran across the water and Bay and T-top quickly dismounted their horses and followed suit. The big three ran across the shallow canal, up the hill and an argument ensued.

"I wish like the fuck you would shoot at my sisters, old man!" Dawk snapped. "You don't wanna take it there, potner!"

"He damn sure don't!" T-top snapped.

391

Bay, at that moment, was really thinking about riding her horse back to the house and call her daddy, but by then, there was no telling what would have happen because Dawk and Tiva both had hot tempers and she knew they weren't going to back down. They may in fact hop the man's fence and beat him senseless, despite his threats.

"Come on y'all," Bena said, "let's go before something bad happens."

"Something bad on your side!" the man snapped as he watched the three kids walk back across the canal and up the hillside.

Dawk was furious. No one, no one he felt, had the right to threaten his family. The old man didn't know what kind of fuse he was igniting. Dawk may have only been thirteen, but he was well-built, standing just under feet and weighing 140 pounds. He also had it in him to do the man bodily harm on this day. He'd denied his sisters, threatened to use a gun, and was still running off at the mouth while he, Bay and T-top pulled the family's calves up from the canyon. It took everything within Dawk to keep from walking back onto the man's property and taking it to him, but his cool demeanor prevailed.

After everything had settled down, both parties went about their business, but the animosity between the Holland-Dawkins family and their nameless neighbor had just been kicked up a notch. And things got even more heated later in the morning when Naomi and Doss caught wind of the situation via Dawk. Threatening their kids was a no-no. The neighbor on the other side of the canal was now on Naomi and Doss's radar and would be watched closely from now on.

Kimi and Koko, however, even after witnessing the argument, and upon hearing their mother and father's debate over the man's reckless speech, now knew that there were catfish in the pond on the other side of the canal. The possibility of being shot, or shot at, didn't even enter into their young minds, nor did it deter them from their endeavors. The twins knew where the fish lay; and whether they had the right to do so or not, Kimi and Koko were going to get at that catfish someway somehow.

******

As the day wore on, the family and their workers was about ready to take lunch on the patio of Ponderosa. Doss, who wasn't much of a farmer, had spent the entire morning with his youngest three walking down alongside the canal on occasion with them just to see, hoping in fact, that the old white man would say something to him as the rest of the family worked the land, but the old man never showed.

For lunch Doss had grilled boneless chicken breast and Naomi was now out riding her horse around the land gathering everybody. She had just notified Mary and had turned away to ride the horse back to Ponderosa when she caught sight of a small figure exiting a taxi at the entrance to the family's land so she headed that way, believing the person was lost or in need of help. The closer she got, however, the better she could see.

"Siloam! Siloam, you came back! You came back!" Naomi yelled as she tightened the reins on her horse and rode at a fast pace. The rest of the family looked on as they each made their way to the patio.

"Who that, dad?" Bay asked as she stood out in the field eyeing her mother riding her horse across the front portion of the land.

Doss went into the house and grabbed a pair of binoculars and walked out into the field beside the house and focused the lenses on the person standing at the family's front gate. "That's you all's big sister," he stated happily. The eight kids took off running in Siloam's direction, but Doss stopped them. "Wait children," he yelled aloud, slowing their process. "Let your mother and Siloam talk things out first."

Mary and Dimples smiled, happy Naomi's friend, her unofficially adopted daughter had come back as Naomi had often talked about Siloam Bovina and the events leading up to her sudden departure. "You think Siloam is gonna stay, Uncle Doss?" Dimples asked.

"Well, we'll have to see, baby girl. I sure hope so because that would just set Naomi so right. At least until Martha gets home." Doss replied as he watched Naomi dismount her horse and walk slowly towards the white fence separating her and Siloam.

Naomi rubbed her hands together as she stared at Siloam. She hadn't changed much, a few pounds thinner and longer hair, but she still had those beautiful hazel eyes and that warm spirit one couldn't help but to feel when in her presence. Siloam Bovina, now twenty-four, was dressed in a beige, burgundy and white sunflower dress and burgundy boots with her hair in two pigtails. She had a nervous, pleading look on her face as she stared at Naomi. The look on her face saying only that of four words: can you forgive me?

Naomi said nothing. She only nodded her head up and down, answering a question never posed, but with the keen understanding that it had been asked in silence. She watched as Siloam sat her suitcase down and turned the guitar around. "Momma? I'm sorry for what I did," Siloam said as she began to cry. "I never meant to kill—I never wanted to—"

"You don't owe me anything, Siloam. Not an apology. Not an explanation. You didn't cause their deaths and you are not in contempt with me. The question at hand is, can you forgive *me*? Can you forgive *me* for stripping what little endurance you had left within you on that terrible, terrible day? You looked to me for guidance and understanding during that time," Naomi said as her eyes watered. "When you needed me to reassure you, I stomped on your heart."

"That day haunted me for a long time, momma. I went out of my mind," Siloam replied as she chuckled slightly through her tears. "I was confused, hurt and I felt alone in the world."

"I know. And I did that to you. You didn't deserve that. You've been nothing but a loyal ally to this family ever since the day we first met and you belong here. This is your home. This is your family. And we miss you."

"And I missed you all so much. I should've stayed. But I thought you would always hate me for what happened to Kevin and Serena."

"I never hated you, Siloam. The thing with me is that I don't always say or do the right thing. If I could relive that day I would have never said those words. For a long time I regretted saying that, and I still do. I'll never get over that until you come back, will you come home?"

Siloam didn't answer right away. She stepped back and looked at her guitar and said, "I took some music classes at Wichita State."

"You weren't far away."

"I didn't want to go far away really. I was too afraid to come back home, but yet I wanted to remain close because my heart has been here for a long time now."

"What brought you back?"

"I met some interesting people that helped me to appreciate what all I had. One was this little girl at the bus station in Wichita named Samantha."

"What was so special about Samantha?"

"I don't remember how old she was—but she was young— real young. She was running away from home and I helped her. I was so worried about her when I left her behind in Vegas. It bothered me so much that I rented a car and drove to Portland, Oregon. I couldn't stay there any longer knowing I'd helped that child runaway and gave her up to the streets. I joined a small band in Oregon and did a few tours up and down the west coast."

"Did you like it?"

"Momma? I got, I got involved in drugs. Had risky sex with strangers and began hating myself. I told you the day we loss Kevin and Serena that I wanted to be a rock star and I was on my way. That old band is doing good now—opening up for AC/DC and Guns 'n' Roses, U-2—but the drugs, the sex. It wasn't about the music with them to me. I felt out of place. Here is where I belong."

"I'm glad you feel that way, Siloam."

"Thank you. I learned a lot of songs out west, but this was the first one and it's my favorite. I always played it and thought of home. I'm gonna play it for you and I hope you don't get mad at me for doing so." Siloam said as she began strumming her guitar through her tears.

When Naomi heard the tune she leaned forward on the fence and rested on her elbows as she began to cry. Siloam's face was wet with tears also as she began to sing, "*I got a blue telescope... I'm looking at the world tonight...through a blue telescope...I wish I may...wish I might...not see what I see... sheet metal on sheets of ice...I'm looking through this blue telescope... down a moonstruck road tonight..."*

Naomi began sobbing as she listened to Siloam sing John Hiatt's song *Blue Telescope*, a song she knew all-too-well. The young woman's voice was the epitome of soul and the essence of harmony. Ever since Naomi had known Siloam, she'd always sung songs that had heart-warming, thought-provoking lyrics. Just as Siloam had said moments ago, for her, Naomi knew, it was all about the music. Siloam wanted to evoke emotions whenever she performed, and she was doing so on this day. The young, free-spirited Cherokee Indian was singing Kevin and Serena's song, a song Naomi hadn't heard in a long while. And hearing Siloam sing it, had brought back memories, beautiful memories of the lives of two people who Naomi knew loved her unconditionally and asked for nothing in return —except for her to be happy in life. Naomi couldn't help but to think of happier days—the day she and Kevin left Alabama. Times she'd spent in the kitchen with the man who raised her as his own while preparing dinner. The many sparked conversations she and Kevin had. The day Serena gave her those Raggedly Ann and Andy Dolls. The day Serena fought a woman after she'd called Naomi out of her name and trips she, Kevin and Serena had taken with the kids when they were younger. Kevin's loving smile and warm embrace. Naomi reflected upon those happy times and more as she reached out her right hand and touched Siloam's left cheek and Siloam laid her face into her hands and stared into her eyes as she continued to sing, *"Blue breath on my windshield...I came to a frozen place...I shivered when I said good-bye...I wish I didn't have to face...her in that rearview mirror...though she lives in the heart of me...looking through this blue telescope...I guess she'll always be a star to me..."*

So many emotions were running through Siloam's heart as she sang. She wondered if that little girl that had rode the bus with her to Las Vegas was still alive as she thought of her own failings. Repeated sex with strangers, both men and women, while she was on a cocaine drug binge brought about shame and sorrow. Siloam knew better. She knew wild sex parties and traveling from city to city, living amongst strangers who could care less about her well-being and were only using her was not her life. She didn't belong there. Here, in Ponca City, Oklahoma with the only family that had ever cared for her, the place that brought out her best and allowed her to be the free spirit she was born to be was where she belonged. The shame Siloam felt, shame that she would never share with anyone, because her life for the past two years or so was filled with so much debauchery and excess in her eyes, it warranted washing away, something to be tossed into the annals of her life's history and never to be repeated again. Overcome with emotions of the events that had transpired in her life, Siloam was forced to abruptly end the song and fall into Naomi's waiting arms.

"I'm sorry, momma! I'm so sorry!" Siloam said through a heaving chest as she clutched Naomi.

Naomi helped Siloam cross over the fence. She went for her suitcase, but Naomi told her to leave it. "Well get it later my child. Let's go home."

Siloam rode with Naomi astride the horse back towards Ponderosa with her face pressed to Naomi's back and crying aloud, happy to be back home. Work was halted on this day in July of 1998 and a celebration was held for Siloam's return. All was well by night fall, and Siloam Bovina was officially welcomed back into the family as if she had never left.

CHAPTER 30
GOOD EATING WITH KIMI AND KOKO

The ringing of Koko and Kimi's alarm clock awakened the twins at four in the morning in the month of August 1998, about a month after Siloam's return. They both eagerly leapt from their beds and tip-toed out of their room towards the bathroom to wash up. With foam from the tooth paste in their mouths, they eyed one another and snickered, excited about their solo venture. Their siblings and parents were still sound asleep when they deactivated the alarm and exited the house twenty minutes later.

Ten year-olds Kimi and Koko, dressed in cutoff jean shorts, tank tops and rubber slippers, ran to the side of the home and grabbed their fishing poles from the shed along with two plastic buckets and made a mad dash towards the canyon, each holding onto a bucket, a fishing pole, a bag of powdered doughnuts, a soda and a bag of chopped boneless chicken from the day before as the many stars in the sky-lit night lit the way.

Kimi and Koko, like their three older siblings, had learned to fish from their father in the creek that ran behind the guest house. Doss taught his kids a lot about life and encouraged them to explore their land whenever they felt the desire. And on this early morning, Kimi and Koko's desire to explore the land had spilled over into unchartered territory. The twins descended the embankment leading into the canyon and crossed the two foot deep canal and climbed up the other side towards their neighbor's fence where they crossed over onto his property, baited their lines with the scraps of boneless chicken and threw them into the pond. Two plopping sounds broke the silence of the moon-lit, silvery night and the twins popped open their sodas and ate the powder doughnuts as they sat beside the pond waiting for the fish to bite. It wasn't long before the lines were being tugged on and the twins fished for almost an hour. They each had caught ten fish apiece when they stopped and drew their lines back in and headed back home. They made it back to Ponderosa and entered through the back patio door and went up to the upstairs kitchen where they saw Bay, T-top and Dawk. "Momma and daddy woke yet?" Kimi asked.

"No. Well, yeah they up doing what they do. Y'all saw them powder doughnuts Siloam brought here yesterday?" Dawk asked.

"Yeah, they gone. We ate them while we was catching these fish." Kimi replied.

"Damn, y'all ate all the doughnuts?" Dawk exclaimed.

"Hey man, you shoulda been there!" Koko replied as she and Kimi sat the buckets of fish on the island counter.

"Sit that on the floor! And that old man gone shoot at y'all for stealing his fish!" Bay snapped.

"It's just a few fish for breakfast, Bay! Dang! Nobody ain't stealing either!" Koko replied.

"I know he ain't give it to y'all," T-top said.

"What y'all doing up anyway?" Kimi questioned. "When we left everybody was sleep."

"Ahhh," Tiva said through a smile. "You never know when we be up. We was in my room playing the PlayStation game and came in here for a snack when we saw the alarm was off. Checked y'all room and knew where y'all was. Lucky we didn't tell daddy and momma."

"How many fish y'all caught?" Dawk asked.

"Like twenty. We got enough for everybody." Koko answered.

"Already!" Tiva quipped happily. "We thought y'all was gone just look out for y'all selves."

"Shiit! We 'bouta eat good! Y'all need help skinning that

up?" Bay asked as she eyed the fish with delight.

"Yeah," Kimi and Koko replied in unison.

"Let's move this party downstairs. I'm a set up daddy deep fryer on the patio. And don't eat all the damn fish like ya' did with the doughnuts," Dawk said.

"Man! We throw some grits and cheese with that deep-fried catfish and we got us some good eating right there y'all!" T-top stated as activity began to unfold in the Holland-Dawkins household shortly before six in the morning.

****

"Shoot it on my ass! Shoot it on my ass Doss!" Naomi moaned huskily as she knelt on all fours on the edge of her bed. Doss was standing on the floor behind his wife pounding her with uncontrolled animalistic lust as Spoonie and Tyke cried outside their parents' door.

Naomi began thrusting back harder and harder. "It's yours! It's yours, daddy," she screamed as the cries from Spoonie and Tyke grew louder.

This had become Naomi, Doss, Walee, Spoonie and Tyke's morning routine for a while. Six year-olds Spoonie and Tyke just didn't understand what was going on in their parents' bedroom every weekday morning; but Walee knew and understood fully. He came stomping down the hall and kicked the door just as Doss drove forward with a powerful thrust and grunted loudly, spilling his load inside his wife. Naomi shuddered and squirted clear fluid from her vagina that splashed Doss's stomach.

"Awww, shit! Doss, baby," Naomi said in a stuttering manner as her body quivered and she spread herself out onto the bed, her top half on the mattress and her legs hanging off the edge of the mattress. "Whewww! Boy, you a bad mother —"

"Watch your mouth!" Doss stated as he slapped Naomi's ass once more, causing her to shiver again.

"Well, I'm talking 'bout you, Doss! Now that's how you start the day, my love," Naomi said as she got up and threw on a robe and went and opened her door. Naomi was used to seeing Spoonie and Tyke along with Walee in front the door in the morning, but when she opened the door, the three were gone. She then caught a whiff of something delectable in the air. "Doss, you didn't put nothing in the oven this morning did you?"

"No. Why, baby?"

"Something, something smells good. I be back." Naomi said as she traveled down the long hall leading to the Grand Staircase. She stood on the balcony in her home and looked around but saw no one. She then traveled down the stairs and went into the downstairs kitchen and saw T-top in front the stove stirring a huge pot of grits.

"Hey, momma. How'd it go with you and dad this morning?" T-top asked with a chuckle.

"Don't play with me, Tiva. What y'all got going on down here this morning?"

"Catfish."

"From where?"

T-top knew if she told the truth, Kimi and Koko would be in trouble. She stopped stirring the grits and said, "Me and Dawk, we umm, we—"

"Y'all went back there and stole that old man's fish?" Naomi asked in dismay.

"He had it coming, momma. I mean, we went late last night while he was sleep. Snuck in and snuck out."

"Stay from back there! Because if he shoot at y'all, I'm gone —" Naomi caught herself, refusing to say what she would do to the man if ever he did something to her children, whether they were wrong or not. "Just stay from back there. But since we got it, how many y'all caught?"

"Enough for everybody."

Naomi merely shook her head and said, "Well, let me get you all's father together. Mary's up yet?"

"Yeah. She and Dimples helping fry the fish out back."

"Where's the young three?"

"They with Siloam in the theater room watching TV."

"Alright. Well, get everything together. It's warm out this

mornin' so we'll eat on the patio again today." Naomi ended as she headed back towards the staircase to rejoin her husband.

About an hour later, the entire family was out on the patio preparing to eat. Mary had seasoned the fish with salt and lemon pepper and deep-fried them to a crisp, golden brown. There was boneless fish for the youngest three and fish-in-bone for the older family members. When the family bit into the catfish there were multiple sighs of delight from various family members.

"I *knew* that pond had some good fish back there!" Kimi stated proudly as she watched the family gorge themselves off the fish she and Koko had stolen.

For over a month, Kimi and Koko, who were soon joined by Dawk, Bay and T-top, would fish their neighbor's pond. Naomi slaughtered her own cows and pigs; there was plenty of ground beef, spare ribs, the best cut steaks, various cuts of pork chops and sliced bacon and salted ham on the ranch, and fresh cut chicken as well; but the catfish, for a while at least, had taken a front seat. At least two days out the week the family ate fish, good fish. The oldest five were taking at a minimum, thirty fish a week, but after a while, the numbers started to dwindle. The oldest five went fishing one morning in early September and caught none. The thievery had finally run its course. The old man knew particular members of the Holland-Dawkins family had taken his fish, but he couldn't prove it. He approached Naomi one day in early September while she and Flacco were pulling cows up from the canal and asked about his stolen fish.

"If I knew your family was thieves I would've never bought this property."

"What the hell are you talking about now, old man?" Naomi asked. Naomi knew where the fish the family was eating was coming from, but she did nothing to stop it. She hated the old man just as much as anybody and would do, or allow anything to go on that she knew would upset the man. She'd figured out that he couldn't, or didn't get up early enough to catch Dawk, Bay, T-top, Kimi and Koko, so she allowed her kids to steal the man's fish at their leisure.

"I'm talking about y'all stealing my crop of catfish!" the old man yelled from behind his fence. "I put a lot of money into this business and you and your family has ruined my crop of catfish!"

"You accusing me and my family of being thieves?"

"Damn right! Thieves and murderers! How could you just kill a cow so cold-heartedly?"

Naomi really hated this old, annoying ass white man and she could care less about his 'crop'. The family had stolen and eaten his cache of fish and it wasn't a damn thing he could do about it and Naomi knew it. He continued on and on with his rant, repeatedly calling Naomi and her family thieves and murderers, until he finally struck a nerve.

Naomi threw down her lasso, pulled out her .44 magnum and stood in the middle of the canal and said, "Look, mutherfucka! Unless you gone get on your knees and smell the cracks of the asses of the people on this side of the water to see if it smell like fish I suggest you shut the fuck up before I blow a hole in your heart and drag your dead ass back over here and feed it to the hogs!"

The look on Naomi's face was one of rage. The old man knew full-well that the family had taken his fish, but he had no proof. On top of that, the look in Naomi's eyes told him that he'd better shut up and let the situation lie. He pulled his water pump from the canal and never replenished his pond. Naomi smirked as she returned to her duties, hoping that the man would give up his land so it could be placed into the hands of her family. She'd wanted to claim that property for herself for some time now, and the stealing of the old man's fish was only the beginning. A serious game of manipulation and antagonizing would now begin. Ten year-olds Kimi and Koko had started it, but Naomi herself would now lead the way.

****

Ten year-olds Kimi and Koko were now sleeping at the guest house in the latter part of September of 1998 in order to help Mary and Dimples set up the produce stand. The twins were up around five this Saturday morning and as they sat on their beds in the bed room, Kimi couldn't help but notice a small deer sneaking down to the creek. For the last week or so, Kimi had seen the deer every morning around the same time.

"I bet we can catch that deer, Koko." Kimi said to her twin.

"A deer? Kimi, they too fast!"

"If we trap him in the water we can catch him." Kimi said in a confident tone as she and Koko got dressed for the day. The twins helped Mary reap some of her produce from the field and ended the day by asking Siloam to take them to the sporting goods store back in town. Once there, Kimi and Koko went straight to the baseball section and purchased a wooden Louisville Slugger baseball bat. Siloam thought Kimi and Koko were buying the new bat for Spoonie and Tyke, who both loved softball, but the twins had other plans for the new stick.

The following morning, Kimi and Koko were out behind the guest house dressed in camouflaged jean shorts, a camouflaged tank top and a pair of black sneakers. They crossed the creek and they each hid behind a tree underneath the star-lit morning sky, blending in perfectly with the scenery as they waited in anticipation of the small deer that came to drink from the creek around the same time every morning.

As they stood motionless, the twins heard the cracking sounds of twigs and dead leaves, and tree branches being pushed aside. Koko looked over to Kimi and nodded her head, suggesting Kimi take a look. Kimi shook her head rapidly to say no and both twins remained still. A few minutes later, the deer sprinted by the twins. He was closest to Koko, who peeked from behind the tree to her right and saw the deer heading for the creek. She quickly dashed out behind the deer, but the animal broke and ran away from the water and back up the hillside and out of sight.

"Dang! I moved too early!" Koko stated disgustedly.

"Next time, Koko? We should try to get him to run back into the creek. We can catch 'em in the water." Kimi said as the twins headed back to the guest house to start their day.

Mary opened her produce stand in the last week of September of 1998 with a fresh bumper crop of onions, strawberries, cabbage, tomatoes, and mustard, turnip, and collard greens and the pumpkins would be ready in October.

Mary unknowingly had Eileen's gifted hands when it came to agriculture and she was now producing crops that would rival that of her grandmother, whom she didn't have any memories stored up in her mind. Still, through Mary, Eileen Holland lived on.

Dimples, Kimi and Koko were on hand the first weekend Mary opened up for business, the four females stood behind the wooden bins holding the crop as they watched cars whizz by the stand. Mary was wondering why people weren't stopping because when she was setting up her stand, numerous people had asked her when she would be open for business. She'd given them all the date and now that it was here, no one was stopping. About an hour later, an orange Harley Davidson pick-up truck pulled up to the stand and a young male in his early twenties got out and approached the four women. The young man, who Dimples thought was handsome, approached the stand with a smile on his light-brown-skinned face and asked, "Is this produce stand open?"

"Yes! We've been open over an hour ago." Mary stated.

"Your sign says otherwise, though."

"What do you mean, sir?" Mary asked.

"It says not open."

Mary's jaw dropped. She had given Kimi and Koko the task of painting the sign, but instead of painting 'Now Open', Kimi and Koko had painted 'Not Open'. Mary and her nieces walked to the edge of the road and all three looked at the sign, "What's wrong with the sign?" Koko asked.

Mary turned to her nieces wondering how they could have made such a mistake. "I said to paint 'Now Open', you two. Look at what you did! This says 'Not Open'!"

"That's what we thought you said, Auntie!" the twins replied in unison.

"No! No! No! If you would stop thinking about that deer every morning, Kimi and Koko, you can focus! We missed out on a lot of money this morning!" Mary snapped.

"We sorry, Auntie." Kimi and Koko responded sadly.

"Hey, it's all right. Now you know and you can fix it. In the meantime, I need a bunch of turnip greens and a bag of onions. My momma's gonna be glad to be able to fix some fresh greens for daddy," the young man stated. Dimples bagged the young man's items and handed them to him with a sexy smile. There was an instant attraction on her part, but the man merely thanked Dimples and walked away, bringing about a sigh of disgust.

Ponca City was a town dominated by Caucasians; there weren't many Black people in town, and most of the men that resided in the small town of 26,000 or so people, no matter what their race, be it white, black, Hispanic and or Native American, if Dimples had to tell it, were already taken, or unqualified. Dimples, like her mother, was a 'choosey lover'. She valued her body and didn't want a player, a man with no goals in life or one that was only out for a good time. Race didn't matter with Dimples, however; she only wanted a man. And the man that had caught twenty-one year-old Regina Holland's attention, although he wasn't black as far as she could tell, had piqued her interest. She watched as the young man got into his truck and couldn't help but to say, "That's good eating right there," in hopes of sparking a conversation.

"Well if it is, I'll be back for certain lady, for certain," the young man said as he entered his truck and slowly pulled away, forcing a sigh of frustration to spill forth from Dimples' lips.

The day ended with Mary making a good bit of sales. The following morning, a couple of hours before they were to return to the produce stand with their aunt, Kimi and Koko headed back to the woods shortly before six and awaited their prey's return. They were really focused on catching this deer, if not to eat it, just to be able to say they'd caught one. The last time they'd tried, the twins had failed to corner the deer because they didn't trap him properly. This time, however, instead of lining up beside the deer, they waited until the animal went and drank from the creek. When the deer lowered his head to the water, Koko stepped out from behind a tree and ran towards the animal, forcing it into a panic as it jutted out into the creek. It was then that Kimi emerged from the opposite side of the creek and jumped into the water and hit the deer across the back with the wooden bat.

The deer made a shrieking sound as he made his way through the waist deep water towards the side of the creek on which the guest house sat. The twins were now in the water with the deer and Koko cheered Kimi on as she pounded its backside repeatedly with the wooden bat. The deer emerged from the water with Koko now hot on its trail. Kimi had pelted the creature with numerous blows to the spine as he swam the creek, but the deer was still able to run once he exited the water. Koko, however, was on his ass something fierce. Mary came out onto the porch to start her day and she watched as Koko ran the deer down in front the guest house and put him in a choke hold.

"Hey! Hey! What are you two doing?" Mary yelled aloud just as Kimi ran up and the twins wrestled with the deer, ignoring Mary's question.

"Hold 'em down and let me get the bat! Hold 'em down! Alright I got the bat! Move Koko!" Kimi yelled aloud as she slammed the bat into the deer's hind section. Mary looked on in shock as Kimi beat the deer until it could not stand up on his hind legs. The twins then took off running towards Ponderosa yelling aloud for Bay and leaving Mary behind standing on the front porch with her mouth agape and looking on in shock.

CHAPTER 31
TAK

Kimi and Koko made the long run back to Ponderosa and ran upstairs to Tiva's bedroom and tapped on the door and Bay answered sleepily a minute later. "What are you two doing up so early," she asked.

"Remember that deer?" Kimi asked, gasping for breath.

"That li'l deer y'all been tryna catch for the last week?"

"Yeah, we got 'em and he still alive. We wanna see if you can shoot it from the porch like when you be out in the woods." Koko answered for her sister.

Thirteen year-olds Bay and T-top, and fourteen year-old Dawk were steadily being trained by their father to use the many handguns and rifles he owned. Dawk preferred the handguns and the shotguns, but Bay and T-top loved the rifles with the scope. Bay's slender, dark eyes lit up when she heard Kimi speak and she was no longer sleepy. She placed tennis shoes onto her feet and walked over to the other side of the mansion to her parents' room in her pajamas and placed her ear to the door. "Good, they not doing it," she whispered to Kimi and Koko as she tapped on the door.

Doss answered and his daughters told him about the deer as he grabbed his robe and walked over to his gun cabinet and unlocked it and allowed Bay to retrieve her weapon of choice while Naomi herself climbed out of bed. Bay looked over her father's many choices of guns and selected a Russian Dragunov SVD. The gun held a ten round clip and was a gas operated semi-automatic. The 9.5 pound rifle with a scope on it was accurate up to 900 meters, over one-half mile.

Bay led the way out the room with a big smile on her face. T-top was awakened and so was Dawk, and by the time Bay set up the rifle on the home's patio, the entire family, including Mary and Dimples was outside of Ponderosa.

"That deer is still alive over there." Dimples said as the family watched Bay place the scope on her rifle.

"He won't be for long," Dawk remarked.

"Ohh noo!" Mary sighed. "Don't shoot him!"

"What you want us to do, Mary? Go over there and beat it to death?" Naomi asked.

"That's how they caught it. They beat it with a bat." Mary remarked.

"How'd they do that?" Naomi asked.

"They ran him down," Dimples said through light laughter.

Naomi looked at Kimi and Koko surprised. "How you two do that?"

"We set 'em up and took 'em down like we was bowling. Took us a week, but we got 'em! You ain't know big girls can move like that huh, momma?" Koko stated as the family laughed lowly.

"Watch this here, y'all." Bay said as she placed the rifle against her left shoulder and looked into the scope.

"Brace for the recoil, Bena," Doss reminded.

"I got it, daddy."

The deer was on high ground in front the guest house struggling to walk because Kimi and Koko had broken one of his hind legs. Bay spotted the deer through the scope and adjusted the lens and reconfigured the rifle's barrel to compensate for the wind and gravity, thus preventing the bullet from going off target. Doss watched the deer, which was about a quarter mile away, through the binoculars as it moved about in a circular pattern.

Bay now had the deer in the cross-hairs of the rifle. She squeezed the trigger and the entire family witnessed the deer drop to ground immediately. *"Umm, mmm, mmm,"* Doss hummed as he lowered the binoculars. *"Over a quarter mile away and she hit a moving target with a head shot. Bay good. Real good,"* he said to himself as he went and hugged his daughter. The deer was skinned and cleaned and placed into a freezer. It would be eaten the following Sunday.

Monday after the deer was killed, Dimples was returning to her mother's produce stand after dropping Kimi and Koko off at school. As she rode back to her mother's stand, Dimples heard a thud coming from the right rear of Mary's F-150 and knew right away that she'd caught a flat. She got out frustrated, knowing she didn't have her cell phone on her and didn't know how to change the tire. She stood beside the truck growing angry at herself for leaving her phone behind as she looked around. No one was in sight, so Dimples started walking back towards her mother's stand just as a tow truck pulled up beside her. "Need help miss," a gentle male voice asked.

Dimples turned to the truck and her heart skipped a beat. It was the young man who'd purchased the turnip greens a few days earlier. "Heyyy! I got a flat and don't know how to fix it. Can you help me, please?"

"Be glad to. My name is Takoda by the way. It means friend to everyone."

Twenty-three year-old Takoda Kotori was a full-bloodied Cherokee Indian whose family had been in Oklahoma since the mid-eighteen hundreds. He was 5' 11", weighing 170 pounds with thick, jet black hair that was draped over his shoulder. He had dark brown eyes, a broad smile, broad nose with high cheek bones. He had a friendly, but stern look about himself, but it was his warm smile that was flooring Dimples on this morning.

Takoda parked his truck and got out and went to assist Dimples as she introduced herself. She then stood behind Takoda, who had on a black silk wife beater and denim jean shorts, as he knelt down to look at the tire. When he placed his left hand on the trucks fender, Dimples saw he wasn't wearing a wedding ring. *"Yes!"* she said to herself.

Dimples was admiring Takoda's physique from behind, and when he turned to look up at her, she quickly turned her head away as if she wasn't staring. Takoda only smiled, he'd felt

Dimples' eyes gazing upon him but he didn't acknowledge the fact. "You have a spare underneath. I can put that on and you can drive over to my shop and I can have a new one put on. There's a deli nearby, maybe we could have breakfast while we wait for my guys to fix it," he said as he stood up.

"Okay. That sounds good, Tak."

"Tak? Tak? You nick-naming me?"

"I like Tak. Can I call you Tak?"

"Call me Lucky."

Dimples laughed and said, "My aunt and uncle's friend name is Lucky. I can't call you by that name— Tak."

Takoda smiled and went to work on Mary's truck and an hour later, after allowing her mother to meet 'Tak', Dimples and Takoda rode to his repair shop where the two had a good conversation over lunch. The young man then departed when the truck was ready; but he was sure to give Dimples his number. As Dimples and her mother rode home from the produce stand, she asked her what she thought of 'Tak'.

"He seems nice, Regina." Mary responded as she drove through town.

"I know, momma. He has his own business and no kids and stays with his mother and father. He used to date but he says he's single right now. He asked me out Friday and I think I'm a go."

"Well, go on baby. Ain't many available men here and you never know. But at the least, you do have a date for Friday night."

"Heyyyy!" Dimples said as she and Mary high-fived one another inside the truck.

Dimples and 'Tak' went out that Friday night and the young man was very cordial. The budding couple had met up at the Olive Garden that night and the two hit it off well, just as they'd done when they had lunch at the start of the week. The conversations were positive, the laughter was sincere and the stares and admiration was constant and pleasant. It was fair to say that both young adults liked one another, and Dimples was fast becoming attracted to 'Tak' and 'Tak', in turn, was falling head over hills for Dimples. He had never seen such a beautiful young woman.

The date ended with a brief hug and a kiss on the cheek although both 'Tak' and Dimples wanted more. Before she got into her mother's truck, Dimples decided to invite 'Tak' to the ranch. Doss was leaving for Chicago the following week and she wanted her uncle's opinion of the man she now had a sincere interest in wanting to know better before he left. Takoda accepted and Dimples asked him if he liked deer.

"Sure do, Regina. Who's cooking deer?"

"My mother and my aunt Naomi. Come over Sunday about five. I told you about my cousins so be ready for whatever."

"Not a problem. So long as you're around, it'll be all right." Takoda ended as he closed Regina's door and watched her drive away from the parking lot.

****

When Takoda made it to the ranch Sunday around five, Naomi's eight were at the front gate. Bay was holding a .22 rifle; the gun was draped gently over her left shoulder as she eyed a pickup truck rolling towards the front gate. Dawk and T-top were also at the front gate and the young five were standing behind the big three. The entrance to the ranch looked more like a border crossing instead of an entrance to a home. Takoda exited his truck and walked up to the gate and stared down at the youngsters, who looked like they were on patrol this day.

"What's up young ones? I'm here to see Regina Holland."

"You got some identification?" seven year-old Walee asked loudly.

Spoonie and Tyke quickly repeated Walee's question. "Yeah, you got indenti, idetifi—what Walee said Spoonie?" six year-old Tyke asked her twin sister.

"Never mind Tyke. Why you here, mister?" T-top then asked.

"I got invited here by your cousin Dimples."

"What's your name, dude?" Dawk asked.

"My name is Takoda—but Dimples calls me Tak."

"Tak? What the hell is a Tak, man?" Walee asked.

"Yeah, what the hell is a, is a, is a, pac-man?" Spoonie asked.

"Y'all two can't say nothing right! Stop repeating him!" Koko snapped.

"You not the boss of me!" Spoonie snapped back before she stuck out her tongue.

"I can beat you like I'm your boss! Shut up!" Koko yelled.

Takoda laughed at the kids as Dawk hopped the gate and walked around his truck as if he were inspecting it. He then walked to the front of the truck and said, "Regina might have invited you, but it's up to us to decide whether you get in or not. You really like my cousin?"

"He better like her! And her *only!*" Bay then stated as she shifted her Dragunov rifle.

"Hey, how you met my cousin?" T-top then asked.

"I changed her flat tire last week."

"What else you did to her?" Koko then asked.

Takoda laughed once more. Dimples told him about her eight cousins over dinner. They may have been coming off rude, but they cared for Dimples and didn't want nothing to happen to their big cousin, like what happened to Ne`Ne`. He chatted with the kids in a playful tone until they grew tired of asking questions and Dawk finally pushed the gate open,

"Hey mister? Can we ride in your truck back to the house?" Kimi asked.

"Wait a minute! I just got interrogated and now y'all want a ride from me? What kind of security are you people?" Takoda asked playfully.

"We the kind of security that need a ride *right now!*" Walee yelled as his siblings laughed right along with Takoda.

The eight piled into the front and back of Takoda's truck and he drove slowly towards Ponderosa. The young man was really impressed with the lay of the land. Dimples never mentioned her aunt was well-off, but that wasn't what was moving Takoda; truth was, the young man simply liked Regina Holland.

"Hey Dimples, this boy right here looking for you!" Kimi

yelled from the back of the truck as it cruised down the side of the house beside the patio.

Takoda met the whole family and it was fair to say that he made an impression. He was polite, well-spoken, intelligent and mature. When Doss gave his opinion, telling Regina to make him wait as long as possible before she gave in sexually, she obliged. Takoda waited patiently until May of 1999 and he and Dimples made love for the first time. They were already in love with one another beforehand, but their lovemaking had only solidified their bond.

Dimples became pregnant in October of 1999 and she and Takoda married on Mary's birthday, March 22, 2000. She gave birth to a son she named Tacoma on June 22, 2000, which was her twenty-third birthday. Regina Holland- Kotori moved into a newly built home on the north side of Ponca City with her husband and continued working for her mother and aunt. Takoda owned a tow truck business and a small repair shop; this is how he would support his family.

****

All was going well for the Holland-Dawkins family as 2001 got underway. Doss was steadily training his big three in preparation of things to come and he was still making good money from the distribution network he, Lucky, Junior, and Fin were running with JunJie back up in Chicago. Naomi had purchased more cows and was steadily transporting livestock to the meat packaging plant in Iowa. Everybody was making money and enjoying life, and when Martha and her friend Twiggy made it to the ranch in August of 2001, the Holland family was completely united and prepared to live life and enjoy the rest of their years together…

…Naomi sat up and leaned forward from the tree she rested on, having finished reflecting on some of the events that transpired in her life up until August of 2001. She got up and walked down Ne'Ne's Hill and strolled gently back to Ponderosa and rejoined her family.

All was well in Oklahoma now, but a phone call to Doss later on in the day pertaining to events that had transpired one month earlier would set the wheels in motion for a chain of events to unfold that would thrust the Doss and his oldest three children onto a new plateau within the underworld.

CHAPTER 32

ONE MONTH EARLIER

Twenty-five year-old Xiang Nyguen walked briskly around to the driver's side of her 1996 cocaine white Impala and stared at the woman who lay on the ground before her. It was July 12, 2001 and Xiang was on the south side of Las Vegas, Nevada on this day. The woman that lay on the ground was the mother of one of her pimp's prostitutes and had vowed revenge against Asa Spade, the pimp she felt was responsible for her daughter Jaleeza's death.

Rival gang members had kidnapped the sixteen year-old prostitute and tortured her to death and were about to load her body into a jeep to get rid of it, but Asa and his cohorts had killed the men before they could finish the job. It was outside the bloody motel room in North Vegas that the teen's body was discovered by Asa's nephew, Wayne Miller, wrapped up in a bloody comforter.

Asa had to discard the young teen's body to prevent the motel murders from coming back on him. That fact went unbeknownst to the teen's mother and on this day, she opened fire in broad daylight on the crowded Las Vegas Boulevard strip and had shot Asa Spade in the torso. She fired into the driver's side of Xiang's Impala, striking Asa three times as he sat behind the steering wheel of Xiang's car. Still, Asa managed to dodge the four remaining bullets. As the woman reloaded her gun, Xiang, the 5' twenty-five year-old Japanese/Vietnamese sidekick to the pimp stepped from the passenger side of the car and opened fire on the woman with a mini submachine Uzi. The woman fell to the ground and Xiang now stood over the woman as she begged for mercy.

"He killed my daughter!" the woman screamed through her pain.

"You were wrong about that!" Xiang replied coldly as she released another volley of bullets across the woman's stomach, killing her instantly.

Xiang then opened the door to her car and shoved Asa into the passenger seat and sped off down Las Vegas Boulevard as witnesses to the drama stared on in disbelief. Xiang knew she couldn't take Asa to the hospital so she called on an old friend from Seattle, Washington, by way of Nagano, Japan.

"Maruyama Realty Corporation. How may I help you," the pedantic voice on the other end responded.

"JunJie!" Xiang said hysterically as she headed south out of Vegas. "We have—I have—I need help! Asa's been shot and we can't go to the hospital!"

JunJie Maruyama, now forty-three years-old, was well acquainted with Asa Spade as he had introduced Xiang to the man in Vegas one day in 1993. "Is he still alive?" JunJie asked calmly as he hurried his staff out of his high-rise office in downtown Seattle and quickly locked the door.

"Asa!" Xiang called aloud. "I got JunJie on the phone! You still with me, baby?"

Asa coughed up blood as he lay across the front seat in a near state of shock, staring blankly at the floor board of the pristine Impala SS. The thirty-one year-old, muscular, dark-skinned 5'10" 210 pound pimp reached for the phone, but he grimaced in pain as he did so, unable to speak, only nodding his head to let Xiang know he was still coherent.

"He's hanging on, JunJie—but he's hurt bad. Can you help?" Xiang asked in a pleading tone as she wheeled the vehicle down Interstate-15 heading nowhere in particular.

"Take him to my home in Paradise." JunJie requested. "The address is—"

"533 Middle-Valley Lane! I know where it's at. I'm headed that way!" Xiang remarked as she exited the highway and began heading east towards JunJie's home in Paradise, Nevada, a ritzy suburb that lay southwest of the Vegas Strip.

Twenty-five minutes later, Xiang was pulling into JunJie's extravagant, three story, white stucco and glass mansion. When the car stopped in the driveway, a middle-aged white man stepped from behind the steering wheel of a white cargo van that was parked at on the curb in front the home. "I'm Fitzgerald. Doctor Fitzgerald," the man said as Xiang approached him. "JunJie referred me. Said you had a problem," he concluded as he pulled a gurney from the rear of the elongated cargo van.

"He's been shot in the body. I don't know how much, but he's lost a lot of blood." Xiang replied as she and the doctor quickly wheeled the gurney up the driveway and loaded up Asa and rolled it towards the front door.

Xiang found the spare key and unlocked the door and she and the doctor wheeled Asa into a bedroom on the second floor via an elevator and Doctor Fitzgerald quickly began setting up IVs and placed his utensils on the dresser. The doctor inserted a needle into Asa's arm and within seconds he passed out.

"What have you done to him? Why isn't he responding?" Xiang asked anxiously.

"The morphine just has him sedated. The heart monitor here shows his heart rate. He's shutting down, but he'll be fine." Doctor Fitzgerald said in a confident tone.

Xiang leaned back against the bedroom wall and sunk to the floor and placed her head in her lap and cried silently. The doctor looked on in silence as he went about removing the four bullets that were lodged in Asa's torso. Doctor Fitzgerald was a young-looking slender white man with brown eyes and blonde hair and was in his early forties. He was JunJie's poker room partner over at the Venetian Casino and the two had built up a good rapport. The doctor didn't really know what kind of man JunJie was, all he knew was that he was a very rich man from the Pacific North West. Wanting to get down and play dirty ball outside of the law, which was a good money racket for surgeons in Vegas willing to dabble in the life, Doctor Fitzgerald, assuming JunJie had criminal ties, told him if he ever needed help along medical lines to call him.

JunJie had held the doctor to his word on that night and Doctor Fitzgerald knew he had to deliver if ever he wanted to collect what he knew would be a healthy six-figure payout for his services. Doctors were under federal and state law to report all gunshot victims to local authorities, but Fitzgerald, like the people whose company he often kept, bent the rules from time in order to garner more wealth. He worked for about five hours on Asa Spade and Xiang had never moved from against the wall. She only stared at the doctor as she sat on the floor like a little girl who was worried about her father, asking an occasional question or two while watching the doctor's every move as he operated on her man, who lay silently on his back in a comatose state.

"How much longer?" Xiang asked in a calm tone, slowly beginning to trust the good doctor.

"Another two, maybe three hours."

"How many times have you done this?"

"Not as many times as Asa's been shot that's for sure." Doctor Fitzgerald could see the worried look on Xiang's face after he'd answered her question. "I'm sorry," he said as he placed a clamp onto Asa's skin to prepare a stitching, "I thought you, well, I assumed you were referring to my doing this kind of work outside of a hospital. I graduated from Stanford University in the top percentile of my class in 1990 and I'm now a top surgeon over at Sunrise Hospital in Winchester. Trust me. I know exactly what I'm doing"

Xiang could see Doctor Fitzgerald smiling from behind his surgical mask as she looked at her watch and saw that it was almost eight 'o' clock in the evening. Asa was scheduled to meet his daughter, but he obviously wasn't going to make it, so Xiang got up exited the room and headed to bath and stripped her clothes and jumped into the shower. Once she was clean, she ran down the stairs and out the front door to her car butt-naked and went into her trunk and grabbed another outfit and dashed back into the house to dress. She returned to the bedroom and told the doctor she was to be away for an hour or so, but she would return.

"He's in good hands," Doctor Fitzgerald said softly as he nodded towards Xiang.

Xiang went into the three-car garage and opened JunJie's key cabinet and found the keys to the man's jet-black 2001 E-Class convertible Mercedes Kompressor. She hopped into the car and pulled out of the driveway on her way to meet Samantha Holland, Asa's unofficially adopted daughter to tell her the bad news. Xiang knew Samantha was scheduled to go to the Navy shortly and she didn't want her to worry about Asa and give up on her dreams of flying jets so she told the teenager that Asa Spade had been killed. Samantha took it hard, but Xiang knew by telling that one lie, she was in effect, saving Samantha's life by pushing her away.

After more than four hours on the streets, moving about cautiously and making contact with a couple of Asa's other top females, Xiang headed back to JunJie's house exhausted, arriving shortly after midnight. She had stayed away longer than planned because it took her a while to track down Ponita Felton and Francesca Aranello, two of Asa's top females, to tell them what happened and she also had to find out what people knew.

The streets were talking according to Ponita and Francesca. Word had spread quickly of Asa's demise and now, the hunter was becoming the hunted. A few of Asa's street walkers had told Xiang that Grape Street Crip gang members had a hit out on both she and Asa. On top of that, Asa's brother, responsible for killing his own son, Wayne Miller, a couple of months back, was also looking for Asa Spade to seize his life's breath. Alvin was a former Blood gang member, but he'd switched sides when he realized he could earn more money by working with the Crips. Asa was a true Blood member, and that, besides the fact that his own brother wanted him dead, is what would put the two brothers at odds.

Xiang exited the car bearing all of her pimp's burdens. Her slender green eyes were weary, her long, shiny, black hair was matted against her sweaty back and the silk dress she wore was a tangled mess by the time she exited JunJie's car. It was then that she noticed a white Lincoln town car limousine in the driveway. She smiled a weary smile when she saw JunJie Maruyama open the front door wearing an apron. The man had flown down from Seattle to check on his old friends and his slender figure standing in the doorway was a welcomed sight. Xiang walked slowly towards the man and hugged him.

"Asa's fine," JunJie said. "He was talking earlier, but he's resting now. Mister Fitzgerald has one more operation to perform in the morning. Simple routine. Asa should be woke for that one, you can talk to him then. Come now, I've made dinner. Come in and relax, Xiang."

"I'm sorry I took your car, JunJie—but I can't use my car anymore because it's too hot."

"Don't worry about it. Phil and Grover will get rid of that thing. Go and get yourself clean and come have dinner with us."

Xiang walked towards the elevator and rode it up to the third floor, stripping off her clothes as she did so. She stepped off the elevator and walked along the narrow hall staring out through the huge tinted panoramic windows that displayed a stunning view of downtown Vegas from atop the hillside. She gathered a huge robe and towels and entered the bathroom at the end of the hall. This particular bathroom inside JunJie's mansion was enormous. White marble floors and walls, and green leafy plants ran throughout. Xiang stared at the gold initials 'JM' that lay in a circle in the center of the bathroom floor. She had never been this far inside of JunJie's house, but on that day, she couldn't help but marvel over the mansion's interior design. She then reflected on the life she and Asa once led, the huge home on Dry Gulch, the BMW's and Suburbans the man once owned, and most of all, the money, all the items that had been lost a few months ago when the Las Vegas police took Asa Spade and his crew down.

Xiang sighed and looked into the mirror with uncertainty towards the future. She and Asa were independent people, on top of the world once, but now they had to rely on JunJie for shelter and support. Not that it was a bad thing, because JunJie cared for Xiang and Asa dearly. Xiang, however, just wanted things back to normal. She was used to having her own, and if she felt that way about the matter, how much more so would Asa feel once he was back at full strength? Climbing back on top would take a great deal of time, Xiang knew, but she was forever loyal to Asa and she would help the man rebuild his empire no matter how much time it would take to do so. Xiang then had an epiphany as she stood staring at herself in the mirror. For so long she had been Asa Spade's underling, his assistant and confidant. Now, with Asa being on rock bottom, Xiang realized that the playing field was now even. She could now show her man her true skills. She had killed for him already and was willing to do more. Whoring for Asa Spade in Xiang's eyes had come to an end on July 13, 1996. The lifestyle had run its course and now it was time to move on to bigger and better things. It would be a challenge to rise again no doubt, but it would be a welcomed challenge, one that Xiang Nyguen knew she and Asa Spade could achieve over time.

With those happy thoughts running through her mind, Xiang walked up the small flight of stairs and began to run warm water into the huge Jacuzzi style tub and returned to the toilet to urinate. She placed her hands over her face and began to cry the moment she sat down and began riding a roller coaster of emotions going from that of joy, joy that Asa was still alive, to anxiety, anxiety over the prospects of the future, and to downright sorrow over all the possessions and lives lost over the past two months.

Xiang was gathering her composure and was unable to see the muscular intruder as he tip-toed into the bathroom. The lone figure crept through the bathroom door, slowly making his way over to her as she sat on the toilet with her head bowed. A wicked smile spread across the tip-toeing bandit as he neared Xiang, never taking his eyes off the vulnerable, weary woman as he pulled out a sterling silver, pearl-handled vintage Japanese dagger worth over $50,000 dollars.

"You still can't sneak up on me, boy!" Xiang finally said as she looked up and smiled at the intruder.

"You're just as keen today as you were back in Seattle," the man said through light laughter as he paused and sat the dagger down. "One day I will master that move so watch your back."

"You could never hurt me, old friend. What were you planning to do anyway? Slit my throat while I piss?" Xiang asked as she flushed the toilet and stood up.

"I've done worse," the man remarked through a smirk.

The two smiled at one another as the man approached and hugged Xiang's neck tightly. He relinquished his grip, stepped back and stared at Xiang and said, "I haven't seen you since you left Seattle eight years ago! How have you been, old friend?"

"I've been having my hands full down here in Vegas. It's been crazy, Grover." Xiang said as she turned off the water and stepped into the Jacuzzi. "But just because I'm no longer in Seattle, it doesn't mean I have been out of the loop. I've heard many things about you also, 'Tin Man'." Xiang said matter-of-factly as she sunk into the warm water. "I hear what a bad boy you've become, Grover."

"Well, you know how people lie now-a-days."

"Oh no. You are the 'Tin Man'. I've heard of your murderous ways, Grover. So young. So violent." Xiang concluded as she closed her eyes and sighed a sigh of relief, the water was so soothing to her soft feminine body.

Grover 'Tin Man' Kobayashi was a twenty one year-old full-bloodied Japanese from Nagano, the same city in Japan as Xiang. He was JunJie's dead business partner's son and had grown up under JunJie with JunJie's son Phillip 'Phil' Tran, a Japanese/Vietnamese, just like Xiang. Grover had lost his father when he died in a plane crash returning to the U.S. from Japan when he was only seven years-old and he'd been living with JunJie and his son Phil ever since.

Twenty-one year-olds Grover, and Phil were introduced to JunJie's business at the age of eighteen when they were ordered to kill a rival real estate business partner, his wife, and three kids in a home invasion back in Nagano, Japan in 1998. When they returned to the United States, Phillip had grown pale as he described the gruesome tactics Grover used to torture and kill the man and his family to his father. Phillip told JunJie how Grover made the man watch as he cut the tongues out of the mouths of the man's kids. He described the blood-curdling screams coming from the basement as Grover cut flesh from the face of the man's wife. The torture went on for hours before Phillip, tired of hearing the agonizing screams and pleas of mercy, walked downstairs and shot the five family members multiple times at random in order to end their ordeal.

On the flight home, Grover ate and drank until his heart was content, and he had a wicked grin on his face as he slept like a baby after feasting himself until he was stuffed. It was back in Seattle as they stood in JunJie's office on that day back in 1998 that Phillip and his father JunJie had given Grover the nickname 'Tin Man', after a character from the movie *The Wizard of Oz* who had no heart, no feelings.

Phillip and Grover had grown real close over time; they were more like brothers instead of best friends. Many people in Seattle's underworld feared the duel because their reputation preceded them in high fashion, especially Grover. Drug dealers, stick-up clicks and gang bangers alike all knew not to cross the young gangsters lest they ended up in some sort of torture chamber screaming to be put to death. With JunJie backing them, and their violent demeanor leading the way, Grover and Phil controlled a vast portion of the drug trade in Seattle and had been doing so since 1999.

Grover sat beside the tub conversing with Xiang, when in walked Phil. The slender-built Asian with jet-black hair, similar in appearance to his father, smiled at Xiang as he walked up and handed her a glass of champagne.

"This is a pleasant surprise, Xiang, in spite of the circumstances we find ourselves in. Are you and Asa going into business with my father now?"

"Don't know yet. Have you checked on him for me? How is he, Phil?"

"You know Ace, he's a strong one. And the doc's pretty good. Asa will live."

"Who did this to Ace?" Grover asked Xiang.

"She's dead, Grover. I killed her myself, but we have other people after us that want to see us dead."

"You know we won't let that happen. Neither will JunJie." Grover replied.

"I know. When Asa's all better, we'll talk to JunJie."

"My father has been itching to get Asa Spade to join us, Xiang. It's millions up there in the Pacific North West and it's wide open. Asa would be a perfect fit." Phillip remarked.

"Millions?"

"Millions, Xiang. All for the taking. We can own that territory and expand into other territories if Asa agrees."

"We may have no choice in all of this, Phillip. The gangbangers are ruining Vegas, and if I know Asa like I do, there will be more murder on these streets before it's all said and done." Xiang said as she sipped her champagne.

"So you think Ace will want to go after these guys?" Grover asked.

"What would you do," Xiang replied. "Asa's brother killed his own son and as of now he has aligned himself with a rival gang. People were busted, killed and ran out of town. I mean, Ace had a good thing going—but envy has a way of working itself into the hearts of men who've been harboring the seed of jealousy. Yeah," Xiang said through a somber, yet serious tone of voice, "I speak on behalf of Asa Spade when I say I want all who were involved in the events leading up to now killed. We're not done. This is only the beginning, gentlemen. A new day is upon us."

CHAPTER 33
PUTTING THE GANG BACK TOGETHER

A burgundy four door 1996 Cadillac Sedan Deville sped out of the Shorter Housing Projects on Denver, Colorado's north east side just after one in the morning as the driver pulls off his ski mask while making a beeline for Interstate-70. The date was July 13, 2001, the day after Asa Spade was shot. The passenger pulled off his ski mask as he looked back at the crumpled body of a man who was once a mid-level drug dealer. The two men in the Caddy, Percy and Douglas 'Dougie' Hunt, who were cousins, had just killed the man after robbing him out of $4000 dollars in cash.

"You seen how that nigga dropped when you hit 'em?" twenty year-old Percy asked in cool and collective manner as he sped away from the scene.

"Fuckin right," twenty-one year-old Dougie responded calmly in his slow, raspy voice as he counted the stolen money. "Fuck we look like selling a nigga a quarter brick in Shorter Arms this time of night? I thought that boy was gone read that set up."

Percy and Dougie had been on the lam since the day Asa Spade was busted by the Vegas police back in June. The two cousins fled the city when Grape Street Gang members burst into their home and tried to kill them in the early morning hours. By fleeing Vegas the cousins had saved themselves; but they never forgot about Asa Spade, however; the man whom they once sold crack cocaine for before the crew came tumbling down.

The cousins hid out for a few weeks, sleeping in their car and petty hustling for cash. Now, after two months of hiding and staying low key, they had come across a lick that would allow them to return to Vegas and deal with the Crips who had tried to kill them. They had pretended to be drug dealers from California and set up a potential buyer and had robbed and killed the man in cold blood. The lick had put $4000 dollars in cash in their pockets, and when coupled with the two fully loaded AK-47 assault rifles in their possession, the cousins were now ready to wage a war, but they first had to find Asa Spade so they could put all the pieces of the puzzle back together.

The cousins touched down in Vegas after a twelve hour drive and their immediate plan was to find some of Asa's old prostitutes to see if they could locate either him or Xiang. Percy and Dougie had been trying to contact Asa for weeks, but they never made a connection because all the cell numbers to their affiliates were disconnected and they had no way of finding out what went down in Vegas. The cousins rode down the busy Vegas strip and turned into the MGM Grand Casino/Hotel, an old hang out of Asa's, and it was there, under the canopy, where they spotted 24 year-old Ponita Felton, one of Asa's former top prostitutes hanging out front.

"Lady P, what's up?" Dougie yelled from the passenger side of the Cadillac.

"Dougie? Boy, you don't speak to me from no car! Get over here and show me some love, mutherfucka!" Ponita yelled aloud over the scores of patrons and loud traffic that was in the air that warm afternoon.

The cousins got out of the car and tipped the valet one hundred dollars to allow them to park under the huge canopy for a few minutes and walked over and greeted Ponita. The 5' 3" 120 pound Argentinian prostitute was so glad to see a couple of familiar faces. She had only seen Xiang once since Asa had gotten out of jail two months ago and that was the day before, when she found out through Xiang that he'd been shot.

"Man I'm glad ta' see y'all! I thought y'all was dead! Man, everything fucked up down here! Them mutherfuckas from Grape Street done damn near took over everything!" Ponita said in frustration.

"Grape Street?" Percy asked, his dark eyes squinting in disbelief.

"I know Wayne ain't let that shit go down like that." 'Dougie added.

The cousins noticed the sad look that Ponita suddenly displayed when she heard Dougie mention Wayne's name. "Y'all ain't hear? Where y'all been man," she asked somberly.

"Hear what? We been up in Denver." 'Dougie' replied.

"Denver? The hell y'all doing in Colorado? Never mind, umm, y'all umm, y'all did right to skip town though 'cause the Crips got the game on lock down here now. Not too many Bloods left in Vegas."

"What happened?" Percy asked.

"Long story. I betta let Xiang tell y'all."

"That's exactly who we looking for. She know were Ace at?" Percy inquired.

"Yea, she gave me her number where they at. It's in my suite, let me go get it. Come on up."

Ponita led the cousins up to her and Francesca's suite on the seventh floor of the hotel and tapped on the door. "I'm knocking so I could see her reaction. Francesca always wondered what happened to y'all." Ponita said through a sly smile.

"Who the fuck is that?" a voice called out from behind the door as Ponita knocked repeatedly.

"It's Dougie! Open up Francesca."

"Oh Shit! That's my nigga Dee out there?" twenty-five year-old Francesca yelled excitedly as she swung the door open wearing nothing but a smile. When Francesca Aranello came into view, Dougie and Percy couldn't help but to stare at the specimen of woman standing before them. She was a tall, dark-skinned Black/Italian with bowed, shapely legs, curly black hair that she wore in a crop, thick full lips and 36c breasts. Francesca was stacked at 5'9" 160 pounds. She stood naked at the door in a pair of four inch-heeled stilettos as she eyed the cousins. "What's up Dougie and Percy? Man, where y'all boys been? Come on in! Ponita you play too much too, girl! You know your ass had a key! Man I'm glad to see y'all two boys!"

The group all sat down in the living room and Francesca rolled a couple of blunts while Ponita searched for Xiang's phone number. She returned to the living room a few minutes later with the number and a bottle of Grey Goose Vodka and the group sat and talked. Dougie and Percy were filled in on the events that had led up to Asa getting busted, but when Percy asked about Wayne, both Ponita and Francesca grew sad again. Ponita handed Dougie her cell phone and said, "Call Ace so he can fill y'all in on the rest."

****

Meanwhile, back over to JunJie's mansion, Asa Spade was laying back in the bed talking to him, Xiang, Grover and Phil.

"Man, I owe you my life, JunJie. That doctor was a wizard."

"That's what a friend does, Ace. Now, tell me, what's your plan for the future?" JunJie asked as he pulled a stool up and sat down beside Asa.

"I'm like whatever right now. I do have a couple of keys to pick up later this week from the Bloods up in Oakland. I can start there."

JunJie merely laughed and turned to Phil and Grover, who laughed as well.

"What's funny?" Asa asked as he stared at the three men.

"Would you like to make some real money, Asa Spade?"

"What kind of numbers you talking?"

"Six figures for starters."

Asa looked on at JunJie. He knew the man wasn't joking, but things were just too complicated in Vegas for him to enter the game at this particular point, and he told him so.

"You have enemies here in Vegas I know," JunJie said, "but why not relocate to Seattle and take care of your business in Vegas from there? I have people that will help out in every way. What have you got to lose?"

"I'm still sore, JunJie. It'll be weeks before I'm well and can walk again. I can't do shit like this. Plus I got a court date coming up and the police seized all my property. The house, the cars, money, everything."

"I'll help out with that matter. I have contacts all over this town and I can keep you outta jail. In the meantime, you can come to Seattle, check out the operation and decide if you want to take over the network I've set up."

"I know judges myself. But knowing the amount of heat I have on me they wouldn't get close enough to throw a favor my way. Okay, umm," Asa grimaced in pain at that moment. Three bullets to the torso was no easy fix; and although he was strong and fit, the hot lead had really taken a toll on the man. He looked up at the ceiling, squinting his eyes because it now hurt every time he breath. Everybody remained silent as they watched Asa combat the pain. When he regained his composure, he looked over to JunJie and said, "If your lawyer can get me off, I'll come, and when I do, I do things my way."

"Ace, it'll be your operation. You can run it as you see fit."

Asa remained silent. He knew there was nothing left for him to do in Vegas except to murder the Grape Street gang members, including his brother Alvin Spencer, all who wanted him dead. His prostitution ring was defunct and all he would have to work with was two kilos. JunJie said he could make six figures out the gate and Asa Spade knew it would be foolish on his part to pass up the offer. "Alright," Asa said as he stared at JunJie, Grover and Phil, "I'm in. But how this supposed to work. What's the plan out the gate, JunJie?"

"I'm heavy into real estate here in America and overseas back in Japan," JunJie answered. "But I making more money from this white powder right now than I ever did buying and selling property during the same span of time. Three times as much. With you and your newly formed crew working the streets, I can focus on the legitimate side of things. Funnel the money into legitimate ventures and wash it clean and make us all very, very rich."

"What I need first is a few more street soldiers, people with muscle you know?" Asa said. "Because I still got that problem with Alvin and the Crips on the west side. I want them dead just as much as they want me out the picture."

"I have a crew that is more than enough muscle for that

particular job. They will get rid of your enemies for you. What you do is rest and get well. You're done here in Vegas, Asa. It's time to move up the ladder." JunJie remarked.

"You have a crew already? Who are they?"

"They're from Chicago and they're damn good. You just rest. Let the streets be for now."

"JunJie, I don't need no fuckin' rookies going out there and fuckin' this shit up and having that drama come back on me. I'm in enough shit already," Asa stated seriously.

"This crew is the best I've seen. Been dealing with them for nearly ten years and they're very proficient. Expert killers."

"Can they bring Alvin to me alive?"

"That's what you want?"

"I wanna look him the eyes and ask him why he killed Wayne before I kill his ass."

"I'm glad you told me so because this crew would've taken him out. They'll bring Alvin to you, my friend. Hell, I'll even have them gift wrap the son-of-a-bitch if you like."

"Well make it happen then," Asa replied just as Xiang's phone began to ring.

Xiang answered and knew the voice right away so she placed the phone to Asa's ear. "Who this?" Asa asked as he placed the phone to his ear.

"What's going on, Blood?" Dougie asked through laughter.

"My nigga, Dee," Asa said lowly. "Where you at, Blood?"

"Me and Percy is back in Vegas and is on our way out ta' Mister JunJie house soon as you tell us how to get there."

"How y'all found me?"

"We ran into Ponita on the strip and she gave us the number."

"I thought y'all niggas was dead or in jail. Tell Ponita thanks for keeping it real, man." Asa stated as he gave Xiang the phone so she could give the cousins directions to the house.

The cousins pulled into JunJie's driveway about an hour later and were greeted by the man as he welcomed them both into his home and guided them towards Asa. It was a loud roaring reunion when the cousins walked into the bedroom and greeted Xiang and Asa with hugs. "Oww, mutherfuckas watch the wounds. Watch the wounds." Asa said as he lay back down on the bed. "Man, I swear, I never thought I'd see y'all niggas again." he said nearly out of breath.

"We thought the same thing, Blood. We been up in Denver. It's a money pit out there, homie. We thinking 'bout going back. Where Wayne and Samantha? Trudy and Callou?" Percy asked as a glass of gin was handed to him by Grover.

Asa looked up at the ceiling and Xiang ran her hands through her hair as she looked to the marble floor upon hearing Percy's question.

"Nobody can't answer the question? Where the fuck Wayne ass at?" Dougie asked as he sipped a glass of gin.

"Samantha and Trudy all right," Asa remarked somberly. "The rest of 'em, well, it's a long story, young Bloods. Cop a seat and let me tell ya' what went down."

Percy and Dougie were angered by the events that unfolded and had forced them to leave town. And they were unable to believe that Wayne was dead. Let alone the fact that his own father had perpetrated that devious act. "Niggas gotta pay, man," Dougie said. "Alvin was the only one outside the click that could get close to Wayne and he chose this gang shit over family? We gotta get that nigga, Ace."

"We gone be all right, Bloods," Asa said. "JunJie gone get a team on Alvin, so we gone see his ass again before we kill 'em. Now, me and Xiang been talking about getting back in the game and moving some major weight with Grover and Phil outta Seattle. Y'all niggas down?"

"No doubt Ace," the cousins said at the same time.

"That's what I like to hear coming from my nigga. I told y'all JunJie got some people that can handle Alvin," Asa said as he lifted a finger and pointed towards the cousins, "but you two can do one thing for me before we head up north."

"What ya' need done, big man?" Percy asked.

"JunJie got a crew that's gone come in and clean these streets up. We all know it's not how many you kill, but who you kill. Remember them niggas me, Wayne and Callou jumped on outside Bonanza High School and them fools we wasted that night we dumped Jaleeza body?"

"Umm, hmm," Percy answered as he took another sip of his gin.

"It's some niggas out they same crew that's in town looking for me and Xiang—some young niggas I heard. I want y'all to track them boys down, then find Alvin and keep a tab on that boy. When you find them li'l young niggas, get that information back to me so I can pass it on to JunJie and have it set up for this crew he got coming in from outta town to handle that business."

"We got that. It might take a little time, but we gone see it through. We can even get Ponita and Francesca to help us out."

"Get it done any way you see fit, man. Just get it done right. We 'bouta make some serious moves I want all the loose ends tied up before we bounce."

"We can move in on Denver too," Dougie chimed in. "Streets starving for dope up there."

"We gone handle all that. Put eyes on those crabs first and find Alvin for me, though fellas. That's top priority as of today."

"We on it, big homie," Dougie replied as he and Percy headed back out into the streets of Vegas to begin their search.

CHAPTTER 34
MURDER TALK

Forty-eight year-old Finland Xavier was sitting in Anthony's Fish Bar on Alaskan Highway in downtown Seattle talking to JunJie on a mild August day in 2001. Fin now owned his own practice with a team of three criminal lawyers. He'd opened the private law firm with the money he made overseeing cocaine shipments from Seattle. Fin now rarely entered the courtroom; his workers handled the trials as he was busy running Midwest Express, the front for the cocaine operation he, Doss, Lucky, and Junior were running. The 6'2" 190 pound, broad-shouldered man with a slick and shiny bald-head and a thick, black beard sat across from JunJie looking over the files for the family's next hit.

"The guys in Vegas came through in outstanding fashion. I didn't think they would find these marks so quickly," JunJie remarked as he draped a white cloth napkin over his lap. "These four guys hangout in a parking lot behind an elementary school on the west side of Vegas. The address is underneath the photos."

"Who's the lone wolf?" Fin asked as he slid a picture across the table.

"This is my associate's brother. His name is Alvin Spencer and he hangs out at the Sapphire Strip Club on Industrial Avenue, just north of the strip. My associate wants him delivered alive and gift-wrapped as a special request."

Fin looked out the bay window and gazed upon Puget Sound as he smiled to himself.

"Odd ain't it?" JunJie asked as he popped open a Heineken.

"You must be reading my mind."

"I am. We sit here in this nice establishment with such a lovely view discussing—well you know—the demise of others."

"Yes we are," Fin replied as he poured himself a glass of wine. "But I have to say, I enjoy these meetings. You are an interesting individual."

"Everyone has a story, my friend. And we learn from each other. Now, do you think your people can handle this job?"

"Is the price right?"

"One hundred and fifty-thousand dollars."

"That's lower than normal. Much lower." Fin said as two waitresses approached and sat a plate of steaming king crab legs and two porterhouse steaks on the table, forcing the men into silence.

When the waitresses cleared out, JunJie leaned forward and said lowly, "These guys are small potatoes, Finland. The lower the talent of the opposition? The lower the price of the job."

"We're talking about five guys here—nothing's easy about that because my people will be in town for an extended period of time trying to nail these guys all at once, thereby running the risk of getting caught or worse. Not to mention you want one of the marks delivered alive. The price you quote is not worth the effort for the family. That's what they will say."

"Okay. What is fair?"

"When we first started doing business, you paid a million. Why not that price?"

"I'm putting the money up for my associate. He hasn't that kind of money as of now."

"The question still stands." Finland replied as he cracked open a crab leg.

"That first job was out of my pocket and meant a great deal to me. This job is only on behalf of a friend."

"Something tells me that this job is important to you as well, Mister Maruyama. A few minutes ago you said we learn from each and you were right. One of the things I've learned from you is that every job you commission is important. So be straight with me today and don't short change my people."

JunJie laughed as he cut into his steak. "You are on you're A-game, my man," he said. "Three-hundred and fifty thousand dollars on the job, and when the next shipment comes in you'll find an additional ten kilos at no charge."

"That's more like it," Finland replied as he sipped his wine. "I'll get this info over to my people tomorrow night, and from there, the clock starts ticking."

"We have ourselves a deal. Now, let us eat."

"You have any whores around?"

"Asian. Just like you prefer. They're waiting for you at the Four Seasons. Here's the key. My limousine will take you once dinner is done. Me myself? I have my own harem back at my home."

"I love these meetings," Finland said through a smile as he poured another glass of wine.

"Sex, money and murder, my friend. The main three ingredients that makes life worth living." JunJie ended.

****

A week after Finland's meeting in Seattle, Mendoza, DeeDee, Lucky and Junior were turning off the main road of the highway leading onto the Holland Ranch. The kids were eagerly waiting to see their grandfather and his friends ever since DeeDee had called and told them they would be arriving within the hour.

It was a steamy, hot Saturday afternoon when the long, grey four-door Lincoln Continental turned into the entrance. The gate was already open when Lucky turned onto the property with Junior on his side and Mendoza and DeeDee in the backseat staring out at the land with wide smiles. The two old gangsters loved visiting the ranch. What a relief it was to visit the family in an atmosphere of peace on a beautiful span of land far away from the gangster lifestyle the men were living back in Chicago. Here, the gang from Chicago could truly enjoy the good side of life. And what made today really special was the fact that Naomi's other sister, Martha Holland, had just arrived on the ranch and the men all looked forward to a festive celebration with the family.

No soon as DeeDee's car began to traverse the dirt road leading to Ponderosa did the young five come into view. Lucky slowed down and the four men watched and laughed as the kids ran beside their grandfather's car yelling aloud with joy. "Welcome! Welcome, Grandpa!" "Hey, Lucky!" "Welcome, everybody!" the kids yelled at random as they ran beside the car all the way to the house. They were all out of breath by the time DeeDee's car made it to the front of Ponderosa, but it didn't stop them from running up and hugging their grandfather as he exited the car.

Dawk, Bay and T-top stood on the stairs of the patio watching their siblings. The young five, on the other hand, were everywhere—hugging Mendoza, Junior and Lucky, hopping in and out of the car and asking for candy from their grandfather. The big three no longer had the desire to chase the car the way they used to do, however; they were maturing and adapting to the ways of their father in rapid succession and running behind their grandfather's car now seemed to be something reserved for the young five and the young five only. It was fair to say that seventeen year-old Dawk Holland, and sixteen year-olds Bena and Tiva Holland had come of age during the summer of 2001.

DeeDee noticed the big three standing on the porch and quickly realized that this was the first time they had never chased his car. "Now you three is not that grown not to come and greet your family," he yelled out to his oldest three grandchildren. "Come on over here and hug your grandfather's neck!"

Bay and T-top at age sixteen were two petite young ladies standing 5' 7"; and although they only weighed a light 135 pounds, they were a lot stronger than they looked; something that could be attributed to the years they'd spent working on the ranch. The girls were tan-skinned with curvy legs and short, curly black hair and alluring dark brown eyes and both had identical smiles that would melt hearts. The twins leapt from the stairs in unison and ran and hugged their grandfather tightly. "Grandpa, when you gonna let me have this car, man?" Bay asked as she eyed DeeDee's pristine car. "I'm gone take it to Oklahoma City and let 'em flip into something tight!'"

"Hell, it's tight now. I just dropped a new engine in there along with a new paint job so I'm keeping it up. You'll get that car one day, Bena. Just let grandpa keep riding in it for a little longer before he gives it you." DeeDee replied as he eyed T-Top. "Oh my God! Look at you, Tiva! All of y'all! Just a growing! I got some beautiful grandkids!" DeeDee then said with a proud smile plastered on his face.

Dawk at age seventeen stood an even 6' and was a muscular 180 pounds. He was a dark-tan cock strong country boy with long black hair he wore in a single ponytail most days. He walked down the stairs and was greeting Lucky and Junior when the rest of the family began making their way over to DeeDee and company.

"You look good, old man." Mary said as she walked up and hugged DeeDee.

"Old man? Girl, if I was—"

"I would take you down, DeeDee! Take you *down* if you touch my sister!" Martha stated as she and Twiggy laughed and greeted the men.

"You just got out a few days ago, Martha and I know you don't wanna go back in for assaulting an old man," DeeDee joked.

"I heard about you, Doss Dawkins Senior. You might have a high number, but you ain't old."

"I'll take that as a compliment."

"You're welcome," Martha replied.

Naomi and Doss then greeted the men. "Where's Francine and Mildred?" Naomi asked.

"They're flying in tomorrow." Mendoza replied. "We'll have to go down and pick them up from Oklahoma City in the afternoon."

"Okay. I need to get some scrap leather while I'm down there too," Naomi replied.

The family all sat out and ate the food Doss had grilled on the patio before Naomi announced that nine year-olds Spoonie and Tyke had a softball game in an hour. The family piled into four cars and headed to the town's softball field around seven in the evening, just as the sun was beginning to hang low in the sky.

As Spoonie and Tyke, dressed in a Cubs outfit, the teams' uniforms all sponsored by Naomi, practiced on the field, DeeDee, Mendoza, Lucky, Junior and Doss talked about the upcoming job. It was a family atmosphere on the park on this beautiful summer evening, but as the five men stood beside the bleachers, they talked about murdering four people and kidnapping another. The Holland-Dawkins family, to state it plainly, was a well-to-do family that kept a dark secret hidden from most of its family members, that secret being that some of them sold drugs and killed people for large amounts of money. You could never tell just by looking, however, and if you didn't know, the Holland-Dawkins family was just an average, wealthy American family.

"Pop," Doss said lowly as he watched his youngest two daughters practice on the field, "I looked that file over on the way to the park. These guys are small timers. Easy prey. I'm thinking hard about letting the big three take on their first hit."

"You think they ready, son?" DeeDee asked.

"Bay and Tiva are more than ready. Especially Bay. She's a natural with the Dragunov. Bena and Tiva both are pros with the Dragunov now—but Bay? She just got it, dad. It's in her." Doss said in a confident tone.

"And what about Dawk?" DeeDee asked.

"Dawk is more behind the scenes. He's steadily learning the drug trade business and he's a natural leader with good intellect and looks as if he'll be a silent killer. Remind me of myself around the time I met Naomi."

"I think it'll be wise for you to take Dawk and Junior down there, son, and make these guys feel comfortable. What you say, Mendoza?" DeeDee asked.

"Junior and Eddie are tied up Saint Louis with Coban and Benito remember? The shipments are getting larger so they're providing muscle down there for the time being. Our business is expanding because of JunJie—and if Doss says his kids are ready, I think we should allow them to get their feet wet in this line of work because we'll be needing them more and more. But it's your family, and you all's call."

"I have to be honest with you two, four murders and a kidnapping is no easy task. And I don't want to see my grandkids fail their first time out." DeeDee said.

"Dad, trust me. They ready. I been training them for years and it's in them. And I know these kinds of guys. They're just like the guys we hit in Saint Louis back in 1992."

"What about the kidnapping, son?"

"That's the easiest part of the job. Look, Eddie and Junior are tied up right now and I been looking for the perfect job to get Dawk 'nem on the board. Now's the time. You're welcome to join me if that'll make you feel better, but dad, it's time we pass the torch to the next ones up."

"You sound sure of yourself, son. I'll take you at your word. If you say they're ready? I take you at your word." DeeDee ended as the men returned to the bleachers to watch the game.

The crew from Chicago stayed in town for a week and had enjoyed the time spent in Oklahoma. The day after the crew left, Doss, having already informed his big three of the job at hand, loaded two Russian Dragunov rifles into his suburban and he and the big three hopped into the truck and waved goodbye to the family, who were all under the impression that Doss was taking his oldest three kids to Chicago to further train them on the warehouse he was running.

****

"My tears of love...are a waste of time...if I turn away...am I strong enough to see it through...go crazy is what I will do...if I can't have you...I don't want nobody, baby...if I can't have you...ah ha ah..." Naomi was the only one outside of Doss and the big three that knew what was actually going down on this day. She watched from the large bay window on the second floor of the home as her husband and oldest three kids rode off the ranch, telling herself that everything would work out just fine as she listened to Yvonne Elliman's song, *If I Can't Have You* that was playing on the stereo inside the music room just to her left.

"You all right, sis? Hey, nah! Them disco days right there!"

Naomi turned and saw Martha emerging from the grand staircase with a glass of wine in her hand and bouncing to the music.

"I'm fine, Martha. Just observing how things are going. Did you get a chance to say good-bye to Doss?"

"Yeah. We all did. Can I ask you something?" Martha asked over the music.

"Sure."

"Where are Doss and Dawk 'nem really going?"

"To Chicago. Why you ask?"

"A lot of times, from what I've heard, Doss often flies out from Oklahoma City. If he was going to Chicago, why didn't he fly out with Mildred and Francine or didn't just leave with DeeDee 'nem yesterday?"

"He had to gather up some things and wasn't ready until today. And he wanted to give Dawk and the girls a chance to learn how to drive the highways if ever they had to make the trip alone."

"That's all there is to it?"

Naomi could sense that Martha believed that there was much more to the story, and in all actuality, she would love to have informed Martha of all the things that were going on outside the ranch because she knew Martha, unlike Mary, would have an understanding of the lifestyle. Martha, however, had just done nearly eight years behind bars and had been home not even a month. To lay such heavy realities of what was going down on her was a bit too soon and way too much in Naomi's mind.

"Sis?" Martha said, shaking Naomi from her thoughts.

"Yes, Martha. As of now," Naomi said as she looked her sister square in the eyes, "as of now, that is all there is to it."

Martha nodded, hugged Naomi and said, "I guess that is all— for now," before she turned and headed back downstairs, steadily dancing to the music. "I ain't heard that joint in years!"

Once outside, Martha ran into to Twiggy on the back patio. "You seen the wine was drinking, Mar?" Twiggy asked.

"It's on the island in the kitchen."

"Damn, my ass is desert thirsty."

"Hey, Irene," Martha called out.

"Wait! Let me get a glass of the good shit!"

When Twiggy returned to patio with her stem glass, Martha sat on the wall surrounding the patio and asked, "What you think about Doss and my nieces and nephew?"

"They cool! Shiiit! Mar, your family tight!"

"I'm talking about them leaving like they leaving."

"Well," Twiggy said as she took a sip of her wine, "they learning what their father do."

"Exactly. They learning what their father does." Martha replied as she sipped her wine, her left rapidly shaking from side to side.

"What you gettin' at, sister?" Twiggy asked, sensing a little nervousness rising within Martha.

"DeeDee 'nem." Martha said as she looked up at Twiggy.

"What about 'em?"

"They look like they some gangsters. And Doss is DeeDee's son. And Dawk, Bay and T-top is Doss's children."

"You think it's more to Doss than him just running a warehouse in Chi-Town?"

"I do. I don't know what it is exactly? But they just don't look like they going see about a warehouse in Chicago, Irene. I think Naomi hiding something. I wish she would just let me know what's going because I might be able to help her out you know?"

"I feel ya'. But if she is hiding something, her and Doss is damn good at what they do. Look at this place!" Twiggy said as she stood up and faced the back portion of the land. "I never —shit— Noland and Albert Lee never dreamed of going this far in life. Especially Peter Paul wild ass."

"Yeah. It's beautiful ain't it?" Martha asked as she, too, eyed the wide span of land.

"Don't worry about it, Mar. Maybe later on down the road you can get inside your sister's brain. Shiit! You just out of jail, girl! You and me both! So why jump back into the—why get down with that if that's what it really is? Let Naomi do what she do. She been fine all this time and I'm sure if she needs or needed you, she will and would ask for your help."

"You might be right. But you know we always be liking to know what's going on for real." Martha replied with light laughter.

"True. But what's going right now is them horses over to the barn. Siloam and Kimi gone teach me how to ride. You game?"

"That's what's up. Let's go change." Martha ended as she walked over to a golf cart and rode over to the guest house. Martha had quickly sensed that Naomi was hiding something her first week on the ranch; but she wouldn't hold it against her sister because she herself had played the game. Martha, however, had never made it this far, nor did she have the ambition to so. Naomi, on the other hand, had exceeded all the expectations and dreams Martha had ever had and then some. She was living the good life for real. Whatever she and her husband was doing, they were undoubtedly good at it, and they kept it well-hidden from the family. And it would be for that reason that Naomi, no matter what she was involved in, would earn Martha's utmost respect. She would silently ride with Naomi, waiting in the wings for the day, if ever it should arrive, that she would be called upon. From this day forth, Martha would remain loyal to Naomi, even in blindness.

CHAPTER 35
THE BIG THREE'S FIRST HIT

Doss and the big three had $9000 dollars cash, four Dragonuv rifles, six .380 caliber handguns stashed in the rear of the SUV when they left the ranch along with four pairs of binoculars and a taser. The journey to Vegas would be one of the more risky parts of the job because of the artillery stashed away inside the pristine, dark tinted vehicle. Doss always preferred to travel by car to his destination when doing a hit so as not to leave a paper trail as one would do when flying. He also traveled with under $10,000 dollars in cash to avoid arising further suspicion. If ever the heat came down, Doss knew investigating authorities would be able contact the I.R.S. because of the money, and track his moves and confirm that he was in a particular locale at the time of a murder if he was to ever get fingered.

Dawk, Bay and T-top had been trained by their father for over a period of six years and on this day August of 2001 it was time to see if the many years they'd spent training was worth the time and effort. Doss sat beside his son, who was behind the wheel driving the speed limit on Interstate-35, headed south towards Oklahoma City as he began delving into his kids' psyche. "Okay, kids," he said calmly as he read the Wall Street Journal, watching the numbers on companies the family had stock in, "if we get tagged by the officials, what's our story?"

"We going visit the campus of UCLA," Dawk replied from behind the steering wheel.

"And?"

"You taking me and Bay to Disney Land afterwards," Tiva said from the backseat.

"What does your father do for a living?"

"Works on a ranch in Ponca City, Oklahoma raising livestock," Bay replied.

"How much money I make in my line of work?"

"You don't share that with us. It's enough to get me into UCLA, though," Dawk answered.

"Good. Now, this guy Alvin Spencer, who we plan on kidnapping? There may be collateral damage. Anyone of you three may have to kill an innocent. Any apprehensions?"

"If they with him, then they against us," Bay said as T-top and Dawk nodded in agreement.

"Just want y'all to know that, that umm, what we do, our line of work isn't to be spoken about ever to your brothers and sisters, your aunts or anybody else back home. Everything we do in this line of work starts and stops with me, you three, and you all's mother—understand?"

"We got it," Dawk replied.

"How you three feel about your jobs in the family?"

"We follow you wherever you go, daddy." T-top said.

"Just know that I don't always catch everything," Doss said. "So much can happen out there and things don't always go according to plan. But if we all pay attention to what others say and do our jobs to the utmost perfection, take nothing for granted and stick to the plans laid, we'll be ahead of the game —but it doesn't mean we are infallible—just better than the rest. We will do everything together and know of one another's moves at all times because we will have enemies. You don't wanna be put in a position where you are forced to give up secrets. Men will torture you for information. I speak from experience. Remember the Saint Louis job I told you all about that me and the family did back in 1992?"

"A drill bit through the knee cap gotta hurt," T-top said as she grabbed her knee caps.

"That guy, as tough as he was, that guy offered to do things unimaginable to keep alive."

"You can say what you wanna say, but I can't go out like that. They just gone have to kill me!" Dawk snapped as he wheeled the Suburban down I-35.

"I'm sure that gang banger said the same thing at some point and time in his life, son. Pain, however, pain has a way of changing one's mind. The key to all this is to not allow yourself to be put in that situation to prove that you wouldn't do it because either way you lose. You may die a man, but you're still dead," Doss said as he heard sniggling from the backseat. "What's so funny?" he asked as he peered back at Bay and T-top, both of whom were wearing identical dark tinted Louis Vuitton sunshades.

"Tiva said she would offer to do it and bite somebody penis off," Bay squealed through laughter.

"If I'm going out you can best believe I'm taking somebody with me. Get lock jaw on his behind. Bet he ease up with that drill."

Doss turned around and eyed his young lionesses with slight contempt. They were still full of play, but very much deadly at heart he knew, given their lingo and prowess whenever he was training them and discussing past jobs on the ranch, the things that actually went on when one was on the hunt like the one they were about to engage in. He really didn't like the fact that Tiva seemed to be taking his guidance lightly. His concern was that his kids understood the point about not being caught in a compromising position with potential rivals. The group talked about the up-coming job and Doss gave continuous pointers to his kids regarding the life until they reached Amarillo, Texas where they had dinner and spent the night at an inconspicuous motel, paying cash for two rooms. They awoke the following morning, had breakfast and continued their journey west on I-40 towards Vegas.

The drive went along smoothly, and on the following day, Doss and the big three made it to Vegas and set up in a pay-by-week motel under fictitious names. Doss sat and proudly watched as his oldest three kids went about their business inside the motel room where guns were unloaded and cleaned, and money was recounted and restacked. He'd given each of his children tasks before they left the ranch and they'd all delivered. Tiva had the assignment of routing the drive to Vegas and the planning of fuel and food stops. Dawk was the driver, and Bena had the task of mapping out the city of Vegas where the marks lay. All the play, all the silly antics and plots that had taken place during the ride to Nevada had gone out the window the moment the big three landed in Vegas. Playtime was now over and all three seemed to fully understand the fact that they were involved in a dangerous occupation that warranted high attention to detail.

Doss was watching as Bay sat at the table in the room loading clips into the clip of her and Tiva's Dragunov when he asked, "Do you all understand fully what we are involved in here, family?"

Dawk was rubber banding a stack of twenties as he answered, "We here to kill four people and kidnap a man and deliver him alive."

"What I'm asking is, do you have any regrets about what we're doing?" Doss said as he eyed his three kids.

Doss understood the fact the path he was placing his kids on would be frowned upon by most in society. To train your kids to become criminals was indeed a rare act, but Doss didn't see it that way because he was an outlaw by nature. An outlaw that was able to discern that his oldest three children had it in them to be the man he was, to live the life he was living, and if they did it right, Doss knew his family would reap huge benefits, benefits in his eyes that were worth the risk of prison time and the investment of blood, family blood. On top of that, Doss would have people around him he could literally turn his back on and go to sleep, and they would ride with him to the depths of hell and back because they believed in him that much and were just that capable in his eyes.

"Dad," Tiva said, "you sound like you don't want us to be here really."

"You all's grandfather had the same reasoning. That's not it though, kids. I just wanna be certain that you all are cut out for this life and are not doing what you are doing just because I asked you to and you don't wanna forsake me or let me down."

"Daddy," Dawk said, "we knew a while back through watching granddaddy and Mendoza that you were into something outside the law, but until you told us, we never knew what it was. We talked a lot by ourselves when we were kids playing video games and running around the ranch doing crazy stuff."

"I asked was you serious about us joining you," Bay said.

"I wanted to from the beginning." Tiva added.

"Why?" Doss asked.

"It's what you taught us and it's what we want to do. If we didn't all agree, we would've said no, daddy. But the truth is, we all agreed and we can handle it. This is what we want to do." Tiva said seriously as Dawk and Bay nodded in agreement.

The look on the big three's faces eased Doss conscious tremendously. The man had brief apprehensions about involving his kids in the life, but there was no denying it really, they were built for it. Doss silently told himself that from this day forth, he would never again ask whether or not his children were equipped to live the life of a criminal. The door to wondering had been closed. Now, it was time to get down to business and tackle their first assignment.

"How's about we ride through town, take a look at our marks before we go and have dinner," Doss asked.

"We game," Bay answered just as she finished loading her fourth clip.

Doss and the big three rode through town and laid eyes upon parking lot on the west side where their marks were known to hangout. A Blue Denali with music blasting loudly and several young men in their late teens and early twenties, who were quickly recognized as the family's marks, were smoking weed beside the vehicle. A couple of people were walking up to the Denali and signals were being given as the group cruised pass the area unnoticed.

"You know how you gone go at these guys, Dawk?" Doss asked from the behind the wheel.

"We can follow the Denali and see if we can catch 'em all in one spot."

"That's one step ahead. It'll work, but we missing a step. These guys will sell to anybody," Doss remarked. "Tomorrow, I want you and your sisters to ride up and attempt to buy weed. We'll do that a few times, and work our way in that way."

"What if they think we that police?" Bay asked as Doss rode out of the neighborhood.

"If they think we the police, they gone be cautious and not deal with us. The may think we out to rob them at the highest, but the last thing they gone think is that we in town to kill 'em. The way to play it is like you three are just a bunch of fun-loving teenagers that like to get high and talk shit. You're new in town and just looking to hangout." Doss responded. "That's how I want y'all to play it when y'all get out there. Make 'em feel comfortable as quickly as possible and get the job done in the same order," he ended in cool manner.

****

"And ride on...niggas get your high...while we pump this shit to vibe on...the mutherfuckin' mobster elite...to leave you breathless...when we hit you hit you like this...early in the morning...hop into the Chevy Caprice I'm hurting so thinking of ways of gettin' paid...chedda in the bucket...fifties and hundreds and g's stacks...if I could just hit that big lick I could relax..."

Doss had turned the big three loose the day after the family touched down in Vegas and spied on their marks. Dawk, Bay and T-top now had free reign over the job and were allowed to handle things as they saw fit. Dawk was behind the wheel of the family's Suburban bumping the song *Mobstability* by Twista and The Speedknot Mobstaz as he cruised down Interstate-15 with Bay at his side and Tiva in the backseat bobbing her head to the music.

The colorful lights of Vegas lit up the skyline as the big three traversed through the city preparing to engage the underworld and kill for the first time. Dawk jumped off on West Sahara Boulevard and rode down to South Las Vegas Boulevard and made a right turn onto the strip, which was alive with activity —a traffic jam through the heart of the city amidst the numerous Casinos, shopping malls and strip clubs filled to near capacity, some unfortunate driver receiving a DUI ticket and a couple of fender benders here and there slowing the flow.

Dawk, Bena and Tiva were taking it all in as they listened to the music while making their way through the crowded Vegas Strip towards their destination, slowly sinking into their roles. Their father's words were that they were to be a group of teenagers new in town that loved to get high and have fun and they were following orders—hanging out the window and flirting with people and asking where the happenings were in town. Dawk had even pulled into a gas station and got an older woman to buy him a can of beer. He didn't drink the alcohol, however, because he wanted to remain focused on the task at hand. The move he'd made was just a way of getting in tune with the way people talked and moved about in the city.

After traversing the strip, Dawk jumped back on to I-15 and continued caravanning south towards the area where the marks were known to hangout, weaving in and out of traffic while maintaining the speed limit.

"I tell ya'," Dawk said as he turned the music down, "if we was here for play?"

"It would be off the chain!" Tiva snapped. "I ain't never seen nothing like that."

"That was cool," Bay said. "But let's stay focused, please?"

"We focused," Dawk responded. "You can't say Vegas ain't poppin' though."

"It is. It is. I was just thinkin' how easy it is to lose sight of what we actually here for."

"Ain't nobody losing sight, Bay! You just gotta loosen up! Daddy said we here to have fun! You don't be actin' like a stick-in-the-mud when Aquanina be at the park." Tiva joked.

Bay laughed as she turned around her seat and said, "I'm not a stick-in-the-mud, Tiva. You really think I'm a party pooper?"

"You can be," Dawk answered. "Remember? Tiva? Remember that night with Siloam van and how Bay was driving?"

"She be turtle drivin'. If she had to drive here to Vegas we still be on the road somewhere."

"This the exit coming up, yeah," Bay said.

451

"I almost missed it," Dawk said.

"See? Y'all need my rationale to keep y'all focused."

"Okay you called that one," Tiva said as Dawk moved over to the right lane where he exited the interstate and pulled over to the shoulder of the ramp to allow Bay and T-top to grab the two .380 caliber semi-automatic handguns from the hidden compartment before he continued on through the neighborhood and turned onto Folkstone Avenue. He slowed the Suburban to a roll in front of a field behind Lilly and Wing Fong Elementary School out of sight from their marks and the three sat quietly for a minute and got an up-close view of the area with the aide of their binoculars.

The neighborhood Dawk and his sisters were in reminded him of a neighborhood on the west side of Ponca City where he sometimes hung out with its large apartment complex and numerous people milling about. Kids were out, even at this late hour, and many tenants were moving back and forth copping drugs and just hanging out. Dawk knew he, Bay and T-top were in one of the roughest neighborhoods in Vegas just off Balzar Avenue on the city's west side, but all three were unfazed by it all.

They scanned the area with their binoculars as they sat inside the Suburban for a little while longer until Dawk placed a .380 caliber into his waistband and asked aloud, "Y'all ready ta' connect with these fools?"

"Let's do it," Bay replied as she placed her gun in the door panel.

"It's on." Tiva said nonchalantly as she eyed the men standing beside their whip.

Dawk rode into the parking lot and stepped out the SUV dressed in a pair of white, baggy Girbaud's jeans, a light blue Kansas City Royals baseball jersey, light blue baseball hat and light blue and white Air Force Ones on his feet. T-top calmly exited the ride dressed in a white jean short outfit and light blue and white Air Force Ones. She followed Dawk across the parking lot towards the Denali where music was blasting loudly while Bay remained seated inside the Suburban, her hand slightly draped over the barrel of her gun, ready shoot.

"Eh what's up, homie? What y'all need?" a black male that stood amongst three other males asked coolly as he eyed the two approaching.

"We looking to score some weed. Whatever this can buy." Dawk said as he pulled out five twenty dollar bills and eyed the four men.

The gangbanger stared hard at Dawk for a few seconds before he asked, "Y'all from around here, homie?"

"We just moved down here from Sacramento."

"Sac-town, huh? I never been there."

"Ain't shit up there, man. My family moved down for a better job, you know?"

"You was with that gang shit up there?"

"Never been a banger. Got a few homies ran with some Crips, but that's not my thang."

"We Rolling Sixties, Cuz. You ever wanna get down this where we at. Just ask for Donnell."

"They call me Dawk." Dawk responded as he and Donnell bumped fists.

Donnell looked Tiva over and eyed Bay briefly. Bay was a bit of a ways off sitting inside the darkened interior of the Suburban, but Donnell could tell she was a twin. The nineteen year-old couldn't see it, but Bay had a clutch on her handgun and was ready to bust. Had there not been any witnesses out on this night, all four men would have been dead. A quick kill was not possible this go around and Bay knew it; she and her siblings would have to stick the plan and play things out accordingly.

"Them your girls, Dawk?" Donnell asked as he pointed to Bay and T-top.

"Nahh, Cuz. My sisters."

"Lucky me, then. Say baby what's your name?"

"Who you talking to? Me or my sister?" T-top asked in sassy tone as she turned around and faced Donnell.

"Whichever one of y'all wanna give up a name. Shit, both of y'all sexy as fuck."

"My name is T-top."

Donnell eyed the petite teenager standing a few feet away from him and admired her physique. At sixteen years of age, Tiva and Bena were both 5' 6" and weighed around 135 pounds and had short and curly jet black hair with smooth, tan skin and dark brown eyes. Tiva gave off a radiant smile and licked her lips as she eyed Donnell in his sagging black jeans, blue and white Adidas and crisp, white t-shirt and faded haircut. He was cute in her eyes, and if she weren't in town to kill the young man, she may have given him some play for real; but every move the big three made was with the intent on earning the men's trust to lure them into a vulnerable position.

"T-top? Why they call you that?" Donnell asked.

"Because I like a man that likes to ride with the top down. You got a whip like that?"

"For you I'll buy one tomorrow. Let me get them digits."

While Tiva was talking to Donnell, one his friends went over to the Suburban and tried to talk to Bay. "What's up, shorty? I see you and your sister like to get down." the young man said as he peered into the driver's side window.

"We just do what we do from time to time," Bay replied, never loosing her grip on her .380 nor lowering her eyes as she stared at the young man.

"What they call you, shorty?"

"I'm Bay."

"They call me Whip."

"Where Whip come from?"

"That's what I do. I whip up that product, ya' feel?"

Bay realized right away that Whip was trying to impress her by telling her he sold drugs. She could have played that role with him like she was intrigued, but she shut him down by telling him she liked women. To her surprise, however, her revelation only fueled Whip on further. The two talked, Bay being as cordial as she could be because she'd rather put a slug dead center in between Whip's eyes, until Dawk purchased the weed from another young man that was hanging with Donnell.

"This that Indo, homie. We got it for ya' right here all day after nine at night."

"If it's that fire then we be back, homies," Dawk said as he dapped the men off.

Tiva, meanwhile had given Donnell the number to her Trac-Phone. "I'm a see how real you are next time I see you," she remarked through a sexy smile before walking off.

Dawk and Tiva climbed back into the Suburban and rode off slowly with Dawk behind the wheel. When he was a distance away from the neighborhood, Bay and T-top took the weed and emptied the contents out the window.

"What y'all think about those guys, Bay?" Tiva asked from the backseat.

"Easy, prey, Tiva. Dad was right—they sell to anybody. And all four of 'em hang out there together. We just gotta get at 'em when no people ain't around." Bay replied as she, Dawk and Tiva made their way back to the motel.

The big three exited the SUV and walked into the room and read a note from their father, telling them that he would be back shortly. Doss returned about twenty minutes later carrying three large pizzas and asked, "How'd it go out there?"

"Smooth," Dawk answered. "We think we can get 'em in the parking lot, but we gone make a few more buys and just sit and see how long they stay out there."

"This hit here can be pulled off in that parking lot when nobody ain't around. We can make it look like a rivalry thing and that'll take the heat off us," Bay said.

"Okay," Doss replied. "Remember, though, this is you all's job, so take the wheel and do it as you see fit."

****

Several days later, Dawk, Bay and T-top had earned Donnell and his crew's trust. So much so they'd hung out in the parking lot with the men for a few hours two nights in a row. Dawk talked a lot about life in general, making idol conversation and asking questions about Vegas, pretending he really wanted to learn all he could about the city. He had a certain style about himself that Donnell and his crew liked. They wanted to put him down and Dawk had the young men under the impression

455

that he was interested in joining their crew.

Bay and Tiva were always flirting—dancing to music coming from the crew's Denali and being outright teasers—leading the young men on with promises of sex in the near future and pretending to be enthralled with their lifestyle, and the boys were blindly taking the bait. Seeing Bay and Tiva dressed alike and pussy popping side by side for extended periods of time was a scene Donnell and his crew could never get enough of; but no matter how sincere Donnell and his crew were in extending their friendship towards Dawk, Bay and T-top, no amount of admiration would stop them from killing all four young men the first chance they received. The flirting, dancing and shit-talking was all a part of the act because when it got down to it, Dawk, Bay and T-top weren't in town to make friends. The people they were pretending to befriend were to become their first kills—only time and opportunity—which was rapidly winding down and approaching—stood in their way.

The big three had easily slipped into the lives of their marks and were only waiting the opportune time to strike. Donnell really had a thing for Tiva, going so far as to rent a Porsche 911 to ride her around town in on the third night. Dawk and Bay followed the two around town, not really liking the move Tiva had made, but they knew it was crucial to keeping the men's guards lowered.

Donnell pulled up to a light in front of Fashion Show Mall on the strip, which was thick with cars and people on foot, and cranked the volume up on JaRule's song *Put it on Me...*

"...*Man I feel like you and me been born together... inseparable you chose pain over pleasure...for that you'll forever be a part of me...my body and soul ain't no I in we...*"

Tiva couldn't help but to nod to the music. She wished she didn't have to kill dude because he was cool and had thug-appeal. Tiva liked the bad boys, just like Tonto Jamison back home, a young man she'd given her virginity to on Kaw Lake Park a few days after her sixteenth birthday.

"Hey baby, let's grab a movie or something." Donnell said over the music.

456

The lights of Vegas, the Porsche and Donnell's swagger was taking a toll on T-top. She was enthralled with all that was going on as she'd never been shown anything like this in her life and she was loving it. A movie wouldn't sit right with Dawk and Bay, and T-top knew that to be a fact; so she opted for dinner instead. "Let's go eat something," she said.

"Shiit! I'm looking at what I wanna eat, baby."

"You play your cards right you can do that and then some." T-top replied as she spread her legs slightly and rubbed her inner thighs.

"Alright, baby girl. I like that kinda talk. You cool, people. You cool, people. Let's find us a spot to grub."

Donnell rode over to Peppermill Restaurant where he and Tiva had dinner. The young man was laying it on thick, doing all he could to seduce Tiva, but she remained focused on the job. She knew Dawk and Bay were tailing her, so going off kilter was not an option, although she wanted Donnell to eat her out something fierce. After dinner, Donnell rode back over the parking lot where he hung out and waited with her for Dawk and Bena to pick her up.

"Momma been waiting on you, girl," Bay yelled from the window. "You know you supposed to do her hair tonight! Donnell what you did with my twin?"

"Nothing she didn't let me do, Bay. She back in one piece, homegirl. Dawk you need something?"

"Not tonight. We hanging with moms and she don't play that shit, man. You gone be out, y'all gone be out here tomorrow?"

"Man you know we always out here getting money. Hollar at a nigga. Make sure you bring my baby back."

"I don't think she would let us leave without her, Cuz. We talk," Dawk said as he gave a fist pound to Donnell and blew the horn at his boys as he rode off.

On the following night, Donnell and his boys were out in the parking lot as it began to clear out. "Yo, Donnell, let's be out, Cuz. Don't look like Dawk 'nem coming through." Whip said.

"I called her and everything, man. Damn! I gotta bring the 911 back tomorrow and I was hoping I could get her out from under her brother again so I can fuck."

"What you wanna do, nigga? Fuck that hoe! She ain't tryna give you no pussy anyway!" Whip snapped as he hopped into the Denali.

Donnell hopped into the Porsche and he and his crew pulled away from the now-empty parking lot. When they approached the corner, Dawk, Bay and T-top, who'd been waiting in the wings out of sight, pulled up beside him and Dawk blew the horn.

"What up, homies? Mom's just brought the ride back and we out! Where we going?" Dawk asked happily.

"Downtown, big dog! Say, T-top come ride with a nigga!" Donnell requested.

"You got some weed?" T-top asked from the back passenger seat.

"Got a few bags left, but it's in the Denali."

"Look," Dawk said, "call them boys and tell 'em to swing back to the parking lot so we can score. Me and Bay gone roll up before we follow y'all."

"Okay. Follow me back over there. T-top ride with a nigga!"

"This boy here," Tiva said as she opened her over-sized purse and twisted a silencer onto her .380. "I'm killing his ass tonight if nobody back there."

"We with ya'," Bay remarked as she, too, placed a silencer onto her gun and did the same to Dawk's gun.

Tiva grabbed her purse and jumped out of the Suburban and slid into the Porsche and smiled at Donnell before she leaned over and kissed his cheek. "Let's get this over with so we can go," she said.

"Aite, baby girl. Let's get this party started."

Donnell rode back to the parking lot and T-top quickly scanned the area and saw that the entire lot was void of people. The Porsche slowed to a roll in front of several parked cars where she made her move. "Damn," she said as she reached for her purse. "I got the cigars and shit in my bag."

"Eh, your fam gone need that."

"I know," T-top replied as she unzipped the bag.

Dawk was turning into the parking lot at that moment, Donnell and his boys trailing him closely. When their headlights came into view, T-top came up with her .380, placed it to Donnell's right side and squeezed the trigger three times, shooting him in the lower rib cage before he could react. He slumped over onto the driver's side door and T-top quickly pulled him upright and shot him in the heart before she exited the car with her gun hidden behind her back.

Dawk had just pulled up and he and Bay were exiting the Suburban. "Donnell down. I got the back passenger in the Denali," T-top said as she stood beside Dawk outside the Suburban.

"It's on. Bay, I got the driver. You get Whip from your side," Dawk said lowly as the three walked towards the back of the SUV.

The Suburban the big three were riding in was preventing the three men in the Denali from seeing what was about to go down. They couldn't even see Donnell sitting dead in the Porsche because they were too close behind the Suburban. The driver and the back passenger stepped out of the vehicle just as Dawk, Bay and T-top cleared the rear of the Suburban and opened fire. The front and back windows on the driver's side of the Denali shattered and bullets sliced through both men's bodies. The driver fell dead where he stood, but the back passenger, although hit, began screaming as he reached up under his shirt. He was too late, however, because T-top had ran up on him and shot him point blank in the head before he could pull his semi-automatic handgun.

Bay, meanwhile, had taken down Whip. He was lying back on the front seat moaning when she ran up and shot him two times in the heart at nearly point blank range. Donnell and his crew were killed before they had ever fully realized what was actually going down. Dawk, Bay and T-top had moved swiftly with their silencer-tipped handguns, pulling off the hit successfully without the loud, thunderous sounds of inner city warfare shattering the tranquility of the night.

Dawk and Bay hopped back into the Suburban and waited for T-top to wipe down the interior of the Porsche were she had touched to erase her fingerprints. Once she was done, she grabbed her purse and hopped back into the SUV and the siblings fled the scene, leaving two dead bodies on the ground, one body lying across the seat of the Denali and another dead man sitting upright with the music blasting inside a rented Porsche 911 as they rode way.

It took a little longer than expected for the big three to complete their first hit, but they had pulled it off without a glitch. Their first time out had them completing a quadruple murder successfully and all three would use the lessons learned on their first hit to get better at their newfound profession. They rode back to their motel on the north side eager to share the news with their father and to also plan their next move— which was the kidnapping of a man by the name of Alvin Spencer.

CHAPTER 36
SPECIAL DELIVERY

Within hours after the quadruple homicide, Doss and the big three had moved from their previous motel room into another pay-by-week motel in order to avoid retaliation and apprehension. Donnell and his crew proved to be easy marks, just as Doss had suspected. They never questioned why Dawk, Bay and T-top never smoked weed with them when they were around, even though they bought weed from them nearly every night they were out in the parking lot. The boys never even knew Bay and T-top's real name. They were a good bunch of dudes for the most part, but they were the men who were supposed to kill one of JunJie's associates and for that, they had to die.

Doss was confident that the murders were going to become a cold case, but he wanted to change things up a bit for the next job. The guns used on the hit were thrown into a deep, water-filled rock quarry in a town north of Vegas and the Suburban had been cleaned thoroughly. The tracks of the hit had been covered, but Doss knew time was winding down. He and the big three had been in Vegas for nearly a week and that was long enough. First chance brought forth, Doss was aiming to kidnap Alvin and serve him up to those who were awaiting his delivery.

Doss had been on the tail of Alvin Spencer ever since Dawk, Bay and T-top had made contact with their marks. Alvin hung out at the Sapphire Gentlemen's Club north of the strip every night, just as JunJie's files had stated. Doss went into the club the first night of spying on Alvin and had discerned that the strip club was where he conducted his business as he sat in a sky box overlooking the entirety of the luxurious, 70,000 square foot gentlemen's complex that featured hundreds of exotic dancers, the best wine and fine cigars. Removing Alvin from the club was out of the question; and the parking lot was always packed with potential witnesses. After trailing Alvin for a few days, however, Doss had picked up on the fact that he always requested a limousine to and from the Bellagio Hotel and Casino where he was staying, and the ride back to the hotel was his vulnerable spot.

The night after the big three's first hit found the family waiting in the parking lot inside a white, 1997 four door Crown Victoria Doss had purchased for $4000 dollars in cash from a used Mexican car lot two days before under an alias name. The family watched patiently and in silence as numerous limousines pulled up to the V.I.P. section of the club. Men and women of all races and ages exited pristine, stretched Cadillacs, Hummers, and Mercedes Benzes, just to name a few of the elegant vehicles used to transport people of money and status. Everything seemed brand new and glitzy in this area. People were dressed in their best apparel and emanated money as they walked up the stairs towards the club under its bright neon lights.

Alvin Spencer was no different. He emerged from a silver Cadillac limousine dressed in a white silk suit and black shoes while talking on a cell phone as he walked towards the club's entrance in a carefree state as he trotted up the stairs, pausing a ways from the entrance as he talked, one hand tucked inside his silk slacks, the other holding a cell phone and allowing his wrist and fingers that glistened with diamonds and platinum to be put on full display. He obviously had money, or was giving off that appeal, but he moved about all alone and was ripe for the taking in Doss' eyes.

"There's our mark," Doss said as he sat in the passenger seat with a pair of binoculars. "We'll wait for him to come out and set the plan in motion. Everybody knows their tasks, right?"

"Yeah," the big three answered in unison.

"We shoulda got some donuts," Tiva said from the backseat,

bringing about sniggles from her father and siblings. "For real. It's like we on a stakeout."

"Not many lawmen will do what we are about to do tonight, though." Doss responded.

"You talked to momma, daddy? How everybody back home?" Dawk inquired.

"Everybody's good. Your younger brothers and sisters are missing you all, though."

"I miss them too. Can we stop at that big mall we saw from the highway in Albuquerque on the way home, daddy? I wanna buy Kimi 'nem something." Bay said.

"We can do that, just remember to throw away the receipts," Doss replied.

"Alright."

Shortly after 2 a.m., Alvin emerged from the club and from the way he was walking, Doss could tell he'd had more than his fair share of liquor inside of Sapphire's. "Sometimes I wonder what guys be thinking when they do the type of things they do."

"What you mean, dad?" Dawk asked from behind the steering wheel.

"This guy here killed his own son and has it in for his own brother who's still alive. I mean, he has to know people are looking for him or he may be on someone's hit list for what he did. But he's callous. Getting drunk and moving about by himself like everything is all right," Doss responded casually as he watched Alvin wobble towards a black Mercedes limousine. "Okay, kids. We're on the clock once again. Go ahead and tail 'em son."

Alvin, meanwhile, as the limousine pulled off, uncorked a bottle of champagne and began drinking straight from the bottle as he rolled up a blunt to smoke once he reached the Bellagio. Life was good for Alvin at this particular juncture, but the life he was living came at a high price to those who'd trusted and loved him without fail. A month ago, he'd killed his son, Wayne Miller, and had found $81,000 dollars in cash lying on a desk inside of his younger brother Asa Spade's bedroom. He was now using the money to splurge and live the life of a Vegas High Roller. Alvin, however, was a wanna-be, the complete opposite of his younger brother Asa Spade, who was the real thing. The ex-convict had been harboring a disdain and jealousness towards his younger brother for years and it had never faded. While Alvin was locked up in San Quentin, he'd heard how well Asa Spade was doing out on the streets and he began to resent the fact that his baby brother was beginning to supersede his position within the Blood Bounty Hunter gang; so much so, it had caused him to betray and murder his own son in cold blood in order to reclaim his street status with the Grape Street Crips, the gang he'd joined in order to oppose his own family. Alvin had it in for his younger brother, only he couldn't locate Asa Spade's whereabouts. Last he'd heard, Asa Spade had been shot on the south side of Vegas. Rumor had it that he was dead, others were saying he was alive, but in hiding. Either way, Alvin believed that his younger brother was now on the ropes and he was aiming to finish him off whenever he learned the truth and his brother's whereabouts.

A blue flashing light shook Alvin from his thoughts and he tucked the weed into the back seat of the limousine as the driver pulled over to the curb. "Fuck they want?" Alvin asked through slurred speech as he lowered the partition.

"I don't know man," the chauffeur quipped as he pulled the car into a darkened, small strip mall parking lot. "I wasn't speeding or nothing and I ain't been drinking. Just be calm and I'll handle this."

The chauffeur waited as the officer, who'd exited the passenger side of the unmarked police car, walked up to his window. "Turn the car off and step out, please," the plain clothed officer requested.

"What did I do?"

"Nothing yet. We're just checking for proper licensing and registration. A couple of vehicular escort companies have been operating without a license and we wanna make sure everything is in order."

"I got everything order."

"You can tell me that, but I need you to step out with your

credentials."

The driver exited the car and was escorted back to the Crown Victoria. When Doss opened the rear passenger side door, Bay and T-top, with ski masks over their heads, emerged from behind the car with their Dragunovs and ordered him into the backseat. The man was overcome with fear and was dumbfounded. He raised his hands and fell back into the car and Dawk quickly reached over the front seat and hit 'em with a taser, shocking him into a semi-conscious state.

Alvin was unaware of the situation unfolding as he was nervous about getting caught with marijuana in his possession. He was out on parole and a drug charge would only land him right back behind bars to back up the five years he had remaining on his sentence. He'd barely been out for two months and going back to jail was not an option. He was too drunk to get out and run, and he didn't have a gun on him to wage a battle. His only choice was to stay calm, be as polite as possible, and hope the car wouldn't be searched.

When the officer tapped on his window, Alvin, his whole body trembling, lowered the window and looked up with pleading eyes. "Did I do something wrong, office—" Alvin's remarks were cut short when he was hit in the chest with a taser. He fell back into his seat and Doss unlocked the door and climbed inside.

Dawk, meanwhile, had walked over and got behind the wheel of limousine as Bay climbed behind the wheel of the Crown Victoria. T-top remained in the backseat with the chauffeur, who was now pleading for his life.

"I'm just a driver," the man cried. "I have a family! I'm not a part of that life! Please don't kill me!" the chauffeur pleaded.

"We know all that! Just stay calm and we won't hurt you, man!" T-top snapped from behind her mask as she pressed the barrel of her Dragunov firmly into the back of the man's skull as she placed his hands behind his back and cuffed him. She then duct taped the man's mouth shut and placed one of her boots onto his neck and held him down with the rifle pressed tightly against his back. With both men secured, the family headed towards Paradise to complete their job, Bay leading the way in the Crown Victoria.

Just before the family entered into JunJie's gated community, Bay pulled over alongside a darkened stretch of the palm tree-lined road leading into the neighborhood and she and T-top pulled the driver from the back seat and shoved him towards the trunk of the car. Dawk then exited the limousine and walked over to his sisters with his ear pressed firmly to his Trac-Phone, talking to his father.

"You know what it is! Climb your ass inside," T-top snapped as she and Bay held their assault rifles on the driver.

The driver urinated on himself at that moment, surprising the twins as he began pleading through the duct tape. Tears were streaming down the man's face as Bay pushed him into the trunk of the car, forcing him onto his back.

"We got 'em in place, dad. What you wanna do?" Dawk asked. There was a long pause as Bay and T-top, dressed in all black, stood in a soldier's stance with their ski masks covering their face, only revealing their brown eyes and lips, their rifles aimed on the pleading driver as they both stared at Dawk awaiting orders. When Dawk hung up the phone, he nodded towards the trunk of the Crown Victoria and made a slicing motion across his neck.

Without hesitation, Bay and T-top simultaneously turned towards the driver and both twins fired a single muffled shot from their silencer-tipped rifles, shooting the chauffeur in the heart and killing him instantly. The trunk was quickly slammed shut and Bay and T-top climbed back into the car as Dawk trotted back over to the limousine.

"Give me that phone, son," Doss requested from the back seat.

Doss made a call to a number and a woman answered. "This your man. I got your present."

"This is Xiang. We're waiting."

"I'm two minutes out."

"Okay," Xiang replied before hanging up the phone.

Two minutes later, the door bell rung at 533 Middle Valley Lane and a young black male with a tattoo of a cross on his face opened the door. Dougie was caught off guard when he eyed what lay before his eyes. He knew from Xiang that he was to receive a package, but there were four people, all dressed in black and wearing ski masks to hide their faces standing before him. Dougie could tell the two people standing in the middle were men, and he picked up on the fact the two figures standing on either side of the men were female—maybe —he just didn't know. The rifles the two possible females had aimed at his face, however, let Dougie know that these people —whoever they were—meant serious business.

"Put your eyes down here, son." Doss said calmly from behind his mask.

Dougie looked down and saw Alvin Spencer lying on his back handcuffed with duct tape around his mouth and a red Christmas bow stapled to his suit jacket. Alvin was wide awake now, and when he saw Dougie, he knew right away what this kidnapping was all about: he'd just been delivered alive to his younger brother Asa Spade. He now regretted not running when the chauffeur had pulled over, and if he'd known what he was getting involved in, he would've forced the people who'd kidnapped him to kill him, or at least tried to get them to do so because he knew he was now going to suffer a fate worse than death once Asa Spade laid eyes on him.

Dougie began kicking Alvin in the face repeatedly as Xiang approached the front door toting a duffel bag. "That's enough!" she yelled aloud. "Save it!"

"Boy? We gone work your ass over good before you leave here," Dougie said as he backed away from Alvin. "Nigga thought he could kill Wayne without repercussions? Eh, yo', Percy! Come see what's at the front door!" Dougie yelled happily as he disappeared back into the home.

Xiang then stepped forward and handed the duffel bag to one of the men. "Three hundred and fifty large. Ten kilograms free of charge on your next drop in Chi-Town and we'll get rid of the limousine," she said.

Dawk opened the bag and Doss flipped through the stacks of hundred dollar bills quickly as Bay and T-top held their weapons on the Asian woman standing in the doorway. Satisfied with what his eyes were witnessing, Doss Dawkins eyed the Asian woman, snapped his fingers, and all four kidnappers trotted away from the scene and headed back to the

Crown Victoria to discard the car and the chauffeur's remains.

Doss and his oldest three kids were proficient in their work and was a force to be reckoned with on the streets. They handled their business swiftly and in near flawlessness and made it a point to keep their word at all times. The quadruple murder and the kidnapping and delivering of Alvin Spencer would be the catalyst that would form a lasting partnership between Asa Spade and his crew and the Holland family—two clicks who were ascending to the height of their criminal careers and running in the same circle—yet remaining in obscurity. The only bond that would tie these two parties together would be the crimes they would all have to commit to keep their ships afloat.

Doss and his family had been paid for their job and returned home thousands of dollars richer and with more expertise under their belts. Gifts were bought for the young five and everybody in the family welcomed them back with open arms. Business was good for the family all around—from a legal and illegal standpoint. The family was thriving. And crime was leading the way and getting the job done—propelling the family to more wealth and power.

Dawk, Bay and T-top returned from Vegas hardened to the life. They'd learned many tricks to the trade and had seen and done so much in such a short span of time. They'd committed cold bloodied murder on four people they'd befriended and had killed an innocent man—a man who'd become a casualty of the business they were in—a killing that needed to be done in order to fulfill a contract. They'd also kidnapped another man whom they knew would be killed at a later date and neither crime had faze them one bit.

Dawk, Bay and T-top were every bit of their mother and father. Bred for the life. They were trained to kill and could care less about those who fell by the wayside. Their job was their job and they would do whatever needed to be done in order for the family to succeed. A new generation of killers had been born within the Holland family in August of 2001—and the entire family—either knowing or unknowingly—was along for the ride.

CHAPTER 37
EVERY DOG HAS ITS DAY

"Don't...you   call...me   brother...don't...you   call...me brother...unless you really, really mean it..."

The O'Jays' melodic tune *Don't Call Me Brother* played low on the stereo in the basement of JunJie's mansion as Alvin sat tied to a chair in the center of the room. The basement was more like a dungeon with its concrete floor and walls and low ceilings. Alvin had been tied up and was being worked over repetitiously by Dougie and Percy as Xiang and Grover prepared grilled tuna steaks and shrimp fried rice for everybody to eat inside the small kitchen area.

It was a calm atmosphere inside the small, cozy basement. Music playing lowly, laughter occasionally breaking out between Grover and Xiang as they moved about in the kitchen and the spicy scent of shrimp and fish was filling the basement. If one was under the impression that a celebration was underway they would be right upon first glance—but the sounds of knuckles pounding against flesh and the groans they produced had turned a dainty gathering into an ominous meeting with mankind's most hated foe and unwelcomed ally —death.

Amidst the music and aroma sat Alvin Spencer. Handcuffed to a chair and forced to sit upright, he was now helpless to defend himself and could only sit and take the punishment Dougie and Percy were throwing his way. The cousins repeatedly reminded Alvin that they were whipping his ass over Wayne as they beat him across the head and punched him in the face repeatedly, stopping on occasion to take a few tokes of the blunts they were smoking until they caught their breath, only to return to pounding away on their captive as Grover and Xiang went about their duties, seeing no wrong in what was being done to Alvin, who was by now begging for mercy.

When a pair of legs covered in burgundy silk pajamas and wearing black slippers began to slowly descend the concrete stairs as The O'Jays' song played, Dougie and Percy, who were both taking turns beating Alvin across the face repeatedly at the time, stepped back and wiped their bloody glove-clad hands on their t-shirts and relit their blunts.

Alvin eyed the legs traveling slowly down the stairs and knew who it was right away. He shook his bloodied head from side to side slowly as Asa Spade's figure came into full view.

Asa paused midway down the stairs and eyed his brother coldly as the song played on... *"Don't...you call...me brother...don't...you call...me brother...until you get yourself together..."*

The last time Asa Spade had seen Alvin was when he was locked up in San Quentin. The two brothers had gotten into a fist fight when Asa learned Alvin had given his approval to have his own son killed. The two men parted ways as enemies, but Alvin went ahead with the hit anyway when he was released from prison. Now things had come full circle and Alvin was nearing the end of the line.

"Every dog has its day," Asa Spade said calmly as he continued to slowly descend the stairs, assisting himself with a wooden cane.

"That nigga bitching up over there, big homie," Percy said before he took a hit off his blunt.

"We know you can't work him over, Ace, so we handled that, Boss. We saved you some, though." Dougie remarked as he assisted Asa down the last few stairs.

"I can't believe I used to look up this man once upon a time, Dougie. My mother, my mother had big dreams for my brother. She probably rolling over in her grave over the man he's become today. And I hope she forgives me for what I'm about to do." Asa Spade remarked as he limped pass Dougie and Percy and walked over and stood before Alvin and looked him square in the eyes.

"Ace, what's this shit about? What I did?" Alvin asked, barely able to hold his head up as he peeked out his left eye, an eye that was nearly shut just as tight as his right eye.

Asa looked at his brother in disbelief and said, "You know damn well this all about Wayne. Plus a whole lotta other shit you had planned on doing to me."

"Wayne? You kidnapped me over Wayne? That momma's boy?" Alvin said as he grimaced.

"I don't care what he was, Alvin. Wayne was your son—your own flesh and blood, man. Why you kill him, Al?" Asa asked somberly as he shifted his cane to his other hand and shifted his weight.

"Wayne had ta' go, man," Alvin cried as blood ran down into his one good eye. "Remember, remember that job in Victorville? Grape Street had a hit on your entire crew. Niggas in L.A. wanted to avoid a war so I gave Wayne up. You don't see that? I did that to protect you, li'l brother."

"Don't call me brother. Family don't do family the way you do, Alvin. You coulda prevented my nephew's death. But you not only gave him up—you was the one who pulled the trigger. You chose to kill your own flesh and blood. I told you a while back I was gone deal with your ass. The clock is ticking on your ass. If I wasn't stitched up I'll beat your ass to death my damn self—but I'm gone enjoy watching you die a slow death." Asa said as he turned away from Alvin and was assisted by Grover.

"You kill your own brother?" Alvin yelled aloud.

Asa turned around and said, "You killed your own son, Alvin. I, I just can't get passed that shit. Wayne was more a son to me than he ever was to you. But he tried his best to be like you—to gain your approval—and how you repay him?" Asa said as his eyes began to well up. "How you repay my fuckin' nephew? By blowing his brains out! What kind of man is you to choose money over your own son? Fuck you! Brother!" Asa said as he turned away once again and walked over to where Grover had a seat waiting. "Work his ass over something good, Grover. Do what you do best, my man." he concluded as Xiang placed a small wooden table before him, allowing him to have a front row seat to his brother's demise as he ate the meal she and Grover had prepared.

Grover came over with a bottle of wine and poured Asa a glass full. "Enjoy your meal, my friend. The show is about to start."

"Fuck it man! Get it over with!" Alvin yelled as Grover walked over to him.

"You talk real brave, my man. But you have no idea what's in store for you," Grover said as he slid on a pair of latex gloves.

Grover had been heating four inch needles on the grill while he and Xiang prepared dinner. Once Asa Spade was made comfortable, he gave the order and sat back in a relaxed state as he ate his meal and sipped his wine, watching as Grover walked over to Alvin with a hot needle held by a pair of grip pliers. Alvin now realized he was going to be tortured and he pleaded for mercy, looking towards Xiang, who was standing before him with a bottle of champagne and a sorrowful look on her face. Xiang only looked innocent, however, she wanted to see Alvin suffer for killing Wayne, just as bad as Asa wanted to see it, and just as bad as Grover wanted to do it. Her look of sorrow was because of the fact that she could not believe a man would go so far as to kill his own son for monetary gain. For as long as she had been running the streets, she'd never encountered such a treacherous act. Xiang felt no pity for Alvin and only he hoped he would suffer for as long as possible.

"Make sure he feels every last inch of that needle. In both eyes!" Xiang yelled to Grover in Japanese, leaving Alvin wondering if she was in protest or in support of his demise.

Alvin got the answer when Grover walked over to him and slowly inched the needle towards his left eyeball. He could not move his head either way so he closed his eyes and began screaming aloud, begging and calling out to God. Xiang and Asa looked on as Alvin screamed aloud just as the needle penetrated his closed eyelid and pierced his eyeball. His screams were sickening and he began convulsing and vomiting, nearly knocking the chair over. Grover left the needle in Alvin's left eye and repeated the same act on his right eye, causing Alvin to pass out from the pain.

Grover, Xiang, the cousins and Asa then sat and talked as they ate, drank champagne and smoked, acting as if Alvin was a pile of feces on the ground. Grover would get up and awaken him from time to time, reminding Alvin of his current state and impending death. Alvin could no longer scream, he had lost his voice from screaming so loudly, begging for mercy, begging to be killed.

When Asa grew tired of the show, he decided to have Grover dismantle his brother's body while he was still alive. "Chop off small pieces until he dies, Grover. Take chunks if ya' feel like it—but make sure he feels pain for as long as possible." Asa requested.

It took Grover six hours to kill Alvin that day; and Asa Spade had enjoyed every agonizing minute of pain Grover had inflicted upon his brother. Finally, after he dismembered Alvin's corpse, Grover dug up the basement floor and buried the remains. Alvin would simply vanish from the streets of Vegas without being missed.

Two days later, Asa got a call from Percy. The cousins, along with Ponita Felton and Francesca Aranello, both of whom had given up whoring, had touched down in Denver with two fully-loaded AK-47s and had rented an apartment and were all set to open shop.

In August of 2001 the networking had indeed began to fall into place for Asa and his crew—but unbeknownst to the crew from Vegas, another drug dealer was about to place chips onto the playing table. And just like the crew from Vegas, this player was ruthless and had plenty of white powder to spread around and was looking to seize the reigns of the drug trade as well.

CHAPTER 38
THE RESURRECTION

"Take turns on me, Papi! You can, you can do anything you want to do to me, just don't kill me! Please, Papi! Don't make him kill me! Papi, please! Please! Don't kill—"

The two thundering gunshots that followed had forced twenty-two year-old Carmella Lapiente` to sit upright in her bed and scream aloud. She looked around the room with her mouth agape and her eyes wide open, breathing hard with a rapidly palpating heart. For over two years now Carmella had been having the same reoccurring nightmare and it seemed like the events that had unfolded on a warm spring morning in Memphis, Tennessee back in '99 had just happened the day before. She'd traveled the long road of recovery and had been ready to leave the place weeks ago, but doctors at Presbyterian/Saint Luke's Medical Center in Denver, Colorado still had her under their care in order to make sure that she had full use of her bodily functions and extremities. All was well with Carmella in August of 2001, however, and she knew it, even if the doctors were reluctant to admit that fact. Her memory was fluent, her muscle mass had returned and the metal plate that had been inserted into her head was covered over completely by the skin on her scalp and her silky, auburn hair, which was kept cut short into a crop throughout her rehabilitation.

Carmella turned and placed her feet to the floor and picked up a picture from her night stand inside her private rehabilitation suite and her heart softened. She missed the two men in the picture with her greatly. Damenga and Alphonso Lapiente` were all she'd ever known. The only family she had outside of her mother, who still lived in Valle Hermosa, Mexico. Carmella stared at the picture of her and her brothers, she in between the two lavishly dressed men as the three of them stood before the entrance of The University of Texas down in Austin the day of her arrival in the spring of 1997. She was supposed to be the first of her family to graduate college, but she wanted to be every bit like her older brothers so she dropped out of school her sophomore year, forsook her education and joined her brothers' profession.

Carmella was running Memphis for nearly two years until that fateful night in '99 had uprooted her from her career. She had never known fear until that moment. She'd taken lives herself in times past, but having the tables turned on her that night had nearly made her lose her bowels. She was proud she didn't shit herself, but she was embarrassed because she had begged for her life and had offered up her body in order to be spared. She told herself she would never bitch up again in the face of death and would hold secret her pleas of mercy to all those who still feared and respected her. It was a mark on her street resume` she wanted to erase but couldn't. She would have to live with it, but it would be her secret and hers alone.

After being shot and left dead, Carmella Lapiente`, now fully recovered, was prepared to pick up exactly where she'd left off. She wasn't able to walk, nor could she move her arms or the lower portion of her body a few months after her surgery, a surgery that had saved her life. Doctors said she would never walk again, but Carmella wasn't hearing or having it. She'd proven her two surgeons and their entire staff wrong a little over a year after the prognosis. They could only call her triumph a medical miracle. Carmella Lapiente`, however, viewed it as a resurrection. She was dead. Literally dead. Having died once, flat-lining in Memphis during surgery for four minutes, but she wouldn't let her mother's God take her just yet because she still had business here on Earth.

Ben Holland had destroyed her brothers and she had it in for him and anybody he loved. The whole time she was recovering she had a team of killers hunting down Ben Holland while agonizing and regretting the fact that she'd given her brothers the name of one of the people in the house that night. She wished her brothers would have waited on her so she could join them and get revenge right alongside her family, maybe her brothers would still be alive. All the men responsible for her brothers' death were dead, with the exception of Ben Holland, who Carmella learned through one of her loyal allies, was down in Florence, Colorado at Florence Correctional Center living in maximum security.

Carmella's team had tried to get to Ben Holland on the inside, but he was being protected by an Indian named Yiska Hoka, who was the most powerful prisoner inside the facility, so powerful, he was able to call off hits on Ben Holland and have those who tried to harm the man shipped to another facility. With Yiska around, Ben Holland was Mister Untouchable. And killing Yiska would only perpetuate matters with the Feds and alert Ben to the fact that he was being sought after to be killed so Carmella let his situation lie. Besides, she had more pressing issues on the streets to deal with that she had control over and could handle right away. Ben Holland was serving a life sentence so he was practically dead in her eyes, but if ever she found a way to kill the man, she would give the order. Carmella wiped her teary eyes as she reflected upon the deaths of her brothers and stood up in her robe just as DeAngelo Spires entered the room.

Thirty year-old DeAngelo was the fourth man in charge behind Carmella back in 1999. When Carmella was shot, the slender Colombian with a thick head of jet black hair took her position. When Damenga and Alphonso were killed, DeAngelo took control of the family. He was a trusted man, but people back in Mexico knew the Lapiente` Family was weakened by the loss of the two brothers. They also knew Carmella was in rehab recovering from her gunshot wounds. Workers within the family began to steal from the organization and they went up on prices while reducing shipments to cities like Seattle, St. Louis, Kansas City, and Denver, Colorado, thereby creating a man-made drought and sparking drug wars across the Midwest and Pacific Northwest. DeAngelo tried as best he could to keep things under control, but without a Lapiente` family member running the organization, the Cartel was merely viewed as a loosely-knit drug ring with fast-fading ties to America.

Carmella knew all that was transpiring within the once powerful organization and she was aiming to set things straight. Put the game back in its proper perspective. "We were the kings of white powder," she said to DeAngelo as he approached her bedside. "People feared us once upon a time— but now they treat us like common street whores. It's time for us to take back what's ours. We will rebuild the organization by killing off any dealers here in Denver, and move back in on Houston, Memphis and St. Louis," the 5' 9" 145 pound brown-eyed woman snapped.

"Carmella," DeAngelo said with a hint of uncertainty, "are you sure you're up to this? I mean, it's only been seven months since you learned to walk again. You've been in this place for alomst two years. It's not—"

Carmella raised her hand to DeAngelo's face, silencing him before he could go any further as she walked over to the window and looked out over the city of Denver. "This is ours," she said in her heavy Colombian accent as she stretched forth her arms. "My family once owned everything west of the Mississippi River. I will not let my brothers' death be in vain. We will not lose what we've worked so hard for to build. We will continue on with this business!"

DeAngelo said nothing; he only nodded in agreement. Truth was, DeAngelo didn't really like running the Lapiente` Family, but his loyalty to Damenga and Alphonso had prevented him from walking away. Now that Carmella was seizing control of the family, DeAngelo knew he could work better as an Enforcer for the woman, which was his original position within the organization.

Carmella Lapiente`, although only twenty-two years of age, was the only person willing and able to lead the Lapiente` Family back to power and prosperity. The people who remained loyal, including DeAngelo, weren't leaders. They were loyal followers. Carmella, however, was just like her brothers and she knew it all-too-well. She knew herself through and through and had a love/hate relationship with her own psyche. It was a personality that people around her could only describe as that of being 'crazy'—but her perceived insanity was linked to intelligence, treachery, and courage beyond compare for a female boss—and those attributes are the assets that made twenty-two year-old Carmella Lapiente` a force to be reckoned with on the streets and the rightful leader of the Lapiente` Family.

Carmella was a cold and calculating woman that would trample any and every one that tried to prevent her from accomplishing her goals; but with that aside, it was understood by Carmella herself that no matter how hard she tried, she could not rid herself of the kind heart she often displayed to those in need. It was the one quality she hated about herself, although it was the best quality she possessed. She often felt pity for the poor, having been dirt poor herself when she was growing up in Mexico with her mother. Carmella viewed people that weren't involved in drug trafficking as civilians, helpless individuals too afraid or unable to take the risks involved with dealing large amounts of cocaine, and for those, she showed mercy. To all others, she was downright sadistic.

Carmella stepped away from the window, walked over to DeAngelo and stood before the man and stared at him, a wide smile was draped across her face as she asked lowly, "Do you think I'm sexy, amigo?"

DeAngelo didn't know what to say. He'd always adored Carmella, but he feared Damenga and Alphonso. Now that they were dead, nothing stopped him from being with the young and sexy drug heiress. "Yes, you are very beautiful." DeAngelo replied.

"Don't lie to me!" Carmella said in a sexy voice as she pulled back her hair and revealed the scars in her skull. "Please, don't lie to me."

DeAngelo grabbed Carmella and guided her to a mirror and stood behind her. "Do you think you're ugly, senioretta?" he asked.

The young woman looked at herself in the mirror and smiled. She knew she was beautiful, but she merely wanted DeAngelo to respond to her. She hadn't been fucked willingly in over two years and was craving sex. Carmella's lover, a young woman named Desiree, had not been to the hospital to see her in months. She reflected on Desiree, missing the woman as the two of them often made fierce, passionate love. Carmella went both ways sexually, and men were not her first choice; she loved having sex with a woman, a woman named Desiree. Desiree was not on hand, however, and Carmella was unbelievably horny. Deciding to go with the next best thing, she opened the back of her gown and bent over the sink and called out to DeAngelo. "Fuck me poppy," she moaned.

DeAngelo stared at Carmella's caramel skin as he began running his hands over her soft, pert rear end. He could see Carmella's plum shaped vagina glistening with her juices as he unzipped his pants. "Fuck me, poppy!" Carmella sang in desperation as she felt the heat of DeAngelo's dick nearing her entrance. "Ohh si poppy si, si," Carmella pleaded.

The love-starved woman had an instant orgasm when DeAngelo slid into her and she began speaking Spanish as he pounded her tight-fitting vagina as he stood behind her, his 6' frame pressed firmly against her back. DeAngelo announced he was about to come and Carmella pushed back, forcing his dick to slide out of her creamy pussy. She then turned and dropped to her knees and began to stroke DeAngelo as she sucked on his rigid pole, tasting her own juices that covered his stiffened rod. She stood up as she stroked the man and aimed his dick at her stomach.

DeAngelo's semen spilled onto Carmella's belly and he convulsed through an intense seminal release as Carmella licked and nibbled his earlobes. Just then, a nurse walked into the room with Carmella's lunch. She dropped the tray and ran out of the room when she saw the scene before her eyes and the two laughed aloud as Carmella pranced back to the window butt naked and stared out at the city. "This is my last day inside this depressing place. Here, we'll reopen the club, find Desiree and return to Valle Hermosa to see my ma-ma. As of now, the Lapiente Family is back in business," Carmella said as she smiled back at DeAngelo.

DeAngelo walked over to the closet inside the suite and presented Carmella with her wardrobe. "I'll wait outside for you get ready after I clean up." he said through a smile. "Welcome back, Carmella."

Carmella took her time getting ready. She styled her hair after showering and lotioned her body and sprayed herself with perfume. She then dressed and stared out at the city of Denver one last time, and without notifying her doctors, she walked out of the hospital dressed in tan camouflage pants, brown, knee length leather Dolce and Gabbana boots wearing a brown tank top and two diamond and platinum dog tags worth $140,000 dollars apiece. Shades covered her eyes as she left the main entrance of the hospital and walked towards the silver Hummer that was awaiting her arrival. Carmella hopped into the back seat, removed her shades and said, "DeAngelo, take me to my brothers' jet. Call the pilot on the way and have him meet us there. Before we return to doing business here in America we have to go and see my mama down in Mexico and get things in order with the workers down there."

Carmella Lapiente`, at age twenty-two, was about to forge her brother's empire once again and she was prepared to do whatever needed to be done to reclaim the status the Lapiente` Family held once on the streets.

At the same time, Asa Spade and his crew were just beginning to wet their feet in the vast cocaine drug trade out west starting with the city of Denver, Colorado.

On top of that, Doss Dawkins and his oldest three kids, Dawk, Bay and T-top were now on the scene and the crew from Chicago was beginning to gain a strong grip on the drug trade in the city of Saint Louis, Missouri.

A deadly storm was now in the making. The Lapiente` Family once ran the cities of Saint Louis and Denver and Carmella was aiming to return to both cities and put her product back out on the streets; but Carmella unknowingly would have to confront two heavy-duty clicks who would not go down without a fight, nor could they be scared off by any means.

With the return of Carmella Lapiente, it would be safe to assume that war was now on the horizon. Pieces of a major battle were slowly and unwittingly being maneuvered into place. Cities would be up for grabs. Hearts would be tested. Millions of dollars would be fought over and the lives of the gangsters involved in this imminent conflict would be put in harm's way. The carnage left behind would change the face of the illegal drug trade in America's heartland for years to come and shake not only Asa's crew to the core, but that of the Holland Family as well.

To be continued.

Made in the USA
Monee, IL
18 December 2023

49356709R00266